The Pact of Shadows: The Black Orchard

Clifton Wilcox

Fredericksburg, Virginia

Print ISBN: 978-1-969770-25-8

EBook ISBN: 978-1-969770-26-5

Published by Windward Publishing LLC., Fredericksburg, Virginia.

The characters and events in this book are fictitious. Any similarity to real persons, living or dead, is coincidental and not intended by the author.

Wilcox, Clifton

The Pact of Shadows: The Black Orchard

Windward Publishing, LLC

2026

"If you see your name, run.
If you hear it, it is too late."

Table of Contents

Books by Clifton Wilcox

Fiction

Cool's Last Stand

Where Despair Comes to Play

The Monuments Must Bleed

Keeper of the Fallen Ages

I, Monster

Harvest of Eyes

The Case Against Jasper

Crimson Plume: The Song of Corvus

Framed in Love

Echoes of the Forgotten

Blacktop Harvest

The Plagiarist Game

The Black Forest Protocol

Outcome without Appeal

Deliberation

The Lore Hunter: Brown Mountain

Chapter 1

The Thing in the Root Cellar

The rain had been falling since before dusk, not in clean sheets but in a choking, steady pour that seemed determined to turn Virginia into one long grave. It filled the wagon ruts and old shell craters alike, made rivers of the low places, and softened the ground until a man's boot sank with a sound too much like flesh giving way.

Beyond the last huddled cabins, where the road began to thin into a track and the trees leaned over it like listeners, the orchard house waited. It had once belonged to the plantation up the rise, before the war cracked that world open and let the rot show. Now the big house was a broken silhouette against the clouded sky, its columns scarred by fire, windows gaped out like missing teeth. The orchard, though, still stood.

Apple trees in long, disciplined rows, their branches black with rain. They should have been alive with the last insects and the restless birds that always found shelter in leaves, but there was no movement in them, not even the small, skittish life that clung to ruined places. The trees simply stood, dripping, patient, as if they were waiting for someone to remember what had been buried among their roots.

No one went there after sundown. That was not a rule written anywhere, but it was kept like a Sabbath. Even the men who claimed to fear nothing, who spat in the face of artillery and laughed at sickness, would lower their voices when the orchard house came up. They would glance away, pretending it was only another ruined property, while their hands found their own wrists, as if checking for a pulse.

In the nearest cluster of cabins, a dozen families crowded into one room that still had most of its roof. The air inside was sour with wet wool and woodsmoke and the slow panic of people who had learned the war could take anything and no one would come to stop it. A lantern sat on a crate in the center, its flame struggling, and every face it lit looked older than it should have.

They spoke in fragments at first, in unfinished sentences. No one wanted to be the first to name the thing, because naming it made it closer.

"It ain't soldiers," an old man said, his voice rasping like a saw. "Don't speak of soldiers. Them you can see."

A woman near the wall, her hair tied back with a strip of cloth, pressed her baby's head into her chest and stared at the floorboards as though they might open. "We heard it again."

From the corner came a small sound, not quite a sob. It was a boy, maybe twelve, his knees drawn up. His eyes were too wide, reflecting the lantern like coins. "It was under," he whispered. "Under the house."

The old man's gaze snapped to him. "You weren't there."

."I was by the fence. I went to check the snare line." The boy's voice trembled with the indignation of terror, the need to be believed. "It was quiet, like the whole world had forgot to breathe. Then I heard scraping, slow, like someone dragging a chain through dirt."

At the word chain, someone crossed themselves. A few muttered the Lord's Prayer as if it were a reflex the war had not managed to beat out of them.

A younger man, broad-shouldered and hollow-eyed, shifted his weight. The lantern drew harsh shadows into the angles of his face. "Folks say there's a man down there," he said, as if he could keep the story at arm's length by making it sound simple. "A man they kept. One of them old-time gentlemen. Like from before all this."

"A man don't make the air go wrong," the woman with the baby said. She finally lifted her eyes. They looked feverish, angry. "A man don't make the dogs disappear."

That was true. Three nights ago, the last dog in the cabins had bolted from its chain, yelping so hard it sounded like it was being skinned. When a boy had gone after it with a lantern, he found the broken collar near the orchard road and drag marks that ended where the rain had washed the earth smooth. No blood. No paw prints leading away. Only the collar, wet and empty.

Two days ago, a mule had been found in a ditch, legs folded wrong under it, its throat unbroken. It had no visible wound at all, yet its eyes were wide and glazed, and its tongue hung out as if it had choked on fear.

War did that, people told themselves. Hunger did. Wolves did. Men did, when men were allowed to do anything they wanted. But those explanations did not sit right in the mouth. They tasted like lies.

The boy kept talking, because stopping would mean remembering alone. "I saw a light," he said. "Not lantern light. It was deep, like it come from down in the ground, and it moved under the boards like water."

"That's the storm," someone said too quickly. "Lightning in the cellar, that's all."

The old man shook his head, slow. "There ain't no lightning in a cellar. There ain't no light down there at all, not unless somebody brings it."

He leaned forward. The lantern made his eyes look like dark hollows. "When the plantation still had money, they had a root cellar built under the orchard house. Not under the big house, mind you. Under the little house where they kept preserves and cider and what they called delicacies. That cellar door's thick. Iron on it. Lock big as a fist. Folks say it was a place to keep food cool."

"And folks say," the broad-shouldered man interrupted, "that there's a door beneath that door."

A long silence followed. The rain drummed on the roof. Somewhere outside, a tree creaked.

The woman with the baby swallowed. "My sister worked up there," she said. "Before the Yankees came through. Before the fire. She said there were rooms they didn't go in. Rooms with windows painted black from the inside. She said she heard singing one night, soft, like someone trying not to be heard. She thought it was the master drunk. Then she found nail marks on the inside of the pantry door."

Nail marks. People who had never been locked in a room still understood what that meant. It was a message written without ink.

"Your sister ran," someone said.

"She didn't run," the woman replied, and something inside her voice broke in a quiet, final way. "She vanished. Like she stepped out of the world. And when I went looking, the orchard was so still it hurt."

The boy whispered, "They say it's a grave-man."

At that, the broad-shouldered man spat into the ashes. "Don't call it that."

"Why not?" the boy challenged, too frightened to be polite.

"Because you call something a grave-man, you make it sound like a story. Like a thing you can laugh at in daylight." The man's hands flexed, as if they remembered holding a tool or a weapon. "This ain't a story."

The old man nodded once. "It's older than a story. It's an arrangement."

No one asked him what he meant. They did not want to hear it said plainly, that there were things a family with money could do in the dark that the poor were not even allowed to suspect. There were sins that did not leave records. There were mouths that could be fed without anyone admitting it.

A knock sounded at the door, sudden enough to make several people jerk. The lantern flame jumped. For a moment, no one moved.

Then the broad-shouldered man stepped forward, lifted the bar. The door opened to a slice of wet night.

A woman stood there, hood drawn up, rain dripping from the edge. Her face was pale under the lantern's reach, and her breath came fast, as if she had run through mud.

"They're coming," she said. "A patrol. From the road."

The old man's eyes narrowed. "Who told them?"

"I didn't," she snapped, then softened because they were all too tired to fight. "They asked at the mill what folks seen. Someone spoke. Someone always speaks when there's uniforms nearby. They think it'll buy them protection."

The broad-shouldered man let out a humorless laugh. "Protection. From what?"

The woman's gaze flicked past them, toward the black direction of the orchard, though nothing could be seen through the rain. "They asked about the house," she said. "About the cellar."

At the word cellar, the baby began to fuss, a thin, unhappy sound. Its mother rocked it harder, too sharply, as if she could force silence into it and keep the night from noticing.

The old man pushed himself up with a groan. "No," he muttered. "No, no, no."

"Maybe it's good," someone offered, desperate to turn fear into hope. "Maybe soldiers'll clear it out. Maybe it's deserters or raiders. Maybe it's nothing."

The old man fixed the speaker with a look of pity. "You ever seen a man go down into a hole and come back the same?" he asked quietly. "You ever seen a hole that wanted men?"

Outside, faint through the rain, came the sound of hooves and the clink of tack. A low, muffled voice calling orders. The patrol was close, moving cautiously, but moving.

The broad-shouldered man reached for his coat. "If they go up there," he said, "they ain't going to hear us if we tell them to stop."

"They won't stop," the woman with the baby said. Her voice had gone flat, as if something in her had already accepted the shape of what was coming. "They'll think we're ignorant. Or lying. Or trying to hide something. Soldiers always think folks are hiding something."

The boy stood, swaying a little. "Should we warn them?" he asked. "Should we tell them about the chains?"

The old man stared at him for a long moment. Then he looked toward the door, toward the wet night and the sound of approaching boots. His mouth tightened, not in anger but in the grim concentration of someone watching a cart wheel slide toward a ditch and knowing he has no strength left to stop it.

"Warn them if you want," he said. "But don't go near the orchard. Don't go near that house. Don't even look at it if you can help it."

The lantern flickered again, and for a heartbeat the shadows in the corners seemed to shift, as if something had leaned in to listen more closely.

The rain kept falling. The patrol drew nearer. And beyond the cabins, beyond the ruined plantation bones, the orchard stood in its unnatural silence, holding its breath like a mouth about to open.

The first rider came into view like a piece of the storm given shape, cloak plastered to his shoulders, hat brim streaming water. A second and third followed, their horses careful in the mud, hooves making a thick sound that the rain swallowed. The men carried themselves with the weary authority of soldiers who had long ago stopped expecting gratitude. Their carbines were slung but not loose. Their eyes moved constantly, taking in the dark windows of the cabins, the huddled figures behind the doorways, the way no one stepped fully out into the open.

The broad-shouldered man in the doorway held his ground, one hand still on the bar as if the wood could keep the night out. The hooded woman who had warned them stood off to the side, rain running down her jaw. The old man did not go outside. He remained in the lantern light with his shoulders drawn up, as if bracing for a blow he had already received once in his life.

The lead rider reined in hard enough that his horse tossed its head, annoyed. He looked down at them, face lined and wet, moustache dripping.

"Who's in charge here?" he demanded, though his voice carried the telltale rasp of fatigue.

No one answered for a moment. Then the broad-shouldered man said, "Ain't no charge. Just folks."

The rider's eyes narrowed. He had the look of someone who could smell lies even when there were none, trained to assume the worst because it kept him alive. He dismounted, boots sinking. Behind him, two of his men slid down from their saddles, moving with that practiced care that suggested they had been shot at recently and expected it again.

"We heard there's trouble up this way," the rider said. "House in the orchard."

At the word orchard, the boy flinched as if struck. The woman with the baby tightened her hold; the infant went quiet, not soothed but startled into silence.

The broad-shouldered man's throat worked. "Ain't any trouble you can fix," he said.

"That so?" The rider stepped closer. Rain struck his cheeks and ran into his collar. His eyes flicked over the faces in the doorway, counting them the way officers counted mouths at a ration line. "You telling me you've got deserters holed up and you want to keep your own hide safe by keeping quiet?"

"No, sir," the hooded woman cut in. Her voice was sharp, too sharp, and she seemed to realize it at once. She swallowed and tried again. "It isn't men."

The rider turned his head slowly toward her. “Everything is men,” he said. “Even when you wish it wasn’t.”

From within the cabin, the old man spoke without stepping into the rain. “Don’t go up there,” he said. It was not a plea. It was a statement as flat as a shovel blade. “Don’t go near that house after sundown.”

The rider’s expression shifted, a flicker of irritation and something like interest. He glanced past the cabins, up toward the rise where the ruined plantation lay. The orchard beyond it was not visible from here, but the black mass of trees and the deeper dark of the house could be guessed, a smudge in the rain.

“You heard him,” one of the soldiers behind the rider muttered, half mocking. “Old man thinks there’s haints.”

The rider did not smile. He looked back at the doorway. “What’s in that cellar?” he asked.

No one answered fast enough. Silence pooled between them, heavy and ugly.

The broad-shouldered man shook his head once. “There’s chains,” he said, as if saying it quickly might make it less real. “Bolted in. Folks heard scraping.”

The rider's gaze held. "Chains don't scrape by themselves."

The hooded woman lifted her chin. "Dogs ran," she said. "A mule died like it got scared to death. And that house... it's wrong. Quiet wrong."

The rider's jaw worked. Rainwater slid down his face in thin threads. At last he nodded to one of his men. "Corbin," he said. "Go back to the road. Tell Sergeant Givens we're checking the property. If we don't return by—" He hesitated, as if measuring the night by gut feeling rather than clock. "By morning, bring more."

Corbin looked as though he wanted to argue, but he swung up and rode back into the rain.

The rider faced the cabin again. "You," he said, pointing at the broad-shouldered man. "You coming to show us the way."

The man's mouth opened. Nothing came out.

The old man inside the cabin made a small sound, almost a cough. "Don't," he said, not to the rider but to the man in the doorway. "Don't set foot on that ground."

The broad-shouldered man's eyes flicked back to the lantern light, to the faces watching him. In the war, there were ways to say no to an officer and live; this was not one of them. He stepped out into the rain.

They moved as a small knot of shadow and wet metal up the track, horses left tethered at the edge of the cabins. Four men in all now: the rider who had taken command, two soldiers at his shoulders, and the unwilling guide a step behind, hands held out slightly as if to show he had no weapon.

The civilians did not follow. They stayed under eaves and in doorways, hunched, eyes straining into the black. The boy edged out a fraction, drawn by the same horrible curiosity that made men stare at fires. The woman with the baby did not look up at all.

The path toward the orchard house climbed through a stretch of ground stripped bare by war. Fence posts leaned at odd angles like broken teeth. A cannonball crater held rainwater that reflected nothing. The rain fell hard enough that it blurred the far shapes, yet as they approached the orchard, the world seemed to sharpen in a different way. The air changed. It did not smell only of wet earth and woodsmoke anymore. There was a faint sweetness beneath it, the cloying scent of overripe fruit left too long in heat, though the season was wrong for it.

They passed the first line of apple trees. The branches dripped steadily, each drop slow and separate, a patient kind of sound. No bird stirred.

No insect rose from the grass. Even the rain felt muffled here, as though the orchard absorbed noise the way rich soil absorbed blood.

One of the soldiers cursed under his breath. He shifted his carbine to his hands.

"You said there's a house," the rider snapped at the broad-shouldered man, who had slowed. "Where is it?"

"There," the man said, voice strained. He lifted one hand, pointing.

The orchard house sat lower than the plantation, built squat and practical, with a roof that sagged under years of neglect. Its windows were dark, not with the natural dark of an empty room but with something more deliberate. Rainwater streamed down panes that looked painted from within. The front door hung slightly ajar, rocking in the wind with a small, tired motion.

The rider's men spread out, boots sinking softly into the sodden ground. The rider himself stepped onto the porch, boards creaking. He drew a pistol from under his coat, not dramatic, just careful. He pushed the door open the rest of the way with the barrel.

"Anybody inside," he called, voice loud enough to carry, "come out now. We'll not ask twice."

Nothing answered. Not a footstep. Not a whisper.

He went in.

For a few breaths, the men outside stood listening. The porch roof drummed with rain. The orchard remained still. Then, from inside, came the sound of a chair shifting, wood scraping floor.

"Sir?" one of the soldiers called.

No reply.

The broad-shouldered man took a half step back, as if the porch had tilted. "They had crosses on the doors," he whispered, no one having asked him anything. "Folks said they nailed 'em up."

The soldier nearest him hissed, "Shut your mouth."

A moment later the rider emerged into the doorway again. He looked irritated, more than alarmed. "It's been tossed," he said, and wiped rain from his eyes with the back of his hand. "No one here. But there's signs of folk living in it recent." He glanced over his shoulder, down into the dark of the house's interior. "Basement door?"

The broad-shouldered man did not answer. His gaze had dropped to the porch boards, to where the rainwater ran in narrow streams. He seemed unable to lift his eyes without something inside him snapping.

The rider's patience thinned. "Basement," he repeated. "Cellar."

One of the soldiers, a young man with a narrow face, moved past the guide and stepped inside. "I'll find it," he said, and disappeared into the dark.

The second soldier followed, carbine held high to keep it from bumping walls.

The rider waited one beat, then went in last, as if determined to prove he feared nothing the dark could offer. The broad-shouldered man stayed in the doorway, neither inside nor out, caught between orders and instinct.

The civilians, distant shapes back by the cabins, watched the orchard house swallow the men.

Minutes passed. The rain did not let up. The orchard did not move.

Then the broad-shouldered man heard it: a sound from within the house that made his skin go cold. Not a shout. Not even a scream. A wet, intimate noise, like cloth being torn close to the ear, followed by a brief rasping exhale that could have been pain or surprise. It stopped too quickly. The silence afterward was absolute.

He swallowed hard. “Sir?” he called into the dark, voice cracking on the word.

No reply.

He stepped onto the porch, boards creaking under him. The doorway yawned, smelling of damp wood and that faint wrong sweetness.

From behind him, as if the orchard itself had decided to speak, came another sound: a slow, deliberate clink. Metal against metal, soft but unmistakable. Like a chain shifting.

The broad-shouldered man froze.

Inside the house, deeper now, something moved. Not footsteps with weight and rhythm. More like a glide, a careful displacement of air. The guide’s mind supplied images he did not want: a man crawling, a body dragged, something low to the ground and patient.

He backed off the porch without meaning to, boots slipping in mud. He did not turn and run, because turning would mean showing his back to the open mouth of the house. He stared into the doorway until his eyes watered from rain and terror.

Another minute passed. Then another.

No gunshot cracked the night. No command rang out. No hurried retreat.

Only the rain, and the orchard's stillness, and the sense that three armed men had simply been erased.

The broad-shouldered man stumbled backward, half falling, and ran toward the cabins, splashing through puddles, breath tearing at his throat.

Behind him, the orchard house door rocked gently on its hinges, as if nudged by a hand that had already withdrawn. The porch boards gleamed wet and empty.

In the mud at the threshold, where the soldiers' boots had tracked in clean lines, the prints went in.

None came out.

The broad-shouldered man reached the cabins slick with rain and terror, nearly taking the door off its hinges as he shoved himself inside. The lantern's light caught his face and turned it into something unrecognizable, eyes too bright, mouth working as if language had become another casualty.

"They're gone," he said.

No one asked which they. No one needed it.

The old man rose as if pulled by the words. "How many went in?"

"Three," the guide managed. He pressed a hand to his own chest as though to keep his heart from escaping. "Three besides Corbin that rode back. They didn't shoot. They didn't even shout. It was like…" He shook his head hard, rain spraying from his hair. "It was like the house swallowed them."

A low sound passed through the room. Not disbelief. Something closer to recognition, like a wound being pressed.

The hooded woman who had warned them earlier stared past the guide's shoulder toward the black direction of the orchard. "We told them," she said, and it was not accusation so much as exhaustion. "We told them and they went anyway."

The boy whispered, "They'll send more."

The old man's gaze moved to the door as if he could already see uniformed shapes in the rain. "Yes," he said. "They'll send more. That's what men do. They think more bodies makes a thing stop being real."

Outside, the night stretched on without offering answers. The rain kept its steady insistence, and the orchard remained quiet in the way a shut mouth is quiet, not empty but holding something back.

Corbin did not return before midnight. He did not return before dawn, either. The civilians did not sleep. They dozed in jerks and half-breaths, waking at every change in the wind, every shifting log in the hearth. The baby finally cried from hunger, then fell silent again, its small face pinched in the lantern glow. The guide sat with his back to the wall, knees up, staring at nothing, flinching whenever the house creaked.

When pale morning finally bled into the clouds, it did not bring clarity. It only turned the world the color of old bones. The rain eased into a drizzle, and in that thin light the ruined plantation up the rise looked less like a haunted silhouette and more like a carcass picked clean.

Hooves sounded on the road around midmorning. Not cautious this time, but purposeful. Metal tack clinked, men's voices carried. The civilians rose as one body, drawn to the doorway without deciding to go.

A larger patrol came into view: six mounted men and two on foot leading a packhorse. Their coats were dark with wet; their faces set in the hard neutrality of soldiers who had seen too many kinds of death to be impressed by rumors. At their head rode a sergeant with a red face and a short temper, his moustache bristling with droplets.

He pulled up near the cabins and looked them over as if tallying liabilities.

"Where's Corbin?" he demanded.

The guide stepped forward before anyone else could be chosen. "He rode back last night, sir. Like the lieutenant ordered. He—he never come back."

The sergeant's eyes narrowed. "Lieutenant Rusk was with Corbin."

"No," the hooded woman said quickly, then winced at her own boldness. "Lieutenant went to the orchard house with two men. Corbin rode back."

The sergeant's jaw tightened. He dismounted with the air of a man forcing patience into himself by brute will. "You telling me three-armed men vanished in a house and you didn't come fetch help."

The old man stepped into the doorway at last. The lantern behind him turned his face into sharp planes. "We warned them," he said. "We'd have warned you, too, if you'd listened."

A soldier behind the sergeant snorted. "Old folks and their tales."

The sergeant shot him a look that cut the sound off. He faced the civilians again. "What did you see?"

The guide swallowed. In daylight, the words did not come easier. They only sounded more foolish. "I heard a noise," he said. "Like cloth tearing. And then chain clinking, slow."

"Chain," the sergeant repeated. His gaze flicked toward the orchard rise, toward the place where the trees waited. "Cellar, then."

The hooded woman's voice went thin. "It's locked."

"Everything locks until it doesn't," the sergeant said. He swung back into his saddle. "Two men with me. The rest hold here. If Corbin shows, bring him. If you see anyone come out of that orchard, you fire and you do not ask questions."

As they rode up the track, the civilians watched from the edge of the cabins, bodies angled as if they might bolt at any moment. The drizzle turned the world to glass. The orchard drew closer, tree by tree, and as the patrol passed beneath the first branches, even the soldiers seemed to feel the change. Their horses' ears pinned back. One animal tossed its head and blew hard, smelling something it did not like.

The orchard house stood as it had in the night, squat and damp, its front door still slightly ajar. In morning light, it looked less supernatural, more merely abandoned. That made it worse. Evil that needed shadows could be dismissed; evil that sat plainly in daylight was harder to deny.

The sergeant dismounted on the porch and pushed the door wider with his boot. "Rusk!" he called into the dim interior. "You in there?"

No answer.

He entered, two soldiers behind him. Their boots thudded on warped boards. The air inside smelled of wet wood, smoke long gone cold, and that faint sweetness the guide had noticed, cloying and wrong. The windows were darkened from the inside, not shattered but painted over, so the room held onto its gloom even in daytime.

Furniture lay overturned in the front room, as if someone had tried to build barricades in haste. Nails still bit into doorframes where crude crosses had been hammered up. One wall was blackened by fire, the char pattern reaching higher than a man's head. The sergeant ran a hand along it and brought his fingers away smelling of old soot.

"Looks like panic," one soldier muttered.

"Or theater," the sergeant replied. His eyes moved, reading the scene as if it were a report. "No blood here. No sign of a struggle."

They found the stairs to the cellar in the back, narrow and steep, leading down into a cold that did not belong to the season. The door at the bottom was thick, its iron bands rusted but intact. A heavy padlock hung from the hasp, wet with condensation as if it had been sweating.

The sergeant crouched, studying it. In the dirt on the floor and the thin film of mud dragged from outside, there were boot prints. Several sets. Fresh enough that the edges were still sharp. They went down the stairs, clustered at the door, and stopped.

None returned.

One soldier made a sound between a curse and a prayer. “They didn’t go through.”

“They did,” the sergeant said, but his voice had changed. There was less anger in it now, more carefulness. He reached for the lock, tested it. Solid. He leaned closer, eyes narrowing. “You smell that?”

The sweetness was stronger here, mingled with something metallic. Not blood exactly, but the echo of it, like iron left too long in water.

“Should we break it?” the second soldier asked, and tried to sound like he wanted to.

The sergeant straightened. For a moment he seemed to weigh his authority against his instincts. Then, perhaps because he could not bear the idea of returning to the road with nothing but a story, he nodded.

"Fetch the pry bar," he said. "And if anything moves down there, you shoot it."

The soldier ran back up. The sergeant kept his pistol out; barrel angled toward the lock as if a piece of iron might suddenly become a mouth.

When the bar came, they set its end into the hasp and leaned. The first heave did nothing. The second made the metal groan. On the third, the lock gave with a sharp crack that snapped through the stairwell like a bone breaking.

The door did not swing open. It held, stuck to the frame as though the wood had swollen shut.

The sergeant planted his boot and shoved.

The cellar breathed.

It was not a gust, not a draft. It was an exhale of air so cold and stale it seemed to come from a depth below the house. It carried the smell of rot and damp earth, and beneath that, the intimate scent of something that had been living in the dark too long. The lantern the soldiers had brought down flickered as if the air itself resisted light.

They pushed the door wider, lantern held out, pistol ready.

The cellar was low-ceilinged, lined with stone that glistened with moisture. Crates lay in collapse, half-rotten boards caved in. Broken jars glittered on the floor among old apple press parts and warped shelves. The back wall was shadow deeper than the rest, and the light seemed to die before reaching it.

Something clinked.

Not the random shift of settling wood. A deliberate sound, patient, as if answering their intrusion.

The sergeant's pistol came up. "Lieutenant!" he called again, voice harsher, needing the shape of the word to keep fear from forming.

The lantern light caught iron bolted into stone: rings set into the wall, heavy enough for livestock. Chains ran from them, some snapped and trailing, others disappearing beneath the fallen crates toward the back.

And there, half-buried under the wreckage as if someone had tried to hide him in plain sight, lay a figure.

A man, at first glance. Thin to the point of ruin, his limbs too still. He wore what had once been fine clothes, a waistcoat now stained and hanging loose on him, a shirt open at the throat. His skin was pale in a way that made it seem almost luminous against the cellar's grime, as if the darkness had been drinking color from everything but him. His hands were bound at the wrists with iron, but the chain lay slack, more suggestion than restraint.

His head was bowed. Wet hair clung to his forehead. He could have been dead.

One soldier exhaled, relief trying to take hold. "It's just a man," he whispered, though his voice shook as if he did not believe it.

The sergeant stepped closer, lantern raised. The man's face came into clearer view: sharp cheekbones, lips cracked but oddly composed, as if even starvation could not erase a certain elegance. The skin around his eyes was shadowed, and his lashes were dark against his pallor.

"Sir?" the sergeant said, and it came out quieter than he intended. "Can you speak?"

The chained figure lifted his head.

His eyes opened, and the cellar seemed to narrow around them. Not bright eyes. Not demonic fire. Something worse: eyes that looked almost dead until they focused, and then they were intensely awake, as if they had been waiting in that dark not merely for food or rescue, but for company.

He blinked once, slowly, like a man disturbed from deep thought. Then his gaze slid past the sergeant, over the soldiers, lingering on their throats with a detachment that felt obscene.

"You've brought lanterns," he said, his voice soft and cultured, each word shaped carefully despite the rasp beneath it. "How considerate."

The soldier nearest the stairs swallowed audibly. "Who are you?" he demanded, trying to make his question an order.

The man's mouth curved, not quite a smile. "No one you would recognize," he replied. "Not by any name you have left."

The sergeant's pistol trembled, just slightly. "Where's Lieutenant Rusk?" he said.

The man's eyes flicked to the floor, to the mud tracked in, to the prints that ended at the door. "Gone," he said, as if discussing weather. "You came too late to be useful to him."

The sergeant's face reddened. Anger surged, desperate and familiar, something he could wear like armor. "You're coming with us," he snapped. "You hear me? Up. Now."

For the first time, the man's expression sharpened. Not alarm. Mild annoyance, like a gentleman hearing a servant speak out of turn.

He glanced at his own chained wrists, and then back to the sergeant. "Must we pretend?" he asked quietly.

The lantern flame shivered. In that brief instability of light, the man's shadow on the stone wall seemed to move a fraction too slowly, as though it did not quite match him.

One of the soldiers, the younger one, raised his carbine. His knuckles were white. "Sergeant," he said, "something's wrong."

The chained man's gaze slid to him with a kind of idle curiosity. "Yes," he murmured. "There it is."

The younger soldier jerked, as if the words had touched him.

Then movement happened in the cellar, so swift the mind struggled to keep pace. The chained figure was suddenly not where he had been. The iron at his wrists clinked once, and the sound was the last ordinary thing.

There was a blur of pale fabric and the wet, intimate tearing noise the guide had heard in the night. The younger soldier made a single startled breath, not even a full cry, and then he was dropping, his weapon clattering against stone.

The sergeant fired. The pistol shot thundered in the confined space, smoke blooming and mixing with the cellar's damp. The chained man's head turned toward the sound as if he found it tedious. He was too close now, impossibly close, and the sergeant could see his face with terrifying clarity:

not savage, not frothing, but composed, almost tender.

Something struck the sergeant's wrist. His pistol fell. Pain flared, and then numbness. He staggered back, hitting the stair wall, lantern swinging wild arcs of light across stone and blood-slick floor.

The second soldier turned to run, boots scrabbling on the steps. He managed two strides before he was pulled backward so hard his spine hit the edge of a stair with a crack that made the sergeant's stomach lurch. The man's mouth opened. No sound came out. His breath went out in a thin whistle and did not come back in.

The cellar went quiet again, too quickly for the violence that had just occurred.

The sergeant slid down the wall, clutching his wrist, eyes wide. The lantern lay on its side, flame still lit, throwing light upward in a distorted glow that made the stone ceiling look like it was pressing down.

The pale man stood in the middle of it, breathing evenly. There was blood on his mouth. He wiped it with the back of his hand as if it were an inconvenience.

He looked at the sergeant as one might look at an insect pinned but not yet dead.

"You brought more," he said, and there was the faintest note of satisfaction in it, like gratitude for a delivered meal. "They always do."

The sergeant's lips moved. No words formed. He tried to crawl, tried to move his legs, but his body seemed to have forgotten how to obey him. Terror flooded him not as hysteria but as an awful clarity: whatever this was, it had been chained not because it was dangerous in the way men were dangerous, but because it was dangerous in a way the world did not have language for.

The man stepped closer, and the lantern light climbed his face, revealing the fine bones under starving skin, the calm eyes, the faint darkening at the corners of his mouth.

He crouched, bringing his face near the sergeant's ear, and spoke so softly it felt like a private confidence.

"You should have left the door locked," he said.

What happened next would never be told the same way twice.

Later, the men waiting outside would find only blood in the stairwell, torn cloth snagged on a nail, and drag marks leading down into darkness. Some would claim they heard screaming. Others would swear there was none, only the rain starting up again and a sound like someone drinking.

When they finally dared to descend, the cellar door would be shut.

And from behind it, faint as a memory, would come the soft, deliberate clink of chain on stone, as though whatever lived below had settled itself back into the dark to wait for the next knock.

Chapter 2

Ashes of Virginia

Lieutenant Andrew Mercer had learned to measure the war by what it took away.

In the spring of sixty-four it took fences first, then barns, then whole stretches of forest hacked down for cordwood and breastworks. It took the young men and returned older ones with eyes that did not quite meet the world. It took horses and left skeletons hitched in ditches. It took names off headstones and put them into ledgers no one would ever read again.

That morning, the road was a ribbon of churned clay running between fields that no longer pretended to be fields. The rain had come and gone in cycles, never fully leaving, soaking the land until it held water like a sponge holds blood. Their boots sank and released with a sound Andrew had begun to hate because it resembled a body being pulled free of mud.

He walked at the head of his small column, not because it was brave, but because it kept the men from seeing the weight in his shoulders. The men behind him were the same kind of wreckage he was: survivors by habit, loyal by momentum. Their uniforms had long ago ceased to be uniform, patched with mismatched cloth and stained with everything the body could offer and the road could throw back.

A gaunt private named Rudd carried the company's flag rolled tight around its pole, because even the idea of bright color felt indecent in that landscape. Another man had tied a strip of Bible page around his wrist, the words smeared by sweat and rain, as if God could be worn like a bandage.

Andrew's horse, a bay gelding with ribs showing faintly beneath its coat, followed on a lead held by Corporal Haines. Andrew had been walking more often than riding. It was not a gesture of solidarity; it was a concession to reality. The horse needed the rest more than he needed the height.

He kept his eyes forward, not because there was anything worth seeing, but because looking too long at the ruins on either side could make a man feel like he was walking through the inside of a mouth.

They passed a farmhouse that had been burned so thoroughly only the stone chimney remained, freestanding and absurd, like a monument to a meal. A child's chair lay in the ditch with one leg snapped, rainwater pooled in its seat. A crow watched from the chimney top, head cocked, patient and unafraid.

"Yankees?" Private Rudd asked quietly, as if naming them might draw them out of the trees.

Andrew glanced at the blackened beams, the collapsed roofline. There were too many ways for a place to die now. "Could've been," he said. "Could've been our own. Could've been nobody. Fire doesn't ask who lit it."

Haines gave a short laugh that held no humor. "Fire's the only honest soldier left."

The men murmured, a few bitter agreements. They were exhausted enough to speak truth carelessly.

Andrew did not rebuke them. He had once corrected such talk out of discipline, out of duty to the idea of the cause. These days, the idea felt like a paper map in a flood: still inked with lines, still claiming a shape, but dissolving no matter how carefully you held it.

They trudged on, following a route that had been a supply artery before the war gnawed it down. The command they answered to was thin now, a skeleton of clerks and officers moving pins on maps that bore little relation to the ground. Orders arrived late, delivered by riders who looked half-feral and spoke as if every sentence might be their last.

Three days ago, Andrew had been handed a folded paper with wax already cracked, the ink blurred at the edges.

Assess the viability of the eastern road. Determine presence of enemy patrols, raiders, or civilian obstruction. Report at once.

There was no mention of food. No mention of ammunition. Viability, as if a road could be assessed like a horse. As if the land had not become an open wound.

A mile past the burned farmhouse, they came upon the remains of a wagon. It had broken in the road and been stripped with a thoroughness that suggested hunger rather than malice. The wheels were gone. The iron rim on one had been pried loose. In the ditch, an empty barrel lay on its side, its staves split.

A man was sitting beside it.

He looked old at first glance. Then Andrew saw the smoothness in his cheeks, the thinness of his neck, the way his hands shook. Not old, simply used up.

The man's clothes were civilian, but not clean. Mud had dried in the seams. His hair hung in damp strings. He stared at the soldiers as if he were trying to remember whether they were meant to help him or kill him.

Andrew lifted a hand, and the column slowed. "You alone?" he asked.

The man's eyes darted behind them, toward the gray line of soldiers, then past them into the trees. "No," he said, then reconsidered, then said again, quieter: "Yes."

Andrew's gaze followed the man's instinctive glance. The woods stood wet and silent, their branches dripping. Too many things hid there now: deserters, guerrillas, wolves, men who had stopped being men. The war had taught the land to keep secrets.

"Where you headed?" Andrew asked.

The man swallowed. "Away."

Haines shifted, impatience creeping into his posture. "Away where?"

"Ain't no where," the man said, a sudden sharpness in his voice, like pain. "That's the trouble. There ain't no place that stays safe."

Andrew watched him for another moment. He had seen fear enough to recognize its different flavors. This was not the alert fear of someone who'd heard gunfire. It was a deeper thing, as if the man had been told a story and found it waiting for him at the end of the road.

"You seen bluecoats?" Andrew asked.

The man shook his head quickly. "Not lately."

"Raiders?"

Another shake, slower. "Not the kind you mean."

Haines frowned. "What kind do you mean, then?"

The man's eyes flicked to Andrew's collar insignia, as if trying to find the right shape of speech for an officer. "You from down state?" he asked instead. "You hear about the orchard house?"

Andrew felt something tighten in him, not fear exactly, but irritation at the way rumors traveled faster than rations. "I've heard about a dozen houses," he said. "This country's full of them."

"No," the man insisted, leaning forward. His hands dug into the mud like he needed the ground to hold him in place. "Not like this. Folks say there's a cellar, locked, and men go in and don't come out. They say a patrol vanished. No shots. Just… gone."

Behind Andrew, someone made a small sound, a skeptical snort. Someone else muttered, "Haints."

Andrew raised his hand again, not harsh, just controlling the drift of talk. He looked back at the man. "People say a lot of things," he replied. "They're hungry, they're frightened, they've got time to turn every shadow into a sermon."

The man's lips parted. For a moment Andrew thought he might argue, might beg. Instead, he simply said, "I heard chain," as if that settled it. "Nights back. Like somebody dragging iron through dirt. Like somebody trying to get out."

Andrew held his gaze. The man's eyes were bloodshot and earnest. He was not smiling. He was not enjoying his story. He looked ashamed to be speaking it at all.

"Where is this orchard house?" Andrew asked, already regretting that he was engaging. He could feel the attention of his men sharpen. They lived on scraps of anything that broke the monotony, even if it was dread.

The man pointed with a trembling finger down the road, toward a low rise hidden by trees. "Near the old plantation," he said. "House burned, orchard still standing. Folks don't go there after sundown."

Andrew almost said, *Then they should go somewhere else*. But the road, this miserable road, did not offer many options. Their orders had sent them east, toward the places civilians were abandoning, toward the pockets of land that still had barns and smokehouses, toward anything that could be called supply. Those were exactly the places superstition and hunger would circle.

"What's your name?" Andrew asked.

The man hesitated. "Does it matter?"

Andrew studied him another moment, then reached into his pocket and pulled out a small piece of hardtack wrapped in cloth. It was already softened at the edges from damp. He held it out.

The man stared at it as if it were a trick.

"Take it," Andrew said.

The man took it with shaking fingers and did not immediately eat. He just held it; eyes fixed on Andrew's hand as if expecting it to vanish.

Andrew nodded once. "Move on," he told him. "Stay off the road at night. Keep to the day, keep to company when you can."

The man's throat bobbed. "You going there?" he asked, and there was something like pity in the question.

Andrew's jaw tightened. "We're going where we're told," he said.

That was the truth, the simplest kind. It was also the lie that kept men marching.

They moved again. The civilian remained sitting beside the stripped wagon, hardtack still in his hand, watching them pass as though he were watching a funeral procession.

For a long while there was no conversation. The only sounds were boots, the occasional jingle of equipment, the wet breath of men saving what strength they could. The landscape offered nothing new: broken fence lines, drowned furrows, trees scarred by bullets, a dead cow bloated in a ditch with its hide split and its ribs showing through like fingers.

Andrew's mind tried not to circle the man's story, but it did anyway, as minds do when they are tired. A locked cellar. Vanished men. Chains. It was absurd, and yet it landed in him with an odd weight, like a stone dropped into deep water.

He had seen men disappear in this war without a sound. Not swallowed by houses, but by bureaucracy, by hospitals, by the black arithmetic of marches. He had seen a man step behind a tree to relieve himself and never return, and no one had gone looking, because they were too afraid of what they might find in the woods.

But chains were different. Chains suggested intent. They suggested someone had built a solution and called it a door.

Haines fell into step beside him. "You believe any of that?" the corporal asked.

Andrew kept his eyes on the road. "I believe people are frightened."

"That ain't an answer."

Andrew exhaled slowly. "No," he said. "It isn't."

Haines walked a few paces in silence, then said, "Men don't vanish without a shot unless they're taken close. Knife work. Or a rope. Or… something they didn't see."

Andrew looked at him then, really looked. Haines had been with him since before the Peninsula. He had a scar across his chin where a bayonet had grazed him. His eyes were steady but not calm.

"We'll see what there is to see," Andrew said.

"And if there's something that ain't meant to be seen?"

Andrew's mouth tightened. The rain began again, light at first, then steadier, as if the sky had been listening and chosen that moment to press down.

"If it bleeds," Andrew said, repeating the kind of certainty soldiers used when they had no better prayer, "it can be killed."

Haines did not answer. He only adjusted his grip on the horse's lead and kept walking.

Ahead, the road rose gently, and beyond the rise the trees thickened, their branches knitting together into a darker line. Somewhere beyond them, if the civilian's trembling finger had been honest, stood an orchard that did not sing with birds.

Andrew did not yet believe in monsters. He believed in hunger, and fear, and the way men built traps for each other and then pretended the traps were accidents.

Still, as they marched into the wet, wasted land, he found himself thinking of a locked door beneath another locked door, and the foolish courage it took to put your hand on a latch when every instinct said to keep walking.

By late afternoon the drizzle thinned into a mist that never quite lifted, hanging in the air like breath in a sickroom. The road narrowed as it climbed, its edges eaten away by runoff until they walked in single file in places, boots sliding on clay polished slick by a thousand hurried feet. The trees ahead knitted closer together, their branches making a kind of ceiling. Beneath it, the light dimmed early.

Andrew did not tell the men to hurry. A tired column could not be bullied into speed without breaking. He watched their shoulders, the way their packs rode lower than they should, the way even the youngest among them had begun to move like old men with sore joints. When the world had been normal, sundown meant supper, maybe laughter, maybe a pipe on a porch. Now it meant decisions made under pressure with too little information.

Corporal Haines kept the horse close, leading the gelding carefully around ruts. Private Rudd, still carrying the rolled flag, muttered something that might have been a hymn or might have been a curse disguised as one. A second man, Kellan, wiped his nose with the back of his hand and stared into the tree line as if he expected it to blink first.

They rounded a bend and came upon a cluster of structures set back from the road: not a proper town, just the remains of a crossroads that had once been useful. A blackened frame of what might have been a store leaned against its own collapse. A smithy stood roofless, its anvil half-buried in wet ash. Two cabins remained intact enough to shelter someone, their chimneys smoking low.

Andrew lifted a hand and halted the column. Smoke meant people, and people meant information. It also meant trouble, but that was true of everything now.

He took Haines and Rudd with him and walked toward the nearest cabin. The yard was mud churned by feet and hooves. Someone had hung a strip of cloth in the doorway like a poor man's curtain. It shifted when the wind moved, showing a flicker of lamplight inside.

Andrew called out before stepping closer. "We're Confederate. Lieutenant Mercer, cavalry attached. We need water and directions."

The cloth moved. A woman's face appeared, then withdrew. A moment later a man stepped out, thin and wary, sleeves rolled to the elbow as if he had been working. His hair was wet with sweat or rain. He held nothing in his hands, but his stance was guarded, weight balanced in a way Andrew recognized.

"You got the look of soldiers," the man said. His accent was local, and his eyes were the cautious eyes of someone who had learned uniforms did not guarantee anything. "But that don't mean much these days."

"It means I'll pay for what we take," Andrew replied, and felt the grim humor of it. Pay, with what. He reached into his pocket and produced two coins worn nearly smooth, the last of what he had not already exchanged for food. "Or I'll leave something else of use. We're not here to raid."

The man's gaze dropped to the coins and lifted again, measuring. He glanced past Andrew to the waiting column, the lowered heads, the mud-slick boots. "You're far east," he said. "Roads ain't kind that way."

"We've orders," Andrew said, and the phrase tasted stale in his mouth. "Is this place still called Mill Creek?"

The man gave a short, humorless laugh. "Ain't been a mill in a year. Creek's still there, though. If that's what you're after, it's behind the cabins."

Andrew nodded. "Any blue patrols nearby?"

"Sometimes," the man said. "Sometimes it's your own boys, looking for corn like everyone else. Sometimes it's men without flags. And sometimes…" He stopped. His mouth tightened as if he regretted that his tongue had almost kept going.

Haines, standing just behind Andrew, shifted. "Sometimes what?"

The man's eyes moved to the trees, then back. "You heard the talk," he said quietly.

Andrew held his expression neutral. "We've heard plenty of talk."

This time the man did not laugh. He looked tired enough that fear had become a kind of routine.

"Then you know what folks say about the plantation rise," he replied. "About the orchard."

Rudd's face tightened at the mention, and he looked down, as if avoiding eye contact with the very idea.

Andrew turned his head slightly, listening not only to the man but to the place itself. There were the ordinary sounds of evening: a distant frog, a wet breeze in leaves, the soft crack of a log burning. Yet even here, a mile or two away from that rise, there was a hesitance in the air, as if people spoke around certain words the way a tongue avoids a broken tooth.

"We passed a fellow on the road," Andrew said. "He claimed men vanished near there."

The man's jaw worked. "Fellow with a stripped wagon?" he asked.

Andrew nodded once.

"Then you been warned," the man said. "That boy's got sense enough to run, at least. Most don't. Most go looking. Or they send soldiers."

A flicker of something like irritation rose in Andrew, not at the man, but at the way the war had made everyone a prophet. "We're not chasing stories," he said. "We're assessing the road."

The man's eyes did not soften. "Road goes by it," he replied. "And sundown makes it worse."

Haines spoke before Andrew could. "Worse how?"

The man exhaled. In the lamplight behind him, Andrew could see another figure moving inside the cabin, slow and tense, listening. "You ever seen a place that feels like it's holding its breath?" the man asked. "Like it wants you to be the first one to make noise?"

Rudd made a small sound, almost a scoff, but it died in his throat.

Andrew kept his voice even. "Places don't want," he said. "People want. Animals want."

The man stared at him a moment longer, then nodded, not agreeing, just acknowledging Andrew's need to say it. "Then tell your men to keep wanting daylight," he said. "Because once the sun drops, you can march right past and still feel it watching."

Haines's grip tightened on the horse's lead. "Watching," he repeated, as if tasting the word and finding it bitter.

The man's gaze flicked to Haines's hands. "If you're headed toward the rise, you can camp here," he said, and the offer sounded like a man offering to share his last blanket with a stranger because he couldn't stand the thought of another body turning up in a ditch. "You can take water, rest. Leave at first light."

"We can't lose a full day," Andrew replied automatically. Then he heard his own voice and recognized the old discipline behind it, stubborn as a reflex. He studied the man's face, the mud on his boots, the thinness of his wrists. This wasn't command. This was a civilian trying to stay alive.

Behind them, the light was already turning. The sky, what could be seen of it through branches, had begun to take on that bruised color that came before night. Clouds smeared the horizon so thoroughly there would be no clean sunset, no bright line to mark the boundary. Just a gradual draining, as if someone were pouring the day out.

Andrew looked back at his men. They stood in the road like tired fence posts, some leaning on rifles, some staring at the ground. The thought of pushing them onward into unknown country in failing light stirred something in him that was not superstition but calculation. If they reached the plantation near full dark, they would be navigating ruins and trees and whatever else with tired eyes. If there were raiders, that would be enough. If there were anything stranger, it would be foolishness made into a gift.

"We'll take water," Andrew decided. "We'll camp near the creek and move at dawn."

Haines did not look relieved, exactly, but the tension in his shoulders eased by a fraction. Rudd let out a breath he might not have realized he'd been holding.

The man nodded quickly, as if afraid Andrew might change his mind. "Creek's behind," he said. "Don't go far into the trees. Stay where you can see the road."

Andrew's mouth tightened. "You think something's coming here?"

The man hesitated. His eyes dropped, then lifted again, and in them Andrew saw the particular embarrassment of fear, the shame people felt when they could not justify their dread in sensible terms. "I think," the man said carefully, "that some places draw trouble like a lantern draws moths. And that rise is a lantern."

Andrew held his gaze. "Have you seen anything yourself?"

The man's throat worked. "I heard chain once," he admitted. "Not here. Over that way." He nodded toward the east without pointing, as if a finger might be too bold. "Heard it like somebody dragging iron slow, like they had all night and weren't in a hurry."

Rudd's fingers tightened around the flagpole until his knuckles showed white.

Andrew turned away before his men could see too much of his own reaction. He did not believe in grave-men, not in the way children believed. But the war had taught him that belief was not the point. The point was behavior. People did not alter their lives so thoroughly over nothing. They did not stop going somewhere after sundown out of mere fancy, not when hunger could push a man into a burning house.

They moved to the creek in small groups, filling canteens, letting the horse drink. The water ran brown with churned earth, but it was water. The men settled into the shallow shelter of the trees near the cabins, close enough that the faint lamplight and smoke stayed within sight. A few spoke quietly with the locals, trading cigarettes for a strip of bacon, a handful of dried beans, anything that could be boiled. The civilians spoke in return in the guarded, half-coded way of people sharing information they were afraid to fully name.

Andrew sat on a fallen log and watched the last of the light fade. The air cooled quickly, the damp turning to chill that crept into bones. Somewhere in the distance a dog barked once, then fell silent, as if it had remembered something.

Haines approached and crouched near Andrew, keeping his voice low. “Men are talking,” he said.

“Men always talk,” Andrew replied.

“Not about rations,” Haines said. He glanced toward the locals’ cabins, then toward the east where the road disappeared into trees. “They’re saying the orchard’s quiet. No birds, no insects. Like it’s dead ground.”

Andrew rubbed a hand over his face, feeling grit and fatigue. “Dead ground is half of Virginia now.”

Haines hesitated. “Corporal Jakes says his cousin was near that plantation last winter. Says he saw windows painted black from the inside.”

Andrew felt the phrase hook into him because it matched too neatly with what the civilians at the cabins had whispered in the storm, in that earlier story he’d dismissed as wartime hysteria. He kept his expression flat. “Paint doesn’t kill men.”

“No,” Haines agreed. “But people paint windows black when they’re trying to keep something out. Or keep something in.”

A wind moved through the trees, and the creek’s surface broke into small shivering patterns. The campfire the men had coaxed into life snapped once, a sound too sharp in the gathering dark. Several heads turned at it.

Andrew stood. “Double the sentries,” he said. “Not because of haints. Because of men. We’ll move at first light and be done with it.”

Haines nodded, but his eyes did not leave the eastern trees.

As night settled fully, the cabins behind them went quieter, as if the locals were packing their fear into their walls. Even the smoke from their chimneys thinned, careful, like a man trying not to draw attention. Andrew lay with his coat rolled under his head and stared up at branches that blocked most of the sky. The clouds moved in slow layers, pale against pale, giving no stars to measure by.

He told himself he was simply listening for footsteps, for the crack of a twig, for the human dangers that came with a war’s unraveling. Yet more than once, in the spaces between the creek’s murmur and the fire’s soft consumption of wood, he thought he heard something else: not a voice, not an animal, but a faint metallic suggestion carried and lost again, as if the night itself had bones that shifted.

When he sat up, straining, the sound was gone.

Only the damp dark remained, and the uneasy sense that somewhere beyond the next rise, an orchard waited in a silence too complete to be natural, as if the land had learned a new kind of superstition and was practicing it at sundown.

Dawn came without ceremony. There was no clean break between night and day, only a slow paling of the mist until the trees took shape again and the creek looked less like a strip of moving ink. Andrew rose stiffly, joints aching from the damp, and watched his men blink themselves awake with the same wary rhythm he'd seen a hundred times after a night too quiet to trust.

No one reported trouble. That should have eased him. Instead, it left him with the uncomfortable sense that the night had simply chosen not to spend itself on them.

The locals stayed inside their cabins as the company broke camp. Smoke did not rise from the chimneys now. Doors remained shut. Andrew caught a face once behind a curtain, eyes following the soldiers as if measuring whether they were about to become another story people told in half sentences.

Haines brought the gelding up, its head low, ears turning toward the eastern road. "He's restless," he said, and tried to make it sound like nothing.

Andrew took the reins and felt the animal tremble faintly through the leather. "So are we," he replied.

They moved out just after first light, boots sucking at clay, the road narrowing as it ran toward the rise. Mist clung low between the trees, blurring distance and swallowing sound. It should have been alive with morning birds, with the small commotion of day beginning again. Instead, there was an absence that pressed on the senses. A man could convince himself of almost anything in a quiet like that.

Private Rudd walked a few paces behind Andrew, the rolled flag still under his arm like a wound carried in public. Kellan ranged to the right, rifle held with both hands, eyes flicking into the brush. Jakes, older and tight-lipped, kept glancing back as though expecting the cabins behind them to call them back with a shout.

They crested the rise and the plantation came into view.

The big house was a ruin, as the civilian had described. Charred columns stood like blackened bones. One half of the roof had collapsed inward, and rainwater pooled in the hollow of it. The remaining windows were empty frames, the glass long gone, the interior dark as an open throat. Whatever wealth had lived there once had burned and washed away, leaving only the suggestion of what it had been.

Below it, the orchard stretched in disciplined rows.

Apple trees stood with their branches slick from mist, their trunks dark and wet. The ground beneath them was a tangle of grass and fallen limbs, unkempt but not wild. It looked maintained in the way a graveyard could look maintained: not alive but tended. The orchard house crouched among the trees, smaller than the main house, roof sagging, porch listing slightly. It should have looked merely abandoned.

Instead, it looked inhabited by the lack of everything else.

Andrew halted them at the first line of trees. The men stopped without being told. Even the horse's breathing seemed loud.

"You hear anything?" Andrew asked quietly.

Haines shook his head once, eyes narrowed. "No, sir."

"That's the trouble," Kellan muttered.

Andrew did not answer. He studied the orchard, the way the mist hung between trunks, the way the branches held still as if they were carved. A place could be quiet for innocent reasons. Weather could deaden sound. Fear could make men hear their own blood. He told himself all of that and none of it settled his mind.

"Spread out," he ordered. "Two on the road. The rest with me. Slow, and keep your eyes up."

They moved in, boots brushing wet grass. As soon as they passed under the first branches, the air changed. The faint smell Andrew had caught on the road returned, stronger here: an overripe sweetness, out of season, mixed with damp wood and something metallic buried beneath it. It made his stomach tighten with a memory he couldn't place, like walking past a butcher's shed after rain.

The porch boards creaked under his weight. He could see the front door was ajar, rocking slightly in the weak breeze. He did not like that. A closed door implied neglect. An open one implied either haste or invitation.

Haines stepped to the side of the doorway, rifle angled in. "If it's raiders, they're sloppy," he whispered.

Andrew drew his pistol, more for the comfort of the motion than because he believed it would solve whatever waited inside. "Or they want to be found," he said.

He nudged the door with the toe of his boot, and it swung inward with a soft complaint. The smell inside thickened. The entry room was dim, not because the day hadn't reached it, but because the windows were darkened from within. Not shuttered. Painted, by the look of it. The glass was coated in uneven strokes of black, as if whoever had done it hadn't cared about appearances, only results.

The men stepped in carefully, boots thudding on warped boards. Their breath came out in pale puffs. It was colder inside than it ought to have been.

Furniture lay overturned in the front room: a table on its side, chairs scattered, one leg snapped clean off. Someone had dragged a heavy sideboard across a doorway as a barricade. The wood was gouged with deep scratches. Not the shallow marks of a boot heel or a dropped tool, but long parallel lines that suggested frantic hands or something sharper used without thought.

Rudd stared at the scratches and swallowed. "Looks like they tried to hold it," he said.

"Hold what?" Kellan asked, too quick.

Andrew did not answer. He moved deeper, eyes scanning. On an interior door, someone had nailed up a crude cross made from scrap lumber. The nail heads were bent, hammered in hard enough to split the wood. Another cross hung crooked over a window frame, as if it had been ripped down and put back up again in a hurry.

"Religion," Jakes muttered behind him, and there was contempt in it. Not for God, but for the idea that faith alone could stop what rifles could not.

Andrew ran his fingers along the edge of one cross. The wood was rough, hurriedly cut. He imagined hands making it in the dark, listening for footsteps upstairs, listening for a chain, listening for their own courage to fail.

They passed a room to the left that was blackened by fire. Not the ordinary soot of a fireplace gone wrong. The entire far wall was charred from floor to ceiling, the plaster bubbled and cracked. The smell of old smoke still clung to it, faint but persistent, like a memory that refused to die. On the floor lay the remains of something that might once have been a mattress, now a clumped mass of ash and springs.

Haines leaned in, eyes narrowing. "They burned something," he said.

"Or tried to," Andrew replied.

He forced himself to look at the blackened wall longer than he wanted to. In the soot, there were streaks where something had dragged, leaving cleaner lines through the char, as if someone had leaned their hands against it and slid down. The marks were too long for a child, too low for a man standing. A man crawling, then. A man trying to get away from heat. Or toward it.

Andrew stepped back and felt the room press him away, as if it resented being noticed.

"Sir," Kellan said from the hall, voice tight. "Back here."

They found the cellar stairs in a narrow passage toward the rear of the house. The air coming up from below was cold, and the sweet-metal scent gathered there, heavier. The cellar door itself stood partly open, and for a moment Andrew simply stared at that. Something in him had expected a lock. A barrier. A clean boundary between above and below.

Instead, the door looked as though someone had fled through it and never thought to shut it behind them.

Haines shifted beside him. "We can leave it," he said quietly. It was not a suggestion of cowardice. It was a calculation, the kind good soldiers made when the ground felt wrong.

Andrew heard again the civilian's voice from yesterday: You ever seen a place that feels like it's holding its breath?

He tightened his grip on the pistol. "No," he said, and pushed the door wider.

The stairs creaked under their weight. The cellar below was stone-lined, damp, strewn with collapsed crates and broken jars that caught the weak light in dull glints. Water dripped somewhere steadily, a patient sound. Andrew descended carefully, eyes adjusting.

Then he saw the iron rings bolted into the wall.

They were not decorative. Not the remnants of some farm use. They were set at the height of a man's wrists and ankles, and the stone around the bolts was worn, as if something had strained against them repeatedly over years. Chains lay on the floor, one end still fixed to the wall, the other end snapped. The broken link was twisted open, not cut clean, as though it had been forced apart by strength applied without tools.

Rudd made a small sound behind Andrew, like breath caught. "What in God's name…"

Andrew crouched and lifted the broken end of the chain. It was heavier than it looked, thick enough to hold a mule. The metal was rusted, but the break itself was bright in places where the iron had been torn fresh, as if the rupture was recent. He ran his thumb along it and felt a burr that snagged his skin.

He straightened slowly and looked at the rest of the cellar. The crates were not merely collapsed from neglect. They had been shoved aside, toppled in a pattern that suggested struggle. Drag marks scored the damp floor toward the stairs, then stopped. In the mud near the bottom step were old footprints layered on newer ones, confused and overlapping. He could not tell whose were whose, only that more than one man had come down here and not all of them had walked away calmly.

Haines shone his lantern toward a far corner. For an instant the light caught something dark on the stone: a stain, brown-black, soaked in and spread thin. Not fresh. Not washed away entirely, either. The kind of mark left when blood had time to dry and no one had the strength to scrub it.

Andrew's men stayed close now, shoulders tight, rifles held with both hands. The cellar felt too small for the number of them, as if it were closing around their bodies to learn their shape.

"This isn't a deserter's hide," Jakes said, voice low. "This is… a pen."

Andrew kept his face composed, because officers were meant to be composed, and because if he allowed his own unease to show it would spread through the men like fever. He looked again at the rings, at the snapped chain, at the drag marks that ended without explanation.

He thought of the civilians crossing themselves at the mention of iron clinking in the dark. He thought of boot tracks that went in and did not come out. He thought of windows painted black from the inside, not to keep the sun out, but to keep the world from seeing in.

He did not yet have a name for what this meant. But he recognized its structure.

Terror, he realized, left architecture behind.

“Back up,” he ordered, voice steady. “Everyone out of the cellar. We’ll search the grounds in daylight, and we’ll do it together.”

Haines hesitated. “Sir, do we report this?”

Andrew followed his men up the stairs, each step an effort not to hurry. At the top he paused and looked back once more into the cellar’s dim mouth, at the iron rings catching the weak light like dull eyes.

“Not yet,” he said. “Not until I know what I’m reporting.”

He closed the cellar door gently, without slamming it, as if loudness might invite a reply. Then he turned back into the house, into the overturned furniture and nailed-up crosses, and felt the first true shift inside himself: not belief in ghosts, not acceptance of superstition, but the sober recognition that whatever had happened here had not been a simple crime.

It had been panic, yes.

But panic with reason.

Chapter 3

Orchard of Bones

Outside, the orchard air met them like a held judgment.

Andrew stepped off the porch and paused long enough to let his eyes adjust to the gray day. The mist had thinned but not lifted; it sat in strips between the rows of trees, turning distance into a soft blur. Behind him the orchard house crouched in damp silence, its darkened windows refusing the morning like a man refusing confession.

He felt his men waiting for the next order, felt the twitch in their hands and the way their attention kept sliding back toward the cellar door as if it might open of its own accord. He understood the impulse. He had closed it gently, and the gentleness had not made him feel brave. It had made him feel like he'd laid a lid over boiling water.

"Pairs," he said. His voice came out steadier than his thoughts. "No one walks alone. Haines, take Rudd and work the left row toward the fence line. Jakes, you and Kellan with me. Keep your eyes on the ground and the trunks. If you see sign, you call it, you don't investigate it by yourself."

They nodded, and the column loosened into smaller shapes moving between trees. Boots brushed wet grass, making a soft shushing sound. Every few steps someone's canteen or buckle clicked, and the small noise landed too loud in the orchard's unnatural quiet.

Andrew tried to decide whether the stillness was real or only felt real because they expected it. He looked for birds and found none. He listened for insects and heard only the occasional drip of moisture falling from a leaf. The place was not merely empty of sound. It seemed disciplined about it, as if noise was something it did not permit.

Jakes ranged a little ahead, rifle angled down, eyes narrowed at the ground. He was older than most of Andrew's men, his face cut into lines that had been there even before the war. He had the hard practicality of someone raised on poor land. He trusted dirt more than he trusted men.

Kellan stayed too close to Andrew's shoulder. The young man's jaw worked constantly, as if chewing on words he refused to speak. He kept glancing up at the branches, then back down, like he could not decide whether danger would come from above or below.

The rows of apple trees should have been orderly, but time had softened the discipline. Some trunks leaned. Some branches dragged low and heavy with rain, forming curtains that brushed a man's cap as he passed. Fallen apples, out of place for the season, lay half-rotted in the grass. The smell of them thickened with each step, sweet and sour at once, and beneath it the faint metallic note Andrew could not stop noticing.

Jakes halted and lifted one hand.

Andrew stopped beside him. Kellan nearly collided with them, then caught himself, embarrassed and tense.

"What is it?" Andrew asked, keeping his voice low. The orchard did not seem like a place to raise a shout.

Jakes pointed with the muzzle of his rifle. "Ground's been turned."

At first Andrew saw only mud and grass. Then his eye caught the difference: a patch where the grass lay wrong, not matted by rain but disturbed. The earth there was darker, looser. A depression ran along one edge as if something had been pressed down, then dragged.

"Could be a hog rooting," Kellan offered, too quickly.

Jakes made a small sound that might have been contempt. “Hog don’t cover after.”

Andrew crouched. His gloves were damp already, but he pressed his fingers into the soil anyway. It gave too easily, like a wound. He felt clumps rather than packed ground, the way earth felt when it had been turned recently and not given time to settle back into itself.

He glanced up, measuring distances. The patch lay between two trees, close enough to the trunks that the branches above made a dark canopy. Even in daylight, it was shadowed. A man could work there and be half-hidden from anyone looking from the road.

He stood and looked along the row. There were other patches like it, subtle if you weren’t hunting them. Small irregularities in a place that should have been uniform. It was the kind of thing hunger might miss but fear would find.

“Rudd!” Andrew called, not shouting, but louder than the orchard seemed to want.

A moment later he heard boots approaching through wet grass. Haines appeared first between the trunks, face set, then Rudd behind him with the rolled flag tucked under one arm like a forgotten limb.

Haines took in Andrew's posture and the disturbed ground. "You found something."

"We found turned earth," Andrew said. "I want to know why it's turned."

Kellan swallowed. "Sir, if it's graves…"

Andrew looked at him. "If it's graves, we learn what we can. That's all."

That was not all, of course. Graves meant bodies. Bodies meant questions. Questions meant answers that could break a man's sleep for the rest of his life. But he did not say that part aloud.

Jakes had already moved to another patch a few yards down, testing with his boot, watching the way the ground responded. "More here," he said.

Haines's gaze kept flicking toward the orchard house, then back. "Could be the family," he said, though his voice lacked conviction. "Servants. Soldiers."

"Could be anything," Andrew replied. He took a breath that tasted like rotted fruit. "Rudd, take your bayonet and start careful. Don't plunge. Peel."

Rudd's face tightened at the word carefully, but he nodded. He set the flag against a trunk and drew his bayonet, the steel dull in the flat light.

Andrew crouched beside him. “Slow,” he reminded. “If there’s evidence, we don’t destroy it.”

Rudd began to work the blade into the soil, lifting small sections, turning the earth like he was prying up old boards. The first few inches brought up only wet clods and pale roots. The smell grew stronger as the ground opened, a heavy sweetness mixed with something that made Andrew’s stomach tighten.

Kellan backed a step without noticing he’d moved. Jakes stood with his rifle held across his chest, eyes fixed on the hole as if he expected something to reach out.

Rudd’s bayonet struck something harder than soil. He froze. Looked at Andrew as if asking permission to continue.

Andrew nodded once.

Rudd scraped again, this time with the tip, clearing mud away. A pale curve emerged.

For one brief, stupid moment Andrew thought it was stone. Then he saw the texture, the porous matte of it, and the rounded seam where it met something else.

Bone.

Rudd's breath went shallow. He swallowed and kept scraping because stopping would mean admitting he had crossed a line. The earth came away in wet clumps. More pale emerged. A ridge, then the shape of a jawline. Teeth.

Not animal.

Kellan made a sound in the back of his throat. He turned his head as if to look away, then forced himself to look back, as though the sight might punish him for flinching.

Andrew leaned closer, careful not to step into the disturbed soil. The skull lay tilted, half turned on its side, packed in mud. The body beneath it was not fully decomposed, not clean bone all the way through. There were strands of dark material still clinging, the remnants of hair or cloth, swollen with water and time.

"How deep?" Haines asked, voice tight.

Andrew looked at the shallow pit, the way the skull sat close to the surface. "Not deep enough," he said.

Rudd's hands shook as he cleared more. A shoulder emerged, then ribs, then a forearm bent at an angle that suggested it had been shoved into the ground without care for how it lay. The clothing was in tatters, but enough remained to show it had once been decent. Not a soldier's uniform. A civilian coat, the fabric rotted and dark with damp.

Jakes shifted, boots whispering in the grass. "This ain't proper burial," he said. "This is hiding."

Andrew did not answer. He studied the bones, the scraps of clothing. He tried to place the age of the grave by the state of the remains and found he could not, not with certainty. The war had changed the rules. Bodies decayed differently when the ground stayed wet, when insects avoided a place, when the air itself felt reluctant.

He forced his mind away from speculation and into action. "We check the others," he said. "We don't open them all. We confirm a pattern."

Rudd sat back on his heels, mud on his gloves, face pale. "Sir," he whispered, "why here?"

Andrew stared down at the skull's empty sockets, at the jaw slightly open as if it had wanted to speak but had been packed into silence. The question *Why here* felt childish in a place like this. *Why here* was the kind of question men asked when they still believed the world had to make sense.

"Because someone chose it," Andrew said.

They moved down the row, and with each few yards the ground offered another subtle wrongness. Jakes found one by a tree whose trunk bore old scars, deep cuts grown over. Haines found another close to the fence line, hidden where weeds had been allowed to thicken. At each patch the soil gave too easily, and the smell rose up as if the orchard exhaled through its wounds.

They opened the second grave only enough to see what lay beneath. A hand, skeletal fingers curled inward. A sleeve, the cuff frayed. The bones were cleaner than the first, suggesting more time. Or different conditions.

The third grave held something smaller.

Andrew did not let Rudd dig far. A fragment of skull was enough. The shape was wrong for a grown man. The bones were too slight.

Kellan turned away then, pressing his fist hard against his mouth. His shoulders moved once as if he might vomit, but he swallowed it down, eyes shining with a misery too raw to be hidden.

Haines looked at Andrew with something like accusation, though he did not speak it. You said you didn't believe the stories. You said it was fear. You said it was men. Now what?

Andrew felt a strange steadiness settle into him, not calm, but the numb focus that came when emotion became a liability. He had seen massacres on battlefields. He had stepped over bodies stacked like cordwood in trenches. Those were horrors that happened in public, under flags, with drums and orders and the excuse of necessity.

This was different. This was private.

"These ain't battlefield dead," Jakes said softly, as if even he could not keep his voice hard in the face of what the orchard hid. "These are taken."

Andrew straightened and looked back toward the orchard house. From here it was partially obscured by branches, its porch a pale smear behind dripping leaves. The painted windows stared without reflection.

He thought of the iron rings in the cellar wall. Chains set at a man's wrists and ankles. A snapped link, bright where something had forced it apart. The architecture of terror.

He had been wrong to think the cellar was the center of it. The cellar had been a room. The orchard was the graveyard.

"Mark these places," he ordered. His voice carried farther than he intended in the orchard's quiet, and for a moment he expected the trees themselves to react. Nothing moved. Nothing stirred. The stillness accepted his words like dirt accepted blood.

Haines nodded, though his face remained tight. He broke a fallen branch and jammed it upright beside the first disturbed patch, then another by the second. Crude markers, but visible.

Rudd retrieved the flag from the trunk and held it again, not looking at it, just needing something familiar to anchor his hands.

Andrew turned slowly, scanning the rows. There were more patches. He could see them now that he knew what to look for. Small deviations in grass, low mounds, places where roots had been cut and not allowed to knit back together.

He imagined hands working in the dark, digging fast and shallow, listening for hooves or voices. He imagined someone choosing which tree to use, which patch of ground would hide the evidence long enough for the world to move on. He imagined a body carried not in grief but in necessity, an inconvenient shape disposed of like waste.

And beneath those images another thought crept, unwelcome and cold: What if the graves weren't only for hiding? What if they were storage? What if the orchard had been fed.

Andrew forced the thought down. He would not allow himself to build monsters out of air. Not yet. But the graves were real. The bones were real. The way the men's voices had thinned was real.

Jakes stepped closer, lowering his voice. "Sir," he said, "how many you reckon?"

Andrew kept his eyes on the orchard house. The porch was empty. The doorway hung open, dark inside. The cellar beneath it was shut now, but the iron rings remained in his mind as clearly as if he still stood in that cold stone room.

"Enough," Andrew said.

And in the silence that followed, he realized with a slow, sour certainty that the orchard's stillness was not the peace of a place abandoned.

It was the hush of a place that had been used too often, too well, and had learned that secrecy was its most faithful crop.

Andrew left the crude markers standing like accusations and motioned his men back toward the house. No one argued. Even Jakes, who was never quick to take a notion for truth, moved with the quiet obedience of a man who had seen enough to know that stubbornness could become stupidity.

They crossed the orchard rows without speaking, boots whispering through wet grass. The mist clung lower now, as if the trees had decided to keep what they'd shown. Andrew kept his pistol down but ready, not pointed at anything, simply held in the way a man held the last honest tool left to him.

Near the orchard house, the ground grew harder, trampled by old traffic: wagon wheels long gone, footsteps worn into a faint path. Beyond the porch, half-hidden by a curtain of vines and a collapsed fence, stood the outbuildings that had served the place when it still pretended to be a working estate. A smokehouse with a door hanging open. A narrow shed that might once have held tools. A small cabin set back from the rest, its roof sagging and its chimney cracked.

Haines slowed beside Andrew. “Sir,” he said, pitching his voice low, “that cabin wasn’t mentioned in the talk.”

“No one mentions what they don’t want remembered,” Andrew replied, though he wasn’t sure he meant it as wisdom or bitterness.

They approached with the caution they’d learned on skirmish lines. Kellan ranged right. Jakes angled left, rifle steady. Rudd hung behind them, still carrying the rolled flag as if it were a piece of home he could not put down.

The cabin door was shut. Not barred, not locked. Shut with the simple finality of someone too tired for ceremony.

Andrew lifted his hand and knocked once with his knuckles.

Nothing.

He knocked again, harder. The wood sounded thick with damp.

A faint movement came from inside, not footsteps, but the scrape of something dragged across a floor. Then a sound like a cough, wet and deep.

Haines looked at Andrew, eyebrows lifting slightly. Not fear, exactly. A question: *do we open it?*

Andrew tried the latch. It gave under his hand.

The smell that came out was not the cellar's wrong sweetness. This was ordinary human ruin: sickness, sweat gone sour, old smoke, damp blankets. It should have been comforting in its normality. Instead, it only tightened Andrew's throat, because a human smell meant a human story, and human stories were rarely clean.

The cabin was dim, lit by a single narrow window that had not been painted black, though grime and cobwebs dulled the light. A pallet lay on the floor near the hearth. A man lay on it, half-covered by a thin quilt. He was old enough to have seen the plantation before the war and too thin to look as though he'd survived it well. His skin had the ashy pallor of fever. His eyes were open, tracking the doorway with the slow suspicion of someone who had learned not to expect help.

He tried to push himself up. His arms shook. A groan escaped him; more anger than pain.

Andrew took two steps in, careful not to crowd. "Sir," he said, then corrected himself, because this was no sir and the word landed wrong. "You live here?"

The man stared as though the question were a trick. His lips moved. When sound came, it was a rasp that had to be forced through a throat that didn't want to work. "Ain't lived," he said. "Just… stayed."

Haines shifted at Andrew's shoulder. "He's sick."

Jakes spoke from the other side of the door, voice hard with a farmer's impatience for weakness he couldn't cure. "Could be hiding. Could be one of them raiders."

The man's eyes flicked toward Jakes. Even sick, even pinned to the floor by his own failing body, there was something in the look that made Andrew's skin tighten. Not defiance. Knowledge.

"You soldiers," the man whispered. "Gray."

"We are," Andrew said. "Lieutenant Mercer. We're searching this estate. There are graves in the orchard."

The man closed his eyes for a moment, slow, as if the words were heavy and he was too tired to lift them again. When he opened them, the whites were tinged yellow. "Graves," he echoed. "Yes. Them trees been drinking longer than you been marching."

Kellan, hovering near the window, made a small involuntary sound. Andrew shot him a look that stilled him.

Andrew crouched, keeping his pistol lowered. "What's your name?"

The man's tongue worked, wetting cracked lips. "Moses," he said finally, and the name came out like a confession. "Moses Talley."

Andrew nodded once. He had heard the surname before on lists. Plantation ledgers. In another life, a name like that would have been an entry, not a face.

"Were you the groundskeeper?" Andrew asked.

Moses gave a thin, humorless breath that might have been a laugh if he'd had the strength. "Ground been keeping things," he whispered. "Not me."

Haines stepped forward, canteen in hand. "Water," he said, and held it out.

Moses stared at it with suspicion that looked practiced. Then his gaze lifted past Haines to Andrew's collar, to the insignia that meant command. Something in him settled, not trust, but resignation.

He drank when Haines tipped the canteen, only a few swallows before his throat seized and he coughed, liquid dribbling from the corner of his mouth. Haines lowered the canteen quickly, eyes flicking away as if embarrassed by the intimacy of illness.

Andrew waited until Moses' breathing steadied.

"What happened here?" Andrew asked.

Moses' eyes focused on the hearth stones, not looking at any of them. "Happened slow," he said, each word pulled up from deep. "Folks think evil come like raiders, quick. But it come like rot. Quiet. You don't smell it till you already been breathing it a long while."

Jakes shifted, impatient. "We ain't got time for parables."

Moses' gaze snapped to him. For a moment Andrew saw a flash of something fierce behind the fever. "Time," Moses rasped. "You got plenty time. That's what it takes. It waits."

Andrew held up a hand toward Jakes without looking at him. "Tell me about the cellar," he said. "The chains."

Moses swallowed. His throat bobbed like it hurt. "They built it for keeping," he whispered. "Not potatoes. Not apples. Keeping."

Andrew felt the word settle in him. Keeping. Not storing. Not hiding. Keeping, like an ongoing act.

"The family that owned this place," Andrew said carefully, "they did this?"

Moses' eyelids fluttered. "Family did what family do," he murmured. "Kept their name clean. Kept their table full. Kept their secrets fed."

Haines went still at that, his jaw tightening.

Andrew kept his voice level. "Who was chained down there?"

Moses' mouth pulled into something that was almost a smile and almost a grimace. "He weren't always chained," he said. "At first he was guest."

Kellan blurted, unable to help himself, "A guest?"

Moses turned his eyes toward the young man. "You ever see a man walk in a room and everyone make room for him?" he asked. "Not because he shout. Because he don't have to."

Kellan's cheeks mottled. He looked away.

Andrew pressed, because he could feel the thread of the story and he knew if he didn't hold it, it would snap. "When did this guest arrive?"

Moses' lips moved without sound for a moment, working around time that no longer mattered. "Before," he whispered. "Before you. Before your war. Before my daddy's daddy turned this soil. He come from across water. Talked fine. Smelled clean. Had hands like he never worked a day."

A memory stirred in Andrew of the pale man described by frightened civilians, the way he had been spoken of as a starving gentleman out of another century. Andrew kept his face still, but inside him something tightened like a knot being pulled.

"And then?" Andrew asked.

Moses' voice dropped, forcing them to lean closer to catch it. "Then folks start going missing," he said. "Servants. Travelers. Hired hands. People you can lose without the world stopping."

Jakes' nostrils flared. Rudd stared at Moses as if he'd become another grave opened up.

Andrew felt a cold, practical anger rise. Not moral outrage. Something simpler: the anger of a man seeing a pattern he'd been trained to hate, the quiet selection of who counted and who did not.

"Why didn't you leave?" Andrew asked, and he heard the bluntness of it and did not take it back. In this war, leaving had become its own kind of cruelty.

Moses' eyes softened, not with forgiveness, but with the tired sorrow of someone who had answered that question too many times in his own head. "Leave where?" he whispered. "Roads got patrols. Woods got men. And this place…" He coughed again, then forced himself on. "This place got its hooks. You live near a thing long enough; you start measuring your days around it. You start thinking if you do everything right, it won't look your way."

Andrew thought of his own men, marching by habit and loyalty and geography. He did not like the parallel.

Haines asked, voice roughened, "And the chains? Who put him down there?"

Moses' gaze slid toward the corner of the cabin where old tools leaned against the wall: a shovel handle, a broken rake, things that should have felt ordinary. "When it got bad," he said, "they tried prayers. Then they tried iron. Then they tried fire. They blackened the windows so day couldn't touch him. They carved words in wood, in Latin like that make it holy. They put crosses up like nails could hold back hunger."

Andrew saw again the crude crosses in the orchard house, the wall blackened by an attempt at burning. A single ugly story told in many rooms.

Moses' voice thinned further. "They buried him," he whispered.

Andrew held still. "Buried him," he repeated. "In the cellar?"

Moses shook his head, the motion small but fierce. "Not buried because he was dead," he said, and for the first time the words carried something like clarity, as if fever had burned away everything but the truth. "Buried because he would not die."

The cabin went quiet around the sentence. Even Jakes did not speak.

Andrew felt his pulse in his throat. He kept his face calm because he was still an officer and officers were expected to be made of steadier substance than fear. But he could not keep his mind from returning to the snapped chain link in the cellar, bright where it had been forced open recently.

"What was his name?" Andrew asked.

Moses' eyes drifted, unfocused. "Names," he murmured, and there was contempt in it, faint but real. "He got many. But the mistress… she called him Ambrose. Like it was a hymn."

Ambrose.

The word landed with a weight Andrew could not explain. It sounded too ordinary for what Moses described. That was part of its horror. Monsters in stories had names that warned you. This one had a gentleman's name.

Andrew waited, but Moses' gaze began to slide away again, the fever dragging him under.

"Listen to me," Andrew said, sharper than he intended, and immediately softened his voice. "Moses. Where is he now?"

Moses' lips moved in a whisper that was more breath than sound. Andrew leaned closer, catching it.

"Not in the ground," Moses said. "Not anymore."

A chill traveled through Andrew with the slow inevitability of water seeping into boots. He straightened and looked at his men. Their faces were pale in the cabin's dim light; their eyes fixed on Moses as if he were a prophet and a corpse at once.

Haines spoke quietly, as if afraid to let the walls hear. "Sir," he said, "we need to tell command."

Andrew watched Moses' chest rise and fall in thin, uneven motions. The man looked already half gone, but his eyes opened once more, fixing on Andrew with startling intensity.

"Lieutenant," Moses whispered, and this time the title did not sound respectful. It sounded like warning bells. "You keep your men close. Don't let them wander. Don't let them think daylight mean safe."

Andrew held his gaze. "Why?" he asked, though he already felt the shape of the answer in his bones.

Moses' lips barely moved. "He don't just take," he breathed. "He learns."

Then his eyes rolled slightly, focus slipping, the fever reclaiming him. His head turned toward the hearth stones as if he could rest there.

Andrew rose slowly, every movement controlled. He stepped out of the cabin into the damp air of the orchard and felt, with a clarity that made his stomach tighten, how exposed the rows of trees were, how close together, how easily a man could vanish between them without a sound.

Behind him, inside the cabin, Moses coughed once, a wet, final-sounding noise.

Andrew looked toward the orchard house with its painted windows and its open mouth of a doorway. The graves they'd found were not the whole story. They were the leftovers.

He gathered his men with a look and a gesture, not needing to raise his voice. "Back to the house," he said. "We inventory what we can while it's daylight. And nobody goes off alone. Not for water. Not for piss. Not for prayer."

They moved, and the orchard remained quiet around them, accepting their footsteps the way it had accepted everything else.

As Andrew walked, he could not stop thinking of Moses' last words.

He learns.

And somewhere beneath the stillness, beneath the sweet-metal stench of old blood and rotted fruit, Andrew began to feel something else, faint but undeniable: the sense that they were not simply searching a crime scene.

They were trespassing in a routine.

They went back to the orchard house as if returning to a place they had only imagined and now could not unsee. The porch sagged under their boots; the boards held water in their cracks and gave off the sour smell of old rot. Andrew posted Haines at the front with two men and sent Jakes around the rear, not because he expected a charge from the painted windows, but because the war had taught him the cost of assuming anything was truly empty.

Inside, the air was colder than the day deserved. The blackened windows made the rooms feel as though they belonged to twilight even at noon, and every overturned chair seemed less like the aftermath of hurried looting and more like a memory of people trying to build shelter out of furniture.

"Search it proper," Andrew ordered. "We take what supplies might still be useful, and we find paper. Letters. Journals. Anything that tells us who lived here and who came to visit."

The men moved with reluctant purpose. Rudd and Kellan began opening drawers, lifting warped lids from chests, stepping around the scorched room with the burned wall. Jakes checked behind doors and under a narrow stair as if expecting a man with a knife to spring from old shadows. Haines stood near the entry, rifle loose but ready, watching the open doorway as though the orchard might decide to send something in.

Andrew walked from room to room, reading the place the way he read a field before a fight. A small table had been dragged across one interior doorway and abandoned there, one leg broken. A cabinet lay on its face, the wood split where someone had tried to force it open. Near the kitchen, he found a cluster of crude crosses nailed not only to doors but to the frame around a pantry, the nails sunk deep enough to crack the wood. Someone had been afraid of that pantry. Afraid enough to hammer until their hands hurt.

He stopped by the cellar door and listened.

Nothing answered. No chain. No scrape. Only the steady drip of water somewhere below, patient as a clock.

Andrew had expected the silence to reassure him. It did the opposite. He could not rid himself of Moses's rasped certainty: *it waits*.

Rudd called from a side room. "Sir. Found a book."

Andrew went to him. The room had once been a parlor or a sitting room, but the furniture was shoved aside and one window had been boarded from inside as if the glass alone had not felt solid enough. Rudd held out a small ledger, its cover swollen from damp. The pages stuck together at the edges.

Andrew took it carefully, as if it might crumble. He flipped through until the ink began to show, faded but legible in places. Names, dates, expenses. Then, tucked between pages, a loose sheet written in a finer hand.

He read enough to feel his skin tighten.

Not a confession, not plainly. A mention of a guest arriving, a man of refinement, a man who required discretion. A request to move certain servants away, to "send the boy to the far quarter" and "keep the younger women from the orchard house." The words were polite. The intentions beneath them were not.

Andrew folded the sheet and slid it into his coat.

Kellan hovered at the doorway, face pale, eyes restless. "That him?" he asked in a voice that tried to be casual and failed. "Ambrose."

Andrew looked up. "Names on paper don't mean truth," he said. But he did not deny it.

They found more fragments: a child's primer with the pages torn; a rosary in a drawer, the beads blackened by smoke; a small silver-backed mirror with the glass scratched as if someone had scraped at their own reflection. In the scorched room, Jakes discovered a bedframe with shallow cuts along its underside. He ran his finger over them and swore quietly.

"Letters," he said. "Not English."

Andrew knelt and leaned close. The carvings were crude and hurried, cut deep into the wood. He could not read them. He had learned enough Latin in his schooling to recognize the shape of prayers, or at least the attempt at them. Words meant to bind. To keep. To ward off.

"How long you reckon they been doing this?" Haines asked, when Andrew stood again.

Andrew stared at the carved bedframe and pictured hands working by candlelight, carving as if the knife and the wood were the last line between breath and death. "Longer than the war," he said. "Longer than we want to think about."

They worked until the light outside began to thin and the orchard's gray took on that bruised tone that came before night. Andrew kept checking the windows, the doorways, the gaps in the boards, as if expecting movement to betray itself at last. The orchard remained still. There was no flutter of wings, no distant bark of a dog. Even the horse tied near the porch stood with its head low and its eyes too wide.

When the men began to glance at one another and then away, Andrew understood what they were asking without words: where do we sleep?

He had no good answer.

They could camp in the house, but the painted windows and the cellar beneath their feet made it feel like bedding down on a grave. They could camp in the orchard, but the rows of trees offered too many blind corridors. They could retreat to the road, but they had not come this far to leave without learning what they could, and the thought of abandoning Moses alone in his fevered cabin sat wrong in Andrew's gut.

He chose the least bad option.

"We stay near the house," he said. "Not inside it. On the porch and in the open around it, where we can see. Fire small. No wandering. Haines, you take first watch. Jakes, second. Rudd, Kellan, you rotate after."

The men nodded. No one smiled. No one made a joke. The war had trained them to obey, but obedience did not erase the looks that passed between them, quick and uneasy, as if they were all counting how many throats were present and how many might be missing by morning.

They built a small fire a few yards from the porch, more for the comfort of light than for warmth. The flame licked at damp wood and produced more smoke than heat. Andrew sat on the porch steps and held the ledger on his knee without reading it. The pages felt like they held a contagion, and yet he could not stop wanting to turn them and see if the paper would name what men could not.

Night fell in slow layers. Mist returned, thickening between trees until the orchard seemed to float. The house behind him became a darker mass with darker windows. Somewhere in the distance an owl called once, then did not call again.

Andrew kept his pistol across his lap. He did not tell himself he was guarding his men from a monster. He told himself he was guarding them from raiders, from deserters, from the ordinary human violence that grew wild in places like this. He told himself that because it was a story he could live inside.

But the orchard's silence would not let him forget Moses's words. He don't just take. He learns.

Haines paced on watch with the careful steps of a man who did not want to make noise and did not want to be still. He carried his rifle, and the barrel kept swinging slightly as he turned his head, as if his body could not decide what direction to fear most. Several times he glanced toward the orchard rows and then toward Andrew, as though asking with his eyes if he should say what he thought he heard.

Andrew watched him and thought of the patrol from the civilians' story, the men who had gone into the house and left no tracks coming out. He thought of the cellar door sweating condensation, as if the very iron had known something was waiting behind it.

When Haines's watch ended, Jakes took over with fewer steps and more stillness. He stood near the edge of the firelight and stared out into the orchard as if daring it to move. Jakes had the stubbornness of a man who believed anything could be solved with enough lead and anger. Andrew envied him that simplicity and did not trust it.

The men slept in uneasy shifts. Rudd lay with his boots on and the rolled flag clutched against his side like a child's blanket. Kellan slept with his mouth slightly open, breath visible in the chill, his brow drawn tight even in unconsciousness.

Andrew dozed without surrendering fully. He drifted in shallow starts, waking at changes in the fire's crackle, at the whisper of wind in leaves, at the small metallic click of his own pistol shifting against wood. Each time he woke he expected to see a shape among the trees. Each time he saw only mist and the black lines of trunks.

Near midnight, Jakes came close and spoke low. "Something's off," he said.

Andrew sat up fully at once. "What did you see?"

"Ain't seen," Jakes muttered, irritated with himself. "Heard, maybe. Like… somebody stepping where they don't care if the ground takes their foot."

Andrew listened. Nothing. Only the fire, and beyond it the orchard's refusal.

"Keep your eyes open," Andrew said. "If you hear it again, you wake me."

Jakes nodded and moved back into his post.

Time passed. The fire sank lower. Mist thickened until the nearest trees looked like pillars holding up an unseen roof. Andrew's breath made small clouds that dissolved quickly, as if the air was hungry for warmth.

When Kellan's turn came, he took watch with the nervous diligence of youth. He stood too close to the fire at first, then forced himself to move out to the edge of its light, as if he'd realized that comfort made him more vulnerable. He held his rifle in both hands, knuckles pale.

Andrew watched him for a few minutes and then let his eyes close again, not in trust, but in exhaustion. He felt the ground beneath the porch as a steady pressure. He told himself there was nothing in the orchard but trees and old graves.

A soft sound woke him.

Not a shout. Not a gunshot.

A wet dragging noise, brief, and then quiet.

Andrew sat up, heart already racing. The fire had sunk to coals. The orchard was a wall of mist. Kellan was not at his post.

"Kellan," Andrew called softly. He did not want to give the night more voice than it deserved.

No answer.

Haines stirred from where he lay and pushed up on an elbow. "Sir?" he whispered.

Andrew stood. The porch boards creaked, and the sound seemed to travel farther than it should have in the orchard's hush. He stepped down into the damp grass and moved toward where Kellan had been standing. Jakes rose as well, rifle up, eyes narrowed.

They found the rifle first.

It was leaning neatly against the trunk of an apple tree at the edge of the firelight, upright as if someone had taken care not to let it fall into the mud. The butt was clean. The barrel angled slightly, deliberate. Not dropped in panic. Placed.

Andrew's throat tightened.

Haines reached it first and touched it as if expecting it to be hot. "He wouldn't leave this," he said.

No. Kellan had been too fearful, too desperate to hold onto something that made him feel like a soldier. He would have clung to that rifle even if he had to crawl.

Andrew crouched and swept his gaze over the ground.

In the mud, the marks were plain.

Drag lines, shallow but continuous, leading away from the rifle and into the orchard rows. The grass along either side was bent, slicked down as though something had been pulled across it with weight. A heel mark appeared once, then vanished, as if Kellan had kicked in reflex and then been lifted or gripped tighter.

Jakes swore under his breath. Haines's breathing quickened, sharp and white in the cold.

Andrew followed the drag marks with his eyes and felt the orchard open its corridors. The lines went between two trees and into mist where the firelight could not reach.

"Lantern," Andrew said.

Rudd jolted awake at the word, scrambling up with a noise that made Andrew want to strike him for it. But the boy was already fumbling for the lantern, hands shaking.

Haines held the light low as they stepped to the edge of the drag marks. The lantern's beam cut a small tunnel through mist, making the grass shine wet. The drag trail continued, and beside it, in the soft mud, were prints.

Not boots.

Barefoot impressions, long and narrow, pressed deep as if the body that made them carried more weight than it should have. Toes splayed slightly with each step, as if the foot had gripped the ground.

Andrew stared at them and felt something inside him go cold and very still.

Kellan's boot prints were there too, scattered, interrupted, then gone, swallowed by the drag.

The barefoot prints continued without stumbling.

They led into the orchard as calmly as a man walking home.

Chapter 4

The Gentleman in the Dark

The lantern's light shook in Haines's hand, not from wind but from the small betrayals of muscle and breath. It carved a narrow, jaundiced lane through mist and wet leaves, and beyond that lane the orchard swallowed everything into gray.

Andrew stood over the barefoot prints until his eyes began to insist on reason. Barefoot, in freezing mud. Long and narrow, pressed deep. Toes spread slightly, the way a man's might when he'd been walking without shoes for too long and the ground had taught him to grip it.

He looked again for boot soles, for the familiar geometry of hobnails. Kellan's marks were there in broken, frantic punctuation: a heel skid, a toe dug in, then the long drag line where his weight became an object rather than a body. But the other prints stayed consistent, unhurried, aligned as neatly as if they'd been placed for inspection.

“Sir,” Haines said, and there was a question in it he did not want to shape into words. His eyes kept shifting off the lantern’s beam, as though he expected something to step into it and make it official.

Jakes crouched beside one of the impressions, touched the edge with two fingers, then drew back as if the mud itself might bite. “A man can go barefoot,” he muttered, more to argue with his own nerves than to inform anyone. “Deserter. One of them half-wild boys.”

Andrew heard the stubbornness in it and understood the need. If it was a deserter, it belonged to the war. If it belonged to the war, it could be met with the war’s tools.

But the rifle leaning neatly against the tree trunk did not belong to the war. It belonged to something that had time to arrange a scene.

Rudd hovered behind them with the other lantern, his face pallid, lips parted as if he’d forgotten to close his mouth. The rolled flag lay abandoned near the porch steps where he’d dropped it when Andrew called for light. It looked obscene there, a symbol too clean for what they were doing.

Andrew turned back toward the porch. The men who remained were half-awake and tight with confusion, clutching their weapons, eyes wide in the coals' dim glow.

"Everyone stays here," Andrew said. He kept his voice low, even, the way he would in a skirmish line when panic wanted to spread. "No one moves into the orchard unless I tell them. You keep the fire alive. You listen. If you hear shots, you do not come running blind. You wait for an order."

One of the men swallowed hard. "Sir, Kellan…"

"I know," Andrew said, sharper than he meant, then softened by force. "I know."

He looked at Haines and Jakes. Of all of them, these two had the best chance of not losing their heads. That was a small, ugly calculus, and he hated how natural it felt.

"Haines, you're with me," he said. "Jakes, you're with us. Rudd, you stay. Keep the lantern here and keep the men steady."

Rudd's eyes flashed with wounded pride, then fear drowned it. "Sir, I can—"

"You can follow orders," Andrew said. He met the young man's gaze until it held. "That'll do."

Andrew took the lantern from Haines long enough to adjust the wick, coaxing a steadier flame. The light did not brighten much, but it stopped fluttering like a nervous heartbeat. He handed it back.

"Slow," he said. "We don't rush into a dark row of trees because a boy's missing. That's how you lose three boys instead."

Jakes grunted, a sound that might have been agreement or discontent. He rolled his shoulders once and lifted his rifle into a ready hold. "If it's raiders," he murmured, "they'll regret it."

Andrew did not answer. He stepped into the drag marks as if stepping into a line of scripture he did not want to read but had been given anyway.

They moved between the trees. The lantern lit the lowest branches and the wet grass, made every drip flash briefly and vanish. Mist thickened around their knees. The orchard's sweetness was stronger away from the fire, cloying and wrong, threaded with that metallic undertone that made Andrew think of old pennies held too long in a mouth.

The drag line kept straight for a dozen yards, then angled as though whoever pulled Kellan had chosen a particular corridor between trunks. Andrew's mind tried to picture it. A man hauling another man by the collar, or by the ankles. It would leave uneven furrows, sudden jerks where grip was adjusted. This line was too smooth. Too continuous. It suggested strength applied without strain.

Jakes saw it too. He did not comment, but his jaw tightened, and he began to glance up more often, scanning branches as if expecting to see a rope.

After a short distance the trees grew closer, their branches knitting overhead into a darker canopy. The lantern's reach seemed to shorten, as if the air itself resented light. Andrew tasted damp on his teeth and felt the cold settle deeper under his collar.

Something moved to the left.

Jakes snapped his rifle toward the sound. Haines's breath hitched. Andrew froze, listening.

A rabbit burst from a brush pile and darted across their path, a pale blur vanishing into mist. It did not pause, did not look back. Its panic was pure animal and therefore honest.

Haines let out a thin breath. "Christ," he whispered.

"Keep your voice down," Andrew said, but not harshly. There was no point punishing a man for being alive.

They pressed on. The drag marks began to fade where grass thickened, but the barefoot prints stayed visible in soft patches of mud, and Andrew found himself following those more than the trail. Each print landed with the same measured depth, the same spacing. It was walking, not running, not stumbling. It was leading them.

That thought landed in him with a cold finality: they were not tracking a fleeing man. They were being allowed to follow.

He forced himself to keep moving anyway, because leaving Kellan out there was not an option he could live with. It would poison his men faster than any rumor. Officers could make hard decisions, but there were decisions that turned a unit into something else, something that would not follow you again.

The orchard began to thin. The rows broke down into wilder growth, the apple trees giving way to older woods where trunks were thicker and bark furrowed deep. The ground sloped slightly downward, and the air changed again. The sweetness did not vanish, but it mingled with the smell of wet leaf rot and black soil. A creek ran somewhere nearby, faint and constant, like distant whispering.

Andrew checked behind them once. The lantern's light did not travel far. The orchard house and their fire were gone, swallowed by mist and distance. The world had narrowed to what the lantern could touch, and to the steady sound of their own breathing.

Haines leaned closer. “Sir,” he murmured, “this is past the orchard.”

“I know,” Andrew said.

Jakes spat into the grass. “Then he’s carrying him away from the house,” he muttered. “Why?”

Andrew’s mind offered answers he did not like. Away from witnesses. Away from iron rings and Latin scratches and crosses. Away from the places that had been used before.

Or toward something else.

A faint sound drifted through the trees ahead, and Andrew stopped so abruptly Haines nearly bumped him.

It was not a cry. Not a struggle. It sounded like a low voice speaking, calm and even, the cadence of conversation rather than command. The words were too soft to catch, but there was something in the tone that made Andrew’s scalp tighten: not the rough, clipped sound of local men, not the blunt music of soldiers. This voice was shaped. It belonged to someone who took care with language.

Haines’s eyes widened slightly. He mouthed without sound, “Kellan?”

Andrew raised a hand, silencing them both, and eased forward.

They crept toward the voice, boots careful on wet leaves. The lantern's light bobbed, catching on ferns and slick bark, making the woods look crowded with small, listening faces.

The ground leveled into a small clearing no bigger than a parlor, ringed by trees whose lower branches hung like curtains. Mist pooled there, thicker, turning the space into something half-stage, half-sickroom.

In the center of the clearing, Kellan knelt.

For a heartbeat Andrew could not make the scene make sense. Kellan's posture was wrong. He was not slumped like an injured man. He was upright, head slightly bowed, hands resting loose at his sides as if he'd been told to be still and found obedience easy. His cap was missing. His hair clung damp to his forehead. His eyes, caught by the lantern's edge, looked open but unfocused, reflecting light without truly seeing it.

And in front of him, half-turned so that the lantern did not yet fully claim his face, stood a man.

At first glance he looked like what Moses had described in fevered fragments: a gentleman fallen into ruin. His clothes were dark and once-fine, now worn and wrong for the woods. His posture, however, was unbroken. He stood as if the clearing belonged to him, as if he had always stood there and the trees had grown up around his certainty.

The man spoke softly, and Kellan's head tilted in minute response, like a flower leaning toward sun.

Andrew felt the hair on his arms rise. He lifted his pistol without meaning to, the motion happening before thought could veto it.

Jakes brought his rifle up, sights finding the man's center mass. Haines's lantern hand shook once, then steadied as he forced it.

Andrew took one more step into the clearing.

A twig snapped under his boot.

The gentleman's head turned.

Even before Andrew saw his eyes clearly, he felt the attention land on him with an intimate weight, like a hand placed gently on the throat.

The man smiled, slight and composed, as if he'd been expecting guests.

"So," he said, voice smooth as river stone, "you came after him."

Andrew did not answer at once. The words had been addressed to him as if this were a social call, as if men did not stand with guns raised and fear sweating cold through their collars.

The lantern light found more of the stranger's face when he turned fully. He was pale, yes, but not in the sickly way Moses had been pale. This pallor looked chosen, preserved, as though the sun had never quite had jurisdiction over him. His cheekbones were sharp, his mouth calm, and his eyes were the most unsettling thing: not bright, not wild, not the theatrical glare of a madman. They were steady. They looked at Andrew the way an appraiser looked at a piece of silver, weighing it for flaws.

Kellan remained kneeling, breathing slow and shallow. A thin thread of saliva had gathered at the corner of his mouth and shone when the lantern shifted. His hands trembled once, then went still again.

Jakes's rifle did not waver. "Step away from him," he said.

The stranger's gaze slid to Jakes without turning his head. The motion was small, economical, dismissive. "Is that meant for me," he asked, "or for your own comfort?"

"Step away," Jakes repeated, louder, and now the command carried the brittle edge of a man who knew his voice was all he controlled.

The stranger's smile deepened by a fraction. He lifted one hand, palm slightly up, as if offering a courtesy. "You are too far to stop me," he said. "And yet you believe the distance between us is measured only in feet."

Andrew felt Haines tense beside him. The lantern made a small, involuntary bob as Haines adjusted his grip.

Andrew kept his pistol trained on the stranger's chest. The man's clothing was wrong for this place but not comical. Dark wool, once tailored, now frayed at the cuffs, damp at the hem. A shirt open at the throat with no neckcloth. The look of a man who had once been careful with his appearance and had since stopped pretending he needed to.

"What have you done to my soldier?" Andrew asked.

The stranger's eyes returned to him. "Your soldier," he repeated softly, tasting the possessive. "Does he belong to you?"

"He belongs to himself," Andrew said, and heard the flatness in his own voice, the way it tried to build a wall between fear and reason. "Wake him."

"Wake him," the stranger echoed, as if amused by the simplicity. He glanced down at Kellan. "He is awake. He is simply quiet. You should appreciate quiet. Men like you spend your lives trying to manufacture it."

Andrew did not flinch, but something in him tightened. The stranger spoke as though he knew Andrew's mind, or at least the shape of it. It was not a drunk's ramble, not a raider's bluster. Every word landed where it meant to.

"Who are you?" Andrew asked.

The stranger looked momentarily thoughtful, as if the question were old and the answers all equally tiresome. Then he gave the smallest inclination of his head, a gesture so restrained it felt more insulting than rudeness.

"Ambrose," he said. "At present."

Haines made a sound that he tried to swallow. It came out anyway, a rough breath. The name was too clean for the clearing, too civilized for the drag marks and the kneeling boy and the graves under the orchard trees.

Andrew kept his pistol steady. "At present," he repeated.

Ambrose's eyes flickered, not to the gun, but to Andrew's face. "Names change," he said. "Men change them when the old ones become inconvenient. When they have done something they cannot carry publicly. When they wish to cross a river and have the water forget."

"We found chains," Andrew said. He did not know why he said it, only that he needed to pin this creature to something tangible. Iron. Stone. Evidence. "In the cellar."

Ambrose's expression softened into something like nostalgia. "Yes," he murmured. "I remember those rings. I remember the family's trembling hands. Such righteous industry. They thought they could repair a mistake with hardware."

"You were chained," Haines said suddenly, and his voice cracked on the words. "In that cellar."

Ambrose looked at him as if noticing him for the first time. "I was kept," he corrected gently. "There is a difference. Chains are for animals. Men are kept by promises."

Andrew felt the cold creep higher under his collar. He shifted his stance by an inch, feet finding firmer purchase on wet leaves. He could not afford to be unbalanced.

"Why are you here?" Andrew asked.

Ambrose's gaze did not move, but the attention in it sharpened, like a blade turned a fraction toward skin. "Because you came," he said. "Because you stepped into the orchard with your boots and your orders and your admirable belief that the world is obligated to make room for your explanations."

Jakes gave a short, disbelieving laugh. "Sir, he's talking like a damn preacher."

Ambrose's head turned toward Jakes then, slow, unhurried. "No," he said. "Preachers offer hope. I offer clarity."

Jakes's jaw worked. His finger tightened on the trigger.

Andrew saw it and snapped, "Hold." The word came out low but absolute.

Jakes glanced at him, eyes hot with confusion and anger. "Lieutenant, he's got Kellan on his knees like—"

"Hold," Andrew repeated.

It was not mercy. It was calculation. Something about Ambrose's composure made Andrew distrust any move made in haste. Raiders flinched. Men lied. Men sweated. This thing did none of those. If it wanted them dead, they would already be dead.

Ambrose watched Andrew with visible interest now, as if the order had pleased him. "You have trained them well," he said. "Or perhaps you have trained yourself. That is rarer."

Haines's voice came thin. "Sir, we should take him. We should—"

Andrew did not take his eyes off Ambrose. “Kellan,” he said, raising his voice slightly. “Private Kellan. Look at me.”

Kellan’s head did not lift. His gaze remained fixed somewhere near Ambrose’s boots, unfocused and obedient. His breathing stayed slow, almost peaceful, as though he were kneeling in church instead of in wet leaves.

Ambrose glanced down again. “He cannot hear you,” he said. “Not because his ears fail, but because you do not interest him at the moment.”

Andrew felt his temper flare, quick and controlled. “Release him.”

Ambrose’s smile returned, faint but genuine in a way that was worse than cruelty. “Release him,” he repeated, as if they were negotiating for a borrowed book. “You speak as though you are my superior.”

“I am an officer,” Andrew said. “And you are on my soil, taking my men.”

Ambrose’s eyes widened a fraction, and in that small change Andrew saw something like delight. “Your soil,” Ambrose murmured. “How quickly men adopt the language of ownership. Even now, when everything you claim is collapsing.”

Jakes's rifle remained trained, but his shoulders were tightening toward a lunge, the way a man's body tried to solve what his mind could not.

Andrew forced himself to slow his breathing. "You were kept by the family here," he said. "You took people. We found the graves. Why leave now?"

Ambrose's gaze drifted past Andrew into the darker woods, as if listening for something farther away than human hearing. When he spoke again, his voice had a thoughtful calm that belonged in a drawing room, not a clearing.

"Because the war has made your country hospitable," he said. "Men vanish every day. You bury them in ledgers, in hurried prayers, in the word 'necessary.' What a generous environment you have created for appetite."

The word appetite made Andrew's stomach tighten. It was too honest. It matched the sweetness in the air, the metallic undernote, the way the orchard felt like it had been fed.

Haines whispered, "Sir, what is he?"

Ambrose looked back to Haines. "What I am," he said, "is not as interesting as what you are."

He took a step, not toward them, but slightly to the side, changing the angle so that the lantern caught his face more fully. His features held their elegance even in damp and ruin. There was no mud on his cheeks, no strain in his posture, only the faint dark staining at the corner of his mouth that the lantern light could not quite disguise.

He looked at Andrew as if seeing layers. “Lieutenant Andrew Mercer,” he said.

Andrew’s grip tightened on the pistol. He had not given his name.

Jakes jerked, startled. “How the hell—”

Ambrose continued smoothly, as though the interruption had not occurred. “Not the loudest of your kind. Not the most pious. Not the most cruel, though you have practiced cruelty when told it was duty.” His eyes narrowed slightly, and the weight of them made Andrew feel briefly exposed, as if his uniform were only cloth. “You are careful with yourself. That is why you are emptying so quickly.”

Andrew held his stance, though his pulse hammered hard enough he could feel it in his hands. “You don’t know me.”

Ambrose’s smile softened into something almost affectionate. “No,” he agreed. “Not yet.”

Kellan swayed faintly, as if the air had shifted. Ambrose did not touch him. He did not need to.

Andrew's mind moved fast, trying to anchor itself. The barefoot prints. The neatly placed rifle. The calm voice in the dark. This was no mad deserter. No raider. This was something that had survived long enough to learn manners as camouflage.

"Let him go," Andrew said, and the words came out like a vow. "You can have me instead."

Haines turned his head sharply. "Sir—"

Ambrose's eyes brightened by a fraction at that, and Andrew hated that he had pleased him. "How noble," Ambrose said. "And how predictable. You think sacrifice is a kind of control."

Andrew took one careful step forward, pistol still up. "You want something," he said. "Tell me what it is."

Ambrose regarded him for a long moment. The clearing held its breath around them. Even the mist seemed to wait.

Then Ambrose's gaze slid to Jakes's rifle, to Haines's lantern, to Andrew's pistol, and he smiled as if at a private joke.

"What I want," he said softly, "is to see whether you can stand still."

The words landed with a quiet finality. Not a threat, not exactly. A test. And Andrew understood with a sick clarity that this was not an encounter shaped by their choices. It was an encounter shaped by Ambrose's curiosity.

Jakes's breath went ragged. His rifle twitched a fraction upward; the reflex of a man who could not endure being spoken to that way.

Andrew saw the movement start and knew he could not stop what came next with orders or reason, only with presence. He held his own ground, forcing his feet to stay planted in wet leaves, forcing his shoulders to remain level, forcing his face to remain calm even as every instinct screamed to back away from the thing smiling in front of him.

Ambrose watched him, almost approving.

And in the kneeling silence between heartbeats, with Kellan unmoving at Ambrose's feet and the lantern light trembling against pale skin, the clearing seemed to narrow, as if the woods themselves leaned in to witness what would happen when a frightened man decided whether he would blink first.

Jakes's finger tightened, and the rifle spoke before the rest of him could decide against it.

The shot tore through the clearing with a hard, flat crack that seemed to punch the mist aside. For an instant Andrew saw the muzzle flash paint

Jakes's face in brief, terrible light. He saw the round's path only by consequence, by the way bark on the tree behind Ambrose spat splinters and the leaves shivered as if struck by an invisible hand.

Ambrose did not flinch.

He did not duck. He did not recoil as a man would when death passed close enough to part the air. He only turned his head slightly, as if listening to a sound he found impolite.

Then he moved.

Andrew would later try to place the movement in time, to decide whether it had occurred before the shot or after, whether Ambrose had anticipated it or simply existed too far outside ordinary speed for the distinction to matter. In the moment, it was only this: Ambrose was in front of Kellan, and then he was not, and then he was at Jakes's shoulder as if he had always stood there.

Jakes made a sound that was half curse, half surprise. His rifle jerked downward. His other hand came up instinctively, too late, and Andrew saw the pale blur of Ambrose's fingers brush his throat with a tenderness that belonged to a lover or a surgeon.

The violence was not loud. It was intimate, close enough that the body's small betrayals became the only language. A wet click. A gasp cut short. Jakes's eyes widened in a sudden, bewildered way, not with pain first but with the shock of being touched in the one place a man could not guard.

He dropped to his knees.

Ambrose's face hovered near his ear, as if offering a private benediction. Whatever he did next, he did quickly. Jakes sagged forward, hands clawing at air, and then he toppled onto the leaves with a sound like a sack of grain hitting damp earth.

Haines's lantern swung wildly. "Jesus," Haines breathed, and the word was not prayer so much as the mind reaching for any familiar shape.

Ambrose turned his attention back to them as calmly as if nothing had happened. Jakes lay on the ground and did not move. The mist began to creep in again, reclaiming the edges of the scene.

Andrew kept himself still.

He felt his own blood pounding. He felt the hot, animal part of him urging flight, urging a shot, urging anything that proved he was not prey. But Ambrose had asked a question that was not spoken aloud, a question made of posture and breath: can you stand where you are when you understand you should not?

Andrew held his pistol on Ambrose's chest and did not fire, because he did not trust his hands to hit what his eyes insisted was a man. He did not lower it, because lowering it would be surrender, and he had not yet decided he could afford that.

Ambrose's gaze flicked down to Jakes's body, then back up. "That was unfortunate," he said, voice mild. "He wanted to be brave. Bravery is so often only impatience wearing a uniform."

Haines took one step back, then caught himself, horrified by his own retreat. The lantern's flame wavered.

"You're bleeding," Ambrose observed, and Andrew realized he meant Haines. Only then did Andrew see the thin line of red on Haines's cheek, a shallow cut from flying bark or leaf-blade, already bead-bright in the lantern light.

Haines touched it and looked at his fingers like he didn't recognize the color.

Ambrose's attention returned to Andrew with that same appraising steadiness. "And you," he said softly. "Still."

Andrew swallowed, forcing his throat to work. "Let Kellan go," he said. The words came out level with effort. "You've made your point."

Ambrose's mouth curved faintly. "My point?" He glanced toward Kellan as if Kellan were an object on a table. "He is not the point. He is only what you came to retrieve. Like a lost glove."

Kellan remained kneeling, head slightly bowed, his face slack with a terrible peace. His eyes caught the lantern light and returned nothing meaningful. Seeing him that way, emptied without injury, did something to Andrew's stomach. A man wounded made sense. A man made compliant by a voice did not.

Andrew kept his pistol trained. "What did you do to him?"

Ambrose considered the question with the patience of a teacher deciding how much to give a slow student. "I asked him to be quiet," he said. "And he discovered how badly he wanted permission."

Haines's breathing went ragged. "Sir," he whispered, "we need to get out of here."

Andrew did not answer. He did not move his eyes from Ambrose's face. If he looked away even once, the clearing would change shape. It already felt less like a place in the woods and more like a room Ambrose owned.

Ambrose took a step, slow and unthreatening, as if he were approaching an acquaintance. Andrew's pistol followed the movement by instinct.

"Stay," Andrew said.

Ambrose stopped, obedient in the way a predator could afford to be obedient. His head tilted slightly. "You intend to shoot me," he said, "or you intend to feel as if you could."

Andrew did not deny it.

"Tell me," Ambrose murmured, and his voice had the quiet confidence of someone reading a letter aloud. "When was the last time you were truly alone, Lieutenant Mercer? Not without company. I mean alone in the sense that matters. Alone with the knowledge that no one is coming to rescue what is left of you."

Andrew felt the question dig in under his ribs. He tasted iron in his mouth, sudden and thin. He did not know if it was fear or the memory of blood.

"The war makes everyone alone," Andrew said, and heard how poor an answer it was.

Ambrose's eyes softened as if in sympathy, which was worse than mockery. "No," he said. "The war gives men crowds. Armies. Causes. Noise. It gives them something to blame themselves against, so they do not have to look too closely at the shape of their own hunger."

He let the sentence settle, then added, quietly, "You do not have that comfort anymore."

Andrew's grip tightened on the pistol until his knuckles ached. He wanted to deny it. He wanted to tell this pale stranger in the woods that he knew nothing, that he was only another horror the war would crush. But Ambrose's words landed in places Andrew kept hidden even from himself: the steady hollowing, the sense of being a moving piece on a board that no longer resembled a nation, the way duty had turned into habit and habit into something like numbness.

Ambrose looked past Andrew for a moment, toward the direction they had come, as if he could see through the orchard and mist to the porch fire and the sleeping men. "They will wait for you," he said. "They will tell themselves you are saving the boy. They will let your courage stand in for their own. That is a kind of love, perhaps."

He returned his attention to Andrew. "But they cannot follow you here. Not truly. Not into what you are beginning to understand."

Haines made a small, strangled sound and raised his rifle higher, a useless gesture against the certainty in Ambrose's posture. "Back off," Haines said, voice cracking. "Back off, you—"

Ambrose's gaze moved to Haines. It was not anger. It was mild interest, like watching a dog strain at a leash. "Do not," Ambrose said, very softly.

Haines stiffened.

Andrew saw it in the man's shoulders first, the sudden rigidity, as if his muscles had been seized by a hand inside his skin. Haines's mouth opened. His eyes went wide, not with fear of death but with the panic of losing control of his own body. The lantern dipped, then steadied again as if held by a different will.

Andrew's pulse hammered. "Haines," he snapped. "Look at me."

Haines's eyes flicked toward Andrew for a fraction of a second, pleading, then slid away again as if dragged.

Ambrose spoke as gently as a man calming a horse. "He is not yours at the moment," he said. "Do you see how quickly ownership fails when the right pressure is applied?"

Andrew felt something cold and furious rise in him, not the hot rage of a brawler but a disciplined anger, the kind that wanted to become action. He raised his pistol a fraction higher, sights aligning on Ambrose's sternum.

Ambrose did not react. He only watched Andrew's face with a quiet attentiveness, as if waiting for him to decide who he was.

Andrew breathed in, slow. He forced his finger to tighten.

Before he could fire, Kellan moved.

It was not a lunge or a scramble. It was a simple shift, like a man waking from prayer. His head lifted a few inches. His eyes blinked once, slow and confused. His mouth worked.

"Kellan," Andrew said immediately, voice low and urgent.

Kellan's gaze drifted toward Andrew, unfocused, then sharpened for a heartbeat with recognition that looked like pain. "Lieutenant?" he whispered. His voice was thin, scraped raw, as if he'd been speaking in his sleep for hours.

Ambrose's attention flicked to him, and the change in the air was immediate. Kellan's expression softened again, beginning to slide back into blankness.

"No," Andrew said, and stepped forward before he could stop himself. The leaves slicked under his boot. He went down on one knee without meaning to, a quick, humiliating stumble.

Ambrose's eyes brightened. Not with surprise. With satisfaction.

Andrew forced himself upright again, refusing to look down, refusing to acknowledge the indignity. The pistol remained in his hand, but his careful stillness had been broken.

Ambrose smiled, small and private. "There it is," he murmured. "You can stand still for yourself. But not for them."

Andrew's voice came rough. "What do you want?"

Ambrose's gaze lingered on Andrew a moment longer, as if committing him to memory. Then he stepped back, unhurried, and the mist seemed to welcome him, closing around his figure like a curtain.

"I want very little," Ambrose said. "I want to continue."

He glanced down at Jakes's body with a mild, almost regretful expression. "And I want you to remember that you were given a choice here, even if you did not like the options."

Andrew took another step, and Haines jerked as if released from a string, gasping. The lantern swung and then steadied again in his own hand, his control returning so abruptly it made him stumble.

"Sir," Haines rasped, eyes wild. "Sir, he's—"

Ambrose's gaze returned to Andrew one last time, and in it Andrew felt something like a hand closing around the back of his neck, not violent, simply possessive.

"You are not the bravest man I have met," Ambrose said, voice soft enough that it felt meant for Andrew alone. "Only the loneliest."

Then he was gone.

Not vanishing in a puff of storybook smoke, not dissolving like a ghost. One moment his pale face was framed by lantern light and wet branches, and the next the clearing held only mist and trees and the sound of Kellan's uneven breathing.

Andrew stood rigid, pistol still raised at empty air, as if his body had not yet accepted the absence.

Kellan swayed on his knees. His hands lifted, trembling, and he pressed them to his own throat as if checking that it still belonged to him. He looked at Andrew with dawning terror. "I couldn't… I couldn't move," he whispered. "He told me to kneel and I—"

"Don't," Andrew said, cutting him off, not unkindly but urgently. He glanced toward Jakes's body, then into the woods where Ambrose had retreated. The mist gave nothing back. "You can explain later. Right now, you stand."

Haines moved to Kellan and hauled him up by the arm. Kellan's legs nearly buckled, but he stayed upright, shaking so hard his teeth clicked.

Andrew crouched by Jakes.

There was no dramatic ruin. No torn flesh. No battlefield mess to make death obvious. Jakes's eyes stared open, surprised, and his mouth was slightly parted as if he'd been about to speak a final curse. At his throat, under the lantern's weak light, Andrew saw only a small dark line, neat as a pen stroke, and a dampness spreading into his collar.

Andrew's stomach turned, not from gore but from the precision of it. This had not been slaughter. It had been selection.

"We can't carry him," Haines said hoarsely, and Andrew heard the shame in it, the disbelief.

Andrew swallowed hard and forced his hands to move. He reached down and closed Jakes's eyes with two fingers, a gesture that felt absurdly tender in that clearing.

"We will not leave him like this," Andrew said, though he did not yet know how he intended to keep the promise.

He rose and looked into the mist again.

The woods were quiet. The orchard beyond waited in its disciplined silence. And somewhere within that silence, a presence had turned its attention to him, not as a target alone, but as something worth remembering.

Andrew gathered his men with a sharp gesture. "Back," he ordered. "Now. And keep your eyes up."

As they stumbled toward the orchard, dragging their living and planning how to return for their dead, Andrew felt the sentence Ambrose had left him with cling like wet cloth.

Not the bravest.

Only the loneliest.

He had dismissed superstition as a civilian luxury. Now he understood the deeper truth beneath the stories: people made monsters when they needed a shape for what had already chosen them.

Chapter 5

A Wound That Does Not Heal

They did not run back through the trees. Running invited noise, and noise invited the kind of attention that did not need invitation. Andrew forced them into a fast, controlled walk, the lantern swinging in Haines's hand like a captive star.

Kellan stumbled twice, both times catching himself with a clumsy desperation. He kept looking over his shoulder, not toward any particular shape, but toward the idea of something following. Haines gripped his arm hard enough to bruise, hauling him along whenever his legs hesitated.

Behind them, the clearing with Jakes's body disappeared into mist as if it had never existed. That was its own kind of wrongness, the ease with which the woods swallowed evidence.

Andrew led by memory and instinct, following the faint corridor of their own crushed leaves and the orchard's sour-sweet smell that grew stronger the closer they came to the rows of apple trees. When the first rigid trunks emerged, black lines in gray fog, Andrew felt an ugly relief that tasted like ash. The orchard, at least, was mapped. It had straight lines. It had human intention in it, even if that intention had been twisted.

The porch fire was a smear of coals when they broke from the trees and into the open around the orchard house. Rudd was on his feet at once, lantern lifted, his face white in the weak light.

"Lieutenant!" he hissed, then saw that Jakes was missing and that Kellan was back, alive in the crude arithmetic of bodies. "Where's—"

"Inside," Andrew snapped. "All of you. Now. Quietly."

They moved, not into the house itself, but under the shelter of the porch and the small open space beneath the eaves where the mist thinned a fraction. The men who had remained behind crowded close, eyes darting, rifles held wrong because fear made hands forget habits.

Rudd looked at Kellan, then at Andrew. "Sir?" His voice cracked on the title.

Andrew took the lantern from Haines and held it up, forcing his own face into its steady light, an officer's face, a man who still belonged to the world of orders and patrols. "Jakes is dead," he said. He did not soften it. Softening would have turned it into a rumor, and rumors grew teeth.

One of the men swore under his breath. Another crossed himself so quickly the gesture looked like a twitch.

Haines's voice came hoarse. "It cut him," he said, and then shook his head as if the sentence made no sense in his mouth. "It just touched him and he fell."

Andrew did not correct the pronoun. Let them keep the shape of it vague if they needed to. The truth would not be made kinder by precision.

"We're leaving at first light," Andrew said. "We take what we can carry, and we go back to the road. Nobody sleeps alone. Nobody walks off the porch for any reason. If you need to piss, you do it in pairs and you do it close enough that a man can put his hand on your coat."

Rudd nodded too hard. "Yes, sir."

Kellan sat down abruptly on the porch boards as if his legs had finally remembered they were allowed to fail. He pressed his palms against his own cheeks, then down his throat, then his chest, checking himself like a man inventorying what still belonged to him.

Andrew crouched in front of him. "Look at me," he said.

Kellan's eyes lifted. They were bloodshot and unfocused at the edges, as if sleep clung to him from the inside.

"What did he do?" Andrew asked.

Kellan's mouth worked. "He talked," he whispered. "That's all. He just… talked." His gaze flicked past Andrew's shoulder into the orchard, and his pupils tightened. "He told me to kneel, and it felt like the only thing left in the world I was allowed to do. Like it'd always been true and I'd only just learned it."

Haines made a sound between a cough and a laugh, sick with it. "We ought to burn this damn place."

"We might," Andrew said, and heard how thin it sounded. Fire had rules. Whatever they had met did not seem interested in rules.

He stood and turned his back to the orchard long enough to address the men again. "Keep the coals alive," he ordered. "Light and heat. Not a blaze. A blaze makes you visible."

They obeyed with fumbling hands, feeding damp wood until it caught with a reluctant hiss. The smoke crawled low under the porch roof and clung to clothing, turning their breath into bitter cloth.

Andrew sat with his pistol across his lap and tried to make his mind behave like it belonged to a soldier again. He went over what he knew: graves, chains, Latin carvings, a man named Ambrose who moved like a thought. He tried to reframe it into something that could be reported up the line without sounding like madness.

He found he could not.

When the first gray of morning began to thin the mist, Andrew took Haines and Rudd and went back.

No one wanted to. Their faces said it plainly. But leaving Jakes in the woods would have broken something in them that Andrew could not repair with speeches or punishment.

They moved through the orchard rows with lanterns held low. The place felt different by day, only in the way a corpse looked different when you saw it in sunlight: nothing changed, and yet everything became harder to pretend about. The sweetness clung to the air. The silence did not lift with dawn. No birds greeted the light. No insects warmed and began their small industry. The orchard held still as if listening.

They found Jakes where he had fallen.

His body lay on damp leaves, already stiffening at the joints. The line at his throat had dried to a dark seam. There was no great pool of blood. That was the first wrongness. A man could die from a small cut if it struck the right place, yes, but even then, the body usually told its story messily. This body looked edited.

Haines knelt and swallowed hard. “That’s it?” he whispered. “That’s all it did to him?”

Andrew crouched, studying the wound in the clearer light. The cut was narrow, precise, angled slightly as if whoever made it had known exactly how much pressure to apply. It reminded Andrew of a surgeon’s scalpel, of careful hands, not panic or rage.

Rudd stood behind them, lantern trembling. “He looks… empty,” the young man said, and then looked ashamed as soon as the words left him, as if describing a dead man that way were a kind of insult.

Andrew understood what he meant. Jakes’s skin had a pallor to it that went beyond death. It had the washed-out look of a man bled for a purpose.

They wrapped him in a blanket and dragged him back through the orchard the way they had dragged wounded men from fields. The blanket snagged on roots. Mud soaked through fabric. Each snag felt like the orchard trying to keep what it had been given.

By midmorning they were on the road again, moving west toward the nearest Confederate camp with a field surgeon and a clerk who could at least pretend to make sense of reports. Andrew kept the column tight. He watched his men's eyes. He listened for the slip of sanity, for the first man to start talking too much, too loudly, the way fear sometimes tried to cleanse itself by becoming story.

No one talked. Even Kellan, usually restless with words, rode in silence, staring down at his hands as if they might begin to obey someone else again.

Andrew's own body began to insist on itself only after the first hour of marching, when adrenaline stopped carrying his skin like armor.

A sting flared along his left side beneath his ribs, sharp enough that it made him inhale too hard. He stopped, fingers going to his coat almost without thought.

Haines noticed at once. "Sir?"

Andrew unbuttoned his coat and pulled his shirt aside.

There was a cut there. He had not felt it in the clearing. He had not felt it on the porch. Now it burned with the clean, insistent pain of fresh injury.

The line was shallow but longer than he liked, a thin slash that tracked diagonally, as if something had drawn across him in passing. The edges were too neat for a branch. It looked less like an accident and more like a signature.

"How in God's name…" Haines began.

Andrew tried to remember the moment. His stumble forward. The slick leaves. Ambrose stepping into the mist. There had been a brush of movement near him then, a closeness, as if the air itself had leaned in.

He had not felt a blade. He had not seen a hand.

Rudd leaned in, face pinched. "It ain't deep," he said quickly, trying to make it small, trying to make it manageable. "It'll mend."

Andrew pressed two fingers to the cut. They came away wet and red.

"It's deep enough," Andrew said. And then, quieter, to himself as much as to the men: "He was close."

They bound it with a strip of cloth torn from a spare shirt. The bleeding slowed quickly, almost too quickly, the way blood sometimes did when the body was in shock.

That should have been reassuring.

Instead, Andrew felt, for the first time since the clearing, the chill of something truly personal. Jakes had died because he fired. Kellan had been taken because he stood watch and was young and frightened and easy to bend. Andrew had been spoken to, studied.

And now he was marked.

When they reached the camp by late afternoon, the guards at the perimeter let them through with the weary suspicion of men who had seen too many stragglers and too many bad stories. Andrew reported to the nearest officer with the few hard facts he could offer: a missing sentry recovered, one corporal dead, evidence of bodies buried near the orchard house.

He did not say Ambrose's name. Not yet.

They carried Jakes to the surgeon's tent.

The field surgeon, a man named Whitcomb with gray at his temples and a red rawness around his eyes from too little sleep, looked up as they entered and immediately frowned at the blanket-wrapped shape.

"Another one," he muttered, as if the war were an assembly line and he was the only man left counting. "Set him there."

They laid Jakes on a rough table. Whitcomb pulled back the blanket and leaned in, his hands moving with the practiced efficiency of someone who had stopped pretending death was sacred.

His frown deepened when he saw the throat. He touched the cut with two fingers, then pressed lightly at the collar.

"That's it?" he asked, not looking at Andrew yet. "No other wounds?"

"No, doctor," Haines said. His voice had a strained politeness, the tone of a man asking permission to believe what he was saying.

Whitcomb drew a small knife and gently widened the cut just enough to see beneath. He made a sound of irritation.

"What?" Andrew asked.

Whitcomb finally looked up, meeting Andrew's eyes with the blunt impatience of a man who did not have time for mystery. "I've seen men die from a nick like this," he said. "If it opens the right vessel, it's quick. But this—" He pressed at Jakes's skin again, then at the inside of his arm, as if checking for life by habit even though there was none. “This man has lost more blood than this wound should allow.”

Rudd shifted, swallowing. “Maybe it bled into the ground.”

Whitcomb’s mouth tightened. “Then the ground drank it and left no stain,” he said. He lifted Jakes’s eyelid, stared at the pallor beneath. “He’s white as tallow.”

Andrew felt his cut under the bandage begin to throb, not with pain alone but with awareness, as if the flesh were listening.

Whitcomb wiped his hands on a cloth and nodded toward Andrew. “You’re bleeding too, Lieutenant.”

“It’s nothing,” Andrew said, and hated how quickly the lie came. He had told himself it was nothing the moment he saw it.

Whitcomb stepped closer and reached for the bandage without asking. Andrew did not stop him. An officer could refuse a doctor’s hands only out of pride, and pride was a thin shield in a world that had begun to ignore shields.

Whitcomb unwound the cloth. His expression did not change when the cut showed itself, but something in his eyes sharpened.

"This is a clean slice," he said. "What did it? A saber?"

Andrew held still. He could smell the tent: carbolic, sweat, old blood. The ordinary stink of war. It should have felt like safety after the orchard's sweetness.

"I don't know," Andrew said.

Whitcomb stared at him a moment longer than a man normally stared when examining a wound. Then he took Andrew's wrist, fingers pressing to the pulse with professional detachment that did not quite hide curiosity.

"You should know," Whitcomb said quietly. "Men usually know when they've been cut."

Andrew looked past him at Jakes on the table, at the neat line at his throat, at the absence of the expected mess.

In the orchard, Ambrose had spoken of clarity as if it were a gift.

Andrew had the sick sense that this was the first piece of it. A wound that announced itself only when it chose. A death that left the body altered in ways a surgeon could not account for.

Whitcomb rewrapped the bandage with firmer hands. "Keep it clean," he said. "If it swells or turns, you come back."

Andrew nodded once.

As he stepped out of the surgeon's tent into the late-day light of camp, he found that his relief had not returned. The camp's noise, the clatter of tins, the distant curses, the moans from other tents, all of it sounded suddenly fragile, like a stage set thrown up in front of something older and quieter.

He touched his bandaged side and felt the cut pulse under cloth, not worsening, not mending. Simply present, as if waiting.

And for the first time, Andrew understood that whatever had stepped close to him in the woods had not needed to kill him to do harm.

It had only needed to make itself part of his body.

That night the camp did what it always did when men were too tired to be afraid properly. It turned fear into routine.

Fires were banked low against the damp. Tin cups clinked. A fiddle tried and failed to make something like music near the far line of tents, the tune collapsing into silence when the player's fingers cramped. Somewhere a man prayed aloud and was told to shut his mouth. Somewhere else a man moaned through a fever and no one answered him because answers were in short supply.

Andrew lay on his blanket with his coat folded beneath his head and his bandaged side turned upward, as if keeping the wound away from the ground might keep it honest. He could feel the cut through cloth and skin, a steady, irritant awareness rather than pain. It did not throb the way a fresh injury should. It did not fade the way a shallow slice should.

It simply remained.

Around him, his remaining men settled in uneasy clusters. Haines stayed close, not sleeping so much as resting his eyes with his rifle across his chest. Rudd cleaned mud from his boots with a stick and did not look up at Andrew, as if eye contact might invite questions he could not answer. Kellan sat with his back against a crate, knees drawn up, staring at his own hands again and again like a man checking for invisible strings.

Andrew watched them until he could not stand the helplessness of watching. He closed his eyes.

At first, sleep came only in thin layers. He drifted and rose, drifted and rose, woken each time by the small noises of camp or the louder noises in his own head: Jakes's rifle cracking, the wet click that followed, Ambrose's mild voice in the clearing saying, *So*.

When he finally fell deeper, it was not into rest.

He dreamed he was back at the orchard house, standing in the narrow hall with the painted windows that refused daylight. The air was cold enough to make his breath show, but no breath left his mouth. He lifted a hand and pressed his palm against the black glass. The paint was slick, still wet. It left a smear on his skin like soot mixed with oil.

Behind him, the cellar door creaked.

He turned, expecting to see the iron rings in the wall, the snapped chain, the architecture of terror he had tried to name and contain. But the cellar stairs did not lead down. They led up, climbing into darkness as though the house had been turned inside out, and the earth had become sky.

A sound came from above: not footsteps, not a voice, but the slow drag of iron over stone. Chain, distant and patient.

Andrew stepped onto the first stair. The wood did not creak. It did not protest his weight. It accepted him like soil accepts a coffin.

He climbed. The darkness thickened with every step until it pressed against his eyes. He kept moving anyway, because there was nothing else to do in a dream like that. At the top of the stairs he found a door.

It was the cellar door again, but now it opened into a root cellar dug directly into the living earth, the kind of place that smelled of damp potatoes and old apples and mouse droppings. Only this one smelled too sweet, out of season. It smelled like the orchard's fallen fruit after rain, and beneath that sweetness was the metallic note he could never quite name.

He stepped inside.

Crates lay collapsed around him, half-buried in mud. The ceiling was low and the walls sweated moisture. In the far corner was a mound of dirt that rose like a shallow grave, the soil packed and smooth as if tamped down by careful hands.

Andrew knew without being told that something was under it.

A whisper came from behind him, close enough to warm his ear.

"You understand doors," Ambrose said, voice soft and courteous, as if continuing a conversation begun at dinner. "You understand what men put beneath them."

Andrew spun, pistol in hand, but the cellar was empty. The lantern he expected to see was not there. There was no light at all, and yet he could see the mound, could see the damp sheen on the packed earth.

He tried to speak. His mouth moved and nothing came out.

The ground began to shift.

Not violently. Not like something clawing its way free in frantic panic. The dirt rose and fell in a slow rhythm, as though whatever lay beneath it breathed.

Andrew backed away until his shoulders met the stone wall. His fingers searched for a seam, a crack, any proof that the cellar connected to the ordinary world. His hand found an iron ring bolted into the wall. He closed his grip around it and felt, with sudden clarity, that it was warm.

He looked down.

The ring was not empty. A chain hung from it and ran across the floor to his own ankle, where it was wrapped once, twice, snug as a man's embrace. He had not heard it being fastened. He had not felt the cold bite of iron. It was simply there, as if it had always been.

He pulled. The chain did not give.

He pulled harder. The iron ring did not shift. The wall did not crack. His ankle began to burn, the skin beneath the shackle tightening as if it were being bound from within rather than without.

The mound of dirt in the corner swelled again, higher this time, and he heard, faintly, the scrape of nails through soil.

"Not buried because it was dead," Moses's voice whispered, as if the sick man lay just beyond the stone, fever-dreaming the same dream into the earth. "Buried because it would not die."

Andrew tried to breathe and found the air too thick. It tasted of dirt, wet and loamy, as if someone had packed his mouth full of soil. He opened his jaw to spit and the earth did not fall out. It clung to his tongue like paste.

The cellar ceiling lowered.

He felt it, not on his head at first, but on his shoulders, a pressure that made his ribs protest. He tried to straighten and could not. The chain at his ankle tightened, drawing him down, forcing him into a crouch.

The mound shifted again, and now a pale hand pushed through the packed dirt, fingers elegant even when caked with black soil. The hand did not claw. It rested there, as if testing the air.

Ambrose's voice came again, calm and near. "Lieutenant Mercer," he said, and this time the name slid into Andrew's ear like a key into a lock. "Can you stand still?"

Andrew's throat worked. He managed one sound, a raw and useless breath.

The ceiling pressed harder. The walls leaned inward as if the cellar itself wanted to close around him, wanted to make him part of what it kept. His bandaged side began to sting, not like a cut rubbed raw, but like a brand heating beneath flesh.

He looked down and saw the cloth darken.

The blood did not spread like blood. It seeped in a neat line along the bandage, thin and controlled, as if his body had been instructed on how much to offer and no more.

The chain at his ankle gave one sharp tug.

Andrew stumbled forward into the center of the cellar. The packed earth rose up to meet his shins, climbing him like water rising in a flood. He tried to step back and his legs would not obey. The soil was not heavy, and yet it held him.

He felt himself being lowered.

Not falling. Not collapsing. Being placed.

His mouth filled with the taste of iron.

He woke with a violent gasp, sucking cold night air into his lungs as if he had been underwater. For a moment he lay still, hands splayed on the blanket, certain he would feel dirt under his nails, certain he would hear the scrape of chain close to his ear.

There was only the camp.

A man coughed in the darkness. Somewhere a horse stamped and snorted. A fire popped and sent up a brief shower of sparks. The world looked the same, and yet Andrew could not convince himself it was trustworthy.

He swallowed and tasted iron anyway.

His tongue felt dry, coated. He touched his lips and then his bandage. The cloth was damp. In the weak light from a nearby fire, he could see a narrow line of red seeping through, too precise to be an accident of movement.

Andrew sat up slowly, careful not to wake the men near him. His body felt heavy, as if he had been pressed into the ground and lifted out again. He unwrapped the bandage with controlled fingers.

The cut stared back at him, unchanged.

No swelling, no angry inflammation. No clean knitting of skin. The edges were as neat as Whitcomb had said, and now, in the dark, Andrew had the sick thought that the wound did not look like something healing. It looked like something preserved.

He pressed a fingertip lightly to it. Pain flared, sharp enough to make his eyes water, and then faded into that same steady awareness. His finger came away red.

Behind him, Kellan stirred. “Lieutenant?” The whisper was hoarse, half-asleep. “You all right?”

Andrew did not turn at first. He stared at the blood on his fingertip until it began to cool. Then he wrapped the bandage again, tighter.

“I’m fine,” he said softly, and hated that it was the same kind of lie he had started to hate in other men. The kind meant to keep the night from noticing weakness.

Kellan shifted closer, his voice barely audible. “I dreamed,” he began, then stopped as if afraid of his own mouth.

Andrew finally looked at him. In the dim light Kellan’s face had a pinched, starved look, as though he had lost weight in a single day. His eyes were wide and damp.

“What did you dream?” Andrew asked.

Kellan swallowed. “That I was in the ground,” he whispered. “Not dead. Just… down there. Like I could hear everybody walking above me and none of it mattered. Like I was put away.”

Andrew felt his own skin tighten. He kept his voice even. “It was a dream.”

Kellan shook his head, small and desperate. "No, sir. It felt like… like he was telling me something. Like he was showing me where we belong."

Andrew held Kellan's gaze until the young man's breathing slowed a fraction.

"Sleep," Andrew said. "If you can."

Kellan's eyes flicked to Andrew's bandage, then away. He lay back down, but his body stayed rigid.

Andrew remained sitting long after Kellan's breathing evened into something that pretended to be rest. He listened to the camp's ordinary sounds and tried to fit them back around himself like armor.

He could not forget the cellar in the dream, the soil rising, the chain already fastened as if it had always been there. He could not forget the taste of iron that remained even now, lingering at the back of his tongue like a message he could not spit out.

He had believed burial was an end. In war, it was supposed to be the last mercy you gave a man: to put him under the earth and let him stop being seen.

But in the orchard, in the clearing, and now in his own sleep, Andrew began to understand a darker use for the ground.

Not as an ending.

As a method.

He lay back down at last, staring up at the dark sky beyond the tents, and waited for sleep to return with its dirt-filled mouth. He did not know whether the dreams belonged to fear, or fever, or something Ambrose had left inside him with that neat, effortless cut.

He only knew that when he closed his eyes, the earth felt closer than it should, as if it were leaning in to listen.

Morning did not cleanse the night from Andrew Mercer. It only thinned it, like smoke pulled apart by wind and then gathered again in the corners.

He rose before the camp fully stirred, before the men began their small rituals of living: the clink of tin, the curse at a boot that would not lace, the low cough of someone who had been sleeping too close to damp ground. His bandage sat tight against his ribs, and beneath it the wound held its quiet, stubborn awareness. It did not throb with the ordinary complaint of flesh. It watched.

Andrew walked to the wash line where a barrel of water sat under a canvas awning. The water was cold enough to sting his hands. He splashed his face and waited for the shock to remind his body that it belonged to him.

It did, mostly. Until he lifted his head.

Across the camp, between two wagons, a figure stood where no one had business standing so still.

It was not close enough for detail. It could have been any man, wrapped in a coat, posture upright, simply waiting. But the stillness was wrong. Soldiers shifted even when they tried to be statues. They favored legs, rolled shoulders, scratched beards, adjusted straps. This figure did none of that. He stood as if the world had arranged itself around his patience.

Andrew held his breath without deciding to. Water ran from his chin in a thin line.

The figure's head angled slightly, as though it had noticed Andrew noticing.

Then a teamster passed, carrying a sack of meal. For a moment the moving body blocked the view, and when it cleared, the space between the wagons was empty.

Andrew's fingers tightened on the rim of the barrel until his knuckles whitened. He forced himself to keep his expression blank, because men watched officers for permission to be afraid. He glanced around, slow and deliberate, as if searching for some practical explanation.

A sergeant shouted at two privates near the cook fire. A horse snorted, stamping in mud. Whitcomb's tent flap fluttered as someone went in or out. Nothing else held that hard, unnatural stillness.

Haines approached, rubbing sleep from his eyes with the back of his hand. The cut on his cheek had scabbed over, a thin dark line that made him look marked as well. "Sir?" he asked quietly. "You all right?"

Andrew let his hands drop from the barrel and wiped his face with his sleeve. "Fine," he said, and heard how often he had begun to use that word like a plank laid over a pit.

Haines's gaze flicked toward Andrew's bandage. "It bleeding again?"

Andrew touched the cloth lightly. Dry. "No."

Haines hesitated. There was a question in him that he did not want to ask directly, as if giving the fear a clear shape might make it official. "You sleep any?"

Andrew thought of the cellar in the dream, the earth rising with a slow breath. He thought of the iron ring warm beneath his palm. He forced his tone into something ordinary. "Enough."

Haines nodded, but his eyes stayed fixed on Andrew's face a moment longer, searching for cracks. "Kellan's up," he said. "He ain't said much."

"Keep him close," Andrew replied.

Haines's mouth tightened, a grim acknowledgment. "Ain't any of us wandering, sir. Not after…" He did not say Jakes's name, but it hung between them like a smell.

Andrew started back toward their small cluster of tents and blankets. As he walked, he felt the strange sensation of being followed without footsteps. He told himself it was only vigilance. He told himself his nerves were still stretched from the clearing, from the impossibility of watching a man die without sound. A mind could invent shadows when it wanted to justify its own fear.

But when he passed the line of stacked crates near the quartermaster's wagons, he heard a voice that was not close enough to belong to any man in the nearby path.

"You keep them close," it said, mild, almost approving.

Andrew stopped so abruptly that Haines, a few paces behind, nearly bumped him.

The words had not been shouted. They had not been whispered in his ear. They had the calm presence of a sentence spoken at a dinner table, meant for him and no one else.

Andrew turned his head slowly.

A group of soldiers sat by the cook fire, arguing over something small. Their voices overlapped. None of them had spoken those words. A man in a tattered hat walked by, laughing at a joke Andrew could not hear. No one looked at him. No one waited for his reaction.

Haines moved up beside him, brow furrowed. “Sir?”

Andrew’s throat worked. He made himself walk again. “Nothing,” he said.

They reached Kellan, who stood by their gear with his hands held together in front of him as if he did not trust them to hang loose. His eyes were rimmed red. He looked as though he had been awake all night, even though Andrew knew he had drifted into a thin, haunted sleep.

Kellan’s gaze locked onto Andrew’s bandage, then lifted quickly to Andrew’s face as if caught stealing.

“You eat yet?” Andrew asked.

Kellan shook his head.

“You need to,” Andrew said, though the thought of food made his own stomach tighten. The camp stew smelled of boiled salt pork and old onions, and it should have made a hungry man grateful. Instead the scent turned sour in Andrew’s nose, overlaid by the orchard's sweetness he could not seem to forget.

Kellan swallowed. "Ain't hungry."

"You're a soldier," Haines said, sharper than necessary. "You eat when it's there."

Kellan flinched, but he did not argue. He took the tin cup Haines offered and sipped as if the act of swallowing was a duty rather than comfort.

Rudd arrived with a small bundle of hardtack and a strip of bacon traded off someone who owed him a favor. His face still had that pale, tight look, the expression of a young man who had watched the world break one piece at a time and was trying to keep his own pieces from scattering.

"We moving today, sir?" Rudd asked.

Andrew had already decided they would. Staying in one place gave fear room to root. It also gave Ambrose, wherever he was, time to choose new angles.

"We'll move after midmorning," Andrew said. "Get water. Make sure your powder's dry. We head toward the chapel road."

Haines glanced at him. "Chapel?"

Andrew kept his voice low. "There's a priest out that way. If anyone's heard the old stories, it's a priest."

Haines did not look comforted by that. "Old stories won't mend a wound."

Andrew felt the bandage again, the skin beneath it too attentive. "No," he agreed. "But they might tell us what kind of thing makes one."

They moved out with a small escort granted by a weary captain who seemed relieved to have Andrew's trouble pointed away from his own perimeter. The camp disappeared behind them, swallowed by trees and distance, and the road took them through fields turned to mud and fences chewed down for firewood. Virginia looked the same as it had the day before, and yet Andrew felt a line had been crossed. The land did not need to change to be unfamiliar. It only needed to reveal what it had been hiding.

By noon, the sky darkened again with low, wet clouds. The air held that steady chill that made bones ache. Andrew rode for part of the way, then walked, unable to settle into the saddle without feeling the wound pull wrong. It did not tear. It did not bleed. It simply reminded him, again and again, that it was still open.

Haines rode close. Rudd walked on the other side, flag rolled and strapped to his pack now, as if he had finally realized it drew too much attention. Kellan kept near the middle of the column, eyes constantly sliding to the tree line.

They stopped once near a shallow stream to refill canteens. The water moved over stones with a sound that should have been soothing. Andrew crouched and dipped his hands in, watching the current break around his fingers.

In the water's surface, his reflection looked almost normal: a hard face, tired eyes, stubble darkening his jaw. Then, as the ripples steadied, he saw something behind his reflected shoulder.

A pale shape, upright, close enough to have been standing at the bank with him.

Andrew surged to his feet, hand going to his pistol.

There was no one there except his own men and the thin trees, their branches dripping. Haines had turned at the sudden movement, eyes sharp. Rudd froze mid-step, canteen in hand.

"What?" Haines demanded.

Andrew stared into the woods. The air smelled of wet bark and mud, nothing sweet, nothing metallic. He forced himself to holster the pistol, slow enough that it looked like caution rather than panic.

"Thought I saw a scout," he lied.

Haines studied him. The lie did not satisfy him, but he let it pass, because men learned quickly what truths an officer would not admit.

They moved on.

As the afternoon thinned toward evening, Andrew's head began to ache behind the eyes. His mouth felt dry no matter how much water he drank. He tried to blame it on fatigue, on bad sleep, on the dull illness that lived in camps. But the ache had a particular insistence, as though his own thoughts were being pressed inward, compacted.

They passed a half-burned farmhouse with a collapsed porch. In the yard, an old woman stood watching them, face blank, hands clasped in front of her apron. Her gaze tracked Andrew as he passed, and for an instant he thought she would speak. Instead she only lifted her chin slightly, as if listening to something he could not hear.

Then, from nowhere, the quiet voice came again. Not behind him. Not ahead. Inside the space of his own attention.

"You look for a man of God," it said.

Andrew kept walking. He did not turn his head. He did not quicken his pace. He did not give his men a reason to watch him too closely.

Haines leaned closer. “Sir,” he murmured, “you heard that?”

Andrew’s breath caught. He glanced at Haines and saw, in the corporal’s eyes, the same tight fear.

“What did you hear?” Andrew asked, forcing steadiness into each word.

Haines swallowed. “Nothing,” he said at once, too fast. Then, after a beat, in a smaller voice: “Just… thought I did.”

Andrew nodded once, as if that settled it.

But it did not settle.

The presence was no longer a single figure between wagons, no longer only a trick in water or peripheral vision. It had moved closer to the edge of their shared world, close enough now that another man might brush against it and feel the cold.

As dusk gathered, they made camp in a small hollow sheltered by pines. The men built a fire and kept it modest, and Andrew sat with his back to a tree, pistol across his lap, watching the line where darkness began.

He expected the voice again. He expected the pale figure to step between trunks with that same calm ownership.

Nothing came.

That should have relieved him. Instead, it felt like waiting for a cough in a sickroom and hearing only the patient quiet of someone holding their breath.

When Haines took first watch, he lingered close to Andrew before moving away. "Sir," he said quietly, "what if it ain't done with us?"

Andrew looked up at the tree line where shadows thickened. He thought of Ambrose's eyes, steady and appraising. He thought of the neat cut on Jakes's throat and the way the body had looked edited, drained beyond logic. He thought of his own wound, preserved like a message.

"It's not done," Andrew said.

Haines nodded, as if he had already known and only needed to hear it spoken.

Later, when the men slept in restless shifts, Andrew lay awake with his eyes open. The dark pressed close. The fire popped once, then settled.

At the edge of the hollow, where the trees began, he saw a silhouette that was not shaped like any trunk.

It stood perfectly still, as if carved from the night.

Andrew did not reach for his pistol. He did not call out. He did not wake the men. He only watched, breath shallow, heart heavy with the certainty that the thing in the orchard had not simply encountered them.

It had attached.

The silhouette did not move closer. It did not retreat. It simply remained, a presence at the edge of sight, letting Andrew understand the new rule: distance meant nothing. Doors meant nothing. Miles of wasted Virginia meant nothing.

Ambrose could be absent and still be there.

Andrew closed his eyes for a moment, and the taste of iron rose again on his tongue, faint and unavoidable, like blood remembered.

When he opened them, the edge of the hollow was empty.

But the feeling of being watched stayed, settled deep and patient, as if it had found a place in him and decided to rest.

Chapter 6

The Chapel Without God

Andrew did not sleep. Not truly.

He lay on his blanket with his coat pulled up to his collar and watched the fire degrade into coals, then into a dull orange pulse that seemed less like warmth and more like a wound refusing to close. The men around him shifted and muttered, each of them chasing whatever dream the woods handed them. Even in the hollow's shelter, the night air felt damp enough to soak into thought.

He kept seeing the silhouette at the edge of the trees. When he blinked, it was gone. When he opened his eyes again, it could have been there or not; the uncertainty was the point. Ambrose did not need to stand in the dark to teach Andrew what it meant to be watched. He had already shown him in the clearing, in the edited corpse, in the neat cut that now lived under bandage and refused healing.

Near dawn the sky lightened in a slow, dirty way, not sunrise so much as night withdrawing reluctantly. Haines returned from watch with frost in his eyelashes and a look in his face that said he had counted the minutes until he could hand responsibility back to someone else.

"You see anything?" Andrew asked quietly.

Haines shook his head once. Then, after a hesitation that admitted more than the answer, he added, "Heard owls. Heard wind. Heard things that sounded like nothing."

Andrew understood. He sat up, joints stiff, and pressed his fingers lightly to the bandage. Dry. The cut stayed present anyway, as if dryness were only one kind of honesty.

They broke camp with a speed born not from discipline but from discomfort. Men folded blankets and stamped out coals as if the ground itself might remember their heat. Kellan moved like a sleepwalker, eyes fixed on a point a few feet ahead of him, as though if he looked too far out into the woods the woods would look back. Rudd kept glancing behind them, not in the obvious way of a frightened boy, but in the controlled, frequent way of someone trying to catch a man tailing him on a city street.

Andrew let them do it. Vigilance was not cowardice. Not anymore.

The road toward the chapel was little more than a hard-packed track between pines and broken fields. Here and there they passed fence posts leaning like tired men. They passed a shallow ditch where someone had dumped a dead mule and then covered it with brush, too weak or too hurried for burial. The war had turned the land into a ledger of unfinished tasks.

By midmorning the clouds lowered again, and a fine, steady rain began to fall, not hard enough to drive them to shelter but persistent enough to turn their collars dark and their hair damp. The smell of wet pine should have been clean. Andrew kept waiting for it to sour into orchard sweetness.

It did not. That was a relief, but it was also a reminder of how thoroughly the orchard had rewritten his senses. Every ordinary scent had become suspect.

They came to a fork where an older road branched off, narrower and less traveled. An iron marker post stood half-crooked in the mud, the lettering almost eaten away by rust. Rudd leaned in close, squinting.

“Looks like it says Saint… something,” he murmured.

"Saint Dymphna," Haines read slowly, and then looked up as if the name meant nothing to him. "That a real saint?"

"Saint of the mad," Andrew said, the answer coming from memory without effort. He had heard his mother mention it once, long before the war, when a neighbor's son had started talking to things that weren't there. Andrew had not believed in saints much even then, but he remembered the name because it had sounded like a prayer aimed at the mind.

Haines stared at the post for a beat. "That's cheerful."

Andrew said nothing. He turned his horse onto the narrower road. The men followed.

The trees thickened, and the light under them turned flat and gray. The rain had a different sound here, tapping needles and dripping down in patient clicks. They walked rather than rode, because the path was rutted and slick, and because silence came easier on foot.

Andrew found himself listening for voices that were not there. Not just Ambrose's voice in the private space of his attention, but the ordinary voices of people who still lived in a world that required community: a farmer calling a dog, a woman arguing with a child, a man chopping wood.

The woods offered none of it. Only water and the occasional far-off crow that sounded more like complaint than life.

As the day wore on, they met a man on the road.

He was not a soldier. His hat was too broad and his coat too plain, patched at both elbows. He led a thin mule hitched to a cart with two sacks in it that looked like meal or corn. When he saw the gray uniforms he slowed, eyes narrowing with the caution of a man who had been robbed by both sides and no longer cared which flag did it.

Andrew raised a hand, palm out. "We won't take your goods," he called, keeping his tone level.

The man stopped anyway, mule huffing. "That's a new promise," he said.

"We're looking for a chapel," Andrew replied. "Saint Dymphna's. There should be a priest."

The man's mouth tightened. He glanced past Andrew at the men, at their rifles, at Kellan's hollow stare. Then his gaze returned to Andrew and stayed there a fraction longer, as if something about Andrew's posture told him who was actually holding the reins.

"Ain't no priest worth finding," the man said. "Not these days."

"Is there one?" Andrew asked.

The man spit into the mud. “There’s a man wears black,” he said. “If that’s what you mean. Don’t know what he is beyond hungry and stubborn.”

Haines shifted beside Andrew. “Which way?”

The man nodded toward the trees. “Keep on. You’ll see the steeple before you see the building, if you’ve got eyes. Place sits low. Like it’s ashamed.”

Andrew gave him a short nod. “Thank you.”

The man hesitated, then said, “You Confederates going up there for blessing?”

Andrew almost laughed, but the sound would not have been humor. “No,” he said. “For information.”

The man’s eyes flicked away. “Information’s dangerous,” he muttered, and clicked his tongue at the mule. As he passed, he lowered his voice like a man speaking around a sleeping child. “And Lieutenant? If you hear singing where there ain’t people, don’t follow it.”

Andrew’s head turned sharply, but the man was already moving on, rain darkening his shoulders. Andrew held his gaze on the cart until the trees took it.

Rudd leaned closer. “You know him, sir?”

"No," Andrew said. "But he knows the kind of trouble that lives near a church."

They walked on.

The steeple appeared just as the man had said, a narrow finger of dark wood rising above the tree line. It should have looked reassuring. Instead,

it looked like a bone.

As they drew closer, the chapel revealed itself in pieces: a sagging roofline, a small cemetery fenced with iron that had begun to lean, stones mottled with lichen. The building sat in a shallow dip beside a slow creek, and water had eaten at its foundation over years until the front steps sank unevenly. The windows were narrow and tall, but most of the glass was broken and patched with boards from the inside.

There was no bell.

The air around it felt wrong in a way that had nothing to do with Ambrose. It did not feel hunted. It felt abandoned by the very idea it represented, as if prayer had been tried here too often and the answers had stopped coming.

Andrew halted at the edge of the yard. "No one spreads out," he ordered. "We approach together. Weapons down but ready. No sudden movements."

Haines nodded. Rudd swallowed. Kellan simply stared at the chapel as if he were looking at a mouth.

They crossed the wet grass. The cemetery stones watched them. Some were so old the names had blurred into suggestion. Others were newer, their dates clustered in the last few years. War and sickness had filled this place even without the orchard.

At the chapel door, Andrew paused. The wood was scarred with old marks, shallow cuts like the ones in the bedframe at the estate, though these were older and more deliberate. Not carved in panic. Carved as ritual.

He lifted his hand and knocked.

Nothing answered at first.

Then, from within, came the scrape of a bolt drawn back. A pause. And the door opened a few inches, held on a chain.

A man's face appeared in the gap. He was not old, but his eyes were. Stubble shadowed his jaw, and the collar at his throat was not as clean as it should have been. He looked like someone who had slept in his clothes too many nights in a row.

His gaze flicked over Andrew and his men and settled, inevitably, on their weapons. "You're not parishioners," he said.

"No," Andrew replied. "But we're not here to rob you."

The man's eyes narrowed. "Everyone says that."

Andrew kept his voice calm, though his mouth felt dry. "My name is Lieutenant Andrew Mercer," he said. He watched for any recognition at the name and saw none. "We were sent to assess an estate not far from here. An orchard house. We found graves. We found… evidence of something I don't understand."

The priest's expression did not change much, but something in him went still, the way a man's body goes still when it hears a familiar sound it wishes it had never learned.

"You should leave," the priest said softly.

Haines made an angry sound. "We tried leaving. It followed."

The priest's eyes shifted to Haines, then to Kellan, and held there a beat too long. When he looked back at Andrew, his gaze had sharpened with a kind of reluctant pity.

"You brought it with you," he said.

Andrew felt the wound under his bandage tighten, not in pain but in recognition. He forced himself not to touch it.

"We brought fear," Andrew said. "And a story. That's all."

The priest's mouth pulled tight. He leaned closer into the gap, lowering his voice as if the cemetery stones might be listening. "Fear is how it introduces itself," he said. "A story is how it travels."

Andrew held his ground. Rain slid from the brim of his cap and dripped onto his cheek, cold and steady. "Are you the priest here?" he asked.

"I am what's left of one," the man replied.

Andrew nodded once. "Then I need you," he said. "Because men are dying, and I think the thing doing it is not a man."

For a long moment the priest only studied him. Andrew could see the calculation in the man's eyes, the weighing of risk against obligation. Not the obligation of a Confederate cause or any earthly authority. Something older, thinner, and harder.

At last the priest reached up and unhooked the chain. The door opened wider with a groan that sounded like complaint.

"Come in," he said. "And if you're lying to me, Lieutenant Mercer, I will let God judge you. Because I've grown tired of trying."

Andrew stepped over the threshold. The air inside was cold and smelled faintly of damp wood and old candle wax. The chapel was dim, not with painted windows like the orchard house, but with boards nailed across broken glass to keep the weather out. Rain ticked against the roof overhead like fingers.

Behind him, his men filed in, boots quiet on worn boards.

The priest closed the door and slid the bolt back into place.

The sound of it settling in the bracket was small, ordinary.

It reminded Andrew too much of the cellar door being shut gently over boiling water.

The priest did not offer them pews. He watched them first, as if counting how many ways a man could bring trouble through a doorway.

The chapel's interior had been plain once, built by hands that believed God preferred simplicity to decoration. Now it looked like a place that had survived by subtraction. The altar was bare except for a cracked wooden crucifix and two short candles burned down to stubs. The pews closest to the windows had been dragged inward, away from the boards nailed over broken glass. A thin line of rainwater ran along one wall and collected in a basin like a slow, patient leak of time.

Andrew felt the bolt settling behind them like a memory. He kept his men close by habit, but there was no comfort in closeness here. The air carried damp and wax and something else, faint but sharp, like old smoke trapped in wood. It reminded him of the scorched room in the orchard house, of desperate attempts at purification.

The priest removed a small key from a cord around his neck, unlocked a side door, and gestured them through. “Not out here,” he said. “My study.”

They followed into a narrow room that should have been warmer but wasn’t. A small iron stove sat cold in the corner. A desk, scarred by years of use, was piled with papers weighted down by stones. Shelves held a disorderly congregation of books: worn Bibles, hymnals with torn spines, a Latin missal, and several volumes whose titles were in languages Andrew did not know. A single window looked out on the cemetery. It had been patched with cloth and resin, turning the outside world into a blurred watercolor of leaning stones and wet grass.

The priest closed the door and, only then, exhaled as if he’d been holding his breath since they knocked.

Haines stood with his cap in his hands, uncertain whether respect still applied in a world where things like Ambrose existed. Rudd’s eyes flicked across the books, lingering on the foreign titles. Kellan stayed near the wall, shoulders tight, gaze unfixed, as though the room itself might give him orders.

Andrew faced the priest. "You said we brought it with us."

"I said you brought something with you," the priest corrected. He moved behind the desk but did not sit. He seemed unwilling to place his body too comfortably anywhere. "Maybe it. Maybe its shadow. Sometimes that's enough."

Andrew held his tone level. "What do you know about it?"

The priest's mouth tightened. He rubbed a hand over his jaw, fingers catching on stubble. "You'll tell me exactly what you saw," he said. "All of it. Not what you think it was. What happened. What words were spoken. What it did, and what it did not do."

Haines glanced at Andrew, then spoke before he could stop himself. "It killed Jakes without hardly touching him."

The priest's eyes shifted to Haines. "How?"

Haines swallowed. "Like… like it brushed him. Like a hand at his throat and then he just fell. There weren't no fight."

"And the boy?" the priest asked, nodding toward Kellan without looking directly at him. "The one who came back."

Kellan flinched at the attention. His lips moved, then stopped.

Andrew answered for him. "He was taken from watch. Drag marks. Barefoot prints. We followed into the woods and found him kneeling, awake but not… himself. The man called himself Ambrose."

At the name, the priest's face did not show surprise, but his eyes did something small and telling: a narrowing, a recognition he tried to hide and failed.

Andrew saw it and pressed. "You know the name."

"I know of it," the priest said quietly. "Or I know of something that has worn it."

Rudd spoke, voice thin. "He said, 'Ambrose. At present.'"

The priest's gaze flicked to Rudd, then back to Andrew. "And you saw him clearly? Close enough to judge his clothing, his manner?"

"Yes," Andrew said. He heard his own discipline in the word, the reflex to make it sound like an ordinary report. Then he added, because the truth refused to stay ordinary, "He moved like... like the world was slow around him."

The priest studied Andrew's face as if looking for the place the memory had lodged. "Did he bite?" he asked.

Haines made a confused sound. "Bite?"

"Did you see teeth?" the priest pressed. "Did you see him feed?"

Andrew's bandage seemed to tighten of its own accord. He did not touch it. "No. He killed Jakes. He took Kellan. He talked. That's what he did."

The priest's expression turned inward, as if he were sorting through old drawers in his mind. "Sometimes," he said, more to himself than to them, "they do not show hunger in front of witnesses. Hunger is undignified."

Andrew felt a cold thread run through him. "They," he repeated.

The priest gave a short, humorless breath. "You want a name for it," he said. "A category. A devil you can label in a report and shoot if you find its heart."

Andrew did not deny it. "I want to know what I'm facing."

"You're facing the fact that the world has cracks," the priest replied. "And in war those cracks widen. In famine. In plague. In exile. In any season where men stop keeping proper account of their dead."

Haines's hands tightened on his cap. "Is it a demon?"

The priest's eyes flicked up to the crucifix on the wall and then away, as if unwilling to make cheap promises. "Not in the way you mean," he said. "Not horns and sulfur. Not a creature that fears a Latin phrase the way a dog fears a whip." He tapped the desk with two fingers, soft, steady. "There are things that live alongside us. Not above us. Not below. Alongside. They survive by learning our habits and making use of our collapse."

Rudd's voice came small. "Like sickness."

"Yes," the priest said, and now the word carried weight. "Like sickness. Like appetite."

At that, Andrew remembered Ambrose's voice in the clearing. What a generous environment you have created for appetite. The sentence returned with a clarity that made his stomach knot.

Andrew kept his gaze steady. "The estate had chains. Rings in the wall. Latin carved into wood. Crosses nailed over doors. Moses Talley said the family tried iron, prayers, fire. Does that mean any of it worked?"

The priest's eyes sharpened at the mention of Moses, and something like grief moved behind them. "Moses is still alive?" he asked.

"Barely," Andrew said. "Fever. Weak."

The priest nodded once, as if that matched what he expected of the world. "Those families," he said, "sometimes tried to fight it. Sometimes tried to keep it. Often the two look alike from the outside."

Haines frowned. "Keep it?"

The priest's mouth tightened. He walked to the shelf and pulled down a thin volume bound in cracked leather. He did not open it yet. He held it as if it were heavy. "You found graves in the orchard," he said. "Shallow. Hidden."

Andrew's mind returned to skulls close to the surface, the child's bones, the sweetness in the air. "Yes."

"Then someone was feeding something," the priest said flatly. "Maybe willingly. Maybe because they were afraid it would take more if they did not." He looked at Andrew. "Tell me about your wound."

Andrew felt his men go still. Even Kellan's gaze tightened, as though the room had suddenly narrowed.

"It's a cut," Andrew said. "I didn't feel it when it happened. It hasn't healed right since."

The priest held out a hand. "Show me."

Andrew hesitated only long enough to decide that pride had no place here. He unbuttoned his coat and lifted his shirt enough to reach the bandage. He unwound it slowly. The cloth peeled away with the faint tack of dried blood, though the wound beneath looked too clean for the mess it kept producing.

The priest leaned in. He did not touch it. He studied it like a man studying handwriting.

"It is neat," he murmured. "A mark, not an accident."

Haines's voice broke. "Doctor Whitcomb said Jakes lost more blood than that cut should've let."

The priest's eyes did not leave Andrew's side. "Yes," he said softly. "That is the point. It takes what it wants, not what you think a body can spare."

Andrew swallowed. "What does it mean?"

The priest finally looked up. His gaze was direct, tired, and unkind in the way truth often was. "It means it knows you," he said. "Or it has begun to."

Kellan whispered, barely audible, "He can make you still."

The priest's eyes shifted toward Kellan. This time he looked at him fully. Kellan shrank under it, but he did not look away.

"You heard him speak," the priest said. "What did his voice do to you?"

Kellan's throat worked. "It… settled in me," he whispered. "Like when someone says a thing you already knew but didn't have words for." His hands curled and uncurled. "He told me to kneel, and it felt right. Not good. Just right."

The priest's face tightened with something that might have been pity, or anger, or both. "Compulsion," he said. "Not magic like in stories. Not sparks and smoke. Something older. A pressure on the mind. A suggestion offered with such certainty that your own will steps aside out of habit."

Andrew thought of Ambrose's question. Can you stand still? Not a threat. A measure.

The priest returned to the desk and opened the leather-bound volume. The pages were filled with tight handwriting in the margins, notes added by different hands over years. He ran a finger down a column as if searching for a familiar scar.

"Men call such things by many names," he said. "In the old countries, there are stories that change their clothes each century. They speak of revenants, of blood-drinkers, of the dead who refuse their grave. But those stories are the clothing. What matters is the behavior." He looked up. "This creature, your Ambrose, hides in periods of disorder. He attaches to families with money and secrets. He prefers places where people disappear without inquiry."

Rudd's face pinched. "Like plantations."

The priest's eyes flicked to him, and the silence that followed was not agreement exactly, but recognition. "Yes," he said. "Like plantations. Like armies. Like refugee roads. Like hospitals full of dying men no one can protect."

Andrew felt the room tilt slightly, not physically, but morally. It was too easy to see how the war itself made cover for a thing like Ambrose. Death was everywhere. Records were ash. People fled and never returned, and the world shrugged because it had grown used to loss.

Haines spoke, voice low and rough. "Can we kill it?"

The priest closed the book with a soft thump that sounded too final for such an uncertain question. "Everything can be harmed," he said. "But not everything can be killed the way you mean. Some evils do not die. They relocate. They change names. They find new keepers."

At the last word, Andrew felt his bandage in his hands and the cut beneath it, preserved like a warning. Keeper. The word did not belong in a chapel, and yet it landed there with sick accuracy.

Andrew rewrapped the cloth, tighter than necessary, as if pressure could hold back whatever recognition the priest's words were stirring.

"You've heard of Ambrose," Andrew said. "Then you know more than theory. You know history. Tell me what you know."

The priest hesitated. Rain ticked faintly against the chapel roof. Outside, the cemetery waited with its leaning stones, patient as the earth in Andrew's dreams.

The priest's voice, when it came, was quieter. "I know enough to be afraid," he said. "And enough to understand that fear alone won't save you. Fear can make you run. It can make you pray. It can also make you bargain."

Andrew held his gaze. "And what do you think it will make me do?"

The priest looked at Andrew's face, at the set of his jaw, at the careful control he had carried through war and now carried through something older than war. "That depends," he said, "on what you cannot bear to lose."

The words settled into the room like dust.

Andrew thought of Jakes's surprised eyes, of Kellan kneeling with peace on his face, of Moses fevered on a pallet in a cabin, of the orchard's graves hidden under apple trees like shame planted in rows. He thought, too, of the way Ambrose had spoken his name as if tasting it, as if deciding where it fit.

"I need something practical," Andrew said at last. "Not sermons. Not parables. Something that holds."

The priest nodded once, as if he had expected the demand. He reached under the desk and pulled out a small bundle wrapped in cloth. He set it down carefully, then unwrapped it to reveal a handful of objects: a short length of dull iron chain, a small vial of dark liquid, a strip of parchment covered in cramped Latin, and a heavy wooden rosary whose beads were worn smooth by desperate fingers.

"These are not guarantees," the priest said. "They are tools. Like your rifle is a tool. A tool can fail in the wrong hands, or against the wrong thing. But it is better than empty air."

Andrew stared at the items. The chain looked ordinary and yet the sight of it made his skin tighten. He remembered the warm iron ring in his dream. He remembered real rings bolted into stone.

"What is that?" Haines asked, pointing at the vial.

The priest's expression hardened. "Old remedies," he said. "Old ideas dressed as remedy. Some of them are superstition. Some of them are memory." He looked at Andrew again. "And some of them are meant not to stop it, but to remind you what it is when it tries to speak to you like a gentleman."

Andrew's mouth went dry. He heard, faintly, Ambrose's voice as if from another room: Preachers offer hope. I offer clarity.

Andrew had come to a chapel seeking God's authority. Instead he found a man offering folklore and fear, and calling it wisdom because it was the only currency left that made sense.

The priest gathered the bundle and pushed it toward Andrew. "Take them," he said. "And if you want history, Lieutenant Mercer, you will stay here long enough for me to show you what has been written about your Ambrose across the years."

Andrew placed his hand on the cloth-wrapped tools. The fabric felt cold. The weight of it was small, but the implication was not.

"Show me," Andrew said.

The priest's eyes held on his for a moment, then he nodded, once, like a man beginning a confession he no longer believed would cleanse anything.

"Then listen," he said. "And do not mistake knowledge for safety."

The priest did not sit. He moved around his desk as if the room had angles he did not trust, pulling one of the heavy books down and laying it open with care. The pages were thick and uneven, stitched rather than bound by any modern press, and the ink had browned with age. Margins were crowded with smaller handwriting, cramped notes layered over older notes, like men arguing across decades.

Rain ticked at the window patch. The cemetery beyond it was a blur of slate and wet grass.

Andrew kept his hand on the cloth bundle a moment longer, feeling the dull weight of the chain through the fabric. He did not like how quickly he had accepted tools he did not understand. But he liked emptiness less.

"Start where it starts," Andrew said.

The priest's gaze lifted. "It doesn't start," he replied, and there was no drama in the words, only fatigue. "That's the problem. But I'll begin where it first appears in records that survived long enough to be copied."

He ran a finger down the left page, then stopped at a paragraph marked by a small cross inked in the margin. "These are letters," he said. "Not to a bishop. Not to anyone official. To a brother-in-law in Baltimore, written by a man who wanted to sound rational while describing something he could not afford to describe."

Andrew leaned in, careful not to press too close. The priest read aloud, not performing, simply giving the words a voice again.

"'He calls himself Ambrose,'" the priest read, translating as he went where the phrasing slid into old spellings. "'He was presented as a friend of Father Alphonse, and therefore we received him as a gentleman. His manners are of the Old World, though he gives no clear country, and he speaks of Rome and Paris as though they are rooms in the same house. My wife insists we show him hospitality. I confess the very air seems altered when he enters, as if a window were shut.'"

Andrew listened, his mind pinning each detail. Gentleman. Hospitality. The air altered. It matched too neatly with the clearing, with Ambrose standing in wet leaves as if the woods were his parlor.

The priest continued. "'He has taken an interest in the servants. Not in their labor, but in their movements. He asks when they sleep. He asks who among them is sickly. Yesterday he corrected my son's Latin without being asked. I do not know where he learned it.'"

The priest stopped reading and looked at Andrew as if to make sure he understood what mattered. "He attaches himself to households the way fever does," he said. "Quietly. By being invited."

Haines shifted behind Andrew, boots creaking once on the worn boards. Kellan's breath made a thin, audible sound in the small room, like he was holding too much air in his chest.

Andrew asked, "When was that written?"

The priest tapped the date in the corner. "1792. Copied later by another hand. This chapel did not exist then, not as it is now. But families keep papers. Priests keep what families leave behind. Sometimes in confession, sometimes in fear."

He turned a page. The next sheet was stained along the edge as if it had once been wet with something more than rain. The priest's finger found another note, this time in a different hand, sharper and more educated.

"Here," he said. "A journal entry from a physician. Not a priest, not a folk-teller. A doctor in Richmond during the yellow fever years."

Andrew felt his tongue go dry. War made men familiar with infection, with camps that stank of rot and bodies that failed without bullet holes. Ambrose had said he preferred hospitable environments. Disease was hospitality with a smile.

The priest read. "'There are deaths that do not resemble the illness they are assigned. Several bodies came to my office prepared by family servants for burial. No swelling. No black vomit. Yet the pallor is extreme, and blood is scant as if drained before death. One of the household's enslaved women insisted she had seen a man at the window at night, very pale, standing as if listening. The family calls her hysterical. They call me rude for asking whether they have hosted any stranger in recent weeks. In their parlor, a gentleman sits with perfect composure, and when I speak of blood, he smiles as though the word pleases him.'"

The priest's voice remained even, but the room felt tighter, as if the air itself disliked being forced to carry these sentences. Andrew could smell damp wax and old paper and, beneath it, the memory of orchard sweetness his mind kept trying to summon in places it didn't belong.

Andrew said quietly, "He's been here that long."

The priest's mouth tightened. "Longer. These are only the times he brushed hard enough against people with pens."

He opened another book, smaller, with a torn spine that had been repaired with twine. Inside were lists, not prose. Names in columns. Dates. Short notes in the margins: disappeared, fever, accident, sent away, paid.

Andrew recognized the language at once. It was the same kind of bookkeeping he'd seen in plantation ledgers. The war had its ledgers too, only with different euphemisms.

"What is this?" Andrew asked.

"Copies of copies," the priest said. "And some originals. Records kept by immigrant families who came through this region. Catholics, mostly, because they kept parish ties and wrote to priests when they didn't know what else to do. Protestants tended to keep such fear inside their own walls. They thought admitting it would be surrendering to superstition."

He paused. "There are patterns. The names change, the towns change. He appears near ports, near river routes, near places where people can arrive without being known and leave without being missed. He lingers when a community is weak. Epidemic. Fire. War. Any time the dead begin to outnumber the questions."

Andrew's gaze dropped to the columns. Some names had small crosses beside them. Some had nothing at all, as if even the recorder had gotten tired of marking grief.

Haines spoke, voice roughened. "Does it always call itself Ambrose?"

"No," the priest said. "Sometimes it wears a surname for a decade. Sometimes it takes a title. Sometimes it borrows the name of a man it has already hollowed out." He lifted the edge of a page and showed where several different names had been written in different inks, then bracketed later by one steady hand with a single note: same gentleman.

Andrew stared at that phrase until it stopped being words and became an image: the same pale composure walking through centuries, polite enough to be welcomed, patient enough to wait for a household to rot from the inside.

Kellan made a small sound like a restrained cough. Andrew turned his head slightly and saw Kellan's face tightened, eyes fixed not on the priest but on the books, as if ink on paper could command him the way Ambrose's voice had.

Andrew asked, "How do you know it's the same creature? How do you know you're not collecting stories and forcing them to fit because you want them to?"

The priest looked at him with something like approval, thin and humorless. "Good," he said. "Keep that suspicion. You'll need it." He tapped the page again. "Because the details repeat when details have no reason to repeat. The same complaints: a sweet smell near certain rooms, as if fruit were rotting out of season. The same silence in places where animals should be. The same wounds, small and neat, with bodies left too pale. And always the manners. Always the language of a man who doesn't need to raise his voice."

Andrew thought of Ambrose in the clearing, speaking as if they were interrupting him at dinner. He thought of the rifle placed neatly against the apple tree trunk, upright and composed, like a message: I have time to arrange you.

The priest's finger moved down the list. "Here," he said. "A note from 1814, after a fire. An estate burned near Fredericksburg. They thought they'd ended something. Two years later, a gentleman appeared in Norfolk, staying in a boarding house, paying in gold that looked too old. A girl vanished. The owner said she ran off with soldiers. A priest wrote in the margin: 'I saw him at vespers. He did not kneel.'"

Haines swallowed audibly. "So holy ground—"

"Helps some," the priest said, cutting him off. "Stops others. But do you understand the deeper problem? You can't fence your whole life with consecration. You can't conduct war inside a church and call yourself safe."

Andrew reached into his coat and withdrew the loose sheet he had taken from the orchard house ledger, the one written in a fine hand about discretion and moving servants away. He hesitated, then laid it on the desk.

The priest leaned over it, eyes scanning quickly.

Andrew watched his expression shift, just slightly. Recognition, yes, but also something closer to disgust. Not for the creature, but for the human handwriting.

"This is the more common part," the priest said quietly. "Not the monster. The arrangement."

Andrew's jaw tightened. "You're saying the families helped him."

"Sometimes," the priest said. "Sometimes they thought they were controlling him. Sometimes they thought they were containing him. Sometimes they were simply greedy and afraid and willing to trade lives they did not value in order to preserve lives they did." He looked up. "And sometimes, Lieutenant Mercer, a household becomes accustomed to a hidden appetite the way a man becomes accustomed to a hidden vice. He tells himself he can stop whenever he chooses. Years pass. Then decades. Then his children inherit the habit and call it tradition."

Andrew felt that land inside him like a punch without impact. Tradition. The war itself felt, suddenly, like a tradition of violence inherited and justified by men who could not bear to admit what they were.

The priest reached for another paper, this one folded many times. He opened it carefully, smoothing it flat with his palm. The writing was in a firm hand, but the ink had faded.

"This one is closer," the priest said. "Not in distance, in spirit. It was written during the last big collapse people in this region remember besides this war. The influenza year. The author was a deacon traveling between sick-houses."

Andrew frowned. "Influenza?"

The priest's eyes lifted. "Disease comes in waves. People forget between them because forgetting is more comfortable than preparation. But the records don't forget. Listen."

He read. "'It is easier to hide among the dying than among the living. In the sick-house there is moaning without question, and even the nurses stop counting faces. There is a man who comes and goes without being asked his name. He speaks softly and they obey him because obedience is easier than thinking. He takes from those already leaving. No one calls it murder because the body was already marked. And yet I have seen him step from a shadow with a calmness that does not belong to mortal fear. I have seen a patient wake smiling, eyes fixed on nothing, as if given permission to surrender.'"

Kellan's shoulders jerked, a quick flinch as if struck. Andrew glanced at him and saw his hands clenched so tight his knuckles had gone pale.

Andrew looked back to the priest. "So he feeds where death is expected."

"Yes," the priest said. "Because expectation is a kind of blindness. People see what they've agreed to see."

Andrew's mind returned to Jakes on the table in Whitcomb's tent, the surgeon's irritation: this man has lost more blood than this wound should allow. The edited corpse. The quietness of it. Ambrose had not needed to tear him apart. He had simply taken what he wanted and left the body behind like an emptied container.

Andrew asked, "Why tell me all of this? Why keep these records if it only proves we're outmatched?"

The priest stared at him a long moment, then reached under the desk again and pulled out something else: a thin notebook, its cover plain, its pages filled with names in careful columns.

"This isn't mine," he said. "It belonged to the priest who came before me. He began it after he found a woman in the creek behind this chapel with her throat unmarked and her skin too pale. He didn't know what he was tracking at first. He just knew the deaths didn't fit the excuses. So he wrote them down." He tapped the cover. "Evidence is not a weapon. But it's the only thing that survives long enough to become one."

Andrew felt a strange tightening in his chest that had nothing to do with the wound. He thought of what he'd become in the last week: a man collecting facts in the midst of a horror that did not respect facts. A man trying to build a scaffold of reason around something that slipped through it like smoke.

The priest's voice softened, not kind, but more human. "You asked for something that holds," he said. "This is what holds. Names. Dates. Places. The truth written down when everyone else is too frightened or too guilty to speak it."

Andrew looked at the notebook, at the columns. He imagined starting his own list, his own ledger of losses, not for the Confederacy, not for any cause, but for the simple act of not letting the dead vanish cleanly.

He realized then what Ambrose had meant when he said he learned. It wasn't only about studying a man's face. It was about learning the structures men lived inside, the ways they hid their violence behind paperwork and habit, the way a nation at war could become a field of unguarded throats.

The priest folded the deacon's letter and slid it back into its place. Then he looked at Andrew with the steady seriousness of a man who had said too much to pretend ignorance again.

"Now," the priest said, "you understand what you're dealing with. Not a beast. Not a ghost. A gentleman who has survived by being invited in, and by finding men willing to keep him comfortable when the world gets too bright."

Andrew felt the cloth bundle beneath his hand again. The dull chain. The vial. The rosary beads worn smooth by desperate fingers.

"Is there any record," Andrew asked, "of someone stopping him?"

The priest's mouth tightened into something that wasn't quite a smile. "Stopping?" he echoed. "No. Hurting him, yes. Delaying him, yes. Driving him away from one place into another, yes. But men don't like that word. Delay. They want victory because victory sounds clean. And nothing about this is clean."

He stepped closer, lowering his voice until it felt like a confession offered without absolution.

"There is, however, record of something else," he said. "Record of the way he moves when threatened. He doesn't fight like an animal cornered. He bargains like a landowner. He offers terms. He spares the useful ones. He keeps them."

Andrew's pulse slowed, heavy and deliberate, as if his body were trying to prepare for a blow by becoming stone.

"Keepers," Andrew murmured.

The priest met his gaze. "Yes," he said. "And Lieutenant Mercer, with respect to your uniform and your cause and whatever you still believe you're marching toward, I will tell you plainly: he has already begun to decide whether you are the kind of man he can use."

Andrew held still, hearing again the question in the clearing, the one Ambrose had wrapped in courtesy and curiosity.

Can you stand still?

Andrew had thought it was a test of bravery. Now he understood it might have been a test of suitability. A measure of whether a man could be made to endure horror without breaking into noisy panic. Whether he could carry silence. Whether he could make arrangements.

Andrew drew his hand away from the bundle and folded it into a fist at his side, as if he could keep his own body from being read. "Then tell me what comes next," he said.

The priest's eyes flicked briefly toward the window, toward the cemetery, toward the wet earth that waited with its patient appetite. "What comes next," he said, "is you decide whether you will spend your strength trying to kill him, or trying to keep what's left of your men from becoming the first payment in a bargain you haven't agreed to yet."

In the quiet that followed, Andrew heard only the rain and his own breathing.

But beneath those sounds, deep in the place where fear and duty tangled together, he felt a new understanding settle into him, cold and undeniable.

Ambrose had not simply crossed his path.

Ambrose had history.

And history, like hunger, did not stop because one lieutenant wished it would.

Chapter 7

Feeding Ground

They left the chapel with rain in their collars and the priest's bundle tucked under Andrew's coat like contraband. The priest did not walk them to the cemetery gate. He only unbolted the door and stood in the threshold, watching as if he expected the woods to rearrange themselves the moment Andrew stepped outside.

"Lieutenant," he said, and Andrew paused on the sagging front step.

"Yes?"

The priest's eyes flicked, briefly, to Andrew's men, then back to Andrew. "Do not let him make you feel special," he said. "That is the first kindness he offers, and it is never free."

Andrew held the priest's gaze until the warning stopped being words and became something heavier. "If he comes to this place," Andrew said, "bolt your door and go."

The priest gave a tired, humorless breath. "If he comes, a bolt won't matter. But I will pray anyway. Old habits."

Andrew did not answer. He turned away and led his men back onto the narrow road, the chapel shrinking behind them into trees and rain and the blurred suggestion of leaning stones.

By afternoon the road widened and began to show signs of war again: broken wagon ruts, the charred ribs of a fence line burned for spite or warmth, a discarded canteen half-filled with sour water. Somewhere ahead, beyond the pines, the sound of distant guns rolled like thunder that had learned to speak in intervals.

Haines heard it too. He rode close enough to keep his voice low. "That ain't just skirmish fire," he said.

Andrew listened, counting the cadence. Not the ragged cracking of scattered rifles in brush. This had rhythm. This had reply. "No," he said. "Something's come up."

They encountered the first runner near a crossroads, a mud-splattered private with his cap gone and his hair plastered to his forehead. He nearly collided with Andrew's horse, skidding to a stop with eyes too wide for his face.

"Lieutenant Mercer?" the boy panted.

Andrew's posture stiffened. The war had a way of finding men no matter how far they tried to walk from its center. "Yes."

The private swallowed, working his throat as if his own words were lodged there. "Captain Dorsey requests you at once," he said. "Field hospital's been hit. Not by Yankees. Not… exactly. There's confusion."

Confusion. It was always confusion when men did not want to name the shape of what frightened them.

"Where?" Andrew asked.

"Old tobacco barn off the creek road," the runner said. "They moved the wounded there after the last engagement. Now it's… sir, it's a mess."

Andrew looked at his men. Kellan's face had gone pale in a familiar way, his eyes sliding toward the tree line as if expecting to see a gentleman stepping out with calm ownership. Rudd's mouth tightened, and he adjusted the strap on his pack in a small, nervous motion that looked like readiness and felt like denial.

Andrew touched the priest's bundle beneath his coat, more for reassurance than belief. "Show us," he told the runner.

They rode hard, hooves throwing mud. The rain eased into a thin, persistent mist that made the world look bruised. As they neared the creek road the air began to change. Not the orchard's sweetness, not yet, but the unmistakable stench of bodies kept too close: sweat, sour breath, old blood, lye that could not keep up. The sound reached them next, a low wavering chorus that was not singing, not prayer, not command. It was pain trying to become language.

The barn sat in a shallow dip beside the creek, its plank walls dark with wet and age. Lanterns hung from nails along the eaves, casting small yellow puddles of light into the gray day. Wagons stood crooked nearby, some empty, some piled with bandage cloth and crates stamped with Confederate markings. Men moved between them with the frantic, purposeless energy of insects after a stick had been thrust into the mound.

Andrew dismounted and handed his reins to Rudd. The ground squelched under his boots.

A surgeon stepped out of the barn's wide double doors and nearly walked into him. The man's apron was smeared dark, his hands red to the wrists. He smelled of carbolic and exhaustion.

"Lieutenant," the surgeon snapped, eyes flicking to Andrew's uniform, seeking rank the way a drowning man sought driftwood. "If you've come to ask for miracles, get in line."

"I came because Captain Dorsey sent for me," Andrew said. "What happened here?"

The surgeon laughed once, short and ugly. "What always happens," he said. "We tried to make order out of dying." He glanced back into the barn, where a shout rose and fell. "Now the dying are moving around on their own."

Andrew stared. "Explain."

Before the surgeon could answer, a man in a captain's coat pushed through the doorway, his face pinched with anger that had nowhere to land. Captain Dorsey looked older than Andrew remembered, though it may have been only the way fear carved a man.

"Mercer," Dorsey said, relief and accusation tangled together. "You've been running off with your patrol chasing rumors."

Andrew held his gaze. "I was ordered to assess the estate, sir. We found—"

"Never mind what you found," Dorsey cut in. He lowered his voice as a pair of stretcher-bearers hurried past, burdened by a limp shape that moaned without waking. "We've got wounded disappearing. Not deserting. Not dying and being carried off. Disappearing."

Andrew felt the words settle into him with a quiet, sick inevitability. The priest's warning returned: hospitals full of dying men no one can protect. Feeding ground.

"How many?" Andrew asked.

Dorsey's jaw worked as if he were chewing something bitter. "Six since last night. Maybe more. We can't keep count. That's the trouble." His gaze flicked over Andrew's men. "You've got steady heads?"

"Steadier than most," Andrew said, though he did not know if it was true anymore. He thought of Jakes's body, neat as a line of ink. He thought of Kellan kneeling with peace on his face.

Dorsey gestured sharply. "Come inside. Look for yourself."

The barn's interior hit Andrew like a wall. Heat and damp and the thick smell of blood turned the air into something almost chewable. Lanterns hung from beams, their flames dimmed by smoke. Straw lay in clotted drifts under rows of makeshift cots. Men lay on those cots in every arrangement of ruin: bandaged heads, splinted legs, torsos wrapped tight, faces waxy with shock. Some whispered prayers. Some stared upward with the blank focus of men already halfway gone. Somewhere a man screamed, the sound high and sudden, then broke into sobs as if he had surprised himself by still being alive.

Orderlies moved like ghosts between bodies, stepping over boots, avoiding puddles that were not water. A young nurse, hair stuffed under a scarf, pressed a cup to a soldier's lips and murmured something soothing that did not reach her eyes.

Andrew forced his mind into the hard compartments it used on battlefields. Observe. Measure. Do not drown in the whole.

Dorsey led him along the row nearest the wall. "We moved them here two days ago," he said, talking as if words could nail the world in place. "After the clash near the ridge. Too many wounded for the main camp. Whitcomb's overwhelmed. This barn was supposed to be temporary."

Andrew's bandaged side tightened when he heard Whitcomb's name, as if his body remembered the surgeon's hands and his irritation. He scanned faces, noting pallor, the glazed look of fever, the twitch of men in morphine sleep.

"Who noticed the first missing?" Andrew asked.

Dorsey pointed to a corporal sitting on a crate near the door, his arm bound in a sling. The corporal's eyes were bloodshot from sleeplessness or shock. “Him,” Dorsey said. “He was on inside watch.”

Andrew stepped closer. “Corporal. Tell me what you saw.”

The corporal’s mouth twitched. His gaze slid past Andrew’s shoulder as if he expected to see someone else standing there. “Didn’t see,” he said hoarsely. “That’s the point, sir. I heard a man talking.”

Andrew felt a small chill pass under his skin. “Talking where?”

“Between the cots,” the corporal whispered. “Like he had business. Like it was normal.” The corporal swallowed and licked cracked lips. “I thought it was the surgeon. Thought it was you officers, coming through with orders.”

Haines, behind Andrew, shifted his weight, boots creaking on plank. Andrew did not turn, but he felt Haines listening too hard, as if his ears could prevent what his eyes had failed to.

The corporal continued, voice dropping. “It was polite. That’s what’s wrong. Not drunk talk. Not panic. Polite. Like a gentleman in a parlor.” His eyes darted, then fixed on Andrew with sudden intensity. “I sat up to look and I saw him, I swear I did. Pale as milk. Standing where the lantern light didn't touch him right. And the wounded… they went quiet. Like they was listening."

Andrew kept his face still with effort. "Then what?"

The corporal's throat worked. "Then I blinked," he whispered, ashamed as if blinking were a sin. "And I heard dragging, but no one cried out. No struggle. Nothing. Just… the straw moving a little." He stared at his good hand as if expecting to find proof in his palm. "When I went to count, two beds was empty. Blankets folded like someone had took the time."

Folded blankets. A rifle leaning neatly against a tree. Ambrose's habit of arrangement. His calm. His manners.

Andrew looked down at the long aisle of cots. A figure could walk through here without hurry, without noise, choosing with the patience of appetite. Men would assume it belonged, because the war taught them to accept strangers moving among the dying.

Dorsey watched Andrew's face closely now. "This sound like your orchard trouble?" he asked, and tried to make it contempt, tried to keep it in the shape of rumor.

Andrew's wound gave a small, sharp sting under the bandage, as if in answer.

"It sounds like something that knows where it can feed without interruption," Andrew said.

As if summoned by the word feed, a faint scent drifted through the barn, threading itself beneath carbolic and sweat: a sweetness out of season, like fruit rotting in a hidden barrel.

Andrew's stomach tightened.

Haines leaned in, voice barely moving the air. "Sir," he murmured, "do you smell that?"

Andrew did not answer. He kept his gaze on the aisle, on the pockets of shadow between lantern light. He felt the presence not as a figure he could point to, but as a change in the room's attention, a subtle reorientation, as if something had turned its head.

A wounded man on the nearest cot stopped moaning mid-breath. His eyes opened wider, unfocused, then drifted toward the far corner where the lantern light was weakest. For a moment his face softened with something like relief.

Permission to surrender, the deacon's letter had said.

Andrew's hand went, without fully deciding to, to the inside of his coat where the priest's bundle rested. The dull weight of the chain pressed back through cloth.

The hospital was full of men already halfway gone, and something old and patient had found it.

Not a battlefield.

A feeding ground.

The sweetness did not belong in a barn full of blood and lye. It slipped beneath the sharper smells the way a familiar tune slipped beneath a man's thoughts, quiet at first, then impossible to ignore once recognized.

Andrew walked deeper between the cots. Dorsey and Haines followed a step behind; Rudd lingered near the door with Kellan, both of them pressed into the instinctive safety of daylight and exit. Orderlies watched Andrew with open resentment and hope tangled together, as if any officer might become an answer if he only stood tall enough.

The wounded man who had gone quiet began to murmur, not to anyone in particular. His lips worked around a word that did not fit the barn.

"Angel," he breathed, voice paper-thin. His eyes stayed fixed on the corner where lantern light failed. "An angel's come."

A nurse glanced up sharply. "Hush," she hissed, but her own gaze slid, unwillingly, in the same direction.

Dorsey's face tightened. "They're saying things," he muttered. "Since last night. Calling it an angel. Calling it the devil. Depends on whether they're praying or cursing."

Andrew did not like how neatly those were the only two categories men offered when reason failed. Angel or devil. A comfort or a condemnation. Something sent by God, or something loosed by Hell. Both explanations allowed the speaker to remain small, a witness rather than a participant.

He stopped beside a cot where a boy no older than sixteen lay with his thigh wrapped in a stained bandage. Fever had turned his eyes glossy. The boy's gaze tracked Andrew's uniform without truly seeing it.

"Private," Andrew said quietly.

The boy's mouth twitched. "Sir?" It came out like a question even though Andrew hadn't asked one.

"What happened last night?" Andrew asked. "Tell me what you heard."

The boy swallowed, Adam's apple bobbing like a trapped thing. "I heard… I heard a man talking soft," he whispered. "Polite. Like when the officers come around and pretend not to see we're dying."

Dorsey flinched at that, as if struck. He opened his mouth to reprimand, then closed it. The truth had no rank.

Andrew kept his voice even. "What did he say?"

The boy's eyes drifted toward the shadows again. "He said my name," he whispered. "Not loud. Like he'd always known it." His lips parted, and for a moment there was a strange softness on his face, something like relief that made Andrew's skin crawl. "He said it'd be quiet soon. He said I'd earned rest."

Andrew felt the priest's warning echo in his mind: Do not let him make you feel special. That is the first kindness he offers. Ambrose did not need to promise pleasure. He promised an end to pain, and in a barn full of broken bodies, that was the most persuasive lie in the world.

Haines leaned close, voice rough. "Did you see him?"

The boy shook his head very slightly. "I saw… a coat, I think. Dark. And hands. Clean hands." His gaze flicked back to Andrew's face, sudden fear breaking through fever. "He's not rough, sir. He ain't like the butchers. He's gentle."

Gentle. Andrew thought of Jakes dropping to his knees, eyes wide with bewildered surprise. Of the pale fingers at a throat like a lover's touch. The intimacy had been the worst part, the refusal of drama. Ambrose did not rage. He arranged.

Andrew straightened and looked down the aisle again. Lanterns made islands of yellow light. Between them lay the gaps, the soft black pockets where bodies became shapes and shapes became guesses. A man could walk through those gaps without being seen if everyone agreed not to look too closely. War taught men to cooperate with their own blindness. It was one of its few efficient lessons.

Dorsey's voice lowered. "So, what are you saying, Mercer? You saying this is the same thing you found in that orchard?"

Andrew did not answer at once. He listened instead, forcing his mind to separate noise from meaning. The barn's chorus was constant: low moans, muttered prayers, the scrape of boots, the clink of metal bowls. But under it, he caught something else, a change in the cadence of the room. A thin hush that moved like a draft, not everywhere at once, but in a slow passing, as if attention itself were being drawn along a path.

Andrew followed that hush with his eyes.

A line of cots near the far wall, where the planks were dark with old damp, had gone strangely quiet.

Not silent in the way of sleep or death. Quiet in the way of obedience.

He took a step toward it, then another. Haines matched him. Dorsey hesitated and then followed, anger and fear tightening his mouth.

As they neared, one of the orderlies looked up and began to speak, then stopped mid-word, as if he had forgotten what language was for. His eyes fixed on the aisle ahead. His face took on a careful, composed expression that did not belong to him.

Andrew's bandaged side gave a small sting. Not pain, exactly. Recognition, like a bruise pressed at the center.

The orderly's lips parted. "He's here," the man whispered, and the words sounded neither panicked nor triumphant. Only certain.

Haines's fingers tightened on his rifle. "Sir," he breathed.

Andrew could see no figure. Yet the sweetness thickened, and the men in the nearest cots turned their heads in unison toward an empty strip of air, following a presence his eyes refused to confirm.

A wounded sergeant, face gaunt with loss of blood, pushed himself up on one elbow. His eyes were wet. "Is that you?" he whispered, not to Andrew. "Is it finally time?"

The nurse nearest him made a sound of protest. “No,” she said sharply. “No, you hold on. You hold on, you hear me?”

But the sergeant was smiling now, a quiet, grateful smile that made Andrew’s stomach twist.

“Angel,” the sergeant whispered. “Thank you.”

Something moved at the edge of lantern light. Not a body stepping forward. More like the light itself bending, becoming uncertain, as if it could not decide what to reveal.

Andrew reached under his coat and closed his hand around the priest’s rosary. The beads were worn smooth, too familiar for his callused fingers. He did not know if it was faith or superstition that made him do it. He only knew he needed to hold something that belonged to the human world.

“Show yourself,” Andrew said, voice low, controlled.

Dorsey hissed, “Are you out of your mind?”

Andrew did not look back. His eyes stayed on the corridor of dimness where men’s gazes converged. “If you’re here,” Andrew said again, “be here.”

For a moment nothing happened. Then, very softly, as if spoken beside Andrew’s ear though no breath warmed his skin, a voice answered.

"Such authority," it murmured. "Even in a place like this."

Andrew's spine tightened. He did not turn, because he refused to give the voice the satisfaction of making him flinch. He had learned in the clearing that sudden movement belonged to fear, and fear was a language Ambrose spoke fluently.

Haines's eyes went wide. He heard it too. Dorsey went pale, his anger collapsing into something smaller.

The voice continued, mild and almost amused. "You brought yourself to a sickroom, Lieutenant Mercer. Do you expect a sickroom to behave like a battlefield?"

Andrew kept his breathing steady, though his pulse hammered. "You're taking men from here," he said. "Dying men. Helpless men."

"Helpless," the voice echoed, as if tasting the word. "They are not helpless. They are invited. They are already at the threshold, and they are grateful for a hand to cross it."

The wounded sergeant on the cot gave a small, contented sigh. "Yes," he whispered, as if agreeing with a beloved preacher.

Andrew stepped closer to the cot line. The sweetness became almost cloying, fruit left too long in heat. He could see, now, the faint dark staining at the corner of a mouth as lantern light finally caught a face that should not have been there a heartbeat earlier.

Ambrose stood between two cots as calmly as if he'd been attending patients all morning. His clothing was the same dark ruin Andrew remembered from the woods, wet now at the hem, as if he had stepped through rain without feeling it. His posture was impeccable, and his eyes moved over the wounded with something that could have been pity if it weren't so hungry.

The nurse beside the sergeant froze, cup held mid-air. Her face was slack, not with sleep but with the sudden absence of will. She stared at Ambrose as though she were waiting for instruction.

Ambrose's gaze slid to Andrew. That small, courteous smile appeared.

"You see?" Ambrose said. "It is not so difficult. One only needs to speak to what they already want."

Dorsey's voice cracked. "What are you?"

Ambrose did not look at him right away. His attention lingered on Andrew with a deliberate intimacy, as if the rest of the barn were merely scenery.

Then he answered, politely, as if indulging a child's question. "I am mercy," he said. "To those who are tired of pretending pain has meaning. And I am judgment to those who insist it does."

Haines lifted his rifle a fraction. "Devil," he whispered, and the word came out with the dull certainty of a man naming a storm.

Ambrose's eyes flicked to Haines, not angry, only curious. "Is that what they call me today?" he asked. "How industrious."

Andrew felt the rosary beads bite into his palm. He forced his voice into the shape of command, because command was the only prayer he still knew how to speak. "Leave," he said.

Ambrose's smile deepened by a fraction. "You want me to leave," he murmured, "because you've begun to understand that a hospital is a better orchard than any estate ever was."

The wounded sergeant reached out a trembling hand toward Ambrose, fingers opening like a child reaching for a parent. "Please," he whispered.

Ambrose did not take the hand. He only looked down at it, and the sergeant's face softened further, tears sliding from the corners of his eyes.

Andrew saw then what made this place different from the clearing. In the woods, Ambrose had tested stillness. Here, he did not need to test. The dying offered themselves, and the living were too exhausted to guard them. It was not merely feeding. It was recruitment, a slow training of minds to accept him as comfort.

Ambrose looked back at Andrew. "Listen to them," he said gently. "Angel, devil. Those are your kinds of stories. They are trying to give me a shape that makes their suffering feel governed. But I have no interest in governance." His eyes narrowed slightly, the appraisal returning. "I have interest in use."

Andrew held his ground. The barn seemed to tilt around that gaze, as if Ambrose's attention could rearrange space.

"And you," Ambrose continued softly, "have brought tools under your coat. How earnest."

Andrew's throat tightened. The priest's bundle felt suddenly obvious, as if it radiated guilt.

Ambrose's smile returned, composed and patient. "Tell me," he said, voice low enough that it felt meant only for Andrew, "when they call me angel, do you envy them? When they call me devil, do you feel relief?"

Andrew did not answer. Because he did not know which was worse: envy of men allowed to surrender, or relief that his enemy could be made simple by hate.

Ambrose glanced back at the wounded sergeant, then leaned slightly, close enough that the sergeant shivered with anticipation.

The nurse's cup slipped from her fingers and hit the straw with a dull sound. No one moved to pick it up.

Andrew took one step forward, and the cut beneath his bandage flared, sharp and clean, as if his own body were warning him that proximity had a cost. He felt, suddenly and vividly, how thin the line was between standing and kneeling. Between keeping others safe and being useful.

Ambrose's eyes stayed on him as if he were reading the thought off Andrew's face.

"Careful," Ambrose murmured. "You have a gift for believing you can command what you are only beginning to comprehend."

In the heavy, sweetened air, with men whispering angel and devil like prayers they could not decide between, Andrew understood with cold clarity that this was not simply a monster stalking the wounded.

It was a gentleman offering comfort in exchange for blood, and the war had made that exchange feel, to too many men, like salvation.

Andrew did not raise his pistol. The last time he had trusted a gun to solve Ambrose, Jakes had died for the impulse. Here, among cots and fever, a single shot would ricochet through bodies already torn apart, and Ambrose stood close enough to the wounded that any miss would be paid for immediately.

He kept his voice low, pitched to carry without becoming spectacle. "Step away from him."

Ambrose's gaze dropped to the sergeant's outstretched hand as if considering etiquette. "Step away," he echoed, mild. "You keep trying to make this a matter of distance."

The sergeant's smile trembled. He looked, abruptly, like a man trying to wake from a pleasant dream and failing. "Please," he whispered again, but now the word carried fear. His eyes had found something in Ambrose's face that did not match the promise.

Haines shifted beside Andrew, rifle tight against his shoulder. The nurse still stood with her hands half-raised, empty now, as if her body had forgotten what it had been doing. Captain Dorsey hovered a pace back, pale and angry, the kind of angry that came from realizing a man's authority meant nothing here.

Andrew's fingers eased into his coat. He could feel the priest's bundle: the cold weight of the dull chain, the smooth rosary beads, the folded strip of Latin. He had wanted something that held. Now he was holding it like a child clutching a charm in a storm.

"Mercer," Dorsey hissed through his teeth, careful not to be overheard by the injured. "What are you doing?"

Andrew did not look away from Ambrose. "Buying time," he said.

Ambrose smiled as if he approved of the honesty. "And how will you spend it, Lieutenant? With a prayer? With iron? With fire?"

The mention of iron tightened Andrew's ribcage. He remembered the cellar rings. He remembered the dream; the chain already fastened to his ankle like fate.

He forced his breath to stay even. "You can't take them," Andrew said, and heard the thinness in it. The war took them. Disease took them. Orders took them. Ambrose only had to arrive at the moment they were already being taken.

Ambrose's eyes flicked along the row of cots. Men stared at him with the exhausted reverence of the condemned. "Can't," he murmured. "That word is a habit you learned from ledgers and flags. You think if you say it with enough conviction the world will obey."

He leaned slightly toward the sergeant. The man shuddered. His throat worked. A wet, involuntary sound escaped him, half sob, half hunger. Andrew saw the way the sergeant's gaze fixed on Ambrose's mouth, on the faint dark stain at the corner like spilled wine.

Andrew stepped in, placing himself between Ambrose and the cot. He did it carefully, without the suddenness of challenge, as if he were only shifting position in a crowded aisle.

The cut beneath his bandage flared, a sharp clean line of pain that made his vision narrow for half a heartbeat. He bit down on the reaction and kept his face still.

Ambrose's eyes sharpened with interest. "Ah," he said softly. "There you are."

The barn felt quieter, not because the wounded stopped moaning, but because their attention tilted. The living and dying alike were watching Andrew now the way men watched a gambler approach a table with his last coin.

Andrew drew the chain from his coat.

It was nothing special to look at. Dull links, short length. The priest had offered it with the grimness of a man handing over a tool he did not believe in but used anyway because empty hands were worse. In Andrew's grip it felt heavier than it should have, like it carried memory.

He let it hang where Ambrose could see it clearly. "You know what this is," Andrew said.

Ambrose's gaze rested on the links with a kind of fond contempt. "I know what you want it to be," he replied. "A boundary. A collar. A story where iron means something because men decided it should."

Andrew's thumb found the folded Latin parchment. He did not unfold it. He did not trust his own mouth to pronounce the words properly, and he did not trust that mispronunciation would be harmless. But he let Ambrose see the edge of it anyway, the cramped writing.

Ambrose looked amused, almost indulgent, as if Andrew had brought a child's wooden sword to a duel. "You went to the chapel," he said. "You sat with the man who keeps frightened papers and calls it faith."

"Leave," Andrew repeated, quieter now, because the word felt foolish raised to the level of command.

Ambrose's attention shifted to Dorsey for the first time as if remembering there were other actors on the stage. "Your captain wants me gone because he wants his hospital to behave," Ambrose said. "But this is the truth of it, isn't it? Your hospital is not mercy. It's inventory. It's where you stack the broken parts until they either return to work or stop consuming rations."

Dorsey's face flushed, anger finding a place to stand. "You shut your mouth."

Ambrose turned his head slowly toward him. "Or what?" he asked, and the gentleness of the words made them cruel.

Dorsey's hand went to his pistol. His jaw worked as if he were chewing nails. He did not draw, but the impulse showed, and several of the wounded flinched, the fear of loud violence cutting through their trance.

Andrew saw Ambrose's eyes catch the movement. Not as a threat. As an opportunity.

"Captain," Andrew said sharply, without taking his gaze off Ambrose. "Do not."

Dorsey froze, caught between rank and panic. For a moment Andrew hated him, then forgave him. In war, men were asked to stand in front of horrors that at least had uniforms. This one did not.

Ambrose's smile returned to Andrew. "How familiar you are with giving orders that prevent your own men from getting themselves killed," he murmured. "It's a talent. And talent should be rewarded."

Andrew's grip tightened on the chain until the links bit his palm. "What do you want?" he asked, and he hated the question because it admitted what he'd begun to understand: that Ambrose was not here to be chased off like a raider. He was here to negotiate, to test what men would trade.

Ambrose's gaze moved past Andrew, drifting over the rows of cots. He took in the bloodstained bandages, the empty eyes, the trembling hands. When he spoke, his voice carried without effort, calm enough that it sounded like comfort.

"What I want," Ambrose said, "is not what you imagine."

He looked back at Andrew. "You think I want bodies. I can take bodies anywhere. The world is generous with them. I want the arrangement that allows bodies to vanish without disrupting the story you tell yourselves. I want the quiet machinery that keeps the living from asking why."

Andrew swallowed. The barn's air felt thick, sweetened, as if rot had learned manners.

Ambrose went on, conversational. "This war," he said, "has given you so many excuses. So many ways to call something inevitable. A boy disappears from a wagon and you say 'deserter.' A woman vanishes from her home and you say 'refugee road.' A man bleeds out in his own bed and you say 'fever.'"

His gaze slid briefly toward the sergeant, whose face had tightened into terror now that the promise was fraying. "Do you know what I admire most about you, Lieutenant Mercer?" Ambrose asked.

Andrew said nothing.

Ambrose's tone warmed, almost intimate. "You still believe there is a difference between your violence and mine," he said. "You still want to pretend yours has rules."

Andrew felt heat rise in him, disciplined and sharp. "Mine isn't pleasure."

Ambrose's eyebrows lifted slightly, as if acknowledging a point in a debate. "No," he agreed. "Yours is duty. That's what makes it so reliable."

Behind Andrew, Haines made a low sound, something like a suppressed curse. Andrew did not turn. He could feel Haines's outrage and fear trying to become movement.

Ambrose's eyes flicked to Haines without losing his calm. "Your corporal wants to shoot me," he said. "Your captain wants to shoot me. You want to believe you could shoot me." The smile returned, slight. "And yet you stand still."

Andrew forced himself to speak with care. "I stand still because I've seen what happens when men move wrong."

"Yes," Ambrose said softly. "And because you understand something else you will not admit aloud. If I wished to empty this barn," he said, and his gaze drifted across the cots like a hand, "you would not stop me. Not with rifles. Not with iron. Not with your borrowed prayers."

Dorsey's voice came thin. "Then why haven't you?"

Ambrose turned his eyes to him as if surprised by the question. "Because I have no need to rush," he said. "And because I am not an animal."

He faced Andrew again. "I could take all of them," Ambrose continued. "And you would call it tragedy. Another night of misfortune in a war already drowning in it. But you would remember me as a storm, not a choice."

Andrew felt his mouth go dry. "A choice," he repeated.

Ambrose's gaze held him. "Yes," he said. "I would rather you remember me as something you decided to live with."

The words slid into Andrew's mind like a blade finding an existing seam.

Andrew knew then what the ambush had been meant to be, before he ever set it: a clean moment of righteous action. A trap sprung, a creature contained, a story returned to the proper shape. But in the presence of Ambrose's calm, the idea of clean victory felt childish. The priest had been right. Delay. Hurt. Drive away. Those were the only verbs that fit.

Andrew lifted the chain higher, letting it glint dully in lantern light. "Get out," he said, voice low and steady. "Not because I can stop you. Because you've already done enough here."

Ambrose studied him for a long moment. The barn waited. The wounded seemed to hold their breath as if the argument between a lieutenant and a pale gentleman might decide whether they lived or died.

Then Ambrose smiled, and the smile carried something like approval.

"That," he said, "is the first honest thing you've said to me."

He leaned closer, not to the sergeant, but to Andrew, closing the space with impossible ease. The scent of him was stronger here: sweetness and old metal, like an apple left to rot in a soldier's canteen.

Andrew did not step back. He felt the wound beneath his bandage tighten, as if bracing.

Ambrose spoke quietly, so quietly that even Haines would not hear it clearly. "You came here to lay a trap," he murmured. "To prove you are still the sort of man who can draw a line and call it morality."

Andrew kept his jaw set. "And you came here to feed."

Ambrose's eyes glinted with something colder than amusement. "No," he corrected. "I came here to show you how easy it is."

For a heartbeat, Andrew thought Ambrose might strike him the way he had struck Jakes. A touch. A wet click. Silence.

Instead, Ambrose's gaze dipped briefly to Andrew's bandage. The corner of his mouth stained a fraction darker, as if the sight alone pleased him.

"Tell your men the missing were taken by Yankees," Ambrose said softly. "Tell your captain to add their names to a list. Tell your surgeon to write 'infection' beside them when he gets tired of asking questions."

Andrew felt a surge of anger, but it had nowhere to land. Ambrose was not instructing him. He was describing him.

Ambrose straightened. His voice rose just enough to carry to the nearest cots, gentle as bedside talk. "Rest," he murmured, and several men's faces softened despite themselves, the word slipping into them like morphine.

The nurse blinked, sudden tears on her cheeks, and seemed not to know why.

Ambrose stepped back into the thin corridor of shadow between lantern islands. His figure blurred not because he vanished, but because the room's eyes refused to hold him the way they held ordinary men.

He looked at Andrew one last time. "You will try again," Ambrose said, conversational. "I almost hope you do. It will teach you what you can afford."

Then the sweetness thinned, not gone but withdrawn, like a mouth closing.

Andrew stood rigid, chain still in his hand, listening to the barn's noise return in increments: a moan resuming, a cough, the scrape of a boot as an orderly remembered he had legs.

Dorsey exhaled hard. "Where is he?" he demanded, eyes scanning the aisle as if hatred could make a man visible.

Haines swallowed, voice rough. "Gone," he said. Then, after a beat, quieter: "Or not."

Andrew lowered the chain slowly. His palm ached where the links had bitten him. He looked at the sergeant, who now stared at the ceiling with wide, horrified eyes, as if he'd woken from a beautiful dream to find his own grave waiting.

Andrew felt no triumph. Only the sick certainty that the ambush had failed before it began, because Ambrose had not come to the barn unprepared.

Ambrose had come to argue.

And the argument Andrew realized as he tucked the chain back beneath his coat, was not about whether Ambrose was a devil or an angel.

It was about whether Andrew Mercer would keep pretending he was different from the machinery that made a man like Ambrose possible.

Chapter 8

Terms of Mercy

Andrew left the barn with the chain biting cold against his ribs beneath his coat and the taste of sweetness still ghosting the back of his throat. Outside, the mist had thickened into a light rain again, turning the world to a smear of gray and wet wood. Wagons sat in the mud like exhausted animals. Men stood in small, tight knots, talking in murmurs that kept breaking off whenever someone else looked their way.

Captain Dorsey followed him out, boots sucking at the ground. The captain's face had the strained look of a man trying to convince himself he had not just watched his authority be ignored by something that did not recognize ranks.

"Mercer," Dorsey said, and there was no reprimand in it now, only a brittle need for direction. "Tell me you know what that was."

Andrew did not answer with certainty he did not have. He glanced back toward the barn's doors, where an orderly leaned against the frame, staring into space as if he were still listening to a voice that had withdrawn. The sounds of the wounded had resumed, but something in the cadence had changed; it was the difference between pain that belonged to a man and pain that had been made into a doorway.

"I know it doesn't belong here," Andrew said.

Dorsey let out a harsh breath that might have been a laugh in another life. "Nothing belongs here," he muttered, then lowered his voice. "How do I explain this to command? Six men gone, maybe more. Blankets folded. No blood on the straw."

"Don't decorate it," Andrew said. His own voice sounded flatter than he intended, the tone of an officer forcing a report into a shape paper could hold. "Missing in the night. Likely taken by raiders or scouts. Men get moved; records get lost."

Dorsey stared at him. "That's your advice?"

It was not advice. It was what Ambrose had said, spoken with that polite contempt: Tell your men the missing were taken by Yankees. Tell your surgeon to write infection when he gets tired of asking questions.

Andrew felt the wound beneath his bandage tighten, a small flare of clean pain that seemed less like flesh protesting and more like a reminder that his body was now part of the conversation.

"It's what they'll accept," Andrew said quietly. "And it keeps them from panicking into worse."

Dorsey's mouth worked as if he were chewing the words into something swallowable. His eyes flicked toward Andrew's coat, toward the place where Andrew had hidden the priest's bundle. "You're carrying something," Dorsey said.

Andrew met his gaze. "Tools," he replied. "Superstition, if you prefer. Either way, it didn't stop him."

Dorsey's anger flickered and failed. "Nothing stops anything anymore," he said, and then turned away sharply, as if the admission tasted like surrender.

Haines stood a few steps off, watching the barn with his rifle in both hands. His face had the hard set of a man trying to hold himself together by force. When Andrew approached, Haines' eyes flicked briefly to Andrew's side, to the invisible wound under cloth, and then back up.

"You all right, sir?" he asked.

Andrew did not like how often the question came now, from different mouths. As if the men could feel something shifting in him and needed reassurance that their lieutenant still belonged to them.

"I'm here," Andrew said. It was not an answer to the wound. It was an answer to everything else.

Haines nodded once, grim. "Kellan's been staring at the doors," he said. "Like he expects him to step back out."

Andrew looked toward the nearest wagon where Rudd and Kellan waited. Kellan stood under a sagging canvas tarp, rain darkening his hair, eyes fixed on the barn as though the building were a throat that might open again. Rudd was beside him, too young to look as tired as he did, fingers worrying a strap on his pack.

Andrew started toward them.

That was when the noise changed.

At first it was only a distant rumble, wheels on rutted road, the creak of harness leather. Then voices, more than a handful. The sound carried through the wet air and drew heads the way a gunshot did, with the instinctive question of whether it meant threat or relief.

A supply train crested the slight rise of the creek road: two wagons, mud-splashed, canvas covers sagging with rain, pulled by tired mules. A small escort in gray rode alongside, rifles slung, faces drawn. The sight should have been ordinary. It should have been comfort, food and ammunition and paper orders. Yet the men around the barn tensed, because anything arriving now felt like it might also be another way for the world to go wrong.

The lead wagon slowed as it approached the barn yard. A sergeant in charge raised a hand, calling out to Dorsey's sentries. The wagons stopped with a wet squelch. Men climbed down stiffly.

And then another man stepped from the second wagon.

Andrew saw him in pieces before he recognized him: the way he moved with the quick, purposeful energy of someone who still believed the war could be navigated by effort; the clean cut of his coat compared to the mud-stained fatigue around him; the fact that he paused to look over the barn yard with open, searching concern rather than the dull suspicion everyone else wore now.

He was younger than Andrew by several years, his hair darker, his face less hollowed by sleeplessness. His jawline held the Mercer family's stubborn angle. He carried himself as if he still expected the world to respond to decency.

Andrew felt something in his chest tighten so abruptly it nearly stole his breath.

"No," he said under it, not aloud at first, as if refusal could send the man back onto the road.

The younger man turned, gaze sweeping, and then his eyes found Andrew.

The change in his face was immediate and boyish in a way that hurt. Relief, recognition, a smile that tried to outrun the rain and the smell of blood. He started forward through the mud with long strides.

"Andrew!" he called.

Haines turned sharply. Rudd's head snapped around. Kellan blinked like a sleepwalker jolted awake.

The man reached Andrew and stopped only when he was close enough to grab him. He did, hands clamping onto Andrew's shoulders with an affection that did not bother asking permission.

"Jesus, you look like hell," the man said, and the attempt at humor cracked with genuine fear. "I heard you were posted out this way, and I thought I'd missed you. I thought…" He swallowed, eyes scanning Andrew's face as if searching for injuries in the lines around his mouth. "I didn't know where you'd gone."

Andrew stared at him, trying to reconcile the solid fact of Elias Mercer with everything else that had become unreal.

"Elias," Andrew said. His voice came out rougher than he intended.

Elias grinned, but it faltered. "It's me," he said, as if Andrew might not believe. Then his gaze dropped briefly, catching on Andrew's posture, on the careful way he held himself as though certain movements would cost him. "Are you hurt?"

Andrew almost said no, by habit. Almost gave the easy plank of a lie. But the lie felt too thin in Elias' presence. Too sharp-edged.

"A cut," Andrew said. "Nothing you need to worry about."

Elias' eyes narrowed, not convinced, and then flicked past Andrew toward the barn. His expression changed again, the smile fading into confusion and concern.

"What's this?" he asked. "I thought this was a supply stop. The sergeant said there was a field hospital here, but he didn't say…" He took in the lanterns still burning under the eaves despite daylight, the men standing too still, the damp, sour smell that leaked out each time the barn door cracked open. "How bad is it?"

Andrew felt the world tilt, not from weakness, but from the sudden terrifying clarity of what Elias represented: a remaining tie to a life before the orchard, before the edited corpse, before Ambrose spoke his name like a key turning in a lock. Elias was family, which meant leverage. Elias was goodness that still believed it could stand in a war and remain clean.

Ambrose had spoken in the barn about use. About what could be arranged. Andrew heard the voice as if it were still in the sweetened air: I would rather you remember me as something you decided to live with.

Andrew stepped slightly to block Elias' view of the barn interior. The movement tugged at the bandage under his shirt, and pain sparked cleanly along his ribs. He did not show it.

"It's a relocation point," Andrew said, forcing his tone into the old shape of officer-to-officer explanation. "Wounded from the ridge. Whitcomb's overwhelmed, so they moved some here."

Elias' face tightened with sympathy that made Andrew want to turn away. "And you're assigned to guard them?"

"I was sent to investigate trouble nearby," Andrew said. He kept the words careful, because

Elias' eyes were sharp and his mind still orderly. Too orderly. "I returned and found this."

Elias looked past Andrew again, trying to see around him. His gaze landed on Haines, on Rudd, on Kellan with his haunted stare.

"Your men look…" Elias began, then stopped, as if the word frightened were an accusation. "They look like something's been hunting them."

Haines stiffened. Rudd's eyes dropped. Kellan's mouth twitched as though he were trying not to speak.

Andrew said quickly, "The area's unsettled. Guerrillas. Deserters. Rumors."

Elias' brow furrowed. "Rumors don't fold blankets," he said suddenly, voice low. He nodded toward the barn. "I heard them talking at the wagon line. Men going missing. Is that true?"

Andrew' throat tightened. He had not expected Elias to arrive already carrying the outline of the problem. The war was a net of whispers; nothing stayed contained for long. Still, hearing it from Elias made it sharper. More dangerous.

Before Andrew could answer, Dorsey shouted an order at someone near the wagons, and a wounded man inside the barn cried out, the sound thin and raw. Elias flinched, his eyes widening. He took a half-step toward the barn door on instinct.

Andrew caught his arm.

Elias turned back, startled by the grip. He looked at Andrew's hand on him, then up into Andrew's face, reading something there that the rain could not wash away.

"Andrew," Elias said quietly, "what aren't you telling me?"

Andrew held his brother's gaze. In Elias' eyes he saw thc old faith: in right and wrong, in causes, in the idea that men could make choices without being altered by what they endured.

Andrew felt the priest's warning echo from the chapel doorway: Do not let him make you feel special.

He released Elias' arm gently, as if easing a hand away from a hot stove. "Not here," Andrew said.

Elias' jaw set with familiar Mercer stubbornness. "Then where?"

Andrew glanced toward the wagons, toward the wet line of trees beyond the barn yard, toward the road that led away from this place and yet could not lead away from what had attached itself to him.

He imagined Ambrose watching from somewhere just beyond sight, amused by the timing, pleased by the new piece on the board. A brother. A tender point. A bargaining chip with a beating heart.

Andrew kept his voice steady because he had to. "We'll talk when you're out of earshot," he said. "And you will listen to me, Elias. You will do exactly what I say, even if it offends you."

Elias stared at him a moment, rain clinging to his lashes. Then he nodded once, slow and wary, as if agreeing to a rule he did not yet understand.

"All right," Elias said. "But I'm not leaving you out here. Not after finally finding you."

Andrew felt the words land like a promise and a threat at the same time.

He looked past Elias toward the barn doors, and for an instant he swore he caught the faintest trace of sweetness again, not strong enough to be real, only enough to be remembered.

Terms of mercy, the priest had warned. Bargains made not with equals, but with men made desperate by love.

Andrew turned his face away from the barn and began guiding his brother toward the wagons, already calculating, already dreading how quickly the world could turn a reunion into an offering.

Andrew guided Elias toward the wagons as if he were escorting a valuable officer, not his younger brother. The distinction mattered. Affection made a man careless, and carelessness was what Ambrose harvested.

They passed men unloading sacks of meal and crates of cartridges. The supply sergeant barked orders that sounded too loud in the wet air. The barn behind them breathed its low chorus of suffering, muffled by planks and rain, but never fully contained. Elias kept glancing back, his expression caught between instinct to help and instinct to obey the tone in Andrew's voice.

Andrew stopped beside the second wagon, under the sagging canvas where the rain struck and ran off in steady lines. The mules steamed faintly, ribs rising and falling in patient misery.

"Who sent you?" Andrew asked.

Elias pushed wet hair back from his forehead. "Quartermaster detail out of Hanover," he said. "They needed wagons run to scattered posts. I volunteered when I heard your name attached to this road." He paused. "I thought you'd be grateful."

Andrew heard the accusation he didn't mean. Grateful. As if gratitude were simple. Andrew kept his voice level. "You shouldn't have come looking."

Elias's eyes narrowed. "What does that mean?"

"It means roads are dangerous," Andrew said, and hated how much it sounded like a half-truth, which it was. "This area is worse than you've heard."

Elias leaned in a fraction, lowering his voice as men passed with crates between them. "Andrew, I've seen dangerous. I'm not a child."

Andrew looked at him, really looked, and felt the old protective instinct rise like bile. Elias had seen battle, yes. Elias had seen men torn apart and called it war. But Elias hadn't seen a man die like punctuation, quiet and edited. Elias hadn't watched wounded men smile at the approach of something that wanted them emptied.

"You don't understand the kind of dangerous I mean," Andrew said.

Elias's jaw tightened, stubborn Mercer bone. "Then tell me."

Andrew swallowed. The words did not want to form because naming a thing gave it a foothold. But Elias was here, and silence would not keep him safe. Silence was what Ambrose used.

"We investigated an estate," Andrew said carefully. "An orchard house. Men went missing. There were graves under the trees. Something was kept in the cellar at some point. Chains bolted into stone."

Elias stared at him. "Chains?"

"Yes."

"And you think that has something to do with men disappearing from this hospital," Elias said, already assembling it into a shape his mind could accept. "Guerrillas using tunnels. Raiders."

Andrew almost let him have that. Almost accepted the relief of a human explanation. But he remembered Ambrose in the barn, speaking like a gentleman while men listened like parishioners.

"No," Andrew said. "Not raiders."

Elias held still. "Then what?"

Andrew felt the bandage beneath his shirt tug with the rise of his breath. He did not touch it. "A man," he said, and then corrected himself because the lie was too large. "Something that looks like a man. It calls itself Ambrose."

Elias's expression shifted, confusion turning sharper. "Ambrose," he repeated, as if the name might unlock a category. "Is that one of Mosby's people? A deserter?"

Andrew shook his head once.

Elias's voice dropped. "Andrew. Are you saying you believe in a ghost story?"

Andrew almost laughed at the phrase ghost story, at how small it sounded compared to the reality of a presence that could bend the attention of a room. He leaned closer, so Elias would have to hear without the comfort of distance.

"I've seen it," Andrew said. "Haines has seen it. Kellan has seen it. We lost Jakes to it."

Elias's eyes flicked involuntarily toward the barn, then back. "Lost him how?"

Andrew held Elias's gaze and forced the truth into words that did not tremble. "A touch at the throat. A neat cut. He died without a struggle. Later the surgeon said he'd lost more blood than the wound should allow."

Elias's face went pale in slow stages, as if his body were trying to decide whether to believe his ears. "That's not possible."

"I know," Andrew said. "That's why I didn't want you on this road."

Elias opened his mouth, then closed it. His gaze dropped to Andrew's side, to the way Andrew stood slightly guarded, as if certain angles hurt. "And you," he said quietly. "You're cut too."

Andrew nodded once. “It doesn’t heal right.”

Rain hammered a little harder on the wagon canvas. Nearby, a man laughed at something that wasn’t funny, a quick burst of noise that ended abruptly when another man told him to shut up. The world kept trying to be ordinary around them, and it made Andrew want to tear it open just to stop the pretense.

Elias exhaled slowly, eyes searching Andrew’s face as if looking for proof of madness. “All right,” he said at last, voice controlled. “All right. Say I believe you. What do we do? We tell command. We get more men. We hunt him.”

Andrew felt something cold settle in his stomach. Hunt him. As if Ambrose were a fox and this were still a world where men could win by numbers.

“There’s more,” Andrew said.

Elias’s eyes sharpened. “What more?”

Andrew hesitated only a moment, then spoke because hiding it would not protect Elias from it. “It doesn’t just kill,” he said. “It bargains. It keeps people. People who make arrangements for it when the world gets too orderly.”

Elias’s mouth tightened. “Keeps them how?”

Andrew thought of the cellar dream, the chain already fastened, the feeling of being placed into earth. He forced the memory down. "As caretakers," he said. "As cover."

Elias stared. "You think it wants you."

Andrew did not answer quickly enough.

Elias's eyes widened slightly. "Andrew," he said, and the way he said it was not a question but a recognition of something he didn't want to recognize. "Has it spoken to you?"

Andrew held his gaze. "Yes."

Elias's face tightened with anger, protective and young. "Then we leave," he said at once. "We take your men and we go. Today. We don't stay near this hospital another hour."

Andrew wanted to agree. The desire to say yes rose hot and simple. But he had already learned that distance did not mean absence. Ambrose could be nowhere and still be present at the edge. And now Elias was here, and that changed the arithmetic.

Andrew looked past Elias toward the wet tree line beyond the barn yard. The pines stood black against gray sky, motionless in the rain. For an instant he felt, with the same certainty as the morning he'd seen a figure between wagons, that someone was watching from just beyond the place attention naturally rested.

He lowered his voice further. "Don't say his name loudly," Andrew told Elias.

Elias's brow furrowed. "Why?"

"Because I don't know what he hears," Andrew said. "And I don't know what he likes."

Elias swallowed. "This is insane."

"Yes," Andrew said quietly. "Now you're close."

A shout rose from the barn, a sharp command followed by a man's scream that broke off too suddenly. Elias flinched, eyes snapping back toward the doors.

Andrew caught his shoulder again, gentler this time. "Listen to me," he said. "Stay in sight of me. Stay near people. Do not walk off alone for any reason, not even to piss. If you have to go, you take Haines with you. Do you understand?"

Elias's lips parted, protest ready, then something in Andrew's face made him stop. Elias nodded once, tight. "All right."

Andrew released him and turned toward Haines and the others, who hovered near their gear as if they could feel the pressure around Elias like weather changing. Haines's eyes met Andrew's, and Andrew saw in them a grim I told you so that had nothing to do with pride. It was fear recognizing a new vulnerability.

"We're staying the night?" Haines asked quietly.

Andrew felt the truth of it before he answered. The roads were mud. The wounded needed guarding, even if guards were mostly theater. Dorsey would insist. The supply train would not turn around in rain and dark. And Andrew did not like the idea of Elias riding off alone down any road with the thing's attention freshly caught.

"Yes," Andrew said. "We stay. We keep close."

Elias heard him and stiffened. "Andrew—"

Andrew cut him off with a look that was more officer than brother. "Not now."

Elias fell silent, but his hands clenched and unclenched at his sides, the motion of a man trying not to strike something he could not see.

They made a small camp under the lee of the wagons rather than inside the barn yard proper. It was not much shelter, but it kept them near light and movement. Andrew placed Haines and Rudd where they could watch both the barn doors and the tree line beyond the wagons. Kellan sat with his knees drawn up, eyes fixed on the mud as if it might form words.

As dusk thickened, lanterns were lit and rehung. Their yellow circles carved the yard into islands again, just as they had inside the barn. Andrew hated the pattern. Light surrounded by shadow. Safe pockets separated by blind corridors. It felt like a design Ambrose favored.

Elias tried to speak twice, both times in a low voice, and both times Andrew answered with quiet commands that kept him occupied: help unload the last crate, check the mule tack, make sure no one wanders. It was not kindness. It was control. Control was the only mercy Andrew had left to offer.

When full night finally settled, the rain eased into a thin mist that slicked everything and muted sound. The barn's moans dulled, as if exhaustion had finally taken most of the wounded. Somewhere a man prayed softly and was not told to shut his mouth this time. Men were too tired to argue with God.

Andrew sat with his back against a wagon wheel, pistol in his lap. The priest's bundle pressed under his coat. He could feel the rosary beads through cloth, useless and stubborn. Elias sat beside him, close enough that their shoulders nearly touched. Andrew could feel the heat of his brother's body and the tension in it, coiled and ready.

"I need you to tell me everything," Elias said at last, voice low. "Not pieces. Not warnings. Everything."

Andrew kept his eyes on the yard. "I've told you what matters."

Elias's voice cracked, just slightly. "No, you haven't. You're acting like you're already in a fight you won't explain to me." He swallowed hard. "Are you afraid of him?"

Andrew's wound gave a small, private sting, as if the question touched it. He answered honestly because lying to Elias felt worse than fear. "Yes," he said.

Elias stared at him as if waiting for the rest, the reassurance that Andrew always had a plan. "Then why are we sitting here?" Elias demanded, anger rising. "Why aren't we riding out right now?"

Andrew turned his head a fraction, enough to see Elias's face in lantern light. It looked younger than it should under war's grime, and that youth made Andrew's chest ache. "Because I think he already knows you're here," Andrew said.

Elias went still. "What?"

Andrew's gaze returned to the tree line. The mist moved between trunks like slow breath. "He appears when he wants," Andrew said. "He doesn't need to be invited in the way the stories say. He only needs weakness. Need. A soft place."

Elias's voice lowered, suddenly careful. "You mean me."

Andrew did not answer, and the silence was answer enough.

Elias's breathing quickened. "Andrew, if he comes near me—"

Andrew lifted a hand, not to hush him, but to stop him from finishing. Because finishing felt like tempting fate, and fate had already taken an interest.

A faint sweetness drifted across the yard.

Not strong. Not cloying. Just enough to be unmistakable once known, like the first note of a song that made the body tense before the mind identified it.

Andrew's fingers tightened on his pistol. He did not raise it. He did not move too fast.

Across the lantern-lit mud, between two wagons where the light thinned, a figure stood with perfect composure, coat dark and ruinous, hair slicked back as if he'd had time for a mirror. He looked freshly arrived and yet also as if he'd been there the whole evening, simply waiting for their attention to catch up.

Ambrose.

Elias made a sound beside Andrew, half breath, half disbelief. He did not stand. He did not run. For a heartbeat Andrew was grateful, and then sickened by what that gratitude implied: that stillness was now a measure of survival.

Ambrose's eyes moved over Andrew first, as they always did, and a small smile touched his mouth.

Then he looked at Elias.

The smile deepened, almost pleased.

"Well," Ambrose said softly, as if greeting guests in a parlor rather than two armed men in a war yard. "You've brought me something precious."

Andrew felt Elias stiffen beside him, rage and fear tangled tight.

Ambrose's gaze remained on Elias, appraising without hurry. "The resemblance is charming," he murmured. "You have the same bones, Lieutenant. The same stubbornness. But his hope still shows through."

Elias found his voice, sharp with anger. "Stay away from us."

Ambrose turned his head slightly, regarding Elias as if he'd spoken in a foreign language. Then, politely, "No."

Andrew's pistol stayed in his lap, heavy as shame. "What do you want?" he asked.

Ambrose's attention returned to Andrew, and for a moment the yard seemed to shrink until it was only the space between them. "Terms," Ambrose said. "Not violence. Violence is so common here it scarcely deserves comment." He tilted his head, listening, as if savoring the barn's distant moans. "Mercy, Lieutenant Mercer. Terms of mercy. I am told you admire such things."

Andrew felt Elias shift, preparing to rise, and Andrew's hand closed around his brother's forearm, a silent warning: don't.

Ambrose watched the gesture and smiled as if it confirmed something.

"You are tired," Ambrose said to Andrew, voice gentle. "Tired of deaths that mean nothing. Tired of guarding men you cannot save. Tired of pretending your flag changes the taste of blood."

Andrew kept his voice flat. "Get to your point."

Ambrose's smile did not falter. "Very well," he said. "Here is my offer."

He looked at Elias again, and Elias's face went pale with a fury that could not decide where to strike. Ambrose's eyes lingered on him like a hand.

"I will not take him," Ambrose said calmly. "Not tonight. Not as long as you remain sensible."

Andrew's stomach clenched. Elias's breath hitched.

Ambrose's gaze returned to Andrew, and the warmth drained from his tone without raising its volume. "In exchange, you will provide me what I require when I ask for it," he said. "Safe passage when I wish to move. Silence when I wish to feed. Shelter when I wish to rest. And when the world becomes less convenient than it is now, you will make it convenient again."

Andrew felt the shape of it, the trap hidden inside courtesy. Not a partnership. A leash dressed as a bargain.

Elias whispered, horrified, "Andrew, don't."

Andrew did not look away from Ambrose. "No," Andrew said.

Ambrose's smile held. "Of course," he murmured, as if he'd expected the word. "Men like you always begin with it. You confuse refusal with strength."

Andrew's grip tightened on Elias's arm as Ambrose took one slow step forward, not into full light, but closer to the edge of it. The sweetness thickened, faint but insistent.

"I am not asking because I need permission," Ambrose said softly. "I am asking because I enjoy watching you try to keep your hands clean."

He glanced at Elias again, and his voice remained polite, almost conversational.

"Consider carefully," Ambrose said. "Because you have given me a new way to teach you what you can afford."

Ambrose held the space between the wagons as if it belonged to him by deed. The lantern light did not reach him cleanly; it slid off his coat and left his face pale in a way that looked less like reflection and more like refusal.

Andrew kept his pistol steady in his lap, not lifting it, not lowering it. Beside him, Elias's forearm felt rigid under Andrew's grip, muscle tensed as if he meant to spring.

"You can't teach me anything I haven't learned in this war," Andrew said.

Ambrose's eyes did not leave Andrew. "You've learned to endure," he replied. "Endurance is not wisdom. It is only stubbornness with a uniform."

Elias finally wrenched his arm free. He rose halfway to his feet before Andrew could stop him, boots sliding in mud. "You don't get to talk to him like you know him," Elias snapped. "You don't get to stand there like you're a guest and make demands. We're armed. We can—"

Ambrose turned his head toward Elias with the smallest movement, almost polite.

Elias stopped.

It was not a dramatic freeze. His body simply failed to finish the motion it had begun, as if the connection between intent and muscle had been cut. His mouth remained open on the last word. His eyes stayed wide, furious, and suddenly helpless in a way that made Andrew's stomach knot.

Andrew stood at once, stepping close enough that his shoulder nearly touched Elias's. He did not grab him again. He did not want Ambrose to see his panic as a handle.

"Let him go," Andrew said.

Ambrose's gaze drifted across Elias's face, the resemblance noted again with quiet delight. "He is trying to be brave," Ambrose murmured, almost approving. "It's an attractive habit in young men. It rarely survives."

Elias's throat worked. His eyes flicked to Andrew, and in them Andrew saw the first crack: not fear of dying, but fear of not being able to choose what he did with his own body.

Andrew felt the priest's rosary under his coat. He forced his hand away from it. Tools were not faith, and faith was not control. Ambrose would enjoy watching him fumble for either.

"Enough," Andrew said. "If you want to speak, speak to me."

Ambrose smiled faintly. "Always the shield," he said. "And always the assumption that a shield is virtue."

He turned his attention back toward the yard, past Andrew and Elias, toward the barn's dark outline and the wagons lined like tired beasts. Men moved at the edges of the lantern islands, careful, wary, pretending not to listen while listening anyway. Andrew saw Haines near the first wagon tongue, rifle held wrong because his hands were fighting tremor. Rudd hovered in shadow with the supply sergeant, both of them staring as if their eyes could keep Ambrose pinned in place. Kellan sat on the ground with his back against a wheel, knees drawn up, staring at nothing. When Ambrose appeared, Kellan had not flinched. He had only gone still, like a man already trained.

Ambrose inhaled, a small breath that looked unnecessary. “This is a rich little camp,” he said. “Wounded men stacked in a barn. Hungry men on the road. Supply wagons with names on paper that will never be checked twice. The war is so kind. It makes a man feel as though the world is already halfway to its grave.”

Andrew held his voice steady by force. “You offered terms. I refused.”

“Yes,” Ambrose said. “And yet we are still speaking.”

Elias’s lips moved. A whisper came out, hoarse and furious. “Andrew. Don’t bargain.”

Andrew did not answer him. He watched Ambrose the way he had watched enemy officers on a field: for the moment when talk turned into movement.

Ambrose stepped forward again. Not fully into the light. Just close enough that Andrew could see the faint dark seam at the corner of his mouth, the suggestion of something recently tasted.

“I will simplify it,” Ambrose said, voice calm. “You will do what I ask, when I ask it, and you will continue to breathe. He will continue to breathe.”

His eyes flicked to Elias. "And you may even pretend, for a while, that you are choosing."

Andrew's throat tightened. "And if I don't?"

Ambrose's expression remained composed. "Then you will learn the difference between refusal and consequence."

For a moment Andrew heard only the mist hissing against canvas, the distant moan from the barn. The world held its breath around them.

Then, from the shadows near the supply wagon, someone moved. A young private, face slick with rain and fear, stepped into the light with a pistol in his hand. Andrew recognized him only vaguely, one of Dorsey's men, assigned to watch the wagon line.

"You ain't taking nobody," the private said, voice breaking. "You ain't—"

Andrew opened his mouth to order him back. Too late.

The private fired.

The shot cracked through the yard and snapped the fragile quiet. A mule screamed and lurched against its harness. Men shouted. For a heartbeat everything became war again, loud and stupid.

Ambrose did not flinch. He did not even look startled.

He moved.

Andrew would later try to describe it and find no language that fit. Not a run. Not a lunge. More like the removal of distance, as if the yard had decided to fold. One moment Ambrose stood between wagons; the next he was beside the private, close enough that their coats almost touched.

The private's eyes went wider, confusion overtaking fear. His pistol began to lower, not by choice.

Ambrose touched him at the throat.

It was not a strike. It was not a grasp. It looked, grotesquely, like a correction a tailor might make to a collar.

The private made a small wet sound and sank to his knees, one hand coming up as if to hold his own neck together. His fingers met warm blood, and his face changed from anger to bewilderment, as if his mind could not accept that dying could be so quiet.

He toppled sideways into the mud.

No dramatic spray. No flailing. Just a body laid down, edited into stillness.

A ripple of sound moved through the men watching: a half-swallowed cry, a prayer, someone whispering Jesus like a reflex.

Elias gagged once, hard, and the sound seemed to break whatever held him. He stumbled backward, boots slipping. Andrew caught him by the shoulder, holding him upright without looking away from Ambrose.

Haines raised his rifle.

“Don’t,” Andrew snapped.

Haines froze, eyes wild with hatred and shame. He had wanted permission. Andrew had just denied it.

Ambrose turned slowly back toward Andrew, as if the private’s death had been an interruption, not an act. He looked mildly displeased, like a man whose evening had been disturbed by noise.

“That,” Ambrose said, “is what happens when men insist on making my offers theatrical.”

Andrew’s hands felt cold despite the damp air. He heard himself speak as if from a distance. “You said you wouldn’t take him.”

Ambrose glanced at the dead private, then back. “I have not,” he said. “I am a man of my word, Lieutenant Mercer. In the ways that matter.”

Elias’s breathing came fast and thin beside Andrew, the beginnings of panic he was trying to crush with pride. “Andrew,” he whispered, voice breaking, “tell me you’re not going to—”

Ambrose's eyes slid to Elias again, and Elias's words faltered. Not a full seizure of his will this time, but enough pressure to remind him of the rule: speak when allowed.

Andrew stepped subtly so his body blocked some of Ambrose's view of Elias. It was a small movement, a human gesture, and it cost him. The cut beneath his bandage flared, sharp as a fresh slice, and he nearly inhaled too hard. He swallowed it down.

Ambrose noticed anyway. His gaze dipped to Andrew's side, and the faintest satisfaction touched his mouth.

"You see?" Ambrose murmured. "Your body understands before your mind is ready to admit it."

Andrew forced his voice into steadiness. "You want a keeper," he said. "Someone to arrange things so you can move and feed without noise."

Ambrose's eyes warmed a fraction. "A coarse term," he said. "But yes. Someone who can walk in the daylight and make the world look away."

Andrew stared at him. The yard seemed suddenly full of fragile people. Men with names on paper. Men whose mothers would never know where they fell. Men who would vanish into confusion and be recorded as deserter or taken by Yankees or fevered and buried without a marker.

And Elias. Elias, standing beside him, alive only because Ambrose found the leverage pleasing.

"What do I get?" Andrew asked, and hated himself for asking it because it admitted he was stepping onto the ground of negotiation.

Ambrose's smile returned, not triumphant, simply patient. "You get mercy," he said. "Not for everyone. Don't be childish. Mercy is always selective. You get to name a few and keep them breathing a little longer." His gaze slid again to Elias, lingering. "You get him, if you behave."

Elias shook his head, a small violent motion, as if trying to shake off the air itself. "Andrew, no. If you do this—if you do anything he wants—"

Ambrose's voice cut across Elias's, still quiet, still courteous. "If he does nothing I want," he said, "you will die first. Not because I am angry. Because it will be instructive."

Andrew felt the truth of it like a blade laid flat against his ribs. Not a threat in the usual sense. A lesson planned.

He looked down at the dead private in the mud. The man's eyes were open, staring at the rain. His blood made a thin dark ribbon that the mist was already trying to dilute.

Andrew's mind reached automatically for a report, for language that would make this fit. Shot by unknown assailant. Chaos. Accidental discharge. But he could feel Ambrose inside that instinct, already shaping it, already teaching him what he meant by arrangement.

Andrew lifted his gaze back to Ambrose. "If I agree," he said carefully, "it's to keep him alive. Not to serve you."

Ambrose inclined his head slightly, as if accepting a social nicety. "Call it what you like," he said. "Men always dress their surrender in prettier clothes."

Andrew's jaw clenched. "And tonight?"

Ambrose's eyes flicked toward the barn, toward the wagons, toward the men watching with their breath held. "Tonight," he said, "I will take what I came for. I will not take your brother." He paused, and the pause was deliberate cruelty. "Unless you force me to make a point."

Andrew felt Elias trembling now, contained but real. He put his hand on the back of Elias's neck, not gripping, just anchoring him, the way their father had anchored them as boys when thunder shook the house.

Andrew heard himself speak the words that would haunt him later because they were the first step onto the road he could already see narrowing.

"Fine," Andrew said. "Not in front of my men. Tell me what you want, and I'll decide."

Ambrose studied him as if tasting the concession. Then he smiled, genuinely pleased for the first time.

"Good," he said softly. "Now we are speaking like adults."

He stepped backward into the shadow between wagons. The sweetness thinned with him, retreating like a mouth closing around a secret. For a moment Andrew thought he might vanish entirely.

Instead Ambrose's voice came again, not loud, but carrying through the wet yard as if every ear had been tuned to it.

"Lieutenant Mercer will make sure there is no shouting," Ambrose said. "No running. No heroics. If anyone lifts a rifle, I will take your brother and I will take the loudest man next, and I will do it gently enough that you will dream of it for the rest of your lives."

Andrew felt every eye turn toward him. Haines's gaze burned with accusation. Rudd looked sick.

Kellan looked resigned, as if this was simply the next stage of kneeling.

Elias stared at Andrew, horror spreading across his face as understanding finally caught up. "Andrew," he whispered, "he's making you—"

"I know," Andrew said, and his voice sounded older than it had that morning.

Ambrose moved again, a soft glide into darkness beyond the lantern islands. Somewhere near the barn, a man let out a muffled sob.

Andrew stood in the mud with his brother at his side, and realized with a cold clarity that Ambrose had already won something tonight without needing Andrew's full agreement.

He had made Andrew responsible for the silence.

He had made Elias into value, not as a person, but as a price.

And as the yard held its breath, waiting to see who would be taken next, Andrew understood the true shape of the bargain being forced on him: not a contract written in words, but a conversion. The slow remaking of love into leverage, until the only mercy left in the world was the kind you could purchase with someone else's blood.

Chapter 9

The Burning Estate

The yard did not erupt into chaos the way Andrew expected. It folded inward.

Men who had been quick to shout on battlefields now swallowed their voices as if noise itself could draw teeth from the dark. The lanterns hissed in the mist, throwing weak light on faces that would not meet one another's eyes. Someone dragged the dead private by the heels toward the barn as if distance could make the sight less accusing. The mule that had screamed stood trembling, foam at its bit, whites of its eyes showing whenever it jerked against the harness.

Andrew kept Elias close, not with an arm around his shoulders, but with position: always between him and the gaps where light thinned. He spoke in quiet orders, the kind of orders that sounded like discipline and were, in truth, an attempt to keep fear from turning into a stampede.

"No one goes alone," he told Haines, loud enough for the nearest men to hear. "If you need water, you take two. If you need to piss, you take two. If you hear anything, you do not answer it."

Haines' jaw flexed. His eyes were fixed on Andrew with a hardness that had not been there a week ago. "And if we see him?"

Andrew felt the question like a hook under his ribs. If we see him. As if sight were permission. As if the thing that had stepped through space to touch a throat could be handled by the rules of watch and challenge.

"You don't," Andrew said. "Not unless I say."

The words tasted wrong. He heard Ambrose in them, the way a man could hear a tune inside another tune once it had been pointed out. He did not look at Elias as he spoke, because he could not bear the shape of his brother's expression.

Elias' voice came low beside him, raw with held rage. "This is what he wanted. He wanted you to say that."

Andrew kept his gaze on the shadows between wagons, on the barn doors that breathed suffering, on the tree line where the mist hung like a curtain. "He wanted many things," Andrew replied. "I'm choosing what happens next."

Elias gave a broken laugh that held no humor. "Choosing?"

Andrew did not answer. He could not explain the calculus without sounding monstrous. Not yet. Not even to himself.

Some time after midnight, when even the wounded men in the barn had fallen into exhausted silence, two of the inside watch vanished.

They were not men from Andrew's patrol. They belonged to Dorsey's detail, posted as if bodies and rifles could form a fence around hunger. One moment they were there, silhouettes at the barn door with their caps pulled low; the next, their places were empty. A lantern still burned on a nail where one of them had been told to keep it lit. A rifle leaned carefully against the wall, upright and composed as a sermon.

No one said the word, Ambrose.

Dorsey's face turned gray in the lantern light when the absence was discovered. He grabbed Andrew by the sleeve and pulled him aside behind the supply wagon where the mist muffled sound.

"This is your doing," Dorsey hissed. His eyes were bloodshot, his mouth tight with a man's last belief in blame. "You brought it here. You spoke to it."

Andrew did not deny it. He could have. He could have let the war swallow the truth the way it swallowed everything else. But denial felt pointless now, a child's trick.

"I didn't invite it," Andrew said.

Dorsey's hands shook as he gestured toward the barn. "So, what do I tell command? That a polite ghost took two sentries and folded their blankets?"

Andrew thought of Ambrose's voice, calm as a bedside prayer. Tell your surgeon to write infection when he gets tired of asking questions.

"You tell them raiders took them," Andrew said. He forced the sentence out, each word an act of swallowing glass. "Or deserters. Or you don't tell them anything until you're made to."

Dorsey stared at him as if he'd been struck. "You're helping it."

Andrew stepped closer, lowering his voice further. "I'm keeping your men from panicking and getting more of them killed," he said. "Because if you start shouting about devils in a barn, you'll have men firing into the wounded. You'll have wagons overturned. You'll have the roads filled with screaming. And it will feed on that too."

Dorsey's lips parted and closed again. His anger faltered, not because he agreed, but because the logic was a kind of cruelty he recognized. The war had taught them all to choose the least ruin.

Elias had heard anyway. Andrew saw it in the way his brother's posture changed when Andrew returned: rigid, as if he were holding himself together by muscle alone.

"That's it, then," Elias said quietly. "You're already doing what it said."

Andrew knelt and picked up the dead sentry's cap from the mud where it had been dropped. He turned it in his hands, the cloth soaked and heavy. "I'm doing what keeps you alive," Andrew answered.

Elias flinched, as if the words had physical weight. "Alive for what?"

Andrew had no answer that would not condemn him.

By morning, the supply wagons were ready to move again. The mist had lifted into a low, sour fog that clung to the creek and the barn yard like breath on glass. Dorsey sent a runner toward the nearest command post with a report stripped of everything that mattered: missing men, likely guerrillas, conditions deteriorating, requesting relief. Whitcomb, drawn and furious, refused to look at the places where sentries had stood. He had the fixed expression of a man who could not afford belief.

Andrew gave orders to his own men with the tight efficiency of a man trying not to hear his conscience. He told Haines and Rudd to get powder from the supply crates. He told Kellan to stay at Elias' side and not speak unless spoken to. Kellan obeyed with the dull docility of someone already practiced in surrender. Elias watched it and looked sick.

"What are you doing?" Elias demanded when Andrew checked the powder tins himself, running a thumb over the stamped markings as if verifying they were real.

Andrew did not look up. "Ending it," he said.

Elias made a harsh sound. "By stealing munitions?"

Andrew snapped the lid back on a tin. "By using them," he replied. "You said we should hunt him. We can't hunt him in the woods. We can't drag him into daylight and shoot him like a man. But I know where he was held. I know where the chains were. I know where the graves were planted like a crop."

Elias went still. "The orchard house."

Andrew finally met his gaze. "Yes. If there is any place tied to him, if there is any nest, any tunnel, any den where he thinks the world owes him shelter, it's there."

Elias' face tightened. "And you think burning a house will kill it."

Andrew felt the truth, bleak and humiliating, hovering behind the plan. He didn't know if it would kill Ambrose. He didn't know if anything would. But he needed to do something that was not negotiation. Something that did not involve weighing men's lives against Elias' breathing.

"I think it will take something away," Andrew said. "Records. Rooms. hiding places. Whatever system kept him comfortable. If the families fed him there, if they built him tunnels, if they kept him like a secret vice, I'm going to put it all to flame."

Elias stared as if trying to see his brother through a veil that had suddenly appeared. "And if he's not there?" he asked.

Andrew's wound gave a small sting under the bandage, as if answering in place of his mouth. He looked past Elias toward the road, toward the fog-thick fields and the stripped trees. "Then I will have burned something that deserved burning anyway," he said.

Haines approached, powder secured, his expression grim. "Lieutenant," he said, and hesitated as if choosing his words carefully. "If we go back there… he'll know."

Andrew nodded once. "He knows everything we do," he said. "But he doesn't get to keep everything."

They did not tell Dorsey where they were going. Andrew left the captain only the vaguest outline: scouting the area for raiders, checking the estate again for signs of tunnels. Dorsey looked ready to protest, then looked at the barn and the empty spaces where men had stood, and the protest collapsed into resignation. There was no help coming fast enough to matter. Every man still breathing was already improvising a kind of survival that command would never write down.

Andrew chose only a few to go with him. Haines, because his fear had hardened into obedience rather than panic. Rudd, because he was quick with hands and quiet with questions. Two others from the supply escort who looked steady and sober. Kellan stayed behind with Elias at Andrew's insistence, which Elias hated.

"You're leaving me here," Elias said, voice rising despite his attempt to keep it low. "With that thing loose?"

Andrew gripped his brother's shoulder briefly, firm enough to be felt. "I'm leaving you with men and light and noise," he said. "Not in the woods. Not alone. And you are not to move from the wagons unless Haines returns and tells you I'm dead."

Elias' eyes flashed. "Don't say that."

Andrew let his hand fall. He had already thought it a dozen times. Saying it did not summon it. It only admitted it.

They rode out under a sky that couldn't decide whether to rain again. The road toward the orchard house was a churned scar through low fields and stands of pine. The land looked even more wasted than it had days ago, as if their absence had allowed the world to rot further. Fence posts leaned like exhausted men. A dead horse lay half in a ditch with a tarp thrown over it, the tarp already sagging with decay. They passed a cabin burned to its foundation, the chimney standing alone like a blackened finger.

Andrew carried oil in a sloshing jug tied to his saddle and powder wrapped in canvas. The weight pulled at him with every shift of the horse. It felt like hauling intent made physical.

As the day thinned toward afternoon, the air began to change.

Not at first. Not in the obvious way. Then, as the trees thickened and the road narrowed, a sweetness crept in beneath the damp earth smell, faint and unmistakable, like rot learning to announce itself politely.

Rudd swallowed hard. “Sir,” he murmured, “I smell it.”

Andrew said nothing. He felt it too, and with it came the sense of being expected. Not hunted exactly. Anticipated. Like arriving at a house where the host has been watching from behind the curtain for an hour.

When the orchard finally appeared through the trees, it looked almost peaceful from a distance: rows of bare-limbed apple trees, the house crouched behind them, roofline broken and windows dark. But as Andrew drew closer, the silence hit him again, heavy and unnatural. No birds. No insects. No dog bark from any nearby farm.

The place had the stillness of a mouth closed over a secret.

Andrew dismounted at the edge of the orchard and looked at the house that had started this. His side ached under the bandage, a clean, persistent reminder that he had been marked in a language deeper than wounds.

He took the oil jug from his saddle and handed it to Haines. “We do it quick,” Andrew said. “We soak the lower rooms. We stack kindling. We powder the cellar entrance. We burn the orchard too. No half measures."

Haines' eyes tightened. "And if he shows?"

Andrew looked at the black windows, at the shadowed porch, at the mouth of the cellar door hidden beneath the house like a remembered sin. He felt, very clearly, that fire was not just a weapon. It was a statement. It was the only language he had left that did not sound like bargaining.

"If he shows," Andrew said, "then we light it anyway."

He started toward the house with oil, powder, and men at his back, and the orchard's silence received him like a verdict.

They moved like men robbing a grave, quick and careful, eyes lifting again and again to the black windows as if the house might blink.

The porch boards groaned under Andrew's boots. The sound seemed too loud in the orchard's hush. He paused at the front door long enough to feel the wrongness of the air against his face: cold, damp, and threaded through with that faint sweetness that did not belong to winter or rain. It was not a smell so much as a memory forced into the present.

Haines stepped up beside him with the oil jug, jaw set hard enough to ache. Rudd hovered just behind, clutching a canvas-wrapped bundle of kindling and rags. The two men from the supply escort, both older than Rudd and quieter than Haines, held their rifles without much faith in them. One was a square-shouldered private named Lanier, the other a gaunt corporal called Pritchard. Andrew had chosen them because they had watched the barn yard go still the night before without shouting. Men who could keep their mouths shut lived longer around Ambrose.

Andrew put his hand on the door and pushed.

It gave with a reluctant scrape, swollen by damp, as if the house had been trying to seal itself and failed. The interior breathed out at them: stale soot, old rot, and something coppery beneath it all that made Andrew's stomach tighten. The entryway was dim even in daytime, the boards over the windows turning the world into narrow slits of gray.

"Quick," Andrew murmured. He did not raise his voice. He did not want to teach the place that he could be made to shout.

They spread through the lower rooms in a tight pattern, not separating fully. Andrew had burned buildings before, in war and in spite and in necessity. This was different. A normal house fought fire by accident: damp, plaster, things that smoldered. This house felt as though it had been prepared for it, as if generations had learned what flame could do and how to slow it.

Haines uncorked the jug and began to pour oil along the baseboards, letting it run in dark ribbons. Rudd laid rags in corners and under overturned furniture, hands moving fast, face pale. Lanier and Pritchard dragged splintered chairs and broken table legs into small piles, feeding the future like men stacking bones.

Andrew moved to the blackened room he remembered from the first search, the one burned so thoroughly it seemed less like a fire's aftermath and more like a ritual. The soot had soaked into the wood and would never come out. He crouched and ran his fingers along the floorboards. No fresh ash. No recent burn. An old attempt, then. Someone had tried to cleanse this place before Andrew ever walked into it.

He straightened and forced himself away. Cleansing was a word with too much hope in it.

The cellar door lay beneath the stairs, half-hidden behind a fallen coat rack and a cracked washstand that had been dragged there like barricade. Andrew remembered the architecture of fear from Chapter 2: crosses nailed over doors, furniture shoved into place. People did not build such things unless they had seen what happened when they failed.

He and Haines hauled the washstand aside. Its legs scraped, loud as a scream. Andrew waited for the world to answer. Nothing did. The silence held.

The cellar door was shut, as it had been when others came before them. Not locked now. The lock plate had been torn away at some point, leaving a jagged scar in the wood. Andrew could almost see again the boot tracks that ended here, the locked barrier that turned men's courage into confusion.

Haines swallowed. "This is where they had him," he said, voice rough.

"Where they had something," Andrew corrected. He drew the canvas-wrapped powder charge from Lanier, taking its weight into his hands. Powder and oil. The old human answer to things that refused ordinary death.

He tugged the door open.

Cold rolled up from below, damp and earth-heavy. The sweetness was stronger here, a deep rot like fruit crushed into soil and left to ferment. Andrew's wound tightened under the bandage, that clean sting as if his body recognized a language his mind still fought.

Rudd lifted the lantern. Its flame shook slightly.

They descended.

The cellar steps were narrow and slick with old moisture. Andrew kept one hand on the rail, the other on the powder, and felt the boards under his feet complain. Below, the darkness opened into a low space crowded with collapsed crates and broken barrels. The smell of mold and old apples sat thick against the throat. Water dripped somewhere steadily, patient as time.

"Lord," Pritchard muttered, then cut the word off as if afraid to finish it.

Andrew swept the lantern's light across the stone walls.

The rings were still there.

Iron bolts set into stone, each ending in a heavy loop. The chain marks remained in the mortar like scars. Andrew felt something in him go hard and quiet. Proof did not bring relief; it only made the horror more orderly.

Haines stepped closer, eyes fixed on the nearest ring. "He broke out," he said. "How does a man break iron out of stone?"

"He didn't break out alone," Andrew said.

Haines looked at him sharply, and Andrew knew his own thought had spoken too clearly. The priest's books, the ledgers, the pattern:

arrangements made by human hands. Tunnels. Purchased silence. A system that had held Ambrose like a secret vice.

Rudd angled the lantern toward the far wall.

A section of stonework did not match the rest. The blocks were set differently, the mortar newer than the surrounding wall, though still old by any normal measure. Someone had rebuilt it. Or sealed something behind it.

Andrew walked to it slowly, every instinct warning him not of a trap but of discovery. He pressed his palm to the stone. Cold. Solid. And yet, when he leaned his weight in, he felt the faintest give, not in the stone itself but in a seam.

"Help me," he said.

Haines and Lanier joined him. Together they pushed.

At first nothing happened. Then the seam shifted with a grinding sound like teeth. The wall did not collapse; it swung inward on hidden hinges, stone-faced and cleverly counterweighted. Whoever had built it had wanted it to look permanent, the way respectable men wanted their sins to look like foundation.

A gap opened, black and narrow.

Air breathed out of it, colder than the cellar air and layered with a deeper earth smell, the scent of long-sealed dirt and damp wood. The sweetness threaded through it like a vein.

Rudd stared. "There's more," he whispered.

Andrew held the lantern up.

A passage ran beyond the false wall, low and tight. Not a natural cave. Planks braced the sides in places, old timber shored against collapse. The ground sloped slightly downward. There were tracks in the dirt, faint but visible: repeated scuffs, the marks of something dragged, and the more deliberate prints of boots.

Boots. Not bare feet.

Andrew stepped through the opening and felt the ceiling press close, forcing him to duck. His shoulder brushed the wall. Damp smeared his sleeve.

Haines followed, rifle held across his chest as if that would matter. "Sir," he said, voice strained, "this ain't just a hiding place."

"No," Andrew replied. "This is a route."

He moved forward, lantern bobbing, and the tunnel opened into a wider pocket where the ceiling rose enough to stand upright. Here, someone had been working. A crude table stood against the wall, warped by damp. On it lay glass bottles, corked and empty, and a scatter of metal instruments that looked like a surgeon's tools, though older and less clean. A coil of rope. A small pile of manacles with rusted hinges.

Rudd made a small sound and turned his face away.

Andrew forced himself to look closer. On the table, under a stone paperweight, were papers wrapped in oilcloth.

His heart beat once, heavy. Records. Of course there would be records. Human evil loved documentation when it believed itself safe.

He unwrapped the oilcloth carefully. The paper beneath was thick and yellowed, ink faded but legible. Names. Dates. Amounts paid. Short notes in a practiced hand: moved to Petersburg, sent north, disposed quietly. Another sheet bore a letter with a wax seal long broken, written in the language of men who believed politeness could make anything acceptable.

Andrew read enough to feel his stomach turn.

It was not Ambrose's hand. It was the hand of the household. Of lawyers, perhaps. Of stewards. Men who wrote about missing servants the way they wrote about broken harness: as inconvenience and expense. One line, underlined, stood out as though the writer had wanted it remembered: discretion is the only mercy afforded to those who serve.

"Mercy," Haines muttered, reading over Andrew's shoulder. The word sounded like a curse.

Andrew folded the paper back and forced himself to keep moving. He could not let the tunnel hold him. The longer they stayed below ground, the more he felt the cellar dream trying to become present: the chain already fastened, the earth pressing close, the helplessness presented as inevitable.

The passage continued, branching. One route slanted upward toward the orchard, judging by the faint draft and the way the soil changed, roots pushing through in places. Another ran straighter, deeper under the house. Andrew chose the deeper one, not because it was sensible but because he needed to see the full shape of what had been built.

The tunnel widened again into a chamber with a low wooden platform against one wall. It might once have been a bed. The boards were stained dark. Not with mold. With something older, soaked in and permanent.

A heavy iron ring was bolted into the floor beside it.

Andrew stood still, lantern raised, and felt the wound under his bandage burn cleanly as if answering a call. He imagined Ambrose lying here, elegant even in restraint, waiting with the patience of hunger while men above ground lived their lives and told themselves their evil was contained because it had a room.

Rudd's voice came thin. "They kept him like… like property."

Andrew's jaw tightened. "They kept him like a secret," he said. "And used him like a tool."

Haines shifted, boots scraping dirt. "Sir," he said, and there was fear in it now, not of darkness but of implication. "If there's tunnels, then burning the house—"

"Burning the house is not enough," Andrew finished, because he saw it too. Fire above might collapse a roof, but it would not cleanse a buried system that stretched beyond the visible estate. That was the true horror the priest had warned about. Ambrose was not only a creature. He was part of an arrangement. A machinery made of wealth, fear, and the kind of silence that could be purchased.

Andrew turned back toward the false wall, decision hardening. "We burn the tunnels too," he said. "We pack powder in the passage. We collapse it. We make this place choke on its own secrets."

Rudd nodded quickly, too quickly. Fear made men eager to obey. Lanier crossed himself once, fast and furtive, and Andrew pretended not to see it.

They moved back the way they came, Andrew counting turns, memorizing the branches like a map he never wanted. Behind them, the chamber stayed silent. No movement. No voice. Nothing to confirm Ambrose's presence.

And yet Andrew felt watched anyway, not by eyes in the dark but by history itself, by the patient knowledge that this system had endured long enough to become confident. Even if they burned the house and collapsed the passage, the pattern would persist somewhere else, because men carried it. Men wrote it down and called it necessity.

At the false wall, Andrew paused and looked back into the tunnel one last time.

The lantern light reached only a short distance before being swallowed. In that swallow, in that comfortable darkness shaped by human hands, Andrew understood something with a quiet nausea: the estate had never been a prison meant to hold Ambrose forever. It had been a shelter built for him. A place designed not to stop him, but to keep him fed without inconvenience.

He stepped through into the cellar again and felt the warmer damp of the ordinary underground space, as if the house itself were trying to pretend this was all it had. Haines swung the false wall shut, stone grinding softly until the seam vanished.

Andrew stared at the place where it had been. Invisible again. Respectable again.

"Bring the powder," he said, voice low. "All of it."

Rudd lifted the lantern higher, hands trembling now that the discovery had given his fear a shape. "Sir," he asked, "what if he's not here?"

Andrew thought of the barn yard, Ambrose's calm offer, the way he had turned silence into Andrew's responsibility. He thought of Elias's face, the horror of seeing his brother turned into price. He thought of the papers under oilcloth, the tidy language of paid discretion.

"He's been here," Andrew said. "And that's enough."

He took the first powder charge and set it carefully at the base of the cellar steps, where the stone met wood. Then he looked up toward the ceiling, toward the house above, toward the orchard's bare limbs reaching like hands.

"We light it," Andrew said. "And we make sure this place cannot be comfortable ever again."

Andrew set the last powder charge with hands that did not quite feel like his own. The cellar air was damp enough that the fuse cord seemed to drink it. He kept the lantern close, shielding its flame with his body while Haines crouched beside him, knife in hand, trimming a length of fuse with the careful attention of a man carving his own name into stone.

"Make it long," Andrew said. "Long enough we can clear the porch and the first row of trees."

Haines nodded once. His jaw was locked so tight it looked painful. He did not ask why. They all knew why. There were too many blind corners in this house, too many remembered spaces where a man could stand without being seen until it was too late.

Rudd hovered at the foot of the stairs, lantern raised, his face pale and wet with cellar damp. Lanier and Pritchard kept their rifles angled toward the dark between crates as if something might suddenly decide to take shape. Andrew knew, rationally, that if Ambrose were here, a rifle was a child's threat. But men needed the feel of something in their hands. It was how they stayed human.

When the fuse was set, Andrew climbed out first. The air upstairs felt thin by comparison, though it still carried the orchard's sweetness. He could taste it now, like a lie laid on the tongue. He moved through the house quickly, checking that Haines had soaked the lower rooms properly. Oil had been poured in deliberate trails, along walls and under fallen furniture. Rags sat in corners like small, patient animals waiting to be fed.

The place looked less like a home than a body prepared for burning.

They dragged kindling into the entryway and under the stairs, building a rough nest that would take flame greedily. Andrew stepped into the blackened room and lit a rag there as well, not because it was necessary, but because he wanted that old ritual of desperation to have a new ending. He wanted the soot-stained history of failed purifications to be forced into something final.

"Outside," he ordered.

They spilled onto the porch into gray daylight that had started to thin toward evening. The orchard received them in silence, the bare limbs of the apple trees reaching overhead like hands frozen mid-plea. Haines carried a torch made from a broken chair leg wrapped in oil-soaked cloth. The flame on it was small, careful, almost embarrassed by the damp air, but it lived.

Andrew turned once to look back at the house.

He felt again the architecture of fear in it, the boarded windows, the barricaded cellar door. Not only fear of Ambrose. Fear of neighbors finding out. Fear of God. Fear of consequences in any form that could not be paid away. He thought of the papers under oilcloth, that neat line: discretion is the only mercy afforded to those who serve.

He had brought his own kind of mercy here, and it was fire.

"Light it," Andrew said.

Haines touched the torch to the kindling under the stairs. The cloth caught with a hiss. The flame climbed quickly, hungry for oil. It spread along the trails like a thought turning into certainty. The entryway brightened with a sudden, living orange that made the house look almost warm again, almost inhabited.

They stepped off the porch and moved fast, boots sinking in wet earth. Andrew led them toward the orchard's edge where the trees began to thin. He did not want to be too far when the powder went. He did not want to be so close that the blast took them with it.

Behind them, the fire found a window board and began to chew. Smoke rolled out in low gray ribbons that thickened as they watched. The house started to make noises, small cracks and pops as dry interior timbers remembered what heat did. The sound was not dramatic yet, only the steady complaint of a thing being unmade.

Lanier crossed himself again, this time more openly. “Lord forgive us,” he muttered.

Pritchard snorted without humor. “Lord’s been busy.”

Andrew’s attention stayed on the cellar side of the house. He counted silently, not trusting himself to speak. The fuse burned below, unseen, patient as a snake under floorboards.

Rudd’s voice shook. “Sir. If he’s in them tunnels—if he’s under there—”

Andrew did not look at him. “Then he’ll have to crawl out through fire,” he said.

The sentence sounded braver than he felt. He had said it as if the world still respected pressure and heat, as if there were still rules that could be relied upon. Even as he spoke, he remembered the barn. Ambrose’s calm. His absolute lack of hurry. His amusement at human tools.

The house brightened in its lower windows as flame climbed. One board fell inward with a clatter, and for a moment Andrew saw the fire inside as clearly as if the house’s ribs had been opened. It was almost beautiful, the way it moved, the way it took what it touched and made it something else.

Then the powder went.

The sound was not a single crack. It was a deep, concussive thump that seemed to punch the ground. The porch jolted upward. A section of the foundation near the cellar door bucked and collapsed. Smoke burst from beneath the house in a thick black plume that rolled outward and upward, carrying splinters and dirt like thrown shrapnel. Andrew felt the shock in his teeth. He staggered a half-step, boots sliding in wet grass, and forced himself steady.

Rudd yelped. Haines swore, sharp and quick, then went silent as if the noise had been stolen from him.

For a heartbeat, everything paused. Even the fire seemed to hesitate, as if surprised by the sudden opening of air.

Then flame surged again, greedier now, feeding on broken timbers and the new draft created by collapse. The house began to lean, one side sagging as if tired. Smoke poured from the shattered cellar area in relentless waves. The orchard's sweetness turned bitter under the weight of it, a choking rot made into breath.

Andrew exhaled hard. He realized his hand was clenched so tight around nothing that his fingernails had cut his palm.

"Again," he ordered. "The trees. We burn the orchard."

Haines looked at him, eyes bloodshot with smoke already. "Now?"

"Now," Andrew said. He began to move down the first row of apple trees, torch in hand. He touched flame to dry grass and fallen limbs where he could. It did not catch easily in the damp, but oil dripped from rags he had tied earlier near the trunks, and where the oil touched, the fire held.

The orchard began to answer, reluctantly, with small tongues of flame around roots and dead leaves. The smoke mixed, house smoke and orchard smoke, and the world grew hazy. The trees became silhouettes, black fingers in a gray, living fog.

Andrew kept moving, lighting, moving, lighting, making his statement in a language he could trust. He did not know if it would matter to Ambrose. But it mattered to him. It mattered that he had done something other than swallow terms and keep silence.

A loud crack sounded from the house as part of the roof gave way. Embers shot upward like sparks from a forge. The flames inside roared louder, a low sound that was not quite an animal and not quite a storm. Heat washed outward in pulses that made Andrew's face sting even at this distance.

"Lieutenant!" Rudd called, voice high with panic. "Sir, look!"

Andrew turned.

For a moment he saw only smoke. It rolled out of the ruined cellar opening in thick sheets, black at the base, gray at the edges. The fire behind it turned the smoke red in places, as if it were lit from within by an angry heart.

Then a figure moved through it.

Not stumbling. Not crawling. Walking.

Ambrose stepped out from the smoke as if leaving a theater after a performance. His coat was dark and ruinous, but it did not burn. His hair lay slicked back, untouched by ash. The firelight painted his face in warm tones that made him look almost alive. His eyes found Andrew immediately, and in them there was that familiar calm, that patient amusement that made violence feel unnecessary.

Andrew felt his wound flare under the bandage, sharp and clean. A signal, a recognition, his body answering before thought.

Haines lifted his rifle without being told this time. Lanier and Pritchard followed suit, their fear finally becoming motion. The barrels shook slightly. Rudd stood frozen, mouth open, unable to decide whether he was watching a man or a lie wearing a man's shape.

Andrew raised a hand. "Hold," he snapped, and they held because habit was stronger than terror.

Ambrose's gaze slid briefly to the rifles, then back to Andrew, as if the weapons were a child's rude gesture. He took one slow step forward, the ground wet beneath him, firelight behind him.

And then he laughed.

It was not a cackle. Not a villain's performance. It was a soft, genuine laugh, a small sound of pleasure that carried through smoke and crackling flame with unbearable intimacy. The kind of laugh a man gave when a joke pleased him more than he expected.

Andrew's stomach turned. In the barn, Ambrose had argued. Here, he was amused.

"You did it," Ambrose said, and the warmth in his tone was wrong. "You came back to the place where frightened hands tried to make me a secret, and you tried to cleanse it with spectacle."

Andrew kept his voice steady by force. "If it was your shelter, it's gone."

Ambrose looked over his shoulder at the burning house and the first line of trees beginning to catch. The flames reflected in his eyes as if they belonged there. "Shelter," he murmured, tasting the word. "Yes. A useful one. A comfortable one."

He turned back to Andrew, smile faint. "But you've misunderstood, Lieutenant Mercer. Comfort is not a chain. Not for me."

Andrew swallowed smoke and bitterness. "Are you tied to this place or not?"

Ambrose tilted his head slightly, almost thoughtful. "Tied?" he echoed. "No. That is your language. Your rings in stone. Your vows. Your causes. You keep trying to solve hunger with architecture."

Behind Ambrose the house groaned again, a deep sagging sound as the structure gave more of itself to flame. Embers floated around him like slow, harmless insects. None of them seemed to touch him in any way that mattered.

Andrew felt something cold settle behind his ribs. It was not fear alone. It was the realization that the estate had never been the problem. It had only been one room in a larger house men built for things they did not want to name.

"You're not hurt," Haines whispered, disbelief breaking through his discipline.

Ambrose's eyes flicked to him. "Does that disappoint you?" he asked, polite as ever.

Haines's face twisted with hatred.

Ambrose let his gaze return to Andrew, and his smile widened just enough to show the faint dark stain at the corner of his mouth. "I am pleased," he said. "Not because you burned their records. Those can be rewritten. Not because you collapsed their tunnels. Others exist."

He gestured lightly, encompassing the war-scarred land, the smoke, the orchard. "I am pleased because you wanted this to be a victory," he said. "A clean act. A line drawn. A world corrected by force."

Andrew felt his jaw tighten. "It was necessary."

"Yes," Ambrose agreed, and the agreement was the most insulting thing he could have offered. "Necessary is how men excuse themselves. It is a very old prayer."

He stepped closer, stopping just short of the first line of orchard flame. The firelight painted him gold for a moment, like a saint in a ruined cathedral window.

"I told you," Ambrose said, voice low, so that it felt meant only for Andrew, "you would try again.

And you did." He smiled, that small private curve of the mouth. "You are learning what a keeper must learn."

Andrew felt anger rise, hot and bright, but it had nowhere to go. A rifle would not fix this. Fire would not fix this. The only thing that felt solid was the weight of what Ambrose had already taken from him: certainty.

"You laugh," Andrew said, and his voice sounded strange to his own ears, like a man speaking through cloth. "Because you think you've won."

Ambrose looked genuinely amused by the question, and his laughter came again, soft as breath. "No," he said. "I laugh because you think this was a battle between you and me."

The burning house behind him collapsed inward with a roar, sending a shower of sparks up into the smoke. The sound rolled across the orchard like thunder. For an instant the world was nothing but flame, falling wood, and the thick stink of history burning.

When the sparks drifted down, Ambrose was still there, untouched, watching Andrew with patient interest.

"This is a battle," Ambrose continued, "between what you are and what you pretend to be."

Andrew stood in the wet grass with smoke in his lungs and fire on his face, and understood with a bleak clarity that the estate could burn to ash and it would change nothing essential. The system that had housed Ambrose was human. The silence that fed him could be rebuilt anywhere.

Ambrose's eyes softened by a fraction, not with kindness, but with something like satisfaction. "Go back to your brother," he said gently. "Tell him you tried to kill a story with fire."

Andrew did not move.

Ambrose's smile returned. "And Lieutenant?" he added, almost as an afterthought. "Thank you for the light. I do so prefer to be seen."

Then he turned, stepping away into smoke and shadow as if choosing a door in a familiar hallway. The laughter lingered a moment longer than his body did, a quiet echo that settled into Andrew's mind like ash into lungs.

Andrew stood rigid as the orchard burned behind him, and for the first time he felt, fully and without argument, the true scale of what he faced.

He had brought fire to a thing that lived on collapse.

And it had laughed as if he'd brought it a candle.

Chapter 10

Brother's Blood

They rode back through a countryside blurred by smoke that was no longer behind them.

Andrew could still taste it, the bitter char of the estate and the orchard, caught in the back of his throat like a punishment that refused to finish. Each breath scraped. Each swallow reminded him that he had tried to speak to the thing in a language he trusted, and the thing had laughed as if he were a child striking flint for the first time.

Haines did not talk on the return. He rode with his shoulders hunched, rifle across his saddle like a talisman that had failed him but could not be surrendered. Rudd kept turning in the saddle to look behind them, as if the road itself might fold and deliver Ambrose into their wake. Lanier and Pritchard rode on either flank, faces gray, mouths set, their earlier prayers spent.

Andrew felt his wound under the bandage like a live wire. Not agony. Not the throb of injury. A clean, consistent awareness, as if something beneath his skin had learned a new kind of listening. When his horse's gait jolted him, the pain sharpened briefly, then settled back into that watchful sting. He did not know whether it was flesh refusing to heal or a reminder meant to keep him honest.

They reached the creek road by late afternoon, the sky low and colorless, the light thinning early the way it did when rain threatened but could not commit. The barn came into view in its shallow dip, lanterns already hanging beneath the eaves though it was not yet dark. Wagons stood in the same crooked arrangement, but the yard felt different. Quieter. Not restful, just subdued in the way a room became subdued after a violent argument, when everyone pretended nothing had happened but could not look one another in the eye.

Andrew dismounted before anyone could greet him. His boots hit mud with a wet sound that seemed to carry. Heads turned. Men stared too long, then looked away as if caught. The rumors would be moving faster than any courier: Mercer went into the orchard and came back with smoke in his hair. Mercer spoke to the thing. Mercer can keep it from taking you if he wants.

He hated them for it, and hated himself for giving them reason.

Elias was under the nearest wagon canvas with Kellan. Andrew saw them the moment he entered the yard. Elias rose as if he had been waiting with his muscles already primed, and for an instant Andrew felt a fierce, unsteady relief. Alive. Still intact. Still his brother.

Then he saw Elias's face.

It was not fear alone. It was the look of a man whose belief had been injured and was trying to decide whether it could still stand.

Elias strode toward him through the mud. Kellan remained seated, arms looped around his knees, gaze fixed on some spot just past Andrew as if looking at him directly would be dangerous.

"What did you do?" Elias demanded, voice low enough not to draw the whole yard, but sharp enough to cut.

Andrew kept his posture straight. "I did what I said I would do."

"You went back to the orchard house," Elias said, and the words came out as if they tasted foul. "You took powder. You took men. You burned it."

Andrew did not deny it. There was no point. The smoke was still in his clothes. "Yes."

Elias's eyes searched his face, hunting for something like victory to hate, something like satisfaction to argue with. Finding none, his anger shifted into something rawer.

"And it didn't matter," Elias said, more statement than question.

Andrew felt the memory of Ambrose stepping through smoke as if through a doorway. The soft laugh. The untouched coat. The calm eyes reflecting flame as if flame belonged to him. Andrew forced the image down. "It mattered to me," he said, and heard how small it sounded.

Elias flinched. "To you," he repeated. "That's what this is now? Something you do because it makes you feel like you've done something?"

Andrew's jaw tightened. "Watch your tone."

Elias gave a short, broken breath that might have been a laugh if it had not been full of disbelief. "My tone?" he whispered. "Andrew, men are going missing from a hospital. Sentries vanish and their rifles are leaned up like they were put away by a mother. You stood there last night and you told everyone to be quiet so it wouldn't take me."

Elias stepped closer. "You told them you were responsible for the silence."

Andrew kept his voice level by force. "If men panic, more die."

"That's the line you're using?" Elias said. His eyes shone with something that was not tears but came close. "You're already talking like it. Like you've accepted its rules. Like this is just another ugly necessity."

Andrew felt the yard pressing in, men pretending not to listen while listening anyway. He grabbed Elias's arm and pulled him toward the space behind the supply wagon, where the canvas and crates made a partial wall. Mud sucked at their boots. Elias resisted only long enough to make it clear he could have refused if he wanted, then followed, his anger too focused to be distracted.

Behind the wagon the sound of the barn softened. The air smelled of wet canvas, mule sweat, and old blood. Andrew turned to face his brother.

Elias yanked his arm free. "Tell me the truth," he said. "Not warnings. Not orders. Tell me what happened out there and tell me what you've promised it."

Andrew held his gaze and felt, under that steady stare, how tired he was of lying by omission. Tired of shaping reality into something other people could endure. It was part of the machinery Ambrose had named, and Andrew had been using it long before he knew Ambrose's name.

"It was there," Andrew said. "At the estate. It walked out of smoke like it was stepping from one room to another. It wasn't hurt."

Elias's face tightened, as if the confirmation was a blow. "So, it can't be killed."

"I didn't say that," Andrew snapped, and the sharpness surprised him. He lowered his voice again. "I said fire didn't do it."

Elias stared at him. "And it spoke to you."

Andrew did not answer quickly enough.

Elias's nostrils flared. "It spoke to you," he repeated, and now his voice shook. "What did it say?"

Andrew heard again the words delivered with gentle contempt: You are learning what a keeper must learn. Thank you for the light. I do so prefer to be seen.

"It said it was pleased," Andrew said. "Because I wanted a clean act. A victory. It said I misunderstand the shape of the fight."

Elias's lips parted. "And what do you think now?"

Andrew looked past Elias at the edge of the yard where lantern light fell off into mud and mist. He could almost feel Ambrose standing there, not in body, but in attention, like a weight behind the eyes.

"I think it can be delayed," Andrew said. "Driven away. Hurt, maybe, by the right things." He hesitated. "But it isn't tied to one place. The estate was just one arrangement. There were tunnels. Records. Names. It's been sheltered by men. Fed by systems."

Elias swallowed hard, then said the part he had been circling since morning. "And what about you?"

Andrew's wound gave a small flare beneath the bandage, as if the question pressed directly on it. He kept his face still. "What about me?"

Elias stepped closer until there was barely space between them. "It wants you," he said. "You told me that. It bargains. It keeps people. And now you're acting like you're already in its service."

Andrew felt heat rise in his throat, anger and shame together. "I'm keeping you alive."

Elias's expression broke, just for a moment, into something devastated. "Don't," he whispered. "Don't say it like that. Don't make me the reason you do what it wants."

Andrew's chest tightened. "You are the reason," he said, and it was the truest thing he had said all day.

Elias's eyes widened. Not in fear of Ambrose. In fear of what his brother had become willing to do.

"So you admit it," Elias said. "You're going to bargain."

"I didn't say that," Andrew said, but the denial was weak and both of them heard it. He forced himself to speak with the discipline he used on frightened men. "Listen. If we fight it outright, it will kill whoever it chooses. It will make a lesson of you first. You heard it."

"And if you bargain," Elias shot back, "it will still kill whoever it chooses, only now it will do it with your help."

Andrew's jaw clenched. "Not with my help," he said. "With my silence."

Elias's mouth twisted. "Do you hear yourself?" he demanded. "That's how you talk about it? Like the difference matters?"

Andrew felt something brittle in him begin to crack, not into confession, but into anger sharp enough to be dangerous. "The difference does matter," he said. "Because I've seen what happens when men make noise. I've seen rifles fired. I've seen it touch a throat and drop a man like punctuation. It doesn't need an excuse."

Elias shook his head, disbelief turning into grief. "Andrew," he said, and now his voice lowered into something almost pleading, "if you do what it wants to keep me alive, you will lose yourself. You'll become—"

"A keeper," Andrew finished, and heard how the word sat between them like a curse. He took a breath that hurt. "I know."

Elias stared at him as if waiting for the rest. For the insistence that Andrew would not. For the promise that his brother still lived in a world where men could refuse evil without paying for it in blood.

Andrew could not give him that promise.

Elias's shoulders slumped a fraction, the first visible sign of fatigue that had nothing to do with marching. "Then we're already dead," Elias whispered. "Just walking around with our names still attached."

Andrew's throat tightened. He reached for Elias then, not with words, but with the old instinct to anchor him the way he had in the yard. Elias flinched away.

The refusal landed harder than any blow. It was not rejection of touch. It was rejection of what Andrew represented now: a man who could stand in front of a monster and negotiate the terms under which others would be allowed to breathe.

Elias looked at him with a bleak clarity that made Andrew feel exposed. "I used to think you were the steady one," Elias said quietly. "The one who could endure without becoming like the war. I thought if anyone could come out of this still himself, it would be you."

Andrew said nothing. He could not argue with it because he no longer knew where his own edges were.

Elias's voice sharpened again, anger returning because grief needed a shape to fight. "If it comes again," he said, "and it asks you to do something, you have to refuse. Even if it means—"

"Don't," Andrew snapped, harsher than he intended. "Don't offer yourself like that. Don't be noble for my sake."

Elias's lips pressed together. His eyes glittered. "You mean don't make it easy for you," he said, and the accusation was precise enough to draw blood. "Don't give you a way out that feels righteous."

Andrew felt his face go cold. He looked at Elias and saw, with a sudden sick admiration, that his brother still understood something Andrew was already losing: that evil did not only corrupt by fear. It corrupted by offering relief from responsibility. By making compromise feel like compassion.

Elias stepped back, creating space between them like a boundary. “Whatever survives in you after this,” he said, voice low, “it won’t be my brother.”

The words landed like a sentence.

Andrew opened his mouth to answer, to demand, to plead, he did not know which. Before he could choose, a muffled cry rose from the barn and then cut off. The yard shifted in response like a nervous animal. Men called out, boots moved, lantern light wobbled.

Elias’s head turned toward the sound, and for a brief moment Andrew saw fear flicker across his face, quick and human. Elias looked back at Andrew as if to say, This is what you’re protecting me from. This is what you’re becoming for.

Andrew stepped around him toward the yard, already listening for the shape of silence that moved when Ambrose was near. His wound tightened beneath the bandage, clean and alert. Elias followed a pace behind, but not close now. Not under Andrew’s hand. Not within the circle of trust that had existed yesterday.

Something had broken between them, and Andrew knew, with a clarity that felt like mourning, that it was not easily repaired. It was not a simple argument. It was a fracture in how they saw the world, and in how Elias now saw him.

The war had taken many things from Andrew Mercer.

Now it was taking his brother, even while leaving him alive.

The barn doors slammed inward and then fell still, as if whoever had shut them had done so gently, with consideration for the men inside.

Andrew crossed the yard at a run, boots dragging in mud that wanted to keep him. The lanterns along the eaves trembled in their hooks, their light shaken by the quick movement of bodies. Men turned as he passed, mouths open, eyes wide, as if all of them were waiting for him to tell them what shape their fear should take.

A shout came from inside the barn, then another, and then the sound that cut through everything else: a wet, choked gasp that did not become a scream because it could not find enough air to climb.

Andrew hit the doors and threw them wide.

Heat and stink rolled out. Lantern smoke, old blood, lye that had surrendered hours ago. The cots were a dim grid of suffering, but the grid had broken. Orderlies stood frozen mid-step. A nurse had her hands clamped over her mouth, eyes fixed on a spot between two rows as though she had watched someone walk through a wall.

Captain Dorsey was there, near the center aisle, his pistol out, arm extended, the barrel aimed at nothing Andrew could see.

"What happened?" Andrew snapped.

Dorsey's eyes flicked to him, wild with the relief of having someone else enter the nightmare. "He was here," Dorsey said, voice rough. "I swear to God, Mercer, he was here. Right there." He nodded toward the gap between cots. "And then he wasn't."

"Missing?" Andrew demanded, and hated the word because it sounded like paperwork.

An orderly shook his head hard, as if trying to dislodge a memory. "Not missing," the man whispered. "Taken. Like being pulled under water."

Andrew scanned the cots. Men stared at him with fever-bright eyes, some of them smiling weakly the way they had smiled for Ambrose, as if they still believed a gentle hand might come to end their pain. Others clutched their blankets tight, as if cloth could keep their blood inside.

He saw the empty space where two cots had been, the straw disturbed, blankets folded with careful hands.

He heard the barn's new silence, the wary pause between moans, the way every breath seemed to wait for permission.

And beneath it all, faint as a remembered taste, the sweetness.

Andrew forced himself to turn away. The barn was a mouth, and he could not afford to stand inside it and listen for teeth. He backed out into the yard, mind already running ahead, measuring where danger would go next.

Elias.

Andrew swung toward the wagons.

Kellan was still near the supply canvas, sitting as before, but his posture had changed. He was no longer folded inward. He was leaning forward, elbows on knees, staring at the mud as if he had just watched it swallow something.

"Kellan," Andrew barked.

Kellan blinked slowly, as if waking from a trance. His eyes met Andrew's, and for a moment Andrew saw a shameful resignation there, the look of a man who had learned that horror did not always announce itself with violence.

"Where's Elias?" Andrew demanded.

Kellan's mouth opened. No sound came at first, only breath. Then, hoarse, "He went behind the wagons. Said he needed air. Said he couldn't stay—" Kellan swallowed hard, Adam's apple jerking. "I told him to take someone. He told me to go to hell."

Andrew's skin went cold. He had told Elias, stay in sight, stay near people, no heroics. Elias had heard the words and then tried to reclaim himself by disobeying them.

Andrew moved around the wagon line, boots slipping. Men shifted aside instinctively. Haines appeared near the wagon tongue, rifle held tight, eyes already tracking Andrew's movement as if he knew what question was coming.

"Elias is gone," Andrew said.

Haines's face tightened, anger and fear flaring into the same hard line. "He did it," Haines muttered. "He took him."

Andrew didn't correct him. The pronoun did not matter. The fact did.

Rudd was behind Haines, pale as old paper, hands shaking on his strap. "Sir," he said, voice thin, "maybe he just walked off. Maybe—"

Andrew turned on him, and the look in his eyes shut the hope down. Rudd swallowed and went silent.

Andrew pushed past the wagons toward the shallow slope down to the creek road. The mud there was torn up by hooves and wagon wheels, but beneath that mess he saw it: a line of disturbed earth leading toward the tree line, not quite drag marks, not quite footprints. The ground had been pressed in a pattern that suggested someone had moved quickly without slipping.

And there, beside a broken fence post, Elias's cap lay in the mud.

Andrew stopped long enough to pick it up. The cloth was wet and heavy in his hand, brim bent. It smelled like rain and sweat and his brother's hair oil, familiar enough to make his throat tighten.

He tucked it into his coat as if it were something holy.

"Lantern," he snapped.

Haines shoved one into his hand. Its light was a small, imperfect circle, but it was better than chasing through dark with only imagination.

"Sir," Haines said, stepping close, voice low, urgent. "We need more men."

Andrew shook his head. "He won't leave a trail for a crowd," he said. "He'll leave a lesson. You want him to kill three more just to prove a point?"

Haines's jaw worked. He hated the logic and could not deny it.

Andrew looked at Rudd. "You stay here," he ordered. "You do not move from the wagons. You do not go looking."

Rudd's eyes widened, humiliated. "Sir, I can help."

"You can die," Andrew said. The bluntness was cruel, but it was what Rudd needed. Andrew turned to Haines. "You're with me."

Haines nodded once, grim, and checked the rifle as if the action could turn fear into readiness.

They pushed into the tree line.

The world changed quickly. The lanterns behind them became distant points, then vanished altogether. The wet woods swallowed sound, leaving only the hiss of mist on leaves and the soft suck of boots in mud. Andrew kept the lantern low, not wanting the light to bounce off trunks and blind him. He followed the faint disturbances in the ground, the places where grass had been pressed down as if by a hurried foot.

His wound stung beneath the bandage, clean and persistent. With each step the sensation sharpened, not into pain but into awareness, as if the cut were a compass needle turning toward something it recognized.

“You feel that?” Haines asked quietly, after a few minutes, and Andrew realized Haines had been watching him more than the ground.

Andrew did not answer. There was no point lying. The wound’s sting was not something he could order away.

They reached the creek. The water ran dark and fast under the low fog, carrying small sticks and dead leaves like messages it did not want to deliver. On the near bank, the mud was churned as if a man had slid and caught himself. On the far bank, the reeds were bent in a line.

Andrew stepped into the water without hesitation. Cold shot up his legs, biting through boots and socks. The current shoved at him, eager to knock him down. He braced with one hand on a slick rock, lantern held high. Haines followed, cursing under his breath.

On the far side Andrew climbed out and dropped to a crouch. The bank was soft. Something had climbed here recently.

A boot print. Clear enough that the tread pattern showed. Elias’s.

Then, beside it, another mark: a bare impression in the mud that looked almost like a foot, but wrong in proportion, too long, too smooth at the edges, as if the earth had been pressed by something that did not have the same weight distribution as a man.

Haines stared at it. “God,” he whispered.

Andrew rose and kept moving.

The trail led them through a strip of pines and out into open ground that had been a farm field once. The fence line was broken, posts leaning. A burned-out cabin squatted near the far edge, its chimney a black stump against the fog. Andrew crossed the field quickly, lantern swinging. The mist made distance uncertain; everything looked nearer and farther at once.

At the cabin the scent changed. Old smoke, wet ash, and beneath it the faint sweetness, more pronounced now, as if the land itself had begun to rot politely.

Inside the cabin there was nothing living. A collapsed roof beam. Charred floorboards. A child’s shoe half-buried in soot. Andrew’s lantern light caught a smear on the wall, dark and drying.

Blood.

Not splattered. Wiped. As if a hand had brushed against the boards and then been removed with care.

Andrew's throat tightened. "Elias," he said under his breath, not as a call, but as an involuntary prayer.

Haines moved behind him, rifle up, eyes darting. "Sir, this is—" He stopped, unable to finish without admitting what it meant.

Andrew backed out of the cabin and found the trail again on the far side, where the grass had been flattened toward the road.

They reached the road as the light began to thin further, the day giving up early. The road was rutted and lined with the debris of retreat: a broken wagon wheel, a torn blanket caught on a thorn bush, a shallow ditch where someone had tried to bury something quickly and failed. War's refuse. The nation's discarded skin.

Andrew saw something ahead through the fog: a small structure, roof crooked, steeple broken. A chapel, or what had been one.

"Why there?" Haines murmured, as if the question could keep the place from being true.

Andrew didn't know. But he felt the wound pull, a subtle tightening under the bandage, like a thread drawn toward a needle.

They approached the chapel slowly. Its door hung open, one hinge broken. Inside, pews had been overturned. The altar was stripped bare. Someone had painted over the windows long ago, blackening the panes from within. The air smelled of damp wood and old prayers that had dried and cracked.

Andrew stepped across the threshold and heard, very faintly, a sound from the rear: breathing. Not the rasp of sickness from the barn. Not the steady breath of a sleeping man.

Fast, thin, controlled.

Elias.

Andrew moved down the center aisle, lantern lifted. Haines stayed close, rifle aimed into shadow.

At the rear of the chapel, near a side room that might once have held vestments, Elias knelt on the floor with his hands braced against the boards as if he had been sick. His coat was spattered with mud. His hair was wet and plastered to his forehead. He looked up when Andrew's lantern light hit him, and in his eyes was fury so sharp it almost hid the fear.

"Andrew," he whispered.

Andrew took one step toward him and stopped, because the air shifted.

The sweetness thickened, sudden as a door opening.

A voice spoke from the side room, calm and warm, as if continuing a conversation that had never been interrupted. "You have such devotion," Ambrose said. "It's almost touching."

Andrew's spine tightened. He turned his head slightly, not fully, unwilling to give the shadow the satisfaction of making him whirl.

Ambrose stepped out, and the lantern light found him reluctantly. He looked as he always did: ruined elegance, pale composure, eyes like a patient appetite dressed in courtesy. He was not damp from the creek. He was not winded from the chase. He looked as though he had arrived first and simply waited for the others to catch up.

Haines's rifle jerked a fraction higher. Andrew could feel the tremor in him.

Ambrose's gaze slid to Haines and then back to Andrew, amused. "You brought a witness," he murmured. "How responsible."

Andrew kept his voice level with effort. "Let him go."

Ambrose smiled faintly. "He is here of his own will," he said, and the lie was exquisite. "He wanted to understand what sort of man his brother has become."

Elias surged forward to stand, rage overtaking caution. “Don’t you speak for me,” he snapped.

Ambrose’s eyes flicked to him, and Elias’s movement faltered, not fully stopped this time, but checked, as if an invisible hand had pressed gently against his chest.

Andrew felt something break loose in him, a hard, clean anger that finally found its target. He stepped forward, placing himself between Ambrose and Elias again, and ignored the flare of pain under his bandage.

“You want to teach me,” Andrew said. “Teach me with me. Leave him out of it.”

Ambrose’s smile deepened. “Always negotiating the terms of your own suffering,” he murmured. “As if that is virtue.”

He took a slow step closer. The chapel’s air seemed to tilt toward him, the shadows gathering at his back like obedient servants.

“You’ve been chasing a trail,” Ambrose continued softly. “Through mud, through smoke, through the scraps of your collapsing nation. Do you know what I see when I watch you do that, Lieutenant Mercer?”

Andrew didn’t answer.

Ambrose's gaze held him with intimate patience. "I see a man who cannot bear helplessness," Ambrose said. "Not because he is brave. Because he is proud. You would rather become complicit than become useless."

Andrew felt Elias behind him, trembling with contained hatred. He did not turn. He could not spare the attention.

Ambrose's voice softened, almost gentle. "I told you there would be consequence," he said. "Not as punishment. As instruction."

He glanced at Elias again, and Elias's breath hitched.

Andrew heard his brother whisper, broken despite himself, "Don't."

Andrew stood in the ruined chapel with the smell of damp wood and old prayers, and understood that the pursuit had been allowed. Every step had been permitted. Ambrose had not fled.

He had led.

And now, with Elias close enough to touch and Ambrose close enough to bargain, Andrew felt the trap tighten around them like a chain drawn through a ring in stone.

Outside, the fog pressed against the broken windows as if trying to listen.

Inside, Ambrose smiled at Andrew with patient expectation, and Andrew realized the chase was over.

The choice was next.

Andrew kept his body between Elias and the thing that wore a man's shape. The lantern light made a weak halo around his shoulders, and beyond it the chapel's shadows lay thick, as if the building were trying to remember how to be sacred and failing.

Ambrose stood with the patience of someone who had nowhere else to be.

"Tell me what you want," Andrew said. His voice came out level, but the words scraped on smoke and fatigue. "Name it plainly."

Ambrose's smile did not widen, but something in his eyes did, a slight brightening like a latch lifting. "Plainly," he murmured. "You ask for plainness the way some men ask for prayer."

He shifted his gaze to Elias. The attention landed like a hand on the throat, gentle enough to be called courtesy, firm enough to be called ownership.

Elias swallowed, jaw clenched. He tried to stand straighter, but Andrew could feel the tremor in him through the air, a vibration of fury and fear. "Don't look at me," Elias said, forcing the words out as if they were heavy.

Ambrose regarded him as if considering an interesting painting. "You're the one who came to look," he replied. "You followed your brother into the dark because you couldn't bear not knowing what he'd become."

Elias's hands curled into fists. "I came because you took me," he snapped, and for an instant the pressure on him tightened. Elias's breath caught. His posture faltered.

Andrew felt his own wound flare under the bandage, sharp and clean, as if his body recognized the increase in tension the way a dog recognized thunder.

"Stop," Andrew said.

Ambrose tilted his head. "Stop what?"

"You know what," Andrew answered. He forced himself to keep his feet planted, not to lean forward, not to give Ambrose the satisfaction of movement born from panic. "If you're going to speak to someone, speak to me."

Ambrose's gaze returned to him. The sweetness in the air thickened, not as a smell alone but as a presence, a suggestion of orchards and cellars and folded blankets.

"You want a bargain," Ambrose said. "So be it."

Andrew did not answer immediately. He listened, not for footsteps or breath, but for the subtle shift he had learned to fear: the way a room began to pay attention to Ambrose even when no one wanted to. Even the chapel's broken timbers seemed to lean.

Ambrose stepped closer, stopping just at the edge of the lantern's strongest light. His face, pale and composed, looked almost gentle in that half-illumination, like a man leaning in to speak quietly to the sick.

"You have tried iron," Ambrose said. "You have tried fire. You have tried prayer carried like a weapon under your coat. And still you arrive here with empty hands, asking me what I want, as if you can afford to offer refusal."

Andrew's jaw tightened. "I'm here," he said. "I'm not running. If you want to prove something, prove it on me."

Elias made a low sound behind him, half protest, half disbelief. "Andrew, don't."

Ambrose's eyes slid past Andrew to Elias again, quick as a tongue tasting blood. "It's admirable," Ambrose said softly, "how quickly you offer yourself when you think it will keep him breathing. That is love, isn't it? Or is it only ownership in a nicer coat?"

Andrew felt heat rise into his throat, anger sharp enough to be dangerous because it needed a place to go. He swallowed it down. Rage was what Ambrose expected. Rage was theater.

"Speak," Andrew said.

Ambrose's smile returned, mild. "Very well," he said. "Here are the terms, and you will hear them without flinching."

Andrew held still. He knew the flinch would be the first surrender.

Ambrose lifted one hand, not toward Andrew, but toward the side room behind him, the place he had stepped from as if it were a doorway in his own home. In that dim threshold, something lay on the floor.

A shape.

At first Andrew's mind refused to make it human. Then the lantern's bobble of light caught a boot, a trouser leg, a slack hand.

A man.

Andrew's stomach turned. He recognized the cut of the uniform. One of Dorsey's orderlies, perhaps, or a sentry. Someone from the barn yard. Someone taken without noise and brought here like a message.

The man's eyes were open. His mouth hung slightly parted, as if he had tried to speak and remembered too late that speech required blood.

Elias saw him and recoiled, a hand flying to his mouth. His breath came fast through his nose, and Andrew heard the fight in him, the urge to be sick and the refusal to grant the body that relief.

Ambrose watched Elias's reaction with calm curiosity. "He was loud," Ambrose said. "Not with his mouth. With his thoughts. He wanted to be a hero. A tiresome ambition."

Andrew forced his eyes away from the corpse and back to Ambrose. "If you're trying to frighten me, you're late," he said.

Ambrose's gaze warmed, pleased. "Not frighten," he corrected. "Clarify."

He stepped slightly to the side so Andrew could see the dead man more clearly, and the cruelty of the gesture was in its politeness. Ambrose did not need to gloat. He simply arranged the view.

"I want you to make order," Ambrose said. "Not in this chapel. Not tonight only. In the world around me. I want you to place things back into their proper stories."

Andrew's mouth went dry. He could feel, with sick precision, what Ambrose meant: reports filed, names lost, explanations offered that would settle like dust over absence. A missing man becomes a deserter. A drained man becomes fever. A body with too little wound becomes too much blood loss written off as chaos.

Ambrose continued, voice calm as sermon. “Tonight, you will return to Captain Dorsey and tell him that you found your brother wandering, half-mad with grief and fear, and you brought him back. You will tell him there was an altercation on the road. Raiders. A knife. Something human enough to be believed.”

Andrew stared at him. “And the missing men?”

Ambrose’s smile held. “Will remain missing,” he said. “And you will help them remain so.”

Elias’s voice cracked behind Andrew. “No,” he whispered. “Andrew, don’t listen to him.”

Andrew did not turn. If he turned, he would see Elias’s face and lose what little steadiness he had left.

Ambrose’s eyes flicked to Elias again, and Elias’s whisper faltered into a tight, helpless silence.

“You will do something else,” Ambrose said to Andrew. “Something simple. Something small. A first step that makes the rest easier.”

Andrew's throat tightened. "What."

Ambrose looked down at Andrew's bandaged side, and the glance felt like a finger pressing the wound through cloth. "You carry a charm," Ambrose murmured. "A chain and beads and words in a language you do not speak with conviction."

Andrew's hand drifted, instinctively, toward his coat. He stopped it halfway, forcing it down.

Ambrose's smile deepened as if he'd heard the restraint click into place. "Give them to me," he said.

The chapel seemed to go quieter, as if even the fog pressed closer to listen.

Andrew's mind moved fast, trying to find the trap's seam. The bundle was not only objects. It was the last symbol of refusal he had allowed himself. If he gave it up, he gave up the pretense that he was still hunting.

Elias found his voice again, ragged with desperation. "Andrew. Don't. That's the point. He wants you to hand it over."

Ambrose did not look at Elias this time. His eyes stayed on Andrew with an intimate steadiness, as if the only person in the chapel were the lieutenant standing in lamplight.

Andrew breathed in and tasted damp wood, old ash, and that sweetness that did not belong anywhere living. He imagined returning to the camp empty-handed in the most literal sense, the priest's bundle gone. He imagined the priest's warning at the chapel door: Do not let him make you feel special.

He had thought special meant chosen for death.

Now he understood it also meant chosen for work.

Andrew's fingers went to the inside of his coat, slow and deliberate. He drew the bundle out. The rosary beads slid a little in his grip, worn smooth by another man's faith. The short length of dull chain rested against his palm with cold, honest weight.

Elias made a broken sound. "No," he whispered, and Andrew heard something fracture in that word that would not be repaired.

Andrew held the bundle up, not offering it yet. He forced himself to meet Ambrose's eyes. "If I give you this," he said, "you let him walk out of here. Now. With me."

Ambrose's expression softened by a fraction, almost tender, as if Andrew were negotiating for extra rations. "Yes," he said. "He will walk."

Elias shook his head violently, tears finally spilling despite his effort to keep them contained. "Andrew, I'd rather die," he said, and the statement was not dramatic. It was honest.

Andrew's voice came out low, controlled, and merciless because mercy would get Elias killed. "No, you wouldn't," Andrew said. "Not like this. Not for a point."

Elias's eyes locked on him. The hatred there was not for Ambrose. It was for what Andrew was doing. For the way he was turning love into a calculation.

Ambrose extended his hand.

The gesture was graceful, like a gentleman accepting a glove. His fingers looked clean in the lantern light. Andrew remembered the boy in the barn describing those hands. Clean hands. Gentle.

Andrew placed the bundle into Ambrose's palm.

The instant their fingers touched, Andrew felt his wound flare hard, a clean, bright line of pain that stole breath from his lungs. His vision narrowed. The chapel's shadows swayed. It was not merely injury reacting. It felt like a recognition, an internal nod, as if something in Andrew had just signed its name.

Ambrose's fingers closed around the chain and beads. He did not wince at the iron. He did not recoil from the Latin. He only smiled, faint and satisfied, as if the objects were less important than the act of surrender itself.

"Good," Ambrose murmured. "You learn quickly when your brother is the lesson."

Andrew's breath came back in shallow pulls. He forced his posture straight, refused to bend or stagger. He would not give Ambrose that.

Elias stood rigid, staring at Andrew as if he were seeing him for the first time. "You did it," he whispered, and the words were hollow with shock. "You actually did it."

Andrew could not answer without collapsing into justification, and justification was part of the machinery Ambrose wanted him to become.

Ambrose stepped back toward the side room. He glanced at the corpse on the floor as if considering whether it needed further arrangement. Then he looked at Andrew again.

"You will return," Ambrose said, conversational. "Not because I will chase you. Because you will discover how heavy a secret becomes once you pick it up."

Andrew held his gaze. "This doesn't make me yours," he said, and heard how desperate the sentence sounded.

Ambrose smiled as if indulging a child. "No," he replied. "It makes you practiced."

Then his eyes slid to Elias one last time, and the pressure in the air tightened just enough to make Elias flinch.

"Go," Ambrose said gently. "Both of you. The night is full of other hungers, and I would not want you to think I am the only monster your war has made."

He stepped into the side room, and the shadows seemed to receive him with familiarity. The sweetness in the chapel thinned, not gone, only withdrawn, like a mouth closing after tasting something it liked.

Andrew stood for a heartbeat longer, listening for the shift that would mean Ambrose had changed his mind. Nothing came. Only the fog pressing against blackened windows, only the lantern flame trembling in his hand.

He turned then, slowly, toward Elias.

Elias's face was wet, his jaw trembling with the effort not to plead. He looked at Andrew the way a man looked at a grave that had not finished being dug.

"You saved my life," Elias whispered, and the words were not gratitude. They were accusation.

Andrew's throat tightened until it hurt. He reached out, stopped himself, then forced his hand to Elias's shoulder anyway, firm enough to anchor.

"We're leaving," Andrew said.

Elias's eyes stayed fixed on him. "And what did you give him?" he asked, voice thin. "What did you give him besides beads and chain?"

Andrew could still feel the flare in his side like an afterimage. He swallowed, tasted iron in his mouth that had nothing to do with blood.

"I gave him the first proof," Andrew said quietly, "that I will pay."

Elias's eyes closed for a moment, as if the darkness behind his lids might be kinder than the world in front of him. When he opened them again, the look there was older than it had been the day before.

They walked out of the ruined chapel into fog that clung to their clothes like ash. Behind them, Ambrose remained in the darkness with Andrew's surrendered charm in his hand, and the bargain settled into place with the slow certainty of a chain finding its ring.

Chapter 11

The Keeper's Work

Fog followed them back to the creek like a second skin. It hung in their hair and on their eyelashes, beading there until it looked like sweat. Andrew kept the lantern low and walked with measured steps, not because he feared stumbling, but because he feared what haste looked like from the outside. Panic invited pursuit. Panic made a man theatrical. Ambrose had said he disliked theater only when it wasn't his.

Elias walked beside him, close enough that their shoulders might have brushed if either of them had allowed it. But Elias held himself rigid, as though touch would make something true that he could not bear. His jaw worked in small motions, like he was grinding words down before they could escape.

Haines was waiting near the tree line when they emerged from the fog, rifle in hand, face drawn tight with the expectation of finding only Andrew.

The instant he saw Elias alive, something in him loosened, then twisted into something else.

"He let him go," Haines said, not relief exactly. More like disbelief that made room for a different kind of fear.

Andrew did not correct the sentence. He could not afford to.

They reached the wagon yard just before full dark. Lanterns burned under the eaves, throwing dull yellow coins onto the mud. Men looked up as if the sound of their boots had been announced. A hush moved through the yard the way wind moved through grass. Andrew felt it: the camp had already learned to hold its breath around him.

Captain Dorsey came forward fast, boots slipping once in the muck. His face was set in the hard lines of a man who had been denied sleep by more than pain.

"Mercer," he snapped, then stopped when he saw Elias. His eyes flicked over Elias's mud-smeared coat and wet hair, lingering on the pallor in his face. "Where the hell did you go?"

Andrew kept his voice even. "Lost sight of him in the commotion," he said. "Found him near the old chapel off the road. He was disoriented. Shocked."

Elias's head turned slightly, a sharp movement, as if he meant to speak. Andrew felt it before it happened and stepped half a pace closer, a silent pressure. Elias's throat worked. His eyes stayed on Dorsey, full of a hatred that had no clean target.

Dorsey's gaze narrowed. "Alone?"

Andrew let a beat pass. Raiders was an easy story here. Raiders lived in every shadow the way sickness did. "There were signs of movement," he said. "Boot prints. Blood in a burned cabin. He likely ran into men stripping the road. They cut him, maybe. Not badly." He gestured to Elias's sleeve, where mud could pass for dried blood in lantern light. "He got away."

Dorsey stared, trying to weigh the lie. His eyes flicked to Haines, then back. "And the ones missing from the barn?" he asked, voice roughening. "You find them too?"

Andrew kept his face still. "No."

Dorsey's mouth tightened. For a moment his anger looked like it might become accusation. Then his gaze shifted toward the barn, toward the dark mouth of it, and his anger faltered into something like surrender.

"Get him warm," Dorsey said finally, jerking his chin toward Elias. "We'll talk again, Mercer. Don't think we're done talking."

Andrew nodded once. “Understood.”

As Dorsey turned away, Andrew felt Elias’s stare on the side of his face like heat. When they were beyond earshot of the nearest men, Elias spoke, voice low and stripped of softness.

“Warm,” Elias said, tasting the word like poison. “Like I’m sick.”

Andrew did not answer. He guided him toward the lee of the supply wagon where canvas sagged and the mules steamed faintly. Kellan was there, still folded near the wheel, eyes shadowed, watching as if he expected Elias to vanish again between one blink and the next.

Rudd stood a few paces off, hands worrying his strap. When Andrew approached, the boy’s eyes went to Andrew’s coat, to the place where the priest’s bundle had been hidden. The absence was invisible, and yet Rudd seemed to sense it anyway, the way men sensed missing weight from a familiar pocket.

“You got him back,” Rudd said quietly.

Andrew nodded. “Yes.”

Rudd swallowed. “And the chapel?”

Andrew’s gaze cut to him, not harsh, but final. “You didn’t see anything,” Andrew said.

Rudd's face tightened. He nodded too quickly. "No, sir."

Elias made a sound that might have been a laugh if it hadn't been so raw. "That's it, then," he said. "That's the work. Don't see. Don't speak. Don't name it."

Andrew turned to him. Lantern light caught Elias's eyes and made them look too bright, like fever. "You want to shout the truth into the yard?" Andrew asked. "You want them firing into the trees until one of them hits an orderly? You want Dorsey marching a dozen men into the fog to prove he's still a captain?"

Elias's lips pressed together. His whole body trembled with restraint. "I want you to stop doing what it wants," he said.

Andrew held his gaze. "I am doing what keeps you breathing," he said, and hated that the sentence still came out like a reflex, as if it were armor he could hide behind.

Elias's expression flickered, pain cutting through the anger. "That isn't mercy," he whispered. "That's a chain."

Andrew didn't have an answer that wouldn't be another lie. Instead he said, "Stay with Kellan. Stay where there's light."

Elias stepped back as if the instruction itself offended him. "So you can go do your real business," he said.

Andrew felt something in his chest tighten, but he forced it down and turned away. He could not afford to be pulled into argument now, not when the night still had so many edges.

He found Haines near the wagon tongue, checking the cinches with hands that wanted a task. Haines looked up, and in his eyes Andrew saw what the others would not say aloud: the question of what Andrew had paid.

"We need a place," Andrew said quietly.

Haines's brow furrowed. "For what, sir?"

Andrew kept his voice low, flat. "For him."

The word sat between them like a dead thing.

Haines's jaw flexed. He looked past Andrew toward the barn, toward the wounded and the orderlies and the thin line of men with rifles pretending they could guard anything. Then he looked toward the road that ran away into fog and pine.

"You're telling me to build a nest," Haines said.

Andrew didn't flinch. "I'm telling you to keep him away from the camp," he replied. "As far as we can. Somewhere he can… rest."

Haines's face twisted with disgust at the word rest, the human softness of it. "He rests," Haines muttered, "and men disappear."

Andrew leaned in a fraction. "He disappears men whether he rests or not," he said. "But if he's close, it's easier. And he likes easy."

Haines stared at him, breathing hard through his nose. "And if I say no?"

Andrew held his gaze. "Then he'll take what he wants until there's nothing left to say no with."

Haines looked away first. His shoulders slumped a fraction, not in defeat, but in the grim acceptance of a man choosing between two kinds of ruin.

"There's an old tobacco shed up the creek," Haines said finally. "Half fallen in, but it's got a root pit under it. Farmers used it for storing. Door's thick. Only one way in. No windows."

Andrew's wound gave a small, clean sting, as if something in him approved of the practicality. He ignored it.

"How far?" Andrew asked.

"Half a mile, maybe," Haines said. "Through brush. Hard to see from the road."

Andrew nodded once. "We'll go now. You and me."

Haines hesitated. “And Elias?”

Andrew didn’t look back toward the wagon canvas, because he could feel Elias there without seeing him, a hot point of hurt in the dark. “Elias stays,” he said. “He doesn’t come near this.”

Haines let out a thin breath. “Too late for that,” he murmured.

Andrew did not answer.

They took oil and a shovel and a length of chain scavenged from a broken harness. It felt obscene, carrying tools that belonged to farm work and treating them like instruments of accommodation. Andrew moved through the yard without explaining. Men watched him, then looked away quickly, as if the act of seeing might enlist them.

As they slipped into the tree line, the camp sounds dulled behind them. The fog was thicker here, cold and wet, wrapping trunks until the woods became a hallway of blurred pillars. Andrew kept his steps careful. Not quiet, not sneaking. He had learned that Ambrose did not need silence to find a man. But he also knew that noise could be mistaken for defiance, and defiance was a temptation Ambrose might answer just to prove he could.

The tobacco shed crouched in a low hollow near the creek, half swallowed by weeds and wet leaf rot. Its roof sagged, and one wall leaned outward like a tired shoulder. Haines pushed the door open with a grunt. Hinges squealed, then fell into a damp hush.

Inside, the air was earth-heavy and old. The root pit was in the back, covered by planks that had once been thick and were now softened by years. Haines pried them up with the shovel. The hole beneath yawned dark and cold, lined with rough stone.

Andrew stood over it and felt a familiar nausea, the echo of his dreams. Buried awake. Hearing voices through soil.

Haines cleared his throat. "You sure about this?" he asked, voice strained. "Putting him in the ground again?"

Andrew looked into the pit and tried to make his mind stay human. "It's not a prison," he said, and heard the bitterness in the admission. "It's distance. It's containment. It's…" He searched for a word that didn't sound like surrender. "A boundary."

Haines gave a harsh, humorless exhale. "That's what we called the war too."

Andrew didn't answer. He stepped into the shed, set the lantern on a crate, and began to work with his hands. He dragged loose boards to reinforce the pit cover. He drove nails where he could. He wrapped chain around the door latch twice and secured it with a padlock taken from the supply wagon, the kind meant to protect flour from thieves.

When it was done, the shed looked ordinary again, in the way ordinary things looked when they were built to hide something.

Andrew stepped back, lantern light shaking slightly. He imagined Ambrose inside the pit, elegant even in dirt-dark, listening. Waiting. He imagined those calm eyes opening in the black and the faint sweetness threading out between the boards like breath.

Haines watched him, face pale. “He ain’t here yet,” he said.

Andrew nodded slowly. “No,” he replied. “But he will be.”

The certainty of it settled over the shed like fog.

Haines swallowed. “And when he comes,” he asked, “what do we do?”

Andrew looked at the locked door, at the chain, at the thin, laughable idea that iron could mean anything to a thing that folded distance in the barn yard.

He heard Ambrose’s voice from the chapel, gentle as instruction: You will discover how heavy a secret becomes once you pick it up.

Andrew lifted the lantern and turned back toward the trees, toward the camp, toward his brother's breathing and the fragile, ruined lives clustered around the barn.

"When he comes," Andrew said quietly, "we make it easy for him to stay here instead of there."

Haines's eyes tightened. "And if he wants to feed?"

Andrew felt the wound beneath his bandage flare, clean and sharp, as if it were answering before he could. He held still until the sting faded to its usual watchful ache.

"Then I arrange," Andrew said.

It was the first time he said it aloud, and the words did not sound like a plan.

They sounded like a job.

They walked back to the camp with the lantern hooded, its light reduced to a narrow slit that made the trees look like thin, leaning men. The fog thickened as night settled, and sound carried strangely: the creek's low rush seemed close, then far; a single snapped twig seemed loud enough to be an announcement.

Andrew kept the route in his head, marking it by feel more than sight. A leaning pine with lightning scar. A stump like a chair. A place where the ground dipped and the air smelled faintly of wet iron. He would need to find the shed again without thinking. He would need to find it quickly if Ambrose decided to arrive when someone was watching.

Haines did not speak until the lantern glow from the camp returned, distant and weak through the trees.

"You ever think," Haines said, voice low and rough, "that we're doing the same as them folks at the estate?"

Andrew did not answer at once. The question hit too cleanly, too close to the bone.

"We're not feeding him for comfort," Andrew said finally. "We're not wealthy men keeping a pet sin under the floorboards."

Haines let out a quiet sound that wasn't quite a laugh. "No," he said. "We're poor men keeping a sin under the floorboards. That's the only difference I see."

Andrew felt his wound tighten beneath the bandage, the familiar sting that had become a second pulse. He ignored it and kept walking, as if pace could outpace thought.

"We're keeping him away from the wounded," Andrew said. "Away from the barn. Away from my brother."

Haines's steps slowed half a beat, then matched Andrew's again. "That's what you tell yourself," he muttered.

Andrew said nothing. He knew. That was the point. Telling yourself was a kind of work. It was labor, like lifting a sack of meal, like digging a latrine. It kept the mind from collapsing under the weight of what the hands were doing.

When they emerged into the yard, men looked up and then looked away too quickly. A few pretended to be busy adjusting mule tack or stacking crates, but their bodies were angled toward Andrew, listening with their whole posture. Word moved without speech now. The camp had learned a new kind of attention, tuned to the spaces between lantern islands.

Rudd was waiting near the supply wagon, his face pale in the lamplight. He stepped toward Andrew and stopped as if he'd realized halfway that approaching too eagerly might be mistaken for asking.

"Sir," Rudd said, and swallowed. "Where'd you go?"

Andrew met his eyes and saw the boy's fear trying to be useful. Rudd wanted a role. Men always did. If they had a role, they could pretend the world still had structure.

"Checking the perimeter," Andrew said. "Looking for the same raiders Dorsey thinks are out there."

Rudd nodded too fast. "Yes, sir."

Haines looked like he wanted to speak, then didn't. He turned away toward the mules, hands busying themselves at a harness buckle that did not need adjusting. Work inside work. The way a man hid.

Andrew found Elias where he'd left him, beneath the sagging canvas near the wheel. Kellan sat close by, shoulders rounded, eyes unfocused, as though the world were something he watched from behind glass. Elias's posture was rigid and upright, a defiance held together by muscle. When Andrew approached, Elias looked up with a coldness that made Andrew feel older than the war.

"You've been gone," Elias said.

Andrew crouched, bringing his voice low. "Not far."

Elias's eyes tracked him with the sharpness of a man looking for a lie's seam. "Doing what?"

Andrew heard the answer that would have been honest: building a place for him. Digging comfort into earth. Making a boundary that was only theater, but theater nonetheless.

Instead he said, "Planning."

Elias's mouth twisted. "Planning how to serve him?"

Andrew felt the accusation like a slap, because it was the same line that had formed in his own mind and refused to leave. He glanced at Kellan, at the way Kellan's stare slid away from both of them, and lowered his voice further.

"Not here," Andrew said.

Elias leaned forward, and his voice went tight and furious. "Everything is here," he hissed. "It's all here. You think you can keep it in one shed, one hole, one story you tell Dorsey? You're already building a world around it."

Andrew held his brother's gaze and forced his own face into stillness. "I'm building a world around you," he said. "So you stay alive long enough to leave this place."

Elias's nostrils flared. "Leave?" he repeated, as if the word offended him. "And you stay? You stay to manage it?"

Andrew did not answer, because the truth was too ugly to say aloud: that Ambrose had not told him to stay, but Andrew had already begun to act as though staying was inevitable. As though leaving required permission that no one had granted.

A shout rose near the barn doors. A man arguing with an orderly. A quick flare of panic in a voice that had been quiet too long. Andrew stood immediately, reflexes trained to motion, and looked toward the sound.

Captain Dorsey strode across the yard, coat buttoned wrong as if he'd dressed in the dark and couldn't afford to care. His face was hard, but his eyes kept flicking to the shadows between wagons. He stopped in front of Andrew.

"Mercer," Dorsey said. "Whitcomb wants you."

"Why," Andrew asked, and already knew the answer.

Dorsey's jaw flexed. "Because he's tired of writing fever on men who look like they've been poured out," he said. He lowered his voice. "Because he's talking about sending word up chain, and I don't think he's going to keep his mouth shut much longer."

Andrew felt the wound beneath his bandage sting, clean and sharp, like a reminder that mouths were dangerous and silence was currency.

"I'll speak to him," Andrew said.

Dorsey grabbed his sleeve briefly, fingers digging in. "This is turning into something I can't command," he muttered. "You understand me?"

Andrew looked at the captain's hand on his coat as if it were a symbol of how authority still tried to exist in the middle of collapse. "I understand," Andrew said. "Go back to your post."

Dorsey's eyes narrowed. For a heartbeat Andrew thought he might refuse the order on principle alone. Then Dorsey released his sleeve and walked away, shoulders tight, as if carrying his own shame.

The field surgeon's station was set up in a lean-to beside the barn, a crude table under canvas, lanterns hung from nails. The smell there was lye and old blood and damp straw. Whitcomb stood with his sleeves rolled to the elbow, hands stained despite repeated scrubbing. His face had the drained look of a man who had exhausted his disgust and been left with only anger.

On the table lay a body covered to the chin with a blanket. Only the lower face showed, lips slightly parted, skin drawn. Whitcomb's eyes went to Andrew at once.

"Lieutenant," Whitcomb said. He did not offer a salute. He looked past rank. "Tell me what's happening."

Andrew kept his voice controlled. "Men are being taken," he said, as if the phrasing could make it less monstrous. "In the night. On the road. In the barn."

Whitcomb made a sharp gesture toward the body. "This one wasn't taken far," he snapped. "He was found behind the latrine trench. No struggle. No mud on his knees. And this." He yanked the blanket back slightly, exposing the man's neck.

There was a mark. Not a slash the way a knife would make. Two narrow cuts, neat as if done with a fine instrument, and the surrounding skin looked strangely unbruised.

Whitcomb's voice dropped. "I've cut men open for years," he said. "I've seen what bayonets do. I've seen what rot does. This is neither. And he's empty." He tapped the man's chest with two fingers, a gesture that was almost tender and almost furious. "He's drained like a keg. And yet the wound is small."

Andrew felt his mouth go dry. The sweetness seemed to creep into the air even here, uninvited by memory.

Whitcomb stepped closer, eyes boring into Andrew. "Dorsey says raiders," he said. "You keep saying raiders. But you were at that estate, Mercer. You've seen something. I can see it in your face. So I'll ask you once, and I'd appreciate the courtesy of an answer before I start writing to Richmond like a madman."

Andrew held still. He could feel the camp beyond the canvas, the thin line of men listening even when they pretended not to. He could feel Elias somewhere behind him without needing to see. He could feel the way a rumor could become a stampede if it found the wrong mouth.

"What do you want from me," Andrew asked.

Whitcomb's expression tightened. "The truth," he said.

Andrew looked down at the body again. The man's lips were slightly blue. His eyes were closed, but Andrew could imagine them open, staring at rain, like the private in the mud. Another name that would become a line on paper.

Andrew made his decision with the cold, practiced part of himself that war had sharpened into a tool.

"You want something you can write down," Andrew said quietly. "Something you can put in a report and not be laughed at. You want raiders because raiders are a shape you can fight."

Whitcomb's eyes flashed. "Don't lecture me."

"I'm not," Andrew said. "I'm giving you what keeps men from firing into the dark."

Whitcomb stared, breathing hard through his nose. "So that's it," he said, voice harsh. "You won't say it aloud."

Andrew met his gaze. "I won't give it a parade," he said. "You will write anemia. You will write blood loss. You will write shock. You will write what a reader can accept without losing his mind."

Whitcomb's face went red with anger. "And when the reader asks why there's no wound to match the blood?"

Andrew's wound flared beneath the bandage as if it were laughing silently at the question. Andrew kept his face still.

"You write that rats got to him after death," Andrew said. "You write that the cut was larger before swelling went down. You write whatever you need to write to keep the camp from tearing itself apart."

Whitcomb looked at him a long moment. The lantern light made deep hollows in his cheeks.

"You're asking me to lie," Whitcomb said.

Andrew did not blink. "I'm asking you to practice," he replied.

The word hung there, ugly and precise. Andrew heard it and hated it because it sounded like Ambrose's voice, gentle with instruction. It makes you practiced.

Whitcomb's jaw worked. For a moment Andrew thought the surgeon might strike him, or shout, or do the righteous thing Elias still believed in: refuse.

Instead Whitcomb looked away from Andrew and back down at the dead man.

"Fine," Whitcomb said, the word bitter. "Fine. I'll write it. But you listen to me, Mercer." He leaned in, voice low and shaking with rage that had nowhere to go. "This doesn't make it true. It makes it survivable. For now."

Andrew nodded once. "That's all I'm trying to do," he lied, and felt the lie slide too easily into place.

As he stepped out from under the canvas, he saw how the camp watched him. Not with admiration. With dependence. As if he had become a hinge on which the door of their fear swung. Men wanted someone to tell them what could be endured.

Andrew walked back across the yard, and with every step he felt the shape of his new work assembling itself around him. It was not a single bargain sealed in a chapel. It was a series of small permissions. A note in a surgeon's hand. A sentence offered to a captain. A warning given to a boy like Rudd. Each one a thread, each one tightening until it became a rope.

He reached Elias again and found his brother watching him with a quiet horror that did not need words.

"What did he want," Elias asked softly, and his voice held the tired certainty of a man who already knew the answer.

Andrew looked past him toward the tree line, toward the unseen tobacco shed and its root pit waiting like an open mouth. He kept his own voice calm, because calm was what made lies believable.

"He wanted order," Andrew said.

Elias swallowed. "And what did you give him?"

Andrew felt the bandage against his ribs, the wound beneath it listening like a second ear.

"Not him," Andrew said, and heard how much of his soul he tried to pack into that single defense. "I didn't give him you."

Elias's eyes narrowed, wet with something that might have been grief and might have been rage.

"No," he whispered. "You gave him everyone else."

Andrew didn't answer, because the night had taught him an awful arithmetic: some truths could not be denied without becoming obscene.

He turned away from his brother and began issuing quiet instructions to Haines and Rudd about the watch, about keeping pairs, about keeping lanterns lit. Ordinary military orders dressed in new purpose. Not to repel an enemy. To shape a camp's behavior into something less edible.

And as he spoke, he realized the deepest part of the horror was not Ambrose's hunger.

It was how quickly Andrew Mercer could make himself believe that managing the hunger was the same as resisting it.

Andrew kept his voice low when he spoke to the men, but it carried anyway. It carried because they were listening with their bodies now, shoulders angled toward him, breath held whenever his tone shifted. Haines took the instructions without argument, jaw clenched, eyes refusing to meet Elias's. Rudd nodded too quickly, too eager to be told what to do so his hands would stop shaking. Even Captain Dorsey, passing at the edge of the lantern's reach, slowed as if he might catch a sentence and use it as proof that this was still a problem with edges.

Pairs. Light. No one wandering. No answering voices from the dark.

It was discipline on paper. In practice it was a choreography designed to make the camp less soft.

When the watch was set and the barn had settled back into its exhausted moan, Andrew stepped away from the wagons and walked toward the tree line.

He did not announce where he was going. He did not look back at Elias. He could feel his brother's stare under the canvas like a hand pressing between his shoulder blades, but looking back would have turned it into a conversation, and Andrew could not afford another conversation. Not with Elias. Not with himself.

The night air was wet and cold, but the fog had thinned enough to show the outlines of trunks. The lantern in his hand painted the world in small, wavering pieces. Each step pulled at the mud, as if the land wanted to keep him close. His wound gave its steady, clean sting beneath the bandage, neither worsening nor easing, only reminding him that his body had learned a new kind of attention.

Halfway to the creek the sweetness touched his throat.

Not strong. Just present, the way a familiar face could be recognized in a crowd before you knew why you'd looked.

Andrew stopped.

He listened, and the woods listened back. The creek ran somewhere ahead, dark and patient. A branch shifted in wind. An owl called once and then fell silent, as if remembering the rule about noise.

"Show yourself," Andrew said quietly, and hated the way the sentence sounded like permission.

Ambrose stepped from between two pines with the composure of a man arriving late to a meeting. He was not carrying a lantern. He did not need one. His coat looked dark and wet in the dimness, but the damp never seemed to settle on him the way it settled on ordinary men. His face was pale in the lantern's reach, expression mild, eyes the color of old bruises.

Andrew's grip tightened on the lantern handle until his knuckles stung. He did not draw his pistol. It would have been theater, and Ambrose had already proven what he did with theater.

"You walk alone," Ambrose observed. "I thought you were teaching them caution."

"I didn't bring them," Andrew said. "I came to speak."

Ambrose's mouth curved faintly. "Speak," he echoed. "As if that is a choice you are still afforded."

Andrew held himself steady. "The camp is on edge," he said. "Men are looking for a shape they can shoot. They'll do something foolish."

"Of course they will," Ambrose replied, as though discussing weather. "Foolishness is the only freedom most men have left."

Andrew swallowed against the sweetness. "If you keep feeding near the barn, you'll force them into panic. You'll force me into things I can't control."

Ambrose took one slow step closer, stopping just outside the lantern's brightest circle. The woods behind him looked deeper, as if his presence thickened the dark.

"Control," Ambrose murmured. "You still love that word."

Andrew felt his wound flare, quick and sharp, then settle. He ignored it. "I set up a place," he said.

Ambrose's eyes flicked, slight interest. "Did you?"

"A shed," Andrew continued. "Root pit under it. Away from the wounded. Away from the wagons. You can rest there. You can… stay there."

Ambrose looked pleased, not triumphant, simply satisfied, the way a teacher might look when a student finally stops pretending he hasn't understood the lesson. "You made it comfortable," Ambrose said.

"I made it distant," Andrew snapped, and then reined his voice back in. "I made it less dangerous for the camp."

Ambrose tilted his head. "For the camp," he repeated, as if tasting how Andrew wanted the sentence to be true.

Andrew breathed in through his nose, damp air and pine and sweetness. "If you take men, take them away from there," he said. "Not in the barn. Not where people will see too much."

Ambrose regarded him for a long moment, and Andrew had the sick sense that the creature was not weighing the request but enjoying the fact that Andrew had made it.

"You are learning," Ambrose said softly.

Andrew forced the next words out, because if he didn't speak them, they would rot in his mouth.

"You want me to arrange. You want me to make order. Fine. Tell me what order looks like to you."

Ambrose's smile deepened a fraction. "Honesty," he murmured. "That is progress."

He began to walk, not toward the camp, but alongside the creek's direction. Andrew did not want to follow and yet did. The lantern bobbed with his steps, casting quick shadows that looked like men darting away.

They walked in silence for several paces. Andrew's boots sank in damp earth. Ambrose's steps made almost no sound. The difference was obscene.

Finally Ambrose spoke, voice calm. "Order begins with stories," he said. "Not the grand ones men swear to in uniforms. The small ones. The ones that make absence tolerable."

Andrew stared ahead, jaw clenched. "Deserter," he said.

Ambrose gave a quiet, pleased breath that might have been laughter. "Yes. That is one. Deserter is a wonderful coffin. It requires no body and invites no search."

Andrew felt something cold move through him. "And if it's not a soldier," he asked. "If it's a farmer. A woman."

Ambrose glanced at him, amused by the practicality. "You are thinking ahead," he said. "Good. For civilians you have more delicate tools. Disease. Misadventure. River drownings. Men are always so ready to believe the world is careless."

Andrew's stomach tightened. Images rose unbidden: the groundskeeper's warning, the shallow graves under orchard trees, the way human hands had learned to bury what they could not kill. "You've done this before," Andrew said.

Ambrose's gaze drifted to the creek, as if watching it carry years downstream. "Many times," he replied. "Empires call their dead by different names, but the dead are always useful. Plague taught me that. War taught me that. Famine taught me that. Collapse is an open pantry."

Andrew's wound stung again, almost in agreement. He hated it.

"What do you want from me, exactly?" Andrew asked. "Beyond lies and distance."

Ambrose stopped. In the lantern light his face looked almost carved, elegant even in ruin. He held Andrew with his eyes, and for a moment Andrew felt the chapel again: old prayers dried into wood, the pressure in the air when Ambrose chose to tighten it.

"I want you to stop pretending you are bargaining as an enemy," Ambrose said. "Enemies believe they will win. You are not winning. You are managing."

Andrew kept his voice hard. "So you want obedience."

Ambrose's expression softened with something like indulgence. "I want competence," he corrected. "Obedience is for dogs and saints. You are neither."

Andrew felt heat rise in his throat. "Keep my brother out of your mouth," he said.

Ambrose's eyes brightened with quiet amusement. "There it is," he murmured. "The tether. The thing you pretend is virtue. It is not virtue, Lieutenant Mercer. It is the simplest form of self-preservation. You care for him because he makes you feel like you were not made entirely from war."

Andrew could not deny it, and the inability felt like a humiliation.

Ambrose continued, voice still gentle. "Do you know why I spoke to you at all?" he asked. "It was not because you are brave. Brave men are boring. They die quickly, eager to prove something to a God who does not answer."

Andrew stared, lantern light shaking. "Then why."

Ambrose's gaze slid over him, appraising, intimate. "Because you notice structure," he said. "You walk into a house and see the architecture of fear. You walk into chaos and begin arranging it without being told. Even now you issue orders to keep people in pairs, to keep lanterns lit, to keep noise at a certain pitch. You are a man who builds fences in his mind."

Andrew's mouth went dry. He thought of the tobacco shed, the chain around the latch, the padlock meant for flour. The obscene familiarity of the work.

Ambrose took a half-step closer, and the sweetness thickened slightly, as if the night leaned in with him. "You will learn which men can be made to disappear quietly," he said. "Which men will cause questions. Which men have wives who will come looking and which men will be written off by their own officers with relief."

Andrew's pulse beat hard. "I won't choose victims for you."

Ambrose's smile did not change. "You already have," he said softly. "Every time you keep your brother near light. Every time you tell a boy like Rudd not to see. Every time you tell a surgeon to write anemia instead of truth. You are choosing, Lieutenant. You simply prefer not to name it."

Andrew's wound flared sharp enough that he inhaled too fast. He forced his breath back under control.

Ambrose watched the small crack in Andrew's composure with quiet pleasure, then looked away as if bored by pain. "There are rules," he added, as if offering comfort. "Even for me. I do not feed well on panic. Panic spoils the blood. It makes the body frantic. The taste turns thin."

Andrew stared, sickened despite himself by the casualness. "So you prefer calm," he said.

"I prefer consent," Ambrose replied, and his eyes turned toward Andrew again. "Not always spoken. Not always understood by the giver. But consent nonetheless. A man who has already surrendered will offer himself without needing to be dragged."

Andrew felt the words settle into his mind like ash. Consent. Surrender. The slow conversion of fear into cooperation.

Ambrose's voice softened. "This is why your shed pleases me," he said. "Not the pit. The intention. You are beginning to anticipate my needs. You are beginning to think as a keeper."

Andrew tasted iron, though his mouth was not bleeding. "And if I refuse," he said. "If I decide to stop arranging."

Ambrose regarded him with calm patience. "Then you will be replaced," he said simply. "That is what you do not understand about your position. It is not unique. It only feels special because you are in it."

The priest's warning rose in Andrew's mind with bitter clarity: Do not let him make you feel special.

Andrew stared into Ambrose's eyes, and for a moment he saw the long years inside them, the practiced movements through catastrophe, the way war and plague and hunger were not threats to this thing but seasons.

"What do you want tonight," Andrew asked, voice low. "What is the lesson now."

Ambrose's smile returned, small and satisfied. "Tonight," he said, "you will walk back to your camp and you will sleep."

Andrew stiffened. "Sleep," he repeated, not believing it.

"Yes," Ambrose said. "Because you are exhausted, and exhausted men make mistakes. Mistakes make noise. Noise is inconvenient." His gaze lingered on Andrew's face, on the tightness around his eyes. "And because I want you to learn something important about your new work."

Andrew waited, lantern trembling slightly with the effort of staying still.

Ambrose's tone remained conversational. "You do not need to see what I do in order to be responsible for it," he said. "Responsibility is not a matter of witnessing. It is a matter of arrangement."

Andrew felt cold spread under his ribs. "You're going to take someone anyway," he said.

Ambrose's eyes flicked with faint approval, as if Andrew had finally stated an obvious fact. "Of course," he replied. "But not from the barn. Not from your brother. Not from where your captain will feel compelled to make speeches."

Andrew's mouth tightened. "From where, then."

Ambrose leaned closer just enough that the sweetness became intimate, like breath shared between mouths. "From the road," he said. "A man already leaving. A man who believes he is unnoticed. A man you will not need to name."

Andrew's hands clenched around the lantern. He could picture it already: a soldier stepping out to relieve himself, a sentry sent to check a noise, someone drifting toward the dark to have one private minute. The camp was full of such men.

Ambrose straightened again, as if satisfied the message had landed. "Go," he said gently. "Return to your brother. Continue pretending you are doing this for him alone."

Andrew's throat tightened. "If you touch Elias—"

Ambrose's expression remained mild. "If I touch him," he said, "it will be because you have decided, in some small way, that it is worth the cost. That is what you will learn, Lieutenant Mercer. Not that I can take what I want."

He began to step backward into the trees, the dark accepting him like a familiar room.

"You will learn," Ambrose finished softly, "that you are the one who will start handing things over."

Then he was gone, not with a flourish, not with a rush of wind, simply absent, leaving only the thin sweetness hanging in the damp air like the last trace of a voice after a door closes.

Andrew stood by the creek until the lantern's flame steadied. His wound kept its clean, watchful ache. He looked back toward the camp's distant glow and understood the shape of the instruction with a nausea that had nothing to do with blood.

Ambrose had not taught him how to hunt.

He had taught him how to sleep while the hunger moved.

Andrew turned and walked back to the wagons, each step heavy with the knowledge that exhaustion would come, and when it did, it would not feel like rest.

It would feel like practice.

Chapter 12

Appomattox Night

Andrew reached the edge of the yard and slowed before stepping fully into lantern light, as if the simple act of being seen might make him accountable in a way darkness did not. The camp looked the same at first glance: wagons hunched in mud, the barn a darker block against darker trees, lanterns trembling on nails. But the air had changed. Not the weather. The human air.

Men no longer moved with the cranky rhythm of soldiers enduring another night. They moved like people carrying an ending in their mouths.

Near the barn, someone was arguing again, voices low and urgent, and Andrew heard the words that had been circling for weeks finally landing in place. “Lee’s done,” one man said. “He’s done or near enough.”

Another voice answered, sharp with denial and fear braided together. “You don’t know that.”

"I know what I saw," the first insisted. "Couriers riding like the devil's behind them. Officers burning papers. You don't ride like that unless the world's breaking."

Andrew walked past without turning his head. He could feel eyes tracking him, could feel the camp's dependence trying to fasten itself to his shoulders again. He refused it by refusing to look. The war had taught him that attention could be a weapon. Ambrose had taught him it could be a leash.

Dorsey was near the surgeon's lean-to, coat still buttoned wrong, face raw from a night without sleep. He spotted Andrew and started toward him, then checked himself as if remembering rank and deciding it no longer mattered.

"You've been out," Dorsey said. It wasn't a question.

Andrew stopped a few paces from him. "Checking the line."

Dorsey's eyes flicked toward the tree line, then back, as if expecting to see something pale and composed standing between the trunks. "We had a rider," he said. "Came through an hour ago, headed north. Didn't stop long. Said there's talk Lee's meeting Grant."

Andrew felt the words hit his chest with a dull weight. He had known it was coming. He'd watched the Confederacy thin and fray in every march, every supply run that returned lighter, every farm field stripped to ribs. Still, hearing the shape of the end spoken aloud made something inside him shift, like a foundation giving way.

"Appomattox?" Andrew asked, and hated that he knew the name already. Rumors carried geography like a sickness.

Dorsey nodded. "Maybe. Could be somewhere else. But they're saying it plain now. They're saying surrender."

Behind Dorsey, Whitcomb stood under the canvas, sleeves rolled, hands moving by habit over instruments he could no longer keep clean. The surgeon's eyes met Andrew's and held, not accusing, not pleading, only weary with the knowledge that lies were becoming harder to write when the whole cause was ending.

Andrew looked past the lean-to toward the barn. The wounded men inside would not be carried far if the army broke. They would be left. They would be traded, abandoned, pitied, or shot. The war had always eaten men; now it was preparing to spit them out.

Dorsey lowered his voice. "What am I supposed to do with that, Mercer?" he asked. "Half my detail's talking about slipping off tonight. The other half's talking about dying rather than laying down arms. I've got men looking at me like I'm supposed to hand them a future."

Andrew could have offered the old language: duty, honor, orders. It felt dead in his mouth. He thought of Ambrose by the creek, speaking of stories that made absence tolerable. The Confederacy had been a story too. A grand one, dressed in uniforms and rhetoric, used to make slaughter feel like purpose. Now the story was collapsing, and men were scrambling for smaller ones to hide inside.

"Keep them here until morning," Andrew said finally. "Keep the lanterns lit. Keep them in pairs. No wandering. No drinking."

Dorsey's mouth tightened at the familiar orders. "And after morning?"

Andrew looked at the muddy ground, at boot prints layered over boot prints like years. "After morning," he said carefully, "we see what's left to obey."

Dorsey stared at him as if trying to decide whether that was wisdom or mutiny. Then he gave a short, bitter nod and walked away, already shouldering the work of pretending command still existed.

Andrew turned toward the supply wagon and found Elias awake under the sagging canvas, sitting upright as if sleep were a luxury he refused on principle. Kellan was nearby, chin on his knees, staring at nothing. Haines stood at the wagon tongue, hands busy, eyes too alert.

Elias watched Andrew approach with the steady coldness that had settled into him since the chapel. His face looked thinner, not from hunger, but from the way grief and rage carved a man from the inside.

"They're saying surrender," Elias said before Andrew could speak. His voice was flat, as if he'd scraped emotion out of it to keep himself from shaking.

Andrew nodded once. "Yes."

Elias's gaze sharpened. "And what does that mean for him?"

Andrew understood at once. Not the Confederacy. Not their family. Him, the thing moving through collapse like it belonged to him. Ambrose.

"It means cover," Andrew said. "It means roads full of men without papers. Refugees. Paroled soldiers. People walking away from uniforms and becoming nobody. It means confusion big enough to hide anything."

Elias's mouth twisted. "So it's what he wants."

Andrew didn't answer because the answer was yes, and saying it aloud felt like inviting it.

Haines stepped closer, voice low. "Lieutenant," he said, and nodded toward the far end of the yard. "Rudd's got something."

Rudd stood near a stack of crates, hat in his hands, eyes bright with fear. When Andrew reached him, the boy swallowed hard and leaned in.

"I heard them talking," Rudd whispered. "Two men from Dorsey's. They're leaving tonight. Said there's no point staying. Said they'd rather take their chances on the road than wait to be captured."

Andrew's wound gave its small, clean sting beneath the bandage. He felt, with sick immediacy, how neatly that fit into Ambrose's promise by the creek. A man already leaving. A man who believes he is unnoticed. A man you will not need to name.

Andrew kept his face still. "Who?"

Rudd hesitated, then said, "Fowler and Jakes. They've been talking about it for days."

Andrew nodded once. Fowler and Jakes. Names he could put in a report if he needed. Names that could be turned into deserter and then buried under the larger disaster of surrender.

Elias had been listening, eyes narrowing. "Don't," he said quietly, and there was a tremor in the word despite his effort to keep it steady.

Andrew looked at him. The lantern light made Elias's face look both younger and older, the way firelight could make a man into a ghost of himself.

"What do you think I'm going to do?" Andrew asked.

Elias's jaw tightened. "I think you're going to let it happen," he said. "And then you're going to tell yourself it was better than someone else."

Andrew's throat tightened. He could not deny it without lying. He could not admit it without breaking whatever still held Elias near him.

Haines shifted, uncomfortable, eyes flicking toward the tree line as if the woods were listening. "If them boys leave," Haines muttered, "they'll get caught anyway. Patrols on the roads. Yankees. Guerrillas. Could be anyone."

Elias's gaze snapped to him. "So that makes it right?"

Haines flinched, anger flashing. "It makes it true," he hissed, then bit the rest back as if he'd almost said too much. He looked at Andrew instead, eyes hard. "Sir. We got men about to scatter. If you're going to keep order, you better do it now."

Order. The word felt like ash on the tongue. Andrew had spent the war obeying a structure that was dissolving, and now he was being asked to build a smaller one around a hunger that did not dissolve at all.

Across the yard, two soldiers moved toward the wagon line with careful casualness, packs slung, heads down. Fowler and Jakes, trying to become part of the dark before anyone could stop them. They looked like men doing something shameful and necessary. Their bodies held the particular tension of deserters, the constant readiness to run.

Andrew watched them and felt the terrible clarity of arithmetic. If they left, they would be vulnerable. If they stayed, they might still vanish, but the vanishing would be noticed, would curdle the camp into panic. The war's collapse made every choice uglier and easier at the same time.

Elias stepped closer to Andrew, voice low enough that only he could hear. "If you've got any part of yourself left that isn't his," Elias said, "prove it now."

Andrew looked at his brother and felt the weight of the words Ambrose had left him with: You do not need to see what I do in order to be responsible for it.

Andrew had thought responsibility required action. He was learning that sometimes it required refusal, and refusal was something he had almost forgotten how to do.

He started toward the two deserters.

Not running. Running would be theater. He walked with the calm of an officer going to correct a simple breach of discipline, as if discipline still mattered.

Fowler saw him first and froze. Jakes's hand went to his pack strap like a man reaching for a weapon he did not have.

"Lieutenant," Fowler said, voice too polite, too quick.

Andrew stopped a few feet from them. The lantern light didn't reach here well; their faces were half made of shadow. "Where are you going?" Andrew asked, and kept his tone mild, almost bored.

Jakes swallowed. "Just… taking a piss, sir."

Andrew held the lie in his gaze until it began to sweat. "With your packs on," he said.

Neither man answered.

Andrew glanced past them at the road, at the dark beyond the wagons, at the woods that waited without impatience. He could almost taste sweetness, faint but present, like rot masked by rain.

"You leave now," Andrew said quietly, "and you won't make it a mile. Not because of Yankees. Because the roads are full of men who'll kill you for boots, and because the woods are full of things you don't understand."

Fowler's eyes widened slightly, the expression of a man hearing a rumor he'd tried not to believe. "What are you talking about?" he whispered.

Andrew leaned in just enough to make them feel the weight of his attention. "I'm talking about the fact that you are safer in light," he said. "And I'm telling you this once. Put your packs back. Sit where people can see you. If you need to walk, you walk with two men and a lantern."

Jakes stared, breathing fast. "Sir," he began, and then stopped, as if the rest of the sentence was, Are you threatening us or warning us?

Andrew straightened. "Go," he said.

They hesitated one more heartbeat, then turned back toward the wagons with stiff, quick steps, shame and relief tangled together. Andrew watched them until they disappeared into lantern reach.

Behind him, he felt Elias's stare like a blade between the shoulder blades. When Andrew turned back, Elias was still under the canvas, still rigid, but his expression had shifted into something uncertain and raw.

"You stopped them," Elias said.

Andrew nodded once. His wound stung as if in protest.

Elias's voice tightened. "Why?"

Andrew looked toward the tree line, toward the darkness where Ambrose moved without being seen, toward the nation's unraveling that made every man a potential disappearance. He thought of surrender again, not as a political event, but as a human habit. Men laid down arms. Men laid down names. Men laid down whatever they could not carry.

"I don't know," Andrew said, and the honesty surprised him. He swallowed and forced the rest out. "Maybe because if everything collapses at once, there's nothing left to hold him back. Not even pretense."

Elias stared at him as if trying to find the trick. "So you're still thinking about managing him," he said, bitter.

Andrew felt the truth twist in him. Yes. Always. But there was another truth too, smaller, painful, and stubborn.

"I'm thinking about what happens when no one is watching," Andrew said quietly. "When there's no command. No ranks. No ledgers. No reports. Just hunger and roads full of bodies. That's not order. That's a feeding ground."

Elias's mouth tightened. "And you think you can stop it."

Andrew looked at his brother's face, at the thin line of faith still trying to exist in him. "No," Andrew said. "I think I can fail slower than the world is failing."

The lanterns hissed in damp air. Somewhere near the barn a man coughed and could not stop. The camp's quiet felt like the held breath before a verdict.

Beyond the yard, the Confederacy was folding in on itself, papers burning, officers choosing which truths to carry into surrender. Men who had marched for years were preparing to become strangers overnight.

And in the dark beyond their lanterns, something ancient and patient was preparing to travel with the new chaos, pleased by the shape of the ending.

Andrew stood in the mud and understood that collapse did not mean the end of war.

It only meant the end of rules that had pretended war could be contained.

Andrew did not sleep.

He lay beneath the sagging canvas of the supply wagon with his coat folded under his head, eyes open to the dim yellow sway of lantern light through the cracks. Around him the camp made its small, exhausted noises: a mule stamping, a man coughing until his breath turned ragged, the barn settling with the wooden sigh of an old thing under too much suffering. Somewhere close, Elias shifted once and went still again, the kind of stillness that was not rest but vigilance sharpened into punishment.

Andrew's wound kept its clean, steady ache beneath the bandage. Not throbbing. Listening.

He tried to count the ways out.

If Lee surrendered, the men here would scatter. Some would be paroled. Some would be taken. Some would simply vanish into the woods and become their own small wars. The records would become smoke or mud, and the difference between a missing man and a dead man would be whatever story someone was willing to tell.

That was the opening Ambrose wanted. Not just blood. Not just fear. Transition.

Andrew turned his head slightly and saw Elias watching him from a few feet away, eyes reflecting lantern light like wet stones.

"You're thinking again," Elias said. His voice was low, flat, stripped down to accusation.

Andrew did not pretend otherwise. "I'm planning."

Elias's mouth tightened. "Planning what. Another lie for Whitcomb? Another shed? Another man you tell yourself won't be missed?"

Andrew sat up slowly, careful not to wake Kellan, who lay curled with his back to the wheel like a dog that had learned not to expect gentleness. Haines stood at the wagon tongue, not on watch officially, just present the way a man stayed near the only officer who seemed to understand the shape of the dark.

Andrew's gaze went past them to the barn, to the line of lanterns, to the road disappearing into fog.

"There's a church," Andrew said.

Haines's eyes narrowed. "The one you found him in?"

"No. Not that," Andrew answered. That ruined chapel felt spoiled now, a place where prayer had been used as scenery for negotiation. “Two miles east. Small. White boards. Graveyard behind it. I passed it last month on patrol.”

Elias’s expression did not change. “So.”

“So it’s consecrated ground,” Andrew said. The words tasted strange because he no longer had the priest’s beads, no length of chain from a chapel storehouse to pretend he carried sanctity in his pocket. He had nothing but memory and a plan that wanted to be belief. “If anything can slow him, it’ll be there. If anything can hold him long enough for daylight to matter, it’ll be there.”

Haines’s jaw flexed. “Daylight didn’t matter in the barn,” he muttered.

Andrew’s eyes flicked to him. “He chose not to feed in front of a crowd,” Andrew said. “That’s different.”

Elias gave a short, bitter breath. “You’re still bargaining with his habits,” he said. “Even when you call it a trap.”

Andrew leaned closer, lowering his voice so it would not carry. “You want me to take a clean shot at him,” Andrew said. “You want a moment where a man does the right thing and it ends. That moment doesn’t exist.”

Elias's eyes flashed. "Then make one," he hissed. "For once in your life, stop talking like it's weather."

Andrew felt the flare of anger and something worse behind it: a small, hidden hope that Elias might be right. That there could still be a single decisive act that restored the world to its proper shape.

He looked at Haines. "Get Rudd," Andrew said. "Quietly."

Haines hesitated. "The boy?"

"He's quick and he can carry," Andrew replied. "And he hasn't started drinking yet."

Haines's mouth twitched without humor, then he nodded and moved away into the lantern haze.

Elias stood, shoulders rigid. "You're involving him now," he said. "You said you wouldn't."

Andrew rose too. He felt suddenly older than his rank. "I'm involving whoever keeps us alive long enough to reach morning," Andrew said. "You want to argue, argue after."

Elias stared at him, then looked away, jaw working. When he spoke again his voice was quieter, rougher. "If you're going to do it," Elias said, "do it. Don't talk yourself into hesitation when it matters."

Andrew held that sentence in his chest like a weight. He nodded once.

They moved within the hour, before the night could thin toward false dawn.

Andrew took Haines, Rudd, and Elias. He told Dorsey only that he was checking the road east for any word of the surrender, that he would return before first light. Dorsey looked like he wanted to protest, then saw Elias at Andrew's side and swallowed whatever question had formed. The captain's eyes were too tired to keep fighting mysteries.

Rudd carried a lantern wrapped with cloth to dim its reach. Haines carried rope and two lengths of chain scavenged from harness and wagon hardware. Andrew carried oil in a jug and two powder tins tucked into a sack. Elias carried nothing but a pistol he did not trust and a hate that kept him upright.

They walked rather than rode. Hooves announced men in a way boots did not, and Andrew did not want to announce them to the woods.

Fog lay in strips between the trees. The creek's sound followed them like a low voice. Andrew kept the church in his mind by a series of remembered turns. At times he doubted himself and then, each time, his wound gave that clean, directional sting, as if his body knew where it was going even if his mind wanted to drift.

Rudd whispered once, unable to hold it in. "Sir," he said, "is he following?"

Andrew did not answer at first. He tasted sweetness on the damp air, faint but present, like rot behind a closed door.

"Yes," Andrew said finally. "Or he's letting us think he is."

That did not comfort the boy. Rudd's lantern hand shook harder, and Haines reached over once to steady it without speaking, an act of rough mercy.

The church emerged out of fog as a pale shape, boards washed by moonlight. It was smaller than Andrew remembered, or perhaps everything looked smaller when it was asked to do something impossible. A simple steeple, crooked with age. A single door. Two windows on either side, dark as blind eyes.

Behind it the graveyard rose in a low slope, stones leaning, some half sunk. The ground there looked darker, soaked with years.

Elias stopped at the edge of the yard. His breath came out in a visible plume. "This is it," he said.

Andrew nodded. His throat tightened with the familiar sense of arriving somewhere expected. He motioned them forward.

They did not enter the church. Andrew did not want walls. Walls created corners, and corners belonged to Ambrose. He wanted open ground, the graveyard slope behind them, the road in front, and the sky above that would, eventually, turn gray.

He chose a place between two large oaks near the yard's edge where the grass had been worn thin by feet. There the headstones were sparse, as if the dead preferred distance too.

"Here," Andrew said.

Haines moved immediately, hands practical. He looped chain around one oak and fed the free end toward Andrew. Rudd set the lantern down, crouching as if making himself small would keep him from being noticed. Elias stood rigid, scanning the fog, pistol in his hand.

Andrew poured oil in a rough arc across the grass, then in two lines leading toward the trees. He set kindling along the oil trails, rags and splintered boards from a broken fence near the church. He took one powder tin and wedged it into a shallow depression near the base of a headstone, then scattered loose dirt over it. Not enough to hide it well, but enough to slow its burn.

"What's the idea," Haines asked, voice low.

Andrew kept his eyes on his hands. "He steps where I tell him," Andrew said. "He crosses the oil. He comes between the trees. We pull the chain around him, pin him long enough to light the oil. If he tries to move back, the powder goes. If he moves forward, fire. If he stays, daylight."

Rudd swallowed audibly. "And if he doesn't step where you tell him?" the boy whispered.

Andrew did not answer, because the honest answer was: then nothing here is anything but theater.

Elias spoke instead, voice tight. "He will," he said. "Because he likes watching you try."

Andrew looked at his brother. Elias's eyes were fixed on the fog, not on Andrew, as if looking at Andrew would invite pity he refused to accept.

Andrew finished the last preparations. He took the rope from Haines and looped it once through the chain links, creating something that could be pulled and tightened fast. A crude snare, made for a man, not for what Ambrose was. But they had no better tools.

Then they waited.

The graveyard was quiet in the way the orchard had been quiet, but not identical. Here there were insects, faint and stubborn, and somewhere an owl called again, as if daring the night to disagree. The air felt colder over the stones.

Andrew listened for the sweetness. He felt the wound listening too, the cut beneath his bandage tuned like an ear.

“Do you hear that,” Rudd whispered.

Andrew heard it: footsteps in wet grass, unhurried, coming up the road as if a man had every right to be there.

Ambrose emerged from fog at the yard gate with a composure so complete it made the night look staged around him. His coat was dark, his hair slicked back, his face pale as marrow. He took in the church, the trees, the lantern glow, the four men standing as if they believed in themselves.

His gaze lingered on Elias, and Elias’s grip tightened on the pistol. Andrew saw Elias’s knuckles whiten.

Ambrose smiled faintly. “A graveyard,” he said, voice warm with amusement. “How thoughtful.”

Andrew stepped forward one pace, keeping his voice steady. “You follow collapse,” Andrew said. “You like endings. So come stand where endings are kept.”

Ambrose's eyes returned to Andrew. "You want me in your circle," he murmured. "So the sun can do your work."

Andrew felt the sting under his bandage sharpen, quick as a blade. He ignored it. "Come closer," Andrew said.

Ambrose began to walk, not hurried, not cautious, as if caution would insult him. He stepped over the yard's worn threshold and onto the grass, shoes dark with damp. He did not glance down at the oil. If he noticed it he gave no sign. His attention remained on Andrew, intimate and patient.

As Ambrose approached the space between the oaks, Andrew lifted his hand slightly behind his back, the signal to Haines and Elias to be ready to pull the chain.

Elias moved first, a fraction too eager. His pistol came up.

"Now," Elias said, voice cracking.

Ambrose's eyes flicked to him, and for an instant the air tightened. Elias's arm jerked as if pushed by an invisible hand. The pistol's barrel swung off target. Elias gasped, staggered one step, fighting a pressure that was not quite physical and yet left him trembling.

Haines cursed under his breath, took up slack on the rope, ready to yank.

Andrew had Ambrose almost where he wanted him. Another step and the chain could be pulled tight around the creature's midsection, pinning him between the oaks like an animal in a trap. Another step and Andrew could throw the lantern onto the oil. Another step and he could light a match with fingers that did not shake and watch flame do what flame was meant to do.

Ambrose looked at Andrew as if hearing his thoughts. "Do it," Ambrose said softly, and there was something almost tender in the invitation. "Make your last beautiful gesture."

Andrew's hand clenched.

He saw, in a flash that was too vivid to be imagination, what would happen after. The fire. The smoke. The screaming if the trap failed. Elias too close, Haines too close, Rudd too frightened to move fast enough. Andrew saw the camp beyond the fog, the wounded men, the chaos of surrender spilling down every road. He saw Ambrose stepping through flame again, laughing softly, and then turning his attention, finally, fully, to Elias.

Andrew hesitated.

It was only a heartbeat. Only the smallest pause. But it was the pause of a man who had learned the cost of decisive acts and had begun to fear not death, but consequence.

Ambrose stopped just short of the gap between the oaks, as if he had felt the hesitation like a change in weather.

His smile deepened.

"There," Ambrose murmured, and the pleasure in his voice made Andrew's stomach turn. "That is the truth of you."

Andrew forced himself to move, but the moment was already spoiled. Haines yanked the rope anyway, chain scraping bark. It snapped across the space like a striking snake, but Ambrose was no longer where it needed to be. He shifted with a grace too quick to track, not a run, not a leap, simply elsewhere by the width of a man's shoulders.

The chain slammed into empty air and dropped heavy into wet grass.

Rudd made a small, broken sound.

Elias surged forward with a strangled shout, trying to reclaim his arm, trying to fire, trying to be the righteous man Andrew no longer knew how to be. Ambrose turned his head slightly toward him, and Elias froze mid-step, breath caught, eyes wide with helpless fury.

Andrew stood in the graveyard with oil on the grass and powder under dirt, holding a lantern that suddenly felt like a child's toy. His wound burned bright beneath the bandage, a clean line of pain that felt like a brand.

Ambrose's gaze settled on him again, calm and pleased.

"You brought me to holy ground," Ambrose said, voice low. "And still, you could not commit."

Andrew's mouth went dry. "I can," he said, but he heard the lie in it, thin and panicked.

Ambrose's smile softened, almost kind. "No," he replied. "Not anymore. Not when the act might leave you alone with yourself afterward."

The fog pressed in around the church and the leaning stones. Somewhere in the east, beyond cloud, the sky was beginning its slow shift toward gray.

Andrew felt the dawn approaching like a promise he could no longer trust.

And in that approaching light, he understood with sick certainty that the trap had not failed because Ambrose could not be caught.

It had failed because Andrew Mercer, in the crucial instant, had chosen not to risk a world without Ambrose in it.

Elias did not unfreeze until Ambrose allowed it.

The release came without spectacle. One moment Elias stood locked mid-stride, pistol raised in a posture that wanted to become action; the next his arm dropped as if the joints had suddenly remembered fatigue. He staggered, catching himself on a leaning headstone. His breath came in ragged pulls, each inhale loud in the graveyard quiet.

Rudd's lantern trembled on the grass where he'd set it. A thin ribbon of oil shone faintly, black and wet, tracing Andrew's intentions in the dim light. The chain lay slack between the oaks, heavy as a fallen sentence.

Ambrose watched them as the sky softened by degrees from ink to bruised gray. He looked almost serene in the half-light, his ruined coat hanging straight, his pale face untroubled by cold or damp or consecration. The church behind him was a simple shape, white boards and dark windows, and for a sick instant it looked like a stage built for him alone.

Andrew kept the lantern in his hand because letting it go felt like admitting something. Not defeat. Something worse: that he no longer knew what it meant to fight.

"You arranged all this," Ambrose said, voice gentle with approval. "The oil. The chain. The powder. You even chose a place where men like you believe rules still exist."

Andrew did not answer. His mouth tasted of damp grass and something metallic that had no source except his own body.

Ambrose's gaze shifted to Elias, lingering as if savoring a future. Elias's grip tightened on the pistol again, but he did not raise it. His eyes were wet with rage, and the rage had nowhere to go.

"You see?" Ambrose murmured, as if speaking to Elias about Andrew, or to Andrew about Elias. "He wanted to do it. He wanted to be the clean knife in the story. But he stopped himself."

Elias's voice came out hoarse. "Shut up."

Ambrose smiled faintly. "Or what?" he asked, polite as ever.

Elias took a step, then halted as if remembering the invisible hand. He turned that helpless fury on Andrew instead, the way a man struck the nearest solid thing when the true enemy was smoke.

"You did that," Elias said, and the accusation was not about the trap alone. It was about every small surrender that had led them here. "You stopped."

Andrew kept his eyes on Ambrose. He could not bear to look at his brother's face and see what the hesitation had cost in trust. He spoke carefully, as if each word might be used as a knot. "I didn't know if it would hold," he said.

Ambrose's head tilted. "No," he corrected softly. "You didn't know what you would be if it succeeded."

The words slid into Andrew with an intimacy that made his skin go cold. He felt the truth of them, and worse, he felt how long the truth had been taking shape.

He had been moving toward this moment for weeks, perhaps longer, since the first locked cellar rumor had lodged in his mind like a thorn. He had told himself it was duty. Protection. Strategy. But he remembered the instant in the graveyard when the chain was about to tighten and the lantern was about to become fire, and he had seen a world without Ambrose in it.

The emptiness of that imagined world had frightened him.

Not because Ambrose was comforting. Because Ambrose had given his days a shape. A problem with a name. A purpose that could be pursued even while the Confederacy itself dissolved into mud and smoke.

Andrew's wound burned under the bandage, clean and bright, as if his body agreed with Ambrose's diagnosis. He drew a slow breath, forcing it into control. "What do you want," he asked. "Now."

Ambrose's eyes softened by a fraction, the way a man's eyes softened when he saw a tool finally accept its use. "You will go back," he said. "You will gather your camp and prepare them for surrender, or flight, or whatever form the ending takes. You will do what you have always done: you will make the chaos look orderly enough that men don't begin biting one another."

Andrew felt Rudd's stare on him, wide and terrified. The boy had come here expecting a victory. Now he looked like a child watching adults invent a new kind of sin.

"And you," Andrew said, voice low, "what do you do while we fold?"

Ambrose glanced toward the church, then the graveyard slope, then the road dissolving into fog. "I move," he said simply. "Endings are doorways. You would be astonished how many places open when men start dropping their names."

Elias's laugh came out broken. "He's telling you," he said to Andrew. "He's telling you to help him."

Andrew's jaw tightened. He wanted to deny it. He wanted to tell Elias there was still a plan, still a line he would not cross. But the denial felt theatrical, and Ambrose had no patience for theater he did not direct.

Ambrose stepped closer, not into the oil trail, not into the space where the chain could have caught him, but near enough that his presence thickened the air. The sweetness rose, faint and rotten-sweet, and Andrew's stomach turned with it.

"You are exhausted," Ambrose said. "Not just from marching. From pretending. From holding yourself together with rules that no longer apply."

Andrew held still. The lantern shook slightly in his grip. He steadied it.

Ambrose's gaze dipped, briefly, to Andrew's bandaged side. The look was almost intimate, like a physician's. "That wound listens," he murmured. "It has been listening since I gave it to you."

Andrew's throat tightened. He remembered the flare when he'd handed over the priest's beads and chain in the ruined chapel. The way his body had reacted like a signature being written in pain.

"What are you," Andrew asked, and hated the question because it sounded like fear looking for vocabulary.

Ambrose's smile returned, small and old. "I am hungry," he said, and made it sound like a fact of nature. "But hunger is only the beginning. What matters is continuity. What matters is that I do not starve when the world decides it is civilized again."

The eastern sky was lighter now, a thin bruise turning to gray. The first hints of dawn made the church boards look less like a stage and more like the simple building it was. In the growing light, Andrew saw how crude his trap truly had been. Oil and chain. A child's net thrown at a storm.

Rudd swallowed audibly. "Sir," he whispered, and his voice shook. "Can we go?"

Andrew did not answer him immediately. His eyes stayed on Ambrose, because he felt, with sick clarity, that this was the moment that would be remembered. Not because blood was spilled. Because something was decided without being spoken aloud.

Ambrose seemed to read it. He stepped back half a pace, granting Andrew the illusion of space. "I will not take your brother," he said conversationally, and the casualness of the promise made Andrew want to retch. "Not today. The day is already busy."

Elias's eyes flashed. "Stop talking like you're doing him favors."

Ambrose's gaze flicked to Elias, and the air tightened just enough to make Elias's breath hitch again. Not a full freezing. A reminder. Elias flinched and held himself rigid, refusing to bend more than he had to.

Ambrose looked back to Andrew. "You see?" he said softly. "He is brave in the way brave men always are. He believes anger is a shield. He believes defiance is a weapon. Those beliefs will get him killed one day if you do not teach him a different kind of survival."

Elias's voice went thin with disgust. "Don't you dare."

Andrew spoke before Elias could lunge into another lesson. "We're leaving," he said, and made it an order, because orders were the last form of structure he could still reliably conjure.

Haines moved first, practical and silent. He grabbed the slack chain and began to coil it with stiff hands. His face was gray in the new light, jaw clenched. He did not look at Ambrose. It was the only defiance he could afford: denying the creature attention.

Rudd snatched up the lantern and nearly dropped it, fingers numb with cold and fear. He looked at Andrew as if waiting to be told whether they were retreating or being spared.

Andrew reached down and took the lantern from him for a moment, lowering it to the oil trail. With a deliberate motion, he tipped it and poured a small spill of flame onto the soaked grass.

The oil caught with a low, hungry whoosh. Fire ran along the black line like a thought that had finally become action. It was not meant to trap Ambrose now. It was meant to erase evidence. To deny the graveyard the memory of this arrangement. To close a door behind them, even if the door was only in their own minds.

Elias stared at the sudden flame. For an instant something like hope flickered in his face, then died when he realized what it was and what it was not.

Ambrose watched the fire with mild interest, then looked back at Andrew. "Even now," he murmured, "you think like a man who must manage the story."

Andrew's voice came out tight. "I'm done giving you stages."

Ambrose's smile widened a fraction. "No," he said. "You are done believing you can leave without consequence."

The words landed like a chain finding its ring.

Andrew turned away from the burning oil and started toward the road. Haines fell in beside him.

Rudd hurried behind, too close to Elias's elbow. Elias came last, shoulders rigid, eyes fixed on Andrew's back as if staring hard enough might push him into becoming the brother he remembered.

Behind them the oil fire crackled low, contained by damp grass, more smoke than flame. The smoke drifted toward the church and then away, as if even the wind refused to carry their attempt into daylight.

Andrew did not look back for Ambrose. He forced himself not to. But as they reached the yard gate and stepped onto the road, he felt it anyway: the sense of being watched, not by eyes in a face, but by attention itself.

Ambrose did not need to follow them visibly. He had already moved into a place where following was unnecessary.

He was in Andrew's calculations now. In every decision about lanterns and pairs and roads. In the quiet lies that would become more valuable than ammunition when surrender arrived.

Half a mile from the church, Elias finally spoke, voice low and shaking with restraint. "You hesitated," he said again, as if repeating it might turn it into something Andrew could repair.

Andrew kept walking. The sky above the trees was fully gray now, dawn without warmth. "Yes," he said.

Elias's breath hitched. "Why," he demanded. "Tell me the truth."

Andrew's wound pulsed under the bandage, a clean sting that felt like an answer trying to rise through flesh. He swallowed hard and let the truth come out in its ugliest, simplest form.

"Because I saw what happens after," Andrew said. "If it dies or leaves, the war doesn't stop being a graveyard. The men still scatter. The wounded still get abandoned. The country still tears itself into pieces. And then there's nothing for me to do except watch it fall."

Elias made a sound, half grief, half revulsion. "So you need him," he whispered.

Andrew wanted to deny it. He wanted to say he needed only Elias, only decency, only God. But denial had become another kind of lie he could no longer afford.

"I don't know what I need," Andrew said quietly. "But I know what I've become good at. And he knows too."

Elias stopped walking for a heartbeat, as if his body refused to carry him alongside that confession. Then he hurried to catch up, because stopping alone on a road at dawn was its own kind of invitation.

When they reached the edge of the camp and the first lanterns came into view, Andrew felt the shape of his new bind settle more firmly. The Confederacy was collapsing, and men would soon be looking for someone to tell them what to do when the uniforms no longer meant anything.

Andrew would tell them. He could not stop himself.

And somewhere just beyond their light, in whatever shelter Andrew would prepare next, Ambrose would wait with patient hunger and the calm certainty that the end of one war was only the beginning of the work.

Andrew stepped back into the yard and felt, with a bleak clarity that made his throat tighten, that the chain in the graveyard had missed its target.

But something else had tightened all the same.

Not around Ambrose.

Around him.

Chapter 13

Pact of Shadows

By the time they reached the yard, the lanterns were still burning even though dawn had come. The light looked wrong in daylight, like a lie that had been left out too long. Men moved between wagons with their shoulders hunched, not from cold now, but from the instinct to make themselves smaller while the world decided what to do with them.

Andrew stepped into the mud and felt the camp's attention settle on him the way it always did. It wasn't respect. It wasn't even trust anymore. It was the simple, starving need to believe someone could interpret what was happening.

Dorsey saw him and came over at once, boots slicking in the muck. His eyes went past Andrew to Haines, to Rudd, to Elias last. The sight of Elias returning again, alive again, should have been a relief. Instead it tightened Dorsey's mouth, as if Elias's continued breathing only proved how skewed the rules had become.

"You find anything?" Dorsey asked.

Andrew kept his voice low. "Not news," he said. "But I saw enough to know the roads are turning ugly. Men moving without units. Stragglers. Some armed, some desperate. We shouldn't linger."

Dorsey's face worked, anger and fatigue struggling for the same space. "We're under orders," he said, but the sentence had no spine in it. Orders were made of paper. Paper burned.

Andrew glanced toward the barn. A cough rose inside and ended in a wet rattle. The wounded sounded thinner, as if the night had taken more than blood from them. Whitcomb stood under the lean-to canvas, watching Andrew with hollow eyes. The surgeon's mouth pressed into a line that said he would not ask for truth again. He already had enough of it.

"What do you want me to do, Mercer?" Dorsey demanded, and it was the same question he'd asked the night before, only now it had widened. It wasn't about missing men or raiders. It was about how to behave when your country quietly stopped being your country.

Andrew looked at the wagons, at the crates lashed down, at the mules shifting, ears flicking. He saw the supply train for what it was: not a military detail anymore, but a moving cover. A reason for men to be on the road without being questioned too hard. A place to hide things in plain sight.

"I want you to start thinking like you're already paroled," Andrew said. "Not like you're retreating in formation. We move as civilians with rifles, not as a unit with a destination."

Dorsey stared. "That's desertion."

"It's survival," Andrew said, and heard how easily the word came to him now, how often it stood in for whatever else he couldn't name.

Dorsey's gaze flicked to Elias, still standing a little apart, arms held tight against his ribs as if he was keeping his own body from doing something violent. "And your brother?" Dorsey asked. "He's with you, then."

Andrew nodded once.

Dorsey exhaled through his nose, a sound like surrender disguised as contempt. "Fine," he said. "I'll keep men close. I'll keep the drinking down. But if the Yankees come through—"

"We won't be here," Andrew cut in.

Dorsey looked at him a long moment, as if weighing whether to accuse him of arrogance. Then he glanced toward the tree line, to the darker strip of woods beyond the last wagon, and whatever he saw in Andrew's face made him choose silence instead.

Dorsey walked away barking orders that had changed shape without changing tone. Men obeyed because obeying was easier than deciding. They tightened straps, checked lashings, adjusted harness. The camp became busy in that peculiar way it became busy before a march, only now there was no map anyone trusted and no flag anyone believed in.

Andrew turned toward the supply wagon and found Elias still watching him. Dawn made Elias look harsher. In lantern light his anger had been a bright thing. In daylight it looked like exhaustion that had learned to hate.

"You're going to do it," Elias said. Not a question.

Andrew didn't answer immediately. He could feel Rudd nearby, hovering like a shadow that wanted to be told where to stand. He could feel Haines's attention too, the older soldier's wary readiness to take orders he disliked because disliking them did not change necessity.

Andrew leaned close enough that Elias could hear without anyone else catching words. "We talk later," he said.

Elias's jaw clenched. "No," he replied, equally low. "You keep saying later so you don't have to hear yourself. You hesitated in that graveyard and you called it consequence. Now you're moving pieces. Tell me what you're moving."

Andrew held his brother's gaze and felt the sting under his bandage answer, a small clean flare like a needle. The wound had become an instrument. It reacted not to danger alone, but to direction, to proximity, to decisions that bent toward Ambrose.

"I'm making sure we're not trapped here when the end comes through," Andrew said.

Elias's mouth twisted. "That isn't an answer."

Andrew looked past him toward the wagons again. "Go sit with Kellan," he said.

Elias's eyes sharpened. "Don't order me like I'm one of your men."

Andrew felt impatience rise, and beneath it fear. Not fear of Elias. Fear that if Elias kept speaking, kept pressing, Andrew would either break into confession or break into anger, and either fracture would be useful to Ambrose.

"I'm ordering you because you're breathing," Andrew said, and the old reflex made Elias flinch as if struck.

Elias stepped back. His voice went quieter, almost calm, which was worse. "You promised yourself that as long as I lived, you were doing good," Elias said. "Now you're using my living as a reason no one can argue with you."

Andrew felt something cold settle behind his eyes. "Move," he said, and it came out harder than he intended.

Elias held his gaze for a long moment, then turned away with rigid control and walked back under the canvas, not as obedience but as withdrawal. The distance between them moved with him, a gap that would not close again just because they stood near each other.

Andrew stood still until Elias disappeared among the wagons. Then he turned toward Haines.

"We need paper," Andrew said.

Haines frowned. "For what, sir?"

Andrew kept his voice neutral. "For names. For roads. For explanations." He glanced toward Dorsey and lowered his voice further. "For when the questions start."

Haines's eyes tightened. He did not like being told only part of a thing, but he understood why. "There's a clerk's kit in one of the crates," Haines said. "Ink. Blanks. Seals, if the captain's kept any."

Andrew nodded. “Find it.”

Haines hesitated, then asked the question that carried more weight than it should have. “Are we staying together?”

Andrew looked at him. Haines had lost men, had watched a camp become quiet around missing bodies, had helped build a root pit as if it were a reasonable answer to an impossible appetite. Haines’s loyalty was not romantic. It was the loyalty of a man who’d seen enough to know that leaving alone was another way to die.

“For now,” Andrew said. “Until we can’t.”

Haines gave a short nod and moved off.

Rudd appeared at Andrew’s elbow like a nervous dog. “Sir,” he said, voice thin, “do you need me?”

Andrew almost told him no. Almost sent him away to keep his hands clean a little longer. But he remembered Ambrose’s words by the creek: a man you will not need to name. He remembered, too, that no one stayed un-named for long. Not if Andrew needed them.

“I need you to listen,” Andrew said. “I need you to keep your mouth shut and your eyes open at the same time. Can you do that?”

Rudd swallowed hard. “Yes, sir.”

Andrew nodded once. "Then you're useful."

The words landed wrong in his own ears. Useful. That was how Ambrose spoke. Not cruelly. Practically. As if human beings were tools and the only sin was refusing to admit it.

Andrew walked to the wagon that carried the bulk of their supplies, stepping up onto its wooden lip. He knelt and began shifting crates, checking lashings, feeling for hollow space. The inventory no longer mattered as inventory. It mattered as concealment. Flour sacks could hide more than flour if you arranged them correctly. Broken harness and spare nails could become a top layer of harmless debris. Canvas could be doubled. Boards could be nailed in a way that created a false bottom.

As his hands worked, his mind did too. The end of the war was not a single event. It was a flood. Men would be moving north and west, toward home, toward nowhere, toward new names. Refugees with hollow cheeks and paroled soldiers with bitterness in their throats. In that crowd, a wagon with a Confederate lieutenant at its side was not notable. It was only one more small story among thousands.

He climbed down and crossed the yard toward Whitcomb's lean-to. The surgeon looked up as Andrew approached, his expression already weary with the expectation of another request that would rot his conscience.

"I need a ledger," Andrew said.

Whitcomb's eyebrows rose. "For medicine?"

Andrew held his gaze. "For deaths," he said.

Whitcomb's mouth tightened. "You planning to make more of those?"

Andrew kept his voice low. "I'm planning to make fewer panics," he replied. "If a man dies on the road, we need something to show a patrol. Something that says fever took him. Dysentery. Pneumonia. Anything that keeps strangers from digging into our wagon."

Whitcomb stared a long moment, then looked away in disgust that was also understanding. "You're building a new kind of unit," he said quietly. "Not soldiers. A traveling lie."

Andrew did not deny it. Denial had become decorative.

Whitcomb reached under the table and pulled out a small book with stained pages. "Take it," he said. "It won't stay clean. Nothing will."

Andrew accepted it, feeling the weight of paper and ink as if it were ammunition. "I'll return it," he lied.

Whitcomb's eyes flicked up. "No you won't," he said softly, not accusing, just tired. "You'll keep it because you'll need it. And then you'll tell yourself you're keeping track for justice."

Andrew's wound stung, clean and sharp, as if the truth had touched it. He closed his fingers around the book. "I am keeping track," he said, and the stubbornness in his voice surprised him.

Whitcomb's mouth twisted. "Then I hope you write better than you lie," he said, and turned back to his instruments as if Andrew were already gone.

Andrew stepped out into the yard again. Haines approached with a small wooden box and a bundle of papers, his face set like a man carrying something fragile that he hated.

"Found it," Haines said. "Blank forms, some quartermaster stamps. A seal press too, if you've got wax."

Andrew opened the box and saw the tools: ink that would dry into authority, stamps that could turn a man into an official thing, blank paper waiting for a story.

He imagined writing a name that was not his. He imagined crossing state lines with a wagon that carried something in its dark that did not belong to any jurisdiction. He imagined telling a patrolman they were hauling provisions for a field hospital that no longer existed. He imagined the way men looked away from complicated suffering if you gave them a simple reason to.

He closed the box again as if sealing it.

Rudd was watching, eyes wide. “Sir,” the boy whispered, “what are we doing?”

Andrew looked toward the tree line, toward the invisible line between this camp and whatever waited in the woods. He did not see Ambrose. He did not need to. The sweetness was faint in the air now, but it threaded through everything, present like a memory that had become physical.

“We’re forging a way through,” Andrew said.

Haines’s jaw worked. “Through what?”

Andrew held the box under one arm and the ledger under the other. The weight of them felt like the weight of a new identity assembling itself piece by piece.

“Through the end,” Andrew said. “And into whatever comes after.”

He walked back to the wagon and began arranging the supplies with more care than he’d ever arranged rations in the war. A careful stack could become a wall. A wall could become a hiding place. A hiding place could become a promise.

Behind him, Elias watched from under the canvas. Andrew did not turn to meet his gaze. If he did, he might see the funeral Elias had already held for him. And Andrew did not have time, not yet, to attend his own burial.

The mules shifted and snorted. Men tightened straps. Dorsey's voice carried across the yard, sharp with forced command.

Somewhere in the woods, in whatever shelter Andrew had built and would build again, Ambrose waited with patient hunger for the road to open.

And Andrew, hands stained with ink before he'd even touched it, kept working as if he could construct a life sturdy enough to carry them both.

By midmorning the camp had become a thing in motion, not because anyone knew where they were going, but because staying had begun to feel like waiting for a blade.

The barn's doors were thrown open to let air in, and the sound that came out was not the usual chorus of groans and curses. It was quieter than that, the exhausted murmur of men who had realized they might be abandoned by their own history. Whitcomb's orderlies carried the worst cases on stretchers made from fence rails and blankets. Others, wounded but walking, leaned on rifles like canes. Dorsey moved through it with a brittle kind of energy, barking orders that were still shaped like military commands even as they served a different purpose: to keep men from stopping long enough to think.

Andrew stayed near the supply wagon, hands steady on lashings, eyes taking in what mattered now. Not formations. Not flags. Faces. Which men would remember too clearly what had happened in the night. Which men looked at him with a need that would become resentment later. Which men had already decided that survival meant becoming someone else.

He felt Elias watching him from under the canvas, a fixed pressure. Elias had gone quiet, but it wasn't peace. It was the silence of a man holding himself together with teeth.

Haines came and went with purposeful steps, checking harness, shifting crates the way Andrew had shown him, making layers of harmlessness. Rudd hovered like a shadow that wanted to be told what to do and feared being told. Kellan remained near the wheel, blank-eyed, a man whose mind had learned to step back from his own body when the world got too close.

Andrew kept the clerk's box and Whitcomb's ledger tucked under the seat board where he could reach them quickly. He had already filled the first page with a list of names from the last two nights, written small and neat, as if neatness could make it less obscene. He told himself it was evidence. He told himself it was a record for some future reckoning. He did not examine too closely why it calmed him to put ink to absence.

He heard, now and then, men speaking the word surrender as if it were a disease they didn't want to catch. Lee. Grant. Parole. Terms. The end. Every sentence ended in a pause, because no one knew what to say after the end.

Dorsey approached Andrew with his jaw tight and his eyes bloodshot. He stopped close, lowering his voice the way men did when they were about to share something shameful.

"There's a patrol on the road west," Dorsey said. "Bluecoats, maybe. Or could be state militia. Somebody's wearing a uniform that still fits."

Andrew nodded once. "Then we don't go west."

Dorsey's mouth tightened. "Mercer, I can't keep dodging forever. If they stop us, if they ask—"

Andrew looked at him until Dorsey's voice faltered. The captain's fear was not cowardice. It was the fear of a man who had been trained to believe that if he followed rules, the world would remain legible.

Andrew opened the clerk's box and took out a blank form. He set it on the wagon seat and wrote with quick, practiced strokes, using Whitcomb's ink. He did not need to look for words. The war had given him a library of official phrases that meant almost anything if you stamped them properly.

He wrote that Captain Dorsey's detail was authorized to move medical provisions and convalescents to a temporary field station north of the county line. He wrote dates that were close enough to be believable. He wrote a name for the destination, a town that existed, but far enough away that no one would check. He left gaps where he could add or subtract details depending on who read it.

Haines appeared at his shoulder with wax. Andrew pressed the seal into it with the steady force of a man stamping a coffin lid.

Dorsey stared at the paper. "Where'd you learn that?" he asked, voice rough.

Andrew didn't look up. "I've watched men do it for years," he said. "I just never thought I'd need it."

Dorsey took the paper as if it might burn him. For a moment his expression was pure resentment, and Andrew understood why. This wasn't command anymore. This was manipulation. A lieutenant forging a path by forging lies. A war that ended not with a surrender ceremony but with men smearing ink over the truth until it couldn't be recognized.

"You're good at it," Dorsey said quietly, almost accusing.

Andrew felt shame stir in his chest, not clean enough to become regret, only heavy. "It's just handwriting," he replied.

Dorsey's eyes flicked to Andrew's bandaged side. The wound's outline was visible under the cloth when Andrew leaned. Dorsey didn't ask. He had learned, like the others, that questions were dangerous when the answers were too strange.

"All right," Dorsey said. "We'll move in ten minutes. We're taking who we can. The rest…" He stopped. His throat worked. "The rest will have to take their chances with whoever comes next."

Andrew watched him walk away and felt the lie of that sentence. Whoever comes next. As if the next thing was simply another army, another set of men with rules. He could feel, just beyond the tree line, the truth that moved without uniforms.

The sweetness touched the air faintly, a memory of orchards threaded through mud and sweat. It came and went like a breath that wasn't his.

He climbed down from the wagon and walked a short distance toward the trees, far enough that the camp noises dulled. He did not call out. He did not need to. His wound gave its small, directional sting under the bandage, and with it came that sense of attention turning toward him, intimate as a hand placed lightly between the shoulder blades.

Ambrose did not appear.

That, in itself, felt like a message. Ambrose no longer needed to step into the open to make Andrew move. Presence could be implied. Hunger could remain unseen and still dictate the shape of a man's day.

Andrew stood with the damp wind on his face and realized, with a sudden clarity that made him want to gag, that he was relieved Ambrose was not visible. Relieved, because visibility would mean confrontation, and confrontation required pretending there was still a line to hold.

He turned back to the wagons.

Elias had risen and was standing near the supply wagon's rear corner, arms crossed, face set. His posture was controlled, but the control looked like it hurt.

"You're leaving," Elias said when Andrew drew near.

Andrew nodded. "We're moving north. For now."

Elias's eyes flicked over the wagon. Over the careful stacking. Over the doubled canvas. Over the way Andrew had created spaces where there should not be spaces. Elias was no fool. He had seen tunnels under the burning estate. He understood what hidden places meant.

"You've made room," Elias said.

Andrew felt the words land in his ribs. "For supplies," he said, and hated himself for using the same tone he used on men who didn't deserve the truth.

Elias's mouth twisted. "Don't," he said, voice low. "Don't do that to me. Don't talk like you're still only an officer solving a problem."

Andrew held his brother's gaze. The day around them was bright enough now to show every stain on their clothes, every crust of mud, every hollow under the eyes. There was no dramatic darkness to hide behind, no fog to soften the edges. Shame looked sharper in daylight.

"Elias," Andrew said, and tried to make it a warning and a plea at once.

Elias stepped closer. "Is he coming with us?" he asked.

Andrew's throat tightened. He could have lied. He could have said no and hoped the lie held long enough to get Elias away from him. But Elias's face was set in a way that told Andrew the lie would not survive even a mile.

Andrew did not answer with words. He looked at the wagon again, then back at Elias, and that was enough.

Elias's eyes closed for a moment as if he had been struck. When he opened them, something in him had cooled into a bleak steadiness that frightened Andrew more than anger ever had.

"So this is it," Elias said. "This is what you do after the war. You don't go home. You don't start over. You take that thing and you build a road for it."

Andrew felt his wound listen, a faint sting that was almost rhythmic. He ignored it and forced his voice to remain even. "I'm trying to keep him from taking whoever he wants," he said. "If he moves in the open—"

Elias's laugh cut him off, harsh and brief. "You hear yourself," he said. "You're saying it like you're hauling a sick man to a doctor. Like you're doing a duty."

Andrew stepped closer too, lowering his voice so Rudd and Haines wouldn't hear. "I'm doing what I have to do," he said, and the phrase tasted like rust.

Elias leaned in, his eyes bright with something that had once been faith. Now it looked like grief hardened into a weapon. "No," Elias whispered. "You're doing what you have decided you can live with. That's different."

Andrew's jaw tightened. He wanted to grab Elias, to shake him, to make him understand that the world they had lived in was already gone, and that understanding it did not prevent the world from eating them alive. But his hands stayed at his sides, because he knew how easily force could become habit.

"Get in the wagon," Andrew said. "We're leaving."

Elias's stare held on him. The distance between them felt like a physical thing, a gulf that had been dug in small increments: a whispered bargain, a surrendered charm, a forged report, a trap that failed not because it couldn't be sprung but because Andrew had chosen not to spring it.

"I will," Elias said quietly. "For now."

The words were not surrender. They were an indictment.

Haines called out that the harness was ready. Dorsey's men began to move, wagons creaking, mules snorting, boots slipping in mud as if the earth itself tried to hold them back. The wounded were lifted and settled onto straw with murmured curses and ragged prayers. Some men waved at those left behind, but most did not. It was easier not to make farewells. Farewells acknowledged that something had ended.

Andrew climbed onto the supply wagon's seat and took the reins. His hands did not shake. He felt, distantly, that they should. The absence of shaking was its own kind of horror.

As the wagon lurched forward, mud sucking at the wheels, he looked once toward the barn and saw a few men standing there, watching them go with dull faces. Men too injured to travel. Men too slow. Men who would be found by someone else soon enough.

Shame rose in Andrew's throat like bile. Not because he was leaving them. War had taught him that leaving people behind was sometimes unavoidable. The shame came from knowing he was leaving with something worse than survival.

He felt Elias behind him under the canvas, rigid and silent. He felt Rudd's nervous presence at the side rail, eyes scanning the trees as if expecting pale elegance to step out at any moment. He felt Haines walking alongside for the first stretch, steadying the wagon through ruts, his face set like a man escorting a funeral.

The road ahead was crowded with other endings: small knots of men moving north without banners, families with carts piled high, a loose river of refugees and paroled soldiers already starting to form. The Confederacy was dissolving into bodies and stories.

Andrew guided the wagon into that moving crowd, and the camp behind them shrank until it was only a smudge of barn roof and lanterns that looked ridiculous in full day.

He did not look back again.

He kept his eyes forward, because if he looked back he might see himself more clearly than he could bear: not a lieutenant marching out of a lost cause, but a man driving a wagon that had been prepared like a coffin.

And somewhere in the space he had made, in the hidden dark he had arranged with such care, the sweetness deepened faintly, as if something inside the wagon had breathed in approval.

By late afternoon the road had thickened into a slow, filthy procession. Wagons leaned under furniture and sacks of cornmeal. Men walked with rifles slung like habits they could not quit. A woman in a torn shawl carried a baby that did not cry, its face pressed into her collar as if it had learned early that sound invited attention. No one spoke much beyond what was necessary to keep a wheel from clipping another wheel or to warn of a rut swallowed by puddles.

Andrew kept the team steady with small pulls on the reins. He sat rigid on the board seat, shoulders squared as if posture could keep his thoughts in line. The ledger lay under his thigh where he could feel its edge, a hard little reminder that words were becoming his most reliable weapon. Every so often he glanced at a passing group and measured what they would see if they looked too closely at his wagon: canvas, crates, a Confederate lieutenant with a bandaged side, a handful of tired men guarding supplies.

Nothing worth stopping.

He told himself he was building that nothing on purpose.

Haines walked near the left rear wheel, eyes scanning the treeline when the road dipped between stands of pine. Rudd stayed near the side rail, nervous and eager, as though if he watched hard enough he could prevent whatever lived in dark spaces from becoming real again. Kellan rode under canvas with his back to a crate, knees up, staring at the swaying folds like a man watching his own thoughts drift by.

And Elias sat behind Andrew, under the canvas but close enough that Andrew could feel him as heat and tension. Elias had not spoken since they left the barn behind. The silence was not peace. It was the quiet of a man gathering himself into a shape that would not bend.

They left the main road just before dusk, turning into a rutted farm lane half-swallowed by weeds. Andrew had chosen it when he saw the low smoke of a cooking fire by a stand of trees and decided it was better to make camp near other strangers than alone. Strangers were noisy in a way Ambrose did not prefer. Strangers asked questions, but questions could be answered. Silence was harder.

The lane opened into a field that had been harvested poorly or not at all. Stalks lay flattened in muddy patches. Near the far fence line three other wagons had stopped, their owners keeping close to their own circles of light. A thin fire burned low in a shallow pit. Andrew guided his team to a spot that gave them a view of the lane while still leaving distance between them and the others.

When the mules finally stopped and the wagon settled, the sudden stillness made Andrew's wound sting as if it had been waiting for the moment the road stopped moving. He gritted his teeth against it and climbed down, boots sinking into cold mud.

Haines was already loosening harness. Rudd gathered fallen branches with quick, useless energy. Kellan slid down from the wagon without looking at anyone, as if his body were acting on orders his mind no longer issued.

Elias dropped down last. He stood in the fading light and looked at Andrew with an expression that was almost calm. Almost. The calm was what frightened Andrew. Rage was predictable. Grief was painful but human. This was a kind of clarity sharpened to a point.

Andrew felt, in the back of his throat, the faint sweetness. Not strong. Not a presence stepping into lantern light. Just the suggestion of something content in darkness, listening to the settling of straps and the lowered voices of strangers.

Elias nodded toward the far edge of the field. "Walk," he said quietly.

It was not a request.

Andrew hesitated only long enough to take in who might be watching. Haines glanced up once, as if he understood without being told what this was. He looked away and returned to the harness with exaggerated focus. Rudd pretended not to notice at all, which was his new skill.

Andrew followed Elias toward the fence line where the weeds grew higher and the ground rose slightly. The other camps' firelight did not reach here well. The sky was a dull, bruised color, clouds low and heavy with more rain they had not yet decided to drop.

Elias stopped near a broken fence post and turned. "You made it," he said.

Andrew frowned. "Made what."

Elias's jaw tightened. "You made the wagon," he said. "You made the space. You made the papers. You made it so it can travel without being seen for what it is."

Andrew felt his throat go tight. "Keep your voice down."

Elias's eyes flashed. "There it is again," he said. "Not morality. Not denial. Management."

Andrew stepped closer, keeping his own voice low. "I told you we'd talk later," he said.

"This is later," Elias replied. His hands were clenched at his sides, but he held himself still as if motion might become violence. "You're going to carry him. Through all this." He gestured toward the field, toward the dim lights and the small, huddled families. "Through people who don't even know what they're walking beside."

Andrew stared at him. The honest answer pressed at his teeth: yes. Not forever, he wanted to say. Not willingly, he wanted to pretend. But the road did not care about pretenses. The road only cared about what you carried.

"I don't have another way," Andrew said.

Elias shook his head once, slow. "You do," he said. "You always did. You just don't want it."

Andrew felt heat rise in his chest. "You think I should have lit the oil and taken the risk," he said, and heard the brittle edge in his own voice. "You think I should have killed myself and you with me just to feel clean."

Elias's mouth twisted. "Don't put words in my mouth," he said. Then, quieter, "I think you should have done something that wasn't a bargain."

Andrew swallowed. The wind shifted slightly, and with it came that faint sweetness again, as if the dark inside the wagon had breathed out through the cracks in canvas. Andrew did not look back. Looking back was the beginning of acknowledging, and acknowledging made the arrangement too real.

"I saved you," Andrew said, and hated that the sentence still rose like a reflex.

Elias's face tightened as if in pain. "Yes," he whispered. "You saved me. And you killed something else. Or maybe you just let it die."

Andrew stared at him. "What."

Elias's voice stayed steady, almost gentle, and the gentleness made it worse. "The part of you that would rather lose than compromise," he said. "The part I used to believe was you."

Andrew's wound gave a small, clean sting beneath the bandage, like a reminder that his body had already accepted what his mind still tried to argue with.

Elias took a breath, and when he spoke again his words came out like a decision that had been forming since the chapel. "I'm not staying with you," he said.

Andrew felt the statement hit him with a dull shock. "You can't go alone," he said. "Look at the roads."

Elias's eyes did not soften. "I can't stay with you," he replied. "That's worse."

Andrew stepped forward without meaning to, a sudden instinctive reach. "Elias," he said, low and fierce. "Don't be foolish. Don't be proud."

Elias gave a short, joyless breath. “Proud,” he repeated. “You hear yourself? You sound like him when you talk to me now.”

Andrew froze. The accusation was precise enough to leave him with nothing to grab hold of. He tried to speak and found only air.

Elias looked past him toward the wagons, toward the sagging canvas that concealed what Andrew had arranged. His eyes narrowed as if he could see through boards and cloth by force of hate alone. “He’s in there,” Elias said, voice barely above a whisper. “Isn’t he.”

Andrew did not answer.

Elias nodded slowly, as if confirming something he already knew. “Then I’m already a hostage,” he said. “Not because he’s holding me. Because you are.”

Andrew flinched. “That’s not true.”

Elias’s gaze returned to him, and in it was something like pity that Elias seemed to despise himself for feeling. “You’re going to keep me close forever,” Elias said. “Because you think my breathing justifies your decisions. And I’ll become your excuse the same way you’ve become his tool.”

Andrew's hands curled into fists. "You're alive," he said, and the word came out harsh. "That matters."

"It matters," Elias agreed. "But not like this."

For a moment neither of them spoke. The wind worried at the weeds. Somewhere back in the field a child began to cry and was hushed quickly, the mother's voice urgent with the old instinct to keep sound from drawing attention.

Elias reached into his coat and drew out a small object. In the dim light it took Andrew a moment to recognize it: a narrow strip of cloth, folded. A piece of their mother's ribbon, kept as a keepsake, something Elias had carried through the war like a private prayer. Andrew had seen it once when Elias thought he was asleep and had touched it as if it could summon a safer world.

Elias held it out.

Andrew did not take it at first. "What is this," he asked, though he knew.

"A funeral," Elias said quietly. "Between the living."

Andrew's throat tightened until it hurt. "Don't," he whispered.

Elias's hand stayed extended, steady. "Take it," he said. "Or don't. But I'm done letting you bury yourself and call it protection."

Andrew took the ribbon with fingers that felt clumsy, as if he had forgotten how to hold anything gentle. The cloth was slightly damp, warmed by Elias's body. It smelled faintly of old soap and smoke, an impossible tenderness in a world that had become all mud and blood.

Elias watched him take it, expression hardening again as if softness was dangerous. "I'm leaving at first light," he said. "I'll walk north with the next group I find. I'll take my chances with men. With hunger I can name and shoot."

Andrew's voice came out strained. "And if he follows you."

Elias's eyes flashed. "Then he follows you," he said. "Because you're the one he wants. You're the one making roads for him."

Andrew stood with the ribbon in his hand, feeling the weight of it like a small, quiet condemnation.

Elias stepped back, creating distance the way he had behind the supply wagon days ago, that first boundary that had never stopped widening. "Whatever survives in you after this," Elias said, and his voice did not shake now, "it won't be my brother. I meant it then. I mean it now."

Andrew tried to speak. What came up first was command, and command was useless here. What came up second was apology, and apology felt obscene without change.

So he said the only thing that did not pretend to be clean. "I don't know how to stop," Andrew said.

Elias nodded once, as if he had expected that answer all along. "Then at least stop calling it mercy," he replied.

He turned and began to walk back toward the wagons.

Andrew stood still. He did not follow. Following would have been another kind of restraint, another set of hands on Elias's shoulders disguised as concern. He watched his brother's silhouette cross the dim field until Elias disappeared into the weak circle of lantern light.

Andrew remained by the fence line for several breaths longer, staring at nothing. The ribbon lay in his palm like a small relic he did not deserve.

From the wagon behind him, from the hidden dark he had prepared so carefully, the sweetness seemed to deepen, faint but unmistakable, like a sigh of satisfaction.

Andrew closed his fingers around the ribbon until the cloth creased and warmed under his grip.

Then he turned back toward camp, toward the small fire Rudd had coaxed to life, toward Haines's watchful silence, toward the wagon that looked ordinary to strangers and felt like a coffin to anyone who understood what was inside.

He walked as if attending a burial.

Not of Elias.

Of the last version of himself who might have begged his brother to stay and meant something pure by it.

Chapter 14

Crossroads and Cover Stories

First light came without warmth. It seeped into the field like thin milk, turning last night's shadows into the dull, honest shapes of fences, ruts, and men who had slept poorly. The other camps were already stirring; smoke rose in low, cautious plumes, as if even fire ought to keep its head down.

Andrew had not slept. He sat on the wagon seat with the reins looped over his wrist, staring at the lane they'd come in on. His wound held its familiar, attentive ache beneath the bandage. Not pain that begged. Pain that listened.

Behind him under the canvas, Haines shifted in the straw and cleared his throat once, the sound of a man announcing he was awake without asking permission to speak. Rudd lay on his side near a crate, eyes open and too bright. Kellan was upright already, knees drawn to his chest, staring at the wagon boards as though they might open and show him another place to stand.

Elias moved quietly. There was no drama in it, no hurried packing, no last glance thrown like a knife. Andrew heard him climb down to the mud with careful steps and felt, without turning, that Elias was standing for a moment behind the wagon, looking back at the shape of it. Looking back at Andrew.

Andrew kept his gaze on the lane. He held the ribbon Elias had given him in his coat pocket, folded so tightly it had become a hard little square. A relic. An accusation. Something soft made into something that could be carried without showing.

A low murmur rose from the other camps as groups decided who was leaving and who was staying. Wagon wheels creaked. A baby began to cry and was hushed quickly. Somebody coughed wetly, the sound of lungs scraped thin.

Elias walked to the nearest knot of travelers, a family with a broken cart and two grown sons with rifles held not like weapons but like proof. Andrew saw him there, just beyond the wagon's flank: Elias's posture straight, his face set in that bleak steadiness that had replaced youth's heat. Elias spoke to them briefly, gesturing north along the road. One of the sons nodded, distrustful but willing. The family had learned, like everyone else, that men moved in temporary alliances now. The world had become a chain of short agreements.

Haines climbed up beside Andrew, careful not to look back under the canvas. He followed Andrew's gaze anyway. "He's going," Haines said.

Andrew nodded once. He tasted iron in his mouth and did not know if it was memory or something his body had begun to produce when grief came close.

Rudd whispered, "Sir, are we… are we letting him?"

Andrew kept his voice low. "He made his choice."

Rudd's eyes flicked toward the road, toward Elias. "And if that thing—"

"Don't," Andrew said, sharper than he meant, then forced his tone flat again. "Don't say it. Not out here."

Haines gave a quiet, ugly breath. "He'll be safer with a crowd," Haines muttered, and the sentence held a bitter hope that Andrew could not share. Crowds were safer from bullets. They were not always safer from hunger that preferred to travel unseen.

Elias came back once, just close enough to the wagon that Andrew could see his face clearly. The light made Elias's eyes look pale and tired.

Elias did not climb up. He did not reach for the canvas. He only looked at Andrew and said, "Don't follow me."

Andrew's throat tightened. He managed, "I wasn't going to."

Elias's mouth twitched, not quite a smile. More like a flinch. "Good," he said. "Then you won't be tempted to call it love."

Andrew felt the words land and stay. He could not answer without making it worse.

Elias stepped back, then turned and walked away. He did not look over his shoulder again. The family's cart creaked forward; Elias fell in beside it, a rifle borrowed from someone's shoulder for the moment, his own pistol low in his hand. In the gray morning procession, he became just another man with a haunted face and a direction.

Rudd watched until Elias was a shape among other shapes. "He's really gone," the boy whispered, as if saying it might undo it.

Andrew nodded. "Yes."

Behind them, within the wagon's hidden space, the faint sweetness touched the air and withdrew again. It wasn't strong enough to make anyone retch. It never was when Ambrose was pleased. Pleased was quiet.

Andrew gathered the reins. His hands did not shake. That was the worst part. He had thought letting Elias go might break something open in him, might force a reckoning. Instead it felt like another piece set into place with a craftsman's care.

Haines dropped down to the ground and began checking the harness with a briskness that suggested he could still solve problems by tightening straps. "We should move," he said. "Before the road clogs worse."

Andrew clicked his tongue softly. The mules leaned into the traces; the wagon lurched and then rolled. Mud sucked at the wheels and let go reluctantly.

They eased back onto the main road and joined the slow river of bodies. The landscape around them looked flayed. Farms with fences broken and fields left half-tilled. A house burned down to its chimney, black stones still damp from rain. A church with its bell missing, its steeple intact but useless. Every mile was an argument that whatever had once governed this place had stopped caring.

Andrew kept them behind a wagon loaded with sacks of feed and a bedframe tied on top like a rib cage. The man driving it had the hollow-eyed look of someone who'd decided not to talk anymore unless it was to buy or beg. Andrew understood. Words were currency now, and every currency was unstable.

He watched the ditches. Not for ambushes in the old military sense, but for the shapes of men who might step out with that particular looseness in their posture that meant they had nothing left to lose. Bands of deserters. Guerillas. Boys pretending to be soldiers. Men in mismatched uniforms with private laws.

He also watched for official patrols, which could be worse. Official men wanted papers. Official men wanted categories. Official men panicked when something did not fit.

A mile ahead, the road narrowed where a bridge should have been. Instead there was a washout: rain and wagons and neglect had chewed the bank away, leaving the creek exposed and angry. People had made a crossing by laying boards and fence rails over the worst of it, but it was a bottleneck. Wagons lined up and men argued softly about whose wheels had the right to go first.

Andrew slowed their team and glanced to Haines, who walked alongside the front wheel now, eyes scanning. "If we get stuck here," Haines said quietly, "it'll be easy for someone to look too close."

"Then we don't linger," Andrew replied.

Rudd craned his neck. "There's men up there," he said.

Andrew saw them too: three riders in worn blue coats sitting their horses above the washout. Union, most likely. Not crisp, not parade-ready. Field-worn men with mud on their boots and the bored vigilance of people trying to keep order in a place that did not want it.

Andrew felt his wound sting once, clean and directional, and knew without seeing that Ambrose approved of the complication. Complications were invitations. Complications created reasons to bargain.

He reached down and touched the ledger under his thigh, feeling its hard edge. Then he reached into the clerk's box and pulled out the forged paper he'd stamped for Dorsey, now adjusted in his own mind as a template. He had already written another sheet in smaller script: medical provisions, convalescents, temporary station north. He had learned, quickly, that the best lie was one that gave men a reason not to touch what you carried. Disease was still the most reliable fence.

They rolled forward with the line. Andrew kept his posture bored, irritated, as if the washout was an inconvenience beneath his notice. Officers had survived on that posture for centuries; it was a kind of armor.

When it was their turn, one of the bluecoats raised a hand. “Hold,” he called, voice rough but not cruel. “Where you headed?”

Andrew stopped the team. Haines held the mule’s bridle to keep it from shifting sideways. Rudd stood near the side rail, trying to look like a boy with nothing worth taking.

Andrew lifted the paper, not too fast. Fast looked guilty. “North,” he said. “Temporary field station. Carrying medical supplies and men who can’t move quick.” He nodded toward the wagon canvas, letting the implication hang. Sick men. Wounded men. Contagion. “We’re trying to keep them from spoiling on the road.”

The bluecoat rider leaned in slightly, eyes flicking over Andrew’s uniform and bandage. “Confederate,” he said.

“Was,” Andrew replied, and kept his tone tired, not defiant. Defiance was theater.

The rider’s expression shifted into something complicated and weary. “You got papers?”

Andrew held them out. The rider took them, glanced at the seal, at the neat script, at the place where Andrew had chosen not to include any specific superior officer's name. Specific names created trails. Trails were no longer safe.

The rider's gaze moved to Haines, to Rudd, to the wagon. "Any weapons under there?" he asked.

"Rifles," Andrew said. "Enough to keep wolves and men off us. We're not hunting a fight."

The rider snorted softly, as if he'd stopped believing in men's stated intentions weeks ago. He looked toward the canvas again. "You got sick under there?"

Andrew let a pause stretch just enough to feel real. "Yes," he said.

Inside the wagon, there was no sound. Kellan did not breathe loud. No shifting of straw. Nothing that would invite curiosity. Andrew felt a brief, cold gratitude for Kellan's emptiness.

The rider's mouth tightened. "All right," he said. He handed the paper back with two fingers, as if it might carry fever. "Get across. Don't stop in the middle. And if you see any of your boys trying to cause trouble, you tell them the war's done."

Andrew nodded once. "Understood."

As they moved forward, wheels bumping over the makeshift rails, Andrew kept his face neutral. He did not allow relief to show. Relief was another kind of confession.

They crossed the washout and rejoined the road on the far side. Behind them, the line continued to crawl, and the bluecoats continued to hold their small, failing dam against the flood of wandering men.

Rudd let out a breath he'd been holding. "He didn't look inside," the boy whispered.

"No," Haines said. His voice was flat. "He didn't want to."

Andrew guided the wagon between two burned-out fence posts and felt the truth of that sentence settle. Most men did not want to look inside. Not at wagons. Not at houses. Not at cellars. Not at the places where hunger hid behind boards and called itself necessity.

That was how the country had always been built: by what people refused to see.

The road rose and dipped through ruined countryside. A mile on, they passed a farmhouse where someone had nailed white cloth to the door and then left it there until rain made it sag. A plea that had outlasted the hands that hung it. Farther, they saw a line of shallow graves near a stand of trees, marked with stones that would not last one season of weather.

Andrew kept them moving. He kept the wagon in the center of the road where ruts were deepest, because deep ruts meant other wagons had used them. Other wagons meant safety in numbers and, more importantly, distraction.

His mind built routes the way it had once built patrol schedules. Avoid the bridge where patrols liked to stand. Take the farm lanes where civilians traveled and soldiers did not bother to follow. Stop near other camps so questions had too many possible answers. Keep a story ready like a weapon in a holster.

He was navigating ruins, yes. But he was also navigating the spaces between attention.

And in those spaces, in the hidden dark he had arranged with such careful hands, something traveled with them in silence, content to let the world rebuild itself into new cover.

Andrew felt his wound give its small, clean sting again, like a compass needle turning toward whatever came next.

He did not look back down the road for Elias.

He kept his eyes forward and drove.

The road straightened briefly after the washout, climbing a low ridge where the trees thinned and the land opened into a patchwork of fields left half-claimed by weeds. From that height Andrew could see smoke in three directions, some of it honest cooking fires, some of it the thin, lazy smear of houses burning because no one had bothered to stop it. The war's end had not brought quiet. It had only changed the reasons things burned.

He kept the wagon in the ruts that promised other wagons had survived. Haines walked near the left wheel, eyes flicking between the ditch line and the distant folds of tree cover. Rudd rode on the edge of the seat board when Andrew allowed it, then hopped down again when the road narrowed, never still long enough to look calm. Under the canvas, Kellan made no sound at all. That silence had become a kind of cover, a man-shaped blanket over whatever else traveled with them.

Andrew tasted damp air and, beneath it, that faint sweetness that came and went like a thought he didn't want to finish. It wasn't strong. Strong meant Ambrose was close enough to make the world feel staged. This was only the suggestion of him, the way you could feel someone behind you before you turned.

By midafternoon the procession thinned. People drifted off onto side lanes toward whatever remained of their homes. Others merged into larger knots of travelers, drawn together by fear and the crude safety of numbers. Andrew chose neither. He kept just enough distance to avoid being absorbed, and just enough proximity to avoid looking like prey.

A weathered signpost appeared at a crossroads where two roads met at a shallow angle: one road north toward a larger town, one road east along a creek line. The sign's lettering had been carved and repainted so many times that it looked like scar tissue. One arm of it had been shot through; a bullet hole had widened with rain until it was more wound than puncture.

Haines looked up at it and then at Andrew. "Town'll have patrols," he said quietly.

"And food," Rudd added, too quickly, as if the idea of food was permission to hope.

Andrew slowed the mules and let the wagon roll to a near stop beneath the signpost's shadow. The decision wasn't about hunger. It was about paper.

The forged sheet had carried them past one bored rider at a washout. It would not survive a town where men with desks still existed, men who knew which seals were current and which were old, men who had the time to be suspicious. In open country the right lie only had to be plausible. In a town the lie had to match whatever ledgers the world still pretended to keep.

He felt the ledger under his thigh, remembered the weight of Whitcomb's book in his hands. Deaths recorded as diseases so strangers would not ask what made the bodies so empty. He had taken that habit and sharpened it. Now it wasn't only death he needed to name. It was himself.

"We go east," Andrew said.

Rudd's mouth tightened. "Sir, that road looks worse."

"All roads look worse," Andrew replied, and heard the dullness in his own voice. He did not let himself examine it. "East keeps us away from the main stream. North puts us under eyes that still believe they're in charge."

Haines nodded once, but his gaze was wary. "And how long before we need to pass under those eyes anyway?"

Andrew did not answer immediately. The truthful answer was: soon. The other truth was: always. Eyes were everywhere when you carried what Andrew carried. Even when Ambrose did not show himself, the problem of him shaped every mile.

They turned east.

The creek road ran lower, the ground softer. It followed a line of willows and cypress that drank greedily from the swollen water. Every so often the road dipped into standing puddles where wheel ruts had become little ponds, and the wagon lurched hard enough to make the crates under canvas shift with a low, muffled complaint.

Rudd glanced back at the canvas as if he'd heard something forbidden. "Kellan?" he called, tentative.

No answer.

Andrew felt his wound give a small, sharp sting, quick as a pinprick. Not pain exactly. More like a nudge. A reminder that sound invited attention and attention was a currency Ambrose spent with ease.

"Leave him," Andrew said.

Rudd's face flickered with guilt, then he nodded, eyes down. The boy had learned, in pieces, what could not be said aloud: the quiet rules that now governed them. Don't call into darkness. Don't ask for what might answer.

The road brought them to a narrow bridge made of rough planks over a ditch that fed into the creek. Just beyond it sat a small structure with a slanted roof and an open front: a tollhouse once, perhaps, or a county post. Its porch boards were sagging. Someone had nailed a paper notice to the door and the notice had been soaked and dried until it was illegible, a blur of ink and authority.

A man stood in the porch shadow with a rifle held loosely, not aimed, not slung. He wore a mismatched uniform coat, gray but with blue buttons, the kind of garment that had been traded and stolen so many times it no longer belonged to any side. Two other men sat behind him on a bench, their faces slack with the bored hunger of people who had been waiting for hours and expected to wait for hours more.

Haines's stride changed, his shoulders tightening. "Checkpoint," he murmured.

"Something like it," Andrew said.

Rudd swallowed, and Andrew heard it. The boy's fear had a sound now.

The man on the porch stepped forward and lifted a hand. "Hold there," he called. Not the voice of a trained officer. The voice of a man pretending to be one.

Andrew stopped the mules. Their ears flicked, impatient. A fly-buzz rose around the ditch water and died away again.

"What's your business?" the porch man asked as he approached. His eyes went over Andrew's uniform and lingered on the bandage, not with sympathy but with calculation. He looked young enough that his beard came in patchy. His expression was older than his face.

"Medical provisions," Andrew said, and kept the tone of someone inconvenienced rather than intimidated. "Convalescents. Moving north."

The young man's eyes narrowed. "That's a Confederate coat," he said.

Andrew lifted his chin slightly. "Was," he answered again, as if the word belonged to everyone now.

One of the men on the bench behind the rifleman spat into the dirt and laughed softly. "Ain't nothing 'was' about some of you," he said. "Some of you just ain't been caught yet."

Haines shifted one step closer to the mule's head, hand on the bridle. Not a threat. A promise that if this turned ugly, the mule could become a barrier. Andrew saw it and filed it away. Small preparations. Fences in the mind.

The porch man jerked his chin. "Papers," he said.

Andrew reached into the clerk's box and pulled out the forged form. He handed it down without haste.

The rifleman took it with a grease-stained thumb and forefinger. He frowned at the seal, turning the paper as though rotating it might reveal truth. His lips moved as he sounded out the formal language. The words were correct. That wasn't the problem. The problem was that the man reading them did not care about correctness. He cared about what the paper could be turned into.

"Temporary station north of the county line," the man read aloud, slow. He glanced up. "Where."

Andrew named the town he'd used before, the far-enough one.

The man snorted. "That's a long haul for sick men."

"The main roads are worse," Andrew said. "We keep moving or we lose them."

The rifleman looked toward the canvas as if he could see through it. "How sick?"

Andrew let a pause hang. Disease still worked as a fence, but too much mystery invited the wrong kind of curiosity. He chose a middle truth, something ugly enough to deter but common enough to believe.

"Dysentery," Andrew said.

The man's face tightened. Even the men on the bench shifted, suddenly less bored.

Rudd's eyes flicked to Andrew, impressed and horrified by the ease of the lie. Or perhaps it wasn't a lie. Men did have dysentery. Men had every sickness. That was the beauty of certain stories: they didn't need to be invented. They only needed to be assigned.

The rifleman handed the paper back quickly, as if ink could carry contagion. "All right," he said. "But there's a fee."

Haines's jaw flexed. "Fee," he repeated, and his voice was flat with contained anger.

The rifleman shrugged. "Bridge don't fix itself," he said, and smiled in a way that showed he knew exactly what he was. "Road don't stay safe by prayer."

Andrew felt his wound sting, faint and clean, as if Ambrose had leaned in close enough to listen. The sweetness touched the back of his throat for a brief, intimate moment and then withdrew again. The demand was not surprising. It was predictable. Collapse created little kingdoms wherever a man could stand with a rifle and call himself necessary.

"How much," Andrew asked.

The rifleman's eyes slid over the wagon again. "A sack of flour," he said. "Or a pound of coffee. Or a watch."

Rudd's hand drifted unconsciously toward his own pocket as if checking what could be stolen. He caught himself and let it drop.

Andrew considered shooting him. The thought came with a cold, simple clarity and then passed, replaced by the arithmetic Ambrose had taught him without teaching. A body here would draw attention. A fight would draw more. Even if they won, winning would cost time, and time meant questions from the next armed man down the road.

He could pay and move on.

He could also learn something about this little checkpoint. Who ran it. How long it would last. Whether it was a one-time toll or an invitation that would follow them.

Andrew kept his face neutral. "We have flour," he said. "But it's for the men."

The rifleman lifted his brows. "Then your men can go hungry," he replied, as if it were a reasonable trade. "Or you can turn around."

Haines's hand tightened on the bridle. Andrew saw the tendons stand out. Haines did not speak, but the contempt in his posture was loud.

Andrew took a breath and made himself sound weary rather than cornered. "I'll give you flour," he said. "But you don't open the canvas."

The rifleman smiled, pleased. "Ain't planning to," he said. "Ain't paid enough for that."

Rudd let out a breath that was almost a sob and swallowed it back.

Andrew nodded to Haines. "Get him a sack. Small."

Haines hesitated, then went to the wagon's rear. His movements were controlled, careful. He pulled down a sack from the top layer without disturbing the deeper stacks Andrew had built. Rudd hovered nearby, hands fluttering uselessly until Haines snapped, "Hold the strap," and gave the boy a task that steadied him.

The sack hit the dirt with a soft thud. The rifleman dragged it toward the porch with the satisfaction of a man paid for his own performance.

"Go on then," he said, stepping aside. "And if you see any real patrols, you tell 'em we're here keeping things orderly."

Andrew clicked his tongue. The mules stepped forward, hooves clopping on planks. The wagon rolled onto the bridge.

Halfway across, a muffled sound came from under the canvas. Not a voice. Not a cough. Something like a shifting breath too deep for a man trying to be silent.

Rudd's head snapped around, eyes wide.

Haines did not look back. His eyes stayed forward, jaw clenched so tightly it looked like it might crack.

Andrew kept his hands steady on the reins. He did not turn his head. He did not acknowledge the sound. Acknowledgment was a kind of invitation.

The wagon reached the far side of the bridge. The planks creaked and then fell silent behind them. The checkpoint receded into the willow shadows like an ugly memory.

Only when the road bent and the tollhouse was no longer visible did Rudd whisper, "Sir. Did you hear that?"

Andrew's mouth tasted faintly of sweetness again, as if the sound had been meant for him and him alone.

"Yes," Andrew said.

Rudd's voice trembled. "Was that Kellan?"

Andrew stared at the road ahead, at the wet ruts, at the trees that made the world into narrow corridors. He could lie and say yes. He could lie and say no. Either lie would be a story. The point was not truth. The point was what the story did.

He chose the one that would keep the boy from pulling at the canvas in panic, from demanding a look, from forcing a confrontation that would turn a quiet road into a scene.

"Sometimes men make noise in their sleep," Andrew said. "Sometimes they don't know they're doing it."

Rudd nodded too quickly, accepting the explanation like a drowning man accepting a hand, even if the hand was attached to something that might pull him under.

Haines's voice came out low and rough. "Your papers got us past them," he said.

Andrew heard the unspoken end: but they cost us flour, and flour costs time, and time costs lives.

Andrew kept his gaze forward. "Paper doesn't buy safety," he replied. "It buys distance."

Rudd swallowed. "Distance from what?"

Andrew did not answer right away. The true fear wasn't the rifleman at the tollhouse. It wasn't even the next patrol with better eyes.

The true fear was that every time Andrew used ink to smooth their path, every time he paid a toll in flour or lies, he was proving something to himself. Proving that this could be done. Proving that the world was porous, that authority was only a costume, that you could move a coffin through a rebuilding nation if you learned the right words and stamped them with the right seal.

He felt his wound give its small, approving sting, and hated the way his body had begun to behave as though it belonged to a different set of rules.

"We keep moving," Andrew said finally, and his voice was steady because steadiness was a kind of deception. "We keep our story simple. We don't stop where men with rifles have the time to get curious."

Rudd nodded, eyes fixed on the road as if staring hard enough would prevent it from turning into another trap.

Behind them, under the canvas, the hidden dark remained quiet again. Too quiet. Like something that had made its point and no longer needed to waste effort.

Andrew drove on, the forged paper tucked back into the clerk's box, the ledger pressing against his thigh like a second heartbeat. He understood, with a cold clarity that did not soften, that the papers were not the danger.

The papers were proof.

Proof that the road would open for him if he kept lying.

Proof that he was becoming the kind of man who could carry something ancient and hungry through a world of checkpoints and rebuilding towns, smiling when asked for names.

And that, more than any rifleman's toll, was what made his fear feel true.

The creek road narrowed into a corridor of trees, their branches knitting overhead until the daylight turned the color of old dishwater. The ruts deepened. The mules' hooves made a wet, sucking sound that seemed too loud for how close the woods leaned in. Andrew kept the pace steady, not fast enough to look like flight, not slow enough to invite company.

Haines walked near the wheel for a time and then climbed onto the side rail when the ground leveled, boots hooking over the edge so he could ride without jostling the stacks. He did not ask permission. He no longer did. He only muttered once, as if to himself, "If we keep paying every man with a rifle, we'll be hauling air by next week."

Rudd glanced back toward the canvas, then forward again. His fear had become restless, seeking something to do. "Maybe we should get into town," he said quietly. "Just long enough to buy—"

"No," Andrew replied.

The word came out sharper than he intended. It cut the boy's sentence in half. Rudd flinched and fell silent, eyes fixed on the mud as if the road might offer a better suggestion.

Andrew loosened his grip on the reins by a fraction. He heard Whitcomb's voice in his head, tired and contemptuous: A traveling lie. He tasted that faint sweetness again, almost like bruised fruit left too long in a cellar. It touched the back of his throat and withdrew, as if it had only come close to see whether he would react.

Ahead, the trees thinned. The road bent and revealed a low clearing where smoke rose in thin threads from multiple small fires. It was not a town. It was what happened when too many people needed to stop and nowhere wanted them.

Tents made from quilts and wagon canvas dotted the field. A broken carriage sat on blocks, its wheels removed for firewood. Men stood in knots with rifles held down, not as a threat but as a reminder. Women crouched over iron pots, stirring whatever could be made to stretch. Children moved through the mud with a practiced carefulness, stepping around puddles like old drunks.

Haines leaned forward, eyes narrowing. "Refugees," he said.

"Everybody's a refugee now," Andrew murmured, and guided the wagon toward the edge of the camp instead of through its center. The instinct was to avoid it. But avoidance had its own language. A wagon that skirted a camp looked like a wagon with something to hide.

They rolled into the perimeter and stopped near a fallen fence line where a few other wagons had clustered. The mules lowered their heads and breathed out steam, relieved by stillness.

Andrew did not climb down immediately. He watched the camp the way he watched a checkpoint, looking for the shape of authority. There was no uniformed patrol, but there were men whose posture said they would take it upon themselves to ask questions. There were also men whose posture said they would take it upon themselves to take.

A woman approached with a tin cup in her hand and a scarf wrapped around her hair. Her cheeks were hollow. Her eyes were not pleading. They were assessing.

"You got coffee?" she asked, voice flat.

"No," Andrew answered.

She looked at the bandage at his side and then at his face, as if trying to decide which story he belonged to. "You got medicine?"

Andrew didn't answer at once. Medicine was a word that opened doors and opened mouths.

Haines spoke before Andrew could, voice rough and controlled. "We've got sick," he said, nodding toward the canvas. "Nothing to spare."

The woman's expression tightened, not offended, simply resigned. She glanced at Rudd, at the boy's young face and nervous eyes. Something in her gaze softened for a moment, then hardened again as she turned away. "Sick," she repeated, as if tasting the word like a charm that might keep her from coming too close.

Andrew climbed down. The mud tried to keep his boot. He pulled free with a controlled motion and turned toward Haines and Rudd.

"We change how we look," Andrew said quietly.

Rudd blinked. "Sir?"

Andrew kept his voice low. "Gray coat, officer's seat, stamped paper. It draws the wrong kind of eyes. If we're going to move through crowds like this, we stop looking like anything worth stopping."

Haines's jaw flexed. "You mean take the uniform off."

"Yes."

The word sat between them like another surrender. Andrew had spent years wearing that cloth like a second skin. Now the cloth had become a flag that could get them searched. Or shot. Or simply remembered.

Rudd swallowed. “But won’t that be desertion?”

Haines let out a bitter breath. “Boy,” he muttered, “the desert’s behind us and ahead of us. You just ain’t learned to see it yet.”

Andrew ignored the comment. He was watching a group of men near a fire who were arguing in low voices. One wore a blue cap with the brim torn off. Another wore a gray coat with no buttons. A third wore no coat at all, only a woman’s shawl wrapped around his shoulders. They looked like people who had emptied out whatever identity they used to carry and filled the space with anything that would keep them warm.

“That’s the disguise,” Andrew said, more to himself than to them. “Not a costume. An absence.”

His wound gave a small, clean sting under the bandage. Not pain, exactly. A pulse of attention. He felt, with a nausea that had become familiar, that the thing under their canvas appreciated the lesson. Ambrose had always moved through collapse. This was collapse with faces.

Andrew reached into the wagon and pulled out a plain brown coat from beneath a crate. It was too large in the shoulders and smelled of old sweat.

He'd taken it from the estate weeks ago without thinking, as if even then his hands had begun collecting disguises. He shrugged out of his gray jacket, folded it carefully, and tucked it into the hidden space he'd made, under boards that were too neat to look accidental.

The air under the canvas held a faint, stale sweetness. Andrew kept his movements precise and brief. He did not look deeper. Looking deeper invited recognition, and recognition invited conversation, even if the other party never spoke aloud.

Haines stripped off his own gray coat and replaced it with a patched civilian jacket traded from the dead. He moved like a man who hated the act and understood its necessity. Rudd hesitated, then took off his cap and tucked it away, replacing it with a floppy hat he'd pulled from a crate days earlier. It made him look less like a soldier and more like a farm boy on an errand that had gone wrong.

Kellan did not move.

Andrew lifted the canvas edge and saw him sitting in the dimness, knees drawn up, eyes unfocused. The man's face looked waxy in the low light. He had the expression of someone who had left his body behind and was watching from a distance.

"Kellan," Andrew said quietly.

No answer.

Rudd leaned in, voice trembling. "Kellan, you need to—"

"Leave him," Andrew repeated, and this time the command carried a warning. Rudd drew back.

Haines watched Andrew's hands, his eyes narrowing slightly. "You want to hide, you keep him hidden too," Haines said under his breath. "That's the price."

Andrew did not answer, because yes was too honest and no was too false. Instead he reached for a sack of flour and shoved it closer to the canvas edge, creating a wall of ordinary things between the camp and whatever lay deeper. A man who looked inside would see supplies. He would not want to see beyond them.

Andrew stepped away from the wagon and scanned the camp again. A boy not much younger than Rudd walked by carrying a length of rope. A little girl followed, barefoot, her feet red with cold, holding a spoon like it was valuable.

A man approached them, older, his beard tangled, his coat buttoned wrong. He had a rifle slung but carried it loosely. He stopped at a polite distance, which meant he was not polite at all. He was cautious.

"You boys headed north?" he asked.

Andrew nodded once. "As far as the road lets us."

The man's eyes flicked to the wagon, to the mules, to Andrew's bandage. "You got papers?" he asked, and his tone suggested he did not mean official ones.

Andrew understood immediately. The camps created their own documents: promises, routes, information traded like tobacco. "We got a story," Andrew said.

That made the man smile faintly. "That's all anybody's got."

Andrew reached into his pocket and pulled out a small piece of salt pork, held back for exactly this kind of moment. He offered it without flourish. The man's eyes brightened with hunger, then he took it with a nod.

"Name's Caffey," the man said around the first bite. "There's men on the main road asking questions and taking what they like. Not bluecoats. Just men. They've set up near the county line, calling it a toll. If you got a wagon, they'll want a look."

Haines's jaw tightened. "We just paid a toll," he muttered.

Caffey shrugged. "Then you'll pay again or you'll shoot," he said, as if those were the only two verbs left. "Or you'll go around. Creek road can take you to a ford, but it's slow and the mud'll swallow your wheels."

Andrew absorbed the information, measuring it against the map in his head. Avoid main road. Find ford. Slow might be safer. Slow also meant more nights, more camps, more chances for eyes to linger.

Caffey's gaze slid toward Andrew's face again, sharpening. "You look like you wore stripes once," he said.

Andrew kept his expression dull. "I wore a uniform."

Caffey snorted. "We all did. Or we wore somebody else's. Question is what you are now."

The words hit closer than Caffey could know. Andrew felt his wound sting, quick and clean, as if it enjoyed the question. He kept his voice level.

"I'm a man with sick under canvas," Andrew said. "And not enough flour to be generous."

Caffey's expression tightened at the word sick again. He took another bite of pork and stepped back half a pace, as if disease could travel through conversation. "Then don't stop near those toll men," he said. "And if you camp, camp near noise. Noise keeps thieves away. Quiet is where men get brave."

Andrew almost laughed at the accidental truth of it. Quiet was also where hunger moved easiest.

"Thank you," Andrew said.

Caffey nodded once and wandered off, already scanning for the next trade. Information had become a kind of currency. It did not keep you alive by itself, but it bought you the illusion of choice.

Rudd watched Caffey disappear. "We're going to look like them," he whispered, not quite a question.

Andrew looked around the camp: the mismatched coats, the stolen hats, the missing insignia, the faces that had learned to flatten expression into something unreadable. Disguises among refugees were not masks. They were the stripping away of anything that invited story.

"Yes," Andrew said. "We're going to look like we belong."

Haines's eyes narrowed. "And the wagon?" he asked.

Andrew glanced at the canvas, at the careful stacking, at the hidden space inside that felt less like concealment and more like collaboration. "We make it uglier," Andrew said.

Rudd frowned. "Uglier?"

"Messier," Andrew corrected. "Less deliberate."

He climbed into the wagon bed and began shifting the top layer, not changing what was hidden but changing what was seen. He tossed a broken harness strap over a crate. He smeared mud along the edge where the canvas met wood, making it look like careless travel instead of careful planning. He tied a frayed blanket to the side rail so it hung like a flag of poverty. The work felt obscene. He was disguising the disguise.

All the while, his body listened. The wound remained attentive under the bandage, that second pulse that did not belong to him. He felt, behind his thoughts, the presence of something patient in darkness, pleased not by the mud or the blanket but by the fact that Andrew understood the principle.

If you wished to move a monster through the rebuilding world, you did not dress it as a monster.

You dressed it as need.

When dusk began to settle, Andrew lit a small fire near the wagon, not because he wanted warmth, but because he wanted witnesses. People nearby glanced over and then looked away, relieved to see the shape of an ordinary camp: a wagon, a fire, men hunched in tired silence. Sick under canvas. Nothing worth approaching.

Rudd sat close to the fire, hands extended toward it as if he could burn the fear out through his palms. Haines ate without appetite, eyes scanning the camp's perimeter. Kellan remained under canvas, silent.

Andrew took Whitcomb's ledger out and held it in his lap for a moment, feeling its weight. He did not write yet. He watched the refugees instead: the way they traded stories and objects, the way they avoided names, the way they made themselves smaller so the world would pass over them.

He understood, with bleak clarity, that this was the country Ambrose preferred. Not because it was weak. Because it was willing to look away.

And as the night thickened and the camp's many small fires turned into scattered points of light, Andrew felt that faint sweetness drift through the air again, subtle enough that no one else would name it.

It lingered near him like approval.

Andrew kept his face still and stared into the fire until the flames blurred, and he could almost pretend the heat on his skin was the only presence close enough to matter.

Chapter 15

The Hollowed Land

Andrew woke to the sound of hammers.

For a moment it did not make sense. The refugee field had been full of softer noises: coughing, low voices, babies crying and being hushed, the wet scrape of boots in mud. Hammers belonged to a different world, a world that believed in straight boards and measured nails. He opened his eyes to a pale morning and realized the sound was real.

Beyond the field's fence line, men were setting posts along the road. A small crew, three of them, working with the grim focus of people paid to pretend the future was practical. One man held a post upright while another drove it down with steady blows. The third unrolled wire that flashed dull in the thin light. A new fence, and behind it the bones of an old one still lay half-buried, gray and splintered.

Reconstruction, Andrew thought, and the word felt like an insult to everything it tried to name.

He sat up on the wagon seat. The fire they'd built the night before had burned low and cold, leaving a circle of ash that looked too clean for the mud around it. Rudd slept near it, curled tight, hat pulled down over his eyes. Haines was already awake, sitting with his back against the wheel, sharpening his knife with slow, deliberate strokes. Under the canvas, Kellan did not move.

Andrew felt for the ledger before he fully stood. It was where he'd left it, tucked close. The clerk's box, too, as if ink and stamps were talismans that could keep teeth away. He listened for the faint sweetness and found only damp air and smoke. Still, his wound held its attentive ache, the kind that suggested silence was not absence but restraint.

Haines looked up without asking. "Work crew," he said, nodding toward the fence posts. His voice was flat with suspicion.

Andrew followed his gaze. The men wore no uniforms, but one had a blue forage cap that marked him as either Union or simply fond of Union cloth. Another had a red scarf tied around his neck. All of them looked hungry in the way laborers always had, but now the hunger sat on the surface, unhidden by any pretension of stability.

"They're fencing the road," Rudd murmured suddenly, still half asleep. He pushed himself upright and blinked at the scene as if expecting it to vanish. “Why?”

Haines gave a humorless breath. “Because somebody wants to own it again.”

Andrew climbed down, boots sinking. The mud made a sound like suction, as if the land itself tried to keep what walked across it. He glanced around the refugee camp. People were stirring, folding quilts, tamping ashes, loading wagons with the slow resignation of those who had learned that motion was safer than hope. Faces turned briefly toward Andrew’s wagon and then away again, as if they could smell sickness even without seeing it.

That story had become their strongest protection. Sick under canvas. Nothing to touch. Nothing to steal.

Andrew walked to the rear of the wagon and lifted the canvas edge just enough to look in.

Kellan sat in the dimness, knees drawn up, eyes open. His gaze was fixed on a point in front of him that did not exist. He did not blink when the light shifted.

“Kellan,” Andrew said quietly.

Kellan’s mouth moved once, a small dry motion that might have been the beginning of speech or only habit. Then he went still again.

Behind Kellan, deeper in the space Andrew had made, the shadows looked thicker than they should have. Not darker. Thicker, like cloth folded over itself. Andrew felt the faintest touch of sweetness rise and then settle, as if the air had been stirred by something breathing slowly in comfort.

He lowered the canvas at once, careful, as if the act was only about keeping out cold. His fingers were steady. He hated that steadiness almost as much as he hated the smell.

Rudd approached, rubbing sleep from his face. “Is he…” The boy’s voice caught. He had stopped asking direct questions when he learned answers were weapons. “Is he all right?”

Andrew looked at him. Rudd’s fear had changed shape over the past days. It was less frantic now, more constant, like a low fever. “He’s alive,” Andrew said.

Rudd swallowed. “That’s not what I meant.”

Andrew did not offer him a softer sentence. There were no soft sentences left that did not become lies. “Get the mules ready,” he said instead. “We move as soon as Haines finishes.”

Haines’s knife made one last slow pass along the stone. He stood and slid it into its sheath. “We should leave before those fence men get curious,” he muttered.

Andrew nodded. “Yes.”

They moved with the practiced efficiency of people who had learned to break camp without ceremony. The fire was stamped out. The ash scattered. The mules were harnessed. Rudd fetched water with a tin cup and came back with only a mouthful, his eyes down, because even water had become a thing you begged for or stole.

As the wagon rolled toward the road, the sound of the hammers followed them, steady and indifferent. Andrew glanced back once and saw one of the fence men pause, resting his hand on the post, watching the refugee camp with the expression of someone measuring what could be organized and what would resist organization by simply rotting.

The road carried them past the edge of the camp and into countryside that looked like it had been emptied and then refilled with different kinds of absence. Here and there a chimney rose alone, black against pale sky, like a finger accusing heaven. Fields were torn up by wagon ruts and neglect. A line of trees stood bare and scarred where men had cut them down for breastworks or firewood or simply because they could.

And then, without warning, there were signs of trying.

A house with its roof re-shingled in mismatched wood. A fence rebuilt in crooked confidence. A newly whitewashed church with the paint still too bright, the boards still smelling of lime. A small schoolhouse with fresh glass in one window and the other window still broken, as if the building itself could not decide what year it belonged to.

Ghosts, Andrew thought, not the kind that rattled chains or moaned. The kind that lived in places where a thing had been violently interrupted and then forced to continue.

Rudd pointed at the church as they passed. "They're fixing it," he said, and there was a note in his voice that might have once been wonder.

Haines grunted. "Fixing boards don't fix what happened under 'em."

Andrew watched the churchyard. New graves had been added close to the building, marked with boards that looked freshly cut. Old headstones leaned beyond them, older deaths jostled by new ones. The ground did not care about causes. It accepted everything.

They came into a small town by midday. Not a city, not even a proper county seat, but larger than the scattered farmsteads. There were men in the street laying down planks over a section of mud that had become impassable. A storefront had a new sign hung crookedly, the letters too neat, the paint too bold, like someone trying to shout over memory.

Andrew kept the wagon moving at a steady pace, eyes forward, posture weary and unremarkable. He had dressed himself in the brown coat, kept his hair unremarkable, his face blank. He looked like a man hauling sickness and supplies. He looked like a man no one wanted to talk to for long.

Still, eyes followed them. Not hostile, not curious in a clean way, but watchful. The town had been carved open by war and now it watched every passing thing as if expecting the cut to reopen.

A pair of men stood near a building with a crude sign that read PROVOST. The word looked new, the boards beneath it old. One of the men wore a blue coat unbuttoned, his belt hanging loose. The other wore civilian clothes but carried himself like a soldier, hand resting near a sidearm. Their faces held the bored authority of people assigned to oversee chaos and resentful that chaos kept moving.

Haines's shoulders tightened. He stepped closer to the wagon's side, ready to hand up papers without being asked.

Andrew did not reach for the clerk's box yet. He waited. Too eager looked guilty.

The blue-coated man lifted his hand. “Hold up,” he called.

Andrew stopped the mules. Their harness jingled softly in the sudden quiet. Rudd stood very still at the wagon rail, eyes forward. Haines kept his face flat, as if he had already learned how to become nobody.

The provost man approached, gaze moving over the wagon, the patched canvas, the mud-smeared boards. “Where you headed?” he asked.

Andrew answered with the tired tone of a man who’d been asked too many times. “North,” he said. “Carrying sick and provisions.”

The man’s eyes narrowed slightly. “What kind of sick?”

Andrew did not hesitate. Hesitation was a confession. “Dysentery,” he said again.

The man’s expression tightened. He took half a step back without meaning to. Even authority stepped away from the wrong kind of suffering. “You got papers?”

Andrew reached into the box and produced the form, already stamped, already shaped. He handed it over.

The provost man glanced at it, lips moving as he read, then flicked his eyes up to Andrew’s face.

"You were Confederate," he said, not as an accusation, more as a category being assigned.

Andrew kept his voice dull. "Was."

The provost man held the paper like it was both permission and filth. "War's over," he said.

Andrew met his gaze. "I heard."

The man stared, perhaps expecting bitterness, perhaps expecting defiance, and finding instead only fatigue. He handed the paper back quickly. "Don't stop in town," he said. "If you got sick, you keep it moving."

Andrew nodded once. "That's the plan."

As they rolled on, Rudd let out a breath. Haines did not. Haines's eyes stayed scanning, because he had learned that the most dangerous moment was often after a man decided you were not worth attention. Disinterest could turn into a different kind of curiosity if something changed.

They passed the town's main street. A freed family stood near a storefront, the father holding a sack, the mother holding a child on her hip. Their clothes were plain, their posture careful, their eyes watchful in a way Andrew recognized. Not the watchfulness of soldiers. The watchfulness of people who knew the world could change its rules mid-sentence.

A white man in a vest spoke to them from the doorway, gesturing sharply. The father nodded, mouth tight, and stepped back as if retreating from a blow. The man in the vest went back inside as if the exchange had been nothing at all.

Rudd watched, confused. “What was that?”

Haines’s jaw flexed. “Same as always,” he muttered. “Just with different words on the paper.”

Andrew felt his wound sting faintly, clean and precise, and knew the sting wasn’t about the provost men or the town. It was about the shape of what he was seeing. A country trying to rebuild itself with rules, with offices, with fences, with paper. A country trying to make itself legible again.

A country full of people who did not want to look too hard at what moved in the dark, because looking hard made you responsible.

They cleared the far end of town and took the road that bent back toward trees and open fields. The noise of hammers, voices, and wagons faded behind them.

Rudd shifted closer to Andrew on the seat, voice low. “Sir,” he said, careful, “are we… are we going someplace for good?”

Andrew kept his eyes forward. The road ahead looked like every road now, muddy and uncertain, bordered by signs of ruin and signs of repair that did not quite fit together. He thought of Elias walking north with strangers, carrying his own anger like a lantern. He thought of the ribbon folded in his pocket, the soft thing made hard by being carried.

He felt, faintly, that sweetness again, as if the wagon itself had exhaled.

"No," Andrew said. "Not for good."

Rudd swallowed. "Then what are we doing?"

Andrew's hands tightened on the reins, not enough to show, only enough to feel. "We're passing," he said. "That's all."

But even as he spoke, he knew passing was a kind of life now. The war had ended. The country was trying to rebuild its fences and offices and churches.

And Andrew Mercer was hauling a hidden dark through it, learning the new roads, learning which men stepped back from the word dysentery, learning which towns still believed in stamps.

Ghosts in reconstruction, he thought again. Not only burned houses and fresh graves.

Men, too.

Men who kept moving because stopping would force them to look inside what they carried.

The road narrowed again after the town, slipping between fields that had been worked badly and then abandoned, and thickets that had grown up like scabs over old wounds. The sky stayed a colorless sheet. The air smelled of wet earth and woodsmoke and, beneath it, the faintest suggestion of fruit gone soft.

Andrew kept them moving until the mules began to labor. He did not like stopping in daylight anymore, not because daylight hid less, but because daylight made men feel entitled. In daylight they asked questions. In daylight they counted wagons and decided which ones might be worth the trouble.

By late afternoon the road broke into two rutted tracks where a stand of trees split the land. Andrew chose the lower track that dipped toward a creek line, not because it was better, but because it was quieter. Quieter meant fewer eyes.

Haines walked again, boots sinking, shoulders tight. Rudd rode on the seat board for a time and then climbed down, restless as a dog that couldn't settle. Under the canvas, Kellan remained a silence with skin.

Andrew felt the wound at his side answer the landscape the way a tongue answered a taste. It stung lightly when they passed a farmhouse with people moving inside, worse when they passed a small graveyard behind a church that had been painted too recently. The sting sharpened when the road drifted close to other travelers, then eased when they left them behind.

Ambrose was not only a presence now. He was a kind of pressure in Andrew's body, a way the world arranged itself around a hunger that did not need to announce its direction with sound.

When the sky began to dim toward evening, Andrew spotted a low, abandoned outbuilding near the creek: a smokehouse or a tool shed, half-collapsed, its roof caved in on one side. It stood at the edge of a field where the stalks had been cut and left. No livestock. No dog. Only the creek's slow sound and the distant, muffled clink of a hammer from somewhere far away, as if the country was always building something out of habit.

He brought the wagon off the track and stopped behind a thin line of brush. The mules sighed and lowered their heads.

Haines looked at the smokehouse and then at Andrew. "This?" he asked.

Andrew nodded. "For tonight."

Rudd frowned. "No other fires around."

"Then we make our own," Andrew said, and hated how quickly the thought formed: but small, and close, and ordinary enough to look like any other poor camp.

They moved with practice now. Haines checked the traces. Rudd gathered damp branches and cursed under his breath when they snapped too easily. Andrew circled once, scanning for the gleam of a rifle barrel or the shape of a man deciding whether to approach. There was nothing. The creek and the weeds and the empty field held their silence without interest.

He approached the rear of the wagon and lifted the canvas edge just enough to look in.

Kellan's eyes were open. They always were. The man's face looked paler in the dim, as if his skin had given up trying to match the world. There was a smear of dirt on his cheek where he must have leaned against the boards. His hands rested in his lap, fingers slightly curled, as if he was still holding something he could not set down.

Behind him, deeper in the wagon's arranged dark, the shadows pressed together like folded cloth. Andrew did not see Ambrose. That was not the point. He felt him in the way the air changed, in the faint sweetness that rose and settled again, careful not to be strong.

Andrew lowered the canvas. His fingers lingered on the seam. He did not want to speak into it. Speech felt like a door.

Rudd came up behind him. "Sir," the boy whispered, "we're really staying out here? No town. No—"

"No," Andrew said again, and then softened it by a fraction because the boy was trembling and Andrew could not afford hysteria. "We don't need a town."

Rudd's eyes darted to the smokehouse. "That thing's half fallen down."

"It's cover," Haines said, joining them. His gaze flicked over the brush and the field and then returned to the wagon as if the wagon was the only true terrain now. "And it's empty."

Andrew felt the wound give a small, precise sting at the word empty, and he understood the correction in it. It is never empty anymore, his body seemed to say. You have made it impossible.

They built a small fire in a shallow scrape behind the brush, where the flame would not be visible from the road unless a man came looking. Rudd coaxed it to life with the eager desperation of someone trying to prove usefulness. The smoke rose thin and reluctant. Haines ate a strip of salt pork without tasting it. Andrew sat on the wagon seat with the reins looped near his hand out of old habit, even though no one was trying to steal their team.

As darkness settled, the creek's sound grew louder in the mind, and the quiet spaces between the fire's crackles felt thick. Andrew's thoughts slid toward Elias without permission. He imagined his brother walking with strangers, sharing their food and their suspicion, sleeping with one eye open. Elias would think himself freer out there. Andrew hoped he was right.

Then he imagined Ambrose choosing to follow Elias simply because it would make Andrew run.

The thought tightened something in Andrew's chest until he could hardly breathe.

He forced himself to focus on smaller things: the way the wind pulled at the brush, the way Rudd stared into the fire as if expecting a face to appear in it. The way Haines kept turning his head slightly, listening beyond the obvious sounds.

"What happens when people start settling again?" Rudd asked suddenly. His voice was low and careful, as if he feared the question itself might summon an answer. "When they stop moving."

Haines glanced at Andrew, then back at the dark. "They won't," he said. "Not for a while."

Rudd swallowed. "But they're building fences. We saw them. And offices. That provost sign."

Andrew listened to the creek and felt the wound listening too. It stung in slow pulses, not pain, not warning, but attention turning inward, as if something in the wagon had shifted to hear the conversation more clearly.

"They'll build," Andrew said. "They always build."

"And then what?" Rudd pressed. "Then he can't just—" The boy stopped, unable to find a verb that wouldn't make the world worse.

Haines's jaw flexed. "Then he finds another way," he muttered, and there was something like resignation in it, the tone of a man who had realized the problem wasn't a single creature, but the fact that people made routes for it without knowing they were doing it.

Andrew felt the sweetness rise faintly, as if in agreement.

The fire snapped once. Rudd flinched.

Andrew turned his head slightly toward the wagon. The canvas did not move. There was no sound from within. Kellan remained a mute witness in the dark.

And then Ambrose spoke.

Not loudly. Not as a voice that came from a mouth in a face. It came from the darkness like a thought that wasn't Andrew's, polite and composed, sliding into the air just beyond the firelight where Rudd could not see anything but shadow.

"You are all so convinced," Ambrose said, "that civilization is a wall."

Rudd's head jerked up. His eyes went wide, darting toward the wagon and then toward the brush as if he expected a pale man to step into view. "Sir," he whispered, panic rising.

Haines's hand moved to his knife, not drawing it, only touching it like a habit that pretended to be defense. He kept his face angled away from the wagon as if refusing to offer it direct attention.

Andrew did not move. The wound burned once, clean and intimate, as if his body had been tapped with a finger. He kept his voice low, steady, because steadiness was the only leash he still had on himself and the others.

"What do you mean?" Andrew asked.

A pause, and in the pause the creek sounded like breathing.

"Walls," Ambrose continued, "are for honest things. They keep out weather. They keep in heat. Civilization is not a wall. It is a curtain."

Andrew stared into the dark beyond the firelight. "A curtain," he repeated.

"Yes," Ambrose said, and there was mild amusement in it, as if Andrew had asked for the name of a simple tool. "It hangs wherever men agree not to look too closely. It is stitched from manners, paperwork, propriety, fatigue. It is heavy enough that most will not bother to lift it."

Rudd's breathing came quick. "Stop talking," the boy whispered, not to Andrew, but toward the wagon, toward the darkness. It sounded like a prayer a child made when he realized prayer did not have rules.

Ambrose did not acknowledge Rudd at all. That, Andrew understood, was part of the lesson. Rudd was noise. Andrew was function.

"In war," Ambrose said, "blood is expected. In peace, blood must be explained. That is all."

Haines's voice came out rough, controlled. "So you'll just… what. Start signing papers?"

A soft sound, almost a laugh. "Men will sign for me," Ambrose replied. "They always do. Doctors sign. Clerks sign. Ministers sign. Husbands sign.

Mothers sign when they insist their daughters simply ran away."

Andrew felt the words land with a cold, creeping weight. He thought of Whitcomb's ledger. The way Andrew had told himself records were evidence. The way records could also become camouflage.

"You're adapting," Andrew said, and hated that it sounded like admiration rather than horror.

Ambrose's tone remained courteous, almost instructional. "I do not need chaos," he said. "Chaos is merely convenient. Order is more durable. Order has basements. Order has asylums. Order has respectable men who grow tired of asking where the missing went."

Rudd made a small sound of despair, as if his mind was trying to refuse the image of a future where this could live neatly inside a town.

Andrew's mouth went dry. "Then why travel like this?" he asked. "Why hide in a wagon like a fugitive?"

Another pause. The sweetness thinned, then returned, faint and warm.

"Because the country is between costumes," Ambrose said. "Everything is loose. It is a splendid time to choose a new face."

Andrew heard, in the word choose, the shape of what Ambrose wanted. Not simply shelter tonight, or a sack of flour at a toll bridge, but a settled arrangement that could outlast the road. A cellar. A respectable cover. A name that belonged in a ledger.

Ambrose's voice lowered slightly, intimate enough to make Andrew's skin tighten. "You have already begun," he said. "You learned the word dysentery and watched men step back. You learned to make your wagon look poor. You learned to use paper as a fence."

Andrew's wound stung in three quick pulses, like a quiet applause.

Haines spoke, bitter. "You're proud of him."

"I am satisfied," Ambrose replied, and the distinction was worse. "Pride is human. Satisfaction is practical."

Andrew felt something in him shift at that. Satisfaction. Practical. The way Ambrose could take the language of survival and scrub it clean until it sounded like a trade, not a sin.

Rudd's voice trembled. "What are you going to do?" he asked, and for a moment his fear pushed him into daring. "When we stop. When there's… rules again."

Ambrose's answer was gentle enough to be obscene. "The rules will keep you warm," he said. "They will keep you fed. They will keep you busy. And in that warmth and busyness, you will not notice what slips through the cracks. You will call it misfortune. Illness. Accident. You will call it anything that allows you to sleep."

Rudd covered his mouth with his hand, as if to keep himself from making a sound that would attract attention. His eyes shone with tears that did not fall.

Andrew stared at the fire until it blurred. He understood the horror in a new shape. Ambrose did not need a war. Ambrose needed people who were tired. People who preferred explanations to truth. People who let papers replace seeing.

And Andrew, sitting with a ledger close and a seal in a wooden box, had already proven he could be one of those people. Not only could. Was.

Ambrose's presence receded slightly, as if the lesson was complete. But before the darkness went fully quiet again, the voice returned one last time, directed only at Andrew, quiet enough that it felt like it moved along the bandage at his side and into his blood.

“Reconstruction,” Ambrose murmured, tasting the word as if it belonged to him. “They will rebuild the country. You will rebuild my house.”

Andrew’s hands tightened on his knees. He did not answer.

Across the creek, somewhere far away, a hammer struck a nail with steady rhythm.

Rudd stared at Andrew as if waiting for him to say something that would restore the world’s shape. Haines watched too, wary and grim, his face set in lines that suggested he had already accepted what Rudd still struggled to name.

Andrew felt the ribbon in his pocket, folded hard, a soft thing turned into a small square of pain. He thought of Elias calling it a funeral between the living. He thought of the trap in the graveyard, the moment his hand had not moved.

He understood, in a way that left him hollow, that Ambrose’s adaptation was not only about finding a new cellar or a new doctor or a new town willing to look away.

It was about Andrew adapting too.

And Andrew did not know anymore where the creature’s hunger ended and his own need for purpose began.

Andrew did not sleep that night, but the night still passed through him.

The fire dwindled into coals and then into a faint, pulsing red that seemed less like warmth and more like an eye half-closed. Rudd dozed in fits, jerking awake whenever a branch snapped or the creek changed its voice. Haines stayed on the edge of the light with his knife across his thigh, not as a threat to anything in particular, but as a way to keep his hands occupied so they would not tremble.

Andrew sat with his back against the wagon wheel, the mud cold through his coat, and listened to the dark inside the canvas as if listening could turn it into something he understood.

Ambrose did not speak again. That was the worst part.

When the thing in the dark went quiet, it felt less like absence than like patience. Silence, Andrew was learning, was not a lack of appetite. It was the posture of a creature confident it had already been fed in more ways than blood.

Rudd shifted closer to the wagon at some point, drawn by fear the way men were drawn to fire. He whispered, so low it barely carried, “Lieutenant?”

Andrew looked at him. The boy’s face was smudged with soot and fatigue. The whites of his eyes showed too clearly.

"What," Andrew said.

Rudd swallowed. "When he talks like that," he managed, and then faltered as if even pronouns were dangerous.

Andrew's wound gave a small, clean sting, like a reprimand for refusing to name what controlled them.

"When he talks," Rudd corrected, "is it… is he talking to you? Or to all of us?"

Haines made a rough sound that might have been a laugh if it had any humor in it. He kept his eyes on the treeline and said, "He's always talking to Mercer. We're just close enough to hear the lesson sometimes."

Rudd's mouth tightened. He looked from Haines to Andrew, searching Andrew's face for a denial.

Andrew gave him none. Denial had become another kind of lie, and lies were no longer harmless in his hands. They were tools.

"He wants you scared," Rudd whispered.

Andrew stared at the coals until the red blurred. "No," he said quietly. "He wants you to understand. Fear is just what happens when you do."

Rudd flinched at the coldness in the sentence. Andrew heard it too and felt something twist, a brief sick awareness that he had spoken like

Ambrose without meaning to. Without even noticing until after.

He reached into his coat pocket and touched the ribbon Elias had given him, the small hard square of folded cloth. The gesture was instinctive now, less comfort than a check that something human still existed in him somewhere, even if it had been pressed flat.

The ribbon did nothing. It was cloth. It could not argue with the dark.

Rudd finally lay back down, but he did not close his eyes again. He stared up at the wagon canvas as if expecting it to swell and reveal a pale face pressing through like a birth.

Haines kept watch until the first thin light began to seep into the eastern sky. When dawn came, it came grudgingly, turning the world gray without washing it clean.

Andrew rose stiffly, his joints aching. The wound at his side burned with its familiar attentive ache, the pain not worsening, not healing, simply maintaining itself as a constant reminder that something in him had been altered to keep time with another creature.

He unhitched one mule's harness to let it drink at the creek and watched the animal lower its head, unconcerned. The mule did not know the word civilization. It did not know the word reconstruction. It knew thirst and the taste of water and the simple fact of staying alive.

Andrew envied it with a bitterness that surprised him.

They broke camp quickly. Haines stamped out the coals and scattered the ash. Rudd gathered their few loose things with jerky movements. Andrew climbed into the wagon seat and looped the reins around his fingers as if tying himself to the only forward motion he had left.

Before he clicked the mules on, he turned his head slightly toward the canvas and spoke without raising his voice. "We're moving."

There was no answer.

But the sweetness touched the air faintly, like a breath exhaled through a crack, and Andrew felt the wound respond with a small, satisfied sting. It was enough. Ambrose did not need to acknowledge instructions. Ambrose only needed to be obeyed.

The day's road ran along the creek for a time and then climbed toward higher ground where the fields were wider. They passed a farmhouse with fresh boards nailed over a burned window. They passed men repairing a fence, their backs bent, their movements steady and practiced. The sound of hammer on nail carried across the open space, a rhythm so ordinary it felt obscene.

Andrew kept the wagon rolling at a pace that looked like fatigue, not urgency. He wore the brown coat. He kept his posture slumped just enough to read as civilian. He let his face go blank. He had become good at blankness.

As the sun rose, the land around them filled with travelers again. Small groups on foot, a cart pulled by a thin horse, a family with a wagon piled with bedding. Faces turned toward Andrew's wagon and then away, relieved by the look of poverty and sickness. No one wanted to invite another burden.

That story, sick under canvas, worked too well. It made Andrew's skin crawl with how well it worked.

At midday they stopped near a stand of pines to water the mules. Haines stayed close to the harness, eyes sharp. Rudd wandered a few steps off with a tin cup and came back quickly, as if the trees had whispered something at him.

Andrew climbed down and lifted the canvas edge just enough to look in.

Kellan sat in the same position, knees drawn up, hands in his lap. His eyes were open and unblinking. If he had eaten, it was only because someone had put food into his hands and watched him chew. His face had the waxy pallor of a man whose mind had stepped away and left the body behind as a decoy.

"Kellan," Andrew said.

Kellan's gaze shifted, barely, and for a moment Andrew saw recognition flicker. Not comprehension. Not speech. Recognition like a dying candle flaring when the wind changes. Kellan's mouth opened slightly.

Andrew leaned closer in spite of himself, hungry for a human sound that was not Ambrose.

Kellan whispered something. It was so faint Andrew had to tilt his head to catch it.

"Cold," Kellan breathed.

That was all.

Andrew felt a wave of relief so sharp it almost hurt. A word. A human complaint. Proof that Kellan was still inside his own skin somewhere.

Then the relief curdled as the smell inside the wagon deepened, faint but unmistakable. Not merely sweat and stale straw. Fruit sweetness and old rot threaded together, too subtle to be called a stench, too intimate to be dismissed.

Behind Kellan, in the deeper arranged shadow, something shifted. Not a body moving. A change in density, as if darkness had folded itself to make room for attention.

Andrew froze. The wound at his side burned, a clean flare that made him clench his teeth.

He lowered the canvas at once. His hands were steady. His stomach was not.

Rudd hovered nearby, eyes wide. "Did he say something?" the boy asked, voice tight.

Andrew stared at the wagon boards as if they might confess. "He spoke," Andrew said.

Rudd's face softened with desperate hope. "What did he say?"

Andrew hesitated. The hesitation was small, but he felt it the way he felt every small moral turn now, each one an intersection where he chose what kind of man to be for the next mile.

"He said he's cold," Andrew answered.

Haines's expression tightened. He looked at the canvas as if it were a mouth held shut by nails. "He ain't the only one," Haines muttered.

Andrew turned away and walked a few steps into the pines, pretending to check the road. He needed distance from the wagon, but more than that, he needed to feel like he could still choose where to put his own body.

The ribbon in his pocket felt hard against his palm when he touched it. He unfolded it slightly and then stopped, afraid of tearing it. The cloth smelled faintly of old soap, a scent from before the war, before Ambrose, before Andrew had learned how easily a man could be trained by consequence.

He thought of Elias walking north among strangers. Elias would be hungry and furious and alive. Elias would curse Andrew and mean it. The thought should have hurt more than it did.

That numbness frightened Andrew in a way Ambrose never had.

He went back to the wagon and climbed up. "We move," he said. His voice sounded like an order and like an excuse.

They traveled until late afternoon. The road led them past a small settlement where men were rebuilding a porch. A woman carried water from a well, her face set, her eyes forward. A boy ran past with a length of board on his shoulder as if running made him safe.

Andrew felt the sting in his wound sharpen as they passed the settlement, not warning, not fear, but something else. Interest. Opportunity.

He tightened his grip on the reins and forced the mules onward.

Haines noticed. "You feel him," he said quietly, not looking up at Andrew's face.

Andrew kept his eyes on the road. "I feel my wound," he said.

"That ain't what I mean," Haines replied.

Rudd, listening, whispered, "Sir?"

Andrew did not answer either of them. He could not bear to say aloud what he had begun to suspect: that the wound no longer only reacted to Ambrose's nearness. It reacted to Andrew's decisions. It punished him when he resisted. It rewarded him when he arranged.

As evening approached, they found another place to camp, this time nearer the sound of people, a small cluster of wagons and fires along the edge of a field. Noise, like Caffey had said, kept thieves away. Noise also kept certain kinds of quiet from settling too heavily.

They stopped at the perimeter. Andrew let Haines speak to the nearest group, using the familiar words, sick under canvas, nothing to spare. The group nodded and looked away. No one wanted sickness. No one wanted responsibility.

Andrew sat down by their small fire as if he belonged to an ordinary camp. Rudd ate quickly, eyes darting. Haines ate slowly, watching the other fires.

Andrew took out Whitcomb's ledger when the sky was fully dark. The page he had filled earlier, names and dates and explanations, looked like an attempt to make indecency orderly. He stared at the blank lines below and felt the strange compulsion to fill them, not because anyone demanded it, but because leaving space felt like letting something go unmeasured.

He wrote anyway.

Not names this time. There were no new bodies today. He wrote the places: washout bridge, tollhouse, refugee field, provost sign. He wrote the lies that worked: dysentery, convalescents, medical provisions. He wrote the cost: a sack of flour. He wrote Elias's name once, small, near the margin, and then stared at it until his eyes watered.

Rudd watched him, uneasy. "Why you writing all that?" he asked.

Andrew did not look up. "So I remember," he said.

Rudd's voice trembled. "So someone else remembers?"

Andrew's pen paused. He heard Whitcomb again: You'll tell yourself you're keeping track for justice. He felt the wound sting faintly, like amusement.

He closed the ledger.

“I don’t know,” Andrew said finally.

The admission should have been a crack in him, a place where something human might leak out. Instead it felt like a door quietly closing.

Across the field, a baby cried and was hushed. A man coughed. Someone laughed once, sharply, and the laugh died quickly as if it had startled them all.

Andrew stared into the fire and realized he had begun to measure his days not by miles, not by food, not by weather, but by the creature’s appetite and the country’s willingness to look away. He thought of Ambrose’s words, civilization is a curtain, and understood the deeper truth that made his stomach churn.

Andrew was becoming part of that curtain.

He was learning how to hang it. How to keep it heavy. How to make sure no one lifted it to see what waited behind.

When he finally lay down near the wagon wheel, the ground cold beneath him, he did not pray. He did not even think to. Prayer required a listener who might answer.

He only listened to the wagon's quiet and the soft breathing of men nearby, and he waited for dawn as if dawn were not hope but simply the next shift in a labor he could no longer quit.

In the dark, the faint sweetness lingered and then faded, satisfied.

Andrew closed his eyes and realized, with a calm horror that felt like clarity, that the worst thing Ambrose had done was not give him a wound that would not heal.

It was teach him how to live with it.

Chapter 16

Caretaker of the Night

Morning came with a thin, dry light and the smell of other people's cook fires.

Andrew rose before Rudd, before Haines finished his first circuit of the field's perimeter. The habit of waking early had once been discipline. Now it was vigilance dressed in discipline's old uniform. He stood with his hands in his pockets and watched the small camp wake up: men shaking out blankets, women bending over pots, children stepping carefully through mud that had learned the shape of wheels and bare feet.

No one looked at his wagon longer than a glance. They saw patched canvas and a tired man and the posture of sickness. They turned away the way people turned away from graves they did not dig.

Andrew felt the familiar attentive ache at his side, not worse, not better. The wound had stopped being a wound in his mind. It was an instrument. It told him when to lean forward and when to hold back, when a place had too much attention, when a road had too many eyes.

Haines came up beside him, voice low. “We move?”

Andrew nodded. “Soon as the mules drink.”

Rudd, awake now, crawled out from his blanket with his hat crushed in his hands. He looked older every day, not in face but in the way he moved. He did not ask whether Ambrose had spoken in the night. He did not ask whether Kellan was still alive. He helped with the harness because doing a thing with his hands kept his mind from doing worse things.

Andrew lifted the wagon canvas only enough to slide a tin cup of water inside and a heel of bread. Kellan’s pale face turned slightly, eyes open, and his lips moved in a slow chew that was more reflex than appetite.

“Eat,” Andrew murmured, and the word came out like an order given to a horse.

Kellan obeyed. That obedience, too, had become part of the arrangement: a quiet man under canvas, alive enough to justify the lie, emptied enough not to betray it with talk.

Andrew lowered the canvas. For a moment, as the cloth settled, the faint sweetness rose, bruised fruit and old cellar air. It did not swell into stench. It never did when Ambrose was content. It was almost delicate, as if refinement could be applied to rot.

Andrew stepped back and did not let himself touch the bandage. Touching it felt too much like acknowledging a leash.

They rolled out with the other wagons, not leading, not lagging. Andrew kept their place in the middle of a loose line, close enough that anyone watching would see them as part of the same weary river, separate enough that a sudden stop would not mean hands on his canvas.

By noon they reached a crossroads where a handful of buildings had survived the war by being too small to matter. A general store with boards nailed over one window. A blacksmith's shed with a new patch of roof. A church that stood cleanly whitewashed, as if paint could argue with memory. Beyond the buildings, fields stretched away in ragged squares where men had returned to plows with faces still hollowed by marching.

Andrew felt his wound sting once, sharp and clean, like a warning that this place had rules again, even if they were weak rules held together by habit.

Rudd looked toward the store with open hunger. Haines watched the street edges and the men lingering near doorways.

“We need flour,” Haines said. “Coffee if it exists. Salt. And oats.”

“And paper,” Andrew added.

Haines’s jaw tightened. “More paper.”

Andrew did not answer that. He guided the wagon to a spot near the churchyard fence where other wagons had paused. The proximity to graves was not accident. People respected graves enough to keep their distance. Respect and fear were cousins.

He climbed down and adjusted his coat so the bandage was visible. The bandage did half his speaking for him.

“Rudd,” he said quietly. “You stay by the wagon. You don’t lift the canvas for anyone. Not for water, not for prayer, not for pity.”

Rudd swallowed. “Yes, sir.”

Haines started to follow Andrew toward the store.

“No,” Andrew said. “You stay too.”

Haines frowned. “We can’t both—”

"You stay," Andrew repeated, and this time the tone was flat enough that Haines understood it was not caution about thieves. It was about witnesses. Andrew needed the wagon guarded by men who had seen enough to keep their eyes steady. A lone boy would fail eventually. A single older soldier might be overpowered or distracted. Together they made a shape that said trouble, even in patched coats.

Andrew walked to the general store alone.

Inside, the air smelled of old tobacco, kerosene, and damp wood. Shelves were half-empty. The man behind the counter was gaunt, his beard trimmed too neatly for a poor town, his eyes watchful in the way merchants had learned to be when laws went soft.

Andrew did not give his name. He did not offer a hand. He stood like a customer with fatigue to spend.

"What you need?" the merchant asked, voice neutral.

Andrew kept his own voice mild. "Flour. Coffee if you've got it. Oats."

The merchant's eyes flicked over Andrew's face, then down to the bandage. "War's done," he said, not kindly.

Andrew nodded once. “I heard. Sickness ain’t done.”

The merchant’s gaze sharpened slightly. “You hauling sick?”

Andrew let the pause hang just long enough to feel true. “Dysentery,” he said.

The merchant’s mouth tightened. He did not step back, but his hands moved less, as if he wanted less contact with the air around Andrew. “Then you shouldn’t be in my store.”

Andrew looked at the shelves. “Then sell quick.”

The merchant hesitated, then reached for a sack of flour from beneath the counter, as if he kept the better goods hidden from desperation. “It ain’t cheap,” he said.

“Nothing is,” Andrew replied.

The merchant named a price that was half extortion and half survival. Andrew paid without haggling, because haggling created a conversation, and conversation created memory. He took coffee too, a small tin that looked as if it had been opened and resealed too many times, and a bundle of oats tied in cloth.

When the merchant slid the goods across the counter, Andrew added, quietly, “I need forms. Blank paper.”

The merchant stared. “What for.”

Andrew held his gaze. “So men don’t dig into my wagon.”

A flicker of understanding moved across the merchant’s face. Not sympathy. Recognition. The town lived by other people’s lies now, just as it lived by their labor.

The merchant reached under the counter again and pulled out a small stack of ledger paper and two printed forms that looked like they had been intended for some county office that no longer functioned. “That’s all I got,” he said.

Andrew took them. “I need ink.”

The merchant pointed with his chin toward a bottle near the register. “Take it. And don’t bleed on my floor.”

Andrew almost smiled, not because it was funny, but because it was ordinary. That was how the world continued: a man behind a counter complaining about blood as if blood was merely mess, not meaning.

Andrew carried the goods out, arms loaded, posture careful. He did not look toward the church. He did not look toward the graveyard. He kept his eyes on his wagon and on the men beside it.

Rudd's face lit briefly at the sight of coffee, then fell again as if he remembered that coffee was just another way to pretend the world had edges.

Haines took the flour and oats and stowed them on the top layer, deliberately messy the way Andrew had taught him. He smeared a little mud on the new sack before tying it down, as if the act offended him and soothed him at the same time.

A woman approached from the direction of the churchyard, older, her hair pinned tight under a bonnet that had been mended too often. She held herself with a thin dignity that suggested she had lost men and refused to lose posture too.

"You boys passing through?" she asked.

Andrew answered before Rudd could. "Yes, ma'am."

Her eyes moved to the wagon canvas. "You got sick," she said, not a question.

Andrew nodded. "Yes."

She drew in a breath through her nose, as if the word sick carried a smell. "You can't camp by the church," she said. "Reverend won't have it. Says it invites trouble."

Andrew kept his voice polite. "We're not looking for trouble. We're looking for a night under a roof, if there's a shed to rent."

Haines's head turned slightly, warning in his eyes. Roof meant walls. Walls meant being contained. Contained meant searched.

Andrew saw the warning and ignored it, because he was tired of moving every night like prey and because Ambrose had spoken of basements and asylums and respectable cover. If Andrew wanted to keep the creature quiet, he had to keep the world quiet around it. That meant arranging normalcy, even if normalcy was another trap.

The woman studied him. Her gaze lingered on his bandage and then on his face, as if weighing whether his politeness was real or only practiced. "You got money," she said.

"It depends," Andrew answered.

She made a small sound that might have been a laugh in another life. "Everything depends," she said. Then: "My husband's smokehouse is empty. Roof leaks in one corner, but it's walls and a door that locks. I'll rent it for a night. Two, if you keep your sickness to yourself."

Haines's jaw tightened. "Ma'am," he started, but Andrew cut him off with a glance.

"How far," Andrew asked.

She pointed down a side lane bordered by a new fence that looked too eager. "Past the blacksmith. Behind the apple trees. You'll see it."

Apple trees, Andrew thought, and felt the wound sting faintly, not pain, not warning, but attention. He kept his face still.

"What's your name," the woman asked, still watching him.

Andrew did not give his. Names became roots, and roots were dangerous.

"Mercer," he said, using the truth the way he used every truth now: trimmed and placed where it served. "Lieutenant once. Not now."

The woman's mouth tightened at the title, but she did not comment. Titles had bruised this country enough.

"I'm Mrs. Harrow," she said. "You pay me now. And you don't bring strangers down that lane."

Andrew handed her coin.

As she took it, her fingers brushed his. Her skin was cold. For a moment her eyes flicked toward the wagon canvas again with something like fear.

"Whatever you're hauling," she said softly, as if choosing the words carefully, "folks are trying to make things decent again. You understand?"

Andrew met her gaze. Decent again. As if decency was a quilt you could shake out and lay over rot.

"Yes," Andrew said. "I understand."

Mrs. Harrow nodded once, satisfied by the word even if she did not know what it meant. She turned and walked away with quick, purposeful steps, a woman who had learned the only power left to her was setting terms.

Rudd stared after her. "We're staying in a smokehouse," he whispered.

"For a night," Andrew said.

Haines watched Andrew closely. "That's a locked door," he murmured. "Locks cut both ways."

Andrew climbed onto the wagon seat and gathered the reins. "So do roads," he replied.

They turned down the lane. The town noise fell away quickly, replaced by the softer sounds of work: a hammer striking metal, a dog barking once and then being silenced, men shouting to each other from a field. The apple trees Mrs. Harrow had mentioned stood in a thin line, their branches bare or budding, depending on which had survived neglect. The sight of them made Andrew's mouth taste faintly of sweetness, as if his own body had learned to associate certain shapes with hunger.

The smokehouse sat behind the trees, squat and dark, its door reinforced with an iron latch. A place designed to keep meat safe. A place designed to keep things in.

Andrew brought the wagon up beside it and stopped.

For a moment no one moved. The stillness felt heavy, as if the air itself waited to see what shape Andrew would make of this ordinary structure.

He could hear town life at a distance. He could smell damp wood and old ash. He could feel the wound listening, keen as a needle.

"This is what we do now," Andrew said quietly, more to himself than to the others. "We look ordinary."

Rudd's voice trembled. "Are we?"

Andrew reached into his pocket and touched the folded ribbon, hard as a pressed leaf. He thought of Elias walking north with strangers and the way Elias had said Andrew would call anything love if it kept him from naming it.

Andrew swallowed and kept his face blank.

"We act it," he said.

Then he nodded to Haines.

"Help me," Andrew said. "We're moving the sick inside."

Haines's expression tightened, but he climbed into the wagon bed. Rudd hovered, hands half-raised, afraid to touch the canvas and afraid not to.

Andrew unlatched the smokehouse door. The hinges complained softly, a sound like an old throat clearing. Inside, the air was stale and cold, marked by the faint residue of salt and smoke.

A normal place. A practical place.

A place that could be explained.

Andrew held the door open and listened to the wagon behind him, to the quiet under canvas. He did not hear Ambrose. He did not need to. The sweetness drifted faintly, almost approving, and Andrew felt his wound respond with a small, clean sting, as if his body had been praised for a task done well.

Arranging normalcy, he thought, and stepped aside so the others could carry Kellan down.

It should have felt like shelter.

It felt like construction.

Haines climbed into the wagon bed and pulled the canvas back with the care of a man handling a shroud. The dimness beneath it clung to the boards even in daylight, as if the wagon had learned how to keep its own night.

"Kellan," Haines said, not unkindly, and reached in.

Kellan did not resist. He did not help, either. He let himself be gathered the way a child let himself be lifted when fever took all will. His boots scraped the wagon floor once, then hung limp. His head lolled against Haines's shoulder, eyes open and seeing nothing.

Rudd hovered at the edge, hands half raised. "I can take his feet," he whispered.

Haines looked at Andrew, a question in the set of his jaw: Is this wise?

Andrew answered with a small nod. There was no wise left, only arrangements.

Rudd slid his arms under Kellan's calves. The boy's hands shook at first, then steadied as the weight forced him to focus. Together they carried Kellan down from the wagon and toward the smokehouse door Andrew held open.

The interior was narrow and cold, the air stained with old salt and stale hickory. Hooks still hung from the rafters, dark curved shapes meant for meat. A shallow trough ran along one wall where drippings had once been caught. The floorboards were uneven, blackened at the seams.

Rudd's eyes flicked up to the hooks and then away as if the sight made his thoughts too vivid.

"Lay him there," Andrew said, pointing to the far wall where the light fell weakest.

Haines and Rudd lowered Kellan onto a pile of straw Andrew had dragged in from the wagon earlier, straw that had served as bedding and now served as staging. Kellan's limbs settled without complaint. His mouth opened slightly. He breathed, slow and thin, like a man sleeping at the bottom of a well.

For a moment Andrew stood in the doorway and listened. Town sounds filtered down the lane: a hammer striking metal at the blacksmith, voices carrying in brief bursts, the bark of a dog that sounded more warning than greeting. The world was close enough to offer cover and far enough to pretend ignorance.

Inside, the air held a faint sweetness under the smoke and salt. So faint that if Andrew had not learned to recognize it, he might have called it nothing at all. He felt the old wound at his side answer with a small, precise sting, as if the creature under his care had settled into the idea of walls.

Haines straightened. His gaze moved across the smokehouse interior, measuring angles and shadows like a soldier assessing a defensible position. "We locking him in here?" he asked quietly.

Andrew knew what he meant. Locking Kellan inside meant safety from questions. It also meant that if Kellan woke and wandered, no one would see him. It also meant a door between the town and whatever else might move from the wagon in the night.

"Yes," Andrew said.

Rudd swallowed. "Sir, what if he needs water?"

Andrew looked at the boy. Rudd's face had that strained earnestness of someone who still believed care could change outcomes. "Then we bring it," Andrew said. "And we don't bring anyone else."

Haines stepped to the door and tested the latch with his hand. Iron, old but solid. He leaned close enough that his voice would not carry. "And the other one?" he asked.

Andrew didn't answer with words. There was no way to name it here without making the air wrong. He only felt his wound sting again, quick and intimate, and knew that Ambrose heard everything that mattered.

Andrew closed the smokehouse door and slid the iron bar into place. The sound of it settling into its brackets was heavy, final. Meat-house meant to keep spoilage out. Now it would keep questions out. Now it would keep something else in.

They walked back toward the wagon, each of them moving as if the lane itself watched. Mrs. Harrow's house stood a short distance away, its porch swept, its shutters repaired, the kind of decency that dared the world to leave it alone. Andrew could imagine her inside, counting coins, measuring how long her rented space might remain only a rented space.

Rudd's eyes kept darting to the smokehouse. "He didn't even look at us," he whispered.

"Kellan?" Haines asked, rough.

Rudd nodded.

Andrew kept his voice low. "He's been looking past people for days," he said. "Don't take it personal."

Rudd's mouth tightened. "I wasn't. I just… I didn't think a man could be that empty and still breathe."

Haines gave a short, bitter exhale. "War taught us all kinds of breathing."

Andrew climbed into the wagon and pulled out the clerk's box and Whitcomb's ledger, holding them close to his chest as he stepped down. He glanced up the lane once more, then gestured with his chin.

"Inside the wagon," he told them. "Keep it looking like we're still hauling supplies. Nothing changes for anyone who glances our way."

Haines nodded and began adjusting the visible stacks, shifting sacks so they looked casually piled. Rudd followed his motions, eager to copy, grateful for a task that had rules.

Andrew walked toward the far side of the smokehouse, where the building's shadow fell thickest. He sat with his back against the rough boards and opened the ledger on his knee.

The pages were stained and warped with travel. The ink on the earlier entries had dried into a permanent darkness: names from the patrol, from the hospital wagons, from the burning estate days that still felt like another life. Then the newer entries, smaller, more careful, the records of lies and places. Dysentery. Convalescents. Tollhouse. Provost.

Andrew rested his pen against the paper and stared at the blank lines.

He told himself, as he always did, that the ledger was evidence. A record for a future that might want truth. Proof that if he had become the caretaker of something hungry, he had at least not become its priest.

But sitting there in the smokehouse shadow, he felt the truth shift in his chest. The ledger did not only keep evidence.

It kept order.

Order was what Ambrose had promised would be durable. Order was what made basements possible. Order was what allowed disappearance to be explained as illness, accident, shame.

Andrew wrote the date, as best he could track it now. Dates had grown slippery since Appomattox. He wrote the town's name, the crossroads store, Mrs. Harrow's smokehouse. He wrote Kellan placed inside, the door barred.

He paused, pen hovering, and listened to the sounds around him. The blacksmith's hammer. A wagon wheel creaking. A woman calling for a child. Ordinary life beating its small rhythm, daring the world to behave.

The wound at Andrew's side gave a faint, impatient sting.

He knew what it meant. Not yet, perhaps, but soon. Ambrose had settled. A settled thing fed.

Andrew dipped the pen and turned the page to a cleaner sheet. He wrote a heading without thinking, a habit from military reports.

Ledger of Loss.

The phrase made his stomach tighten, as if his body recognized its honesty even if his mind wished it hadn't been written.

Rudd appeared at the corner of his vision, cautious. "Sir," he whispered, "Mrs. Harrow's coming."

Andrew closed the ledger halfway and rose, smoothing his coat. He tucked the ribbon square in his pocket by reflex, fingers brushing it like a charm.

Mrs. Harrow walked down the lane with measured steps. In daylight she looked like a woman who had lived through three different worlds and learned how to keep her face composed in all of them. She stopped a few paces from the wagon and did not come closer.

"You got your sick put up?" she asked.

"Yes, ma'am," Andrew replied.

Her gaze flicked past him toward the smokehouse door. "He loud?"

"No."

"Good." She hesitated, then added, quieter, "Folks in town don't take kindly to strangers who bring trouble. They got enough trouble they can name."

Andrew nodded. "We'll keep to ourselves."

Mrs. Harrow studied him a moment longer. "You look educated," she said, as if it were an accusation.

Andrew didn't answer that directly. "I learned to read."

"And write." Her eyes flicked toward the edge of the ledger visible under his hand.

Andrew felt a brief spike of tension, then let it settle. "Yes."

Mrs. Harrow held his gaze. "Then write this," she said. "If you hear anything. If you see anything. If you get word of men robbing, or worse, you come tell the provost."

Haines, behind Andrew, made a small sound of contempt that he swallowed before it became a word.

Andrew kept his face polite. "Yes, ma'am."

She nodded, satisfied by the lie in his posture, and turned to go back up the lane.

As she walked away, Rudd leaned close enough to whisper, "She thinks you're respectable."

Andrew watched Mrs. Harrow's back until she disappeared behind her house. "She thinks I'm tired," he said.

Rudd's face pinched. "Ain't that the same thing, sometimes?"

Andrew looked at him, and for a moment he saw how the world was shaping the boy. Rudd was learning the same lessons Andrew had learned: that impressions mattered more than truth, and that decency could be performed.

Andrew sat back down in the smokehouse shadow and opened the ledger again.

He wrote what Mrs. Harrow had asked without meaning to. Provost. Report trouble. A town trying to rebuild its rules. Then he stopped, pen hovering, and listened again, deeper this time, to the smokehouse itself.

Behind the wall, Kellan breathed. Thin. Present. A human sound.

And beneath that, so subtle it might have been imagination if not for the wound's responding sting, he felt another presence. Not in the room, not in the lane. In the idea of the building. In the fact of the lock. In the comfort of a door that could be shut.

Ambrose, satisfied.

Andrew lowered the pen and stared at the ledger's pages until the lines blurred. He understood, with a slow dread, what the ledger could become if he allowed it.

Not a record of what Ambrose did to them.

A record of what Andrew arranged so Ambrose could do it.

He forced his hand back to motion. If he did not write, the day would slide away into the same numbness that had begun to swallow him whole. If he wrote, at least he could pretend he was still separate from the thing he served.

He turned to a fresh page and began a list, not of names yet, but of rules, because rules were easier than confessions.

Do not stop where eyes linger.

Do not let anyone touch the canvas.

Use sickness as a fence.

Sleep near noise.

Keep a door that locks.

Andrew paused, then added another, and the pen pressed hard enough that the paper tore slightly at the end of the line.

Never forget the cost.

The wound stung once, as if amused by the sentiment.

Andrew closed the ledger and held it against his knee, feeling its weight like something alive. He looked up the lane toward town, toward the provost sign, toward the store where he had bought paper and ink as calmly as he had once bought ammunition.

Night would come. Hunger would come with it, whether it came as teeth or as a conversation in the dark.

And when it did, Andrew knew he would open the ledger again.

Because if he could not stop what was happening, he could at least measure it.

And measurement, he realized with quiet horror, was its own kind of permission.

Dusk came early behind the apple trees, thickening the lane with shadow until Mrs. Harrow's swept porch looked like a stage lit from one careful angle. Smoke rose from her chimney in a straight, disciplined line. In the distance the blacksmith's hammer kept time until it stopped and left a silence that felt too sudden, as if the town had inhaled and decided to hold it.

Andrew kept the wagon where it was, close enough to the smokehouse that any passerby would assume all of his business was contained in that locked little building. Haines made a slow circuit of the fence line and returned with his face set, as if he'd seen nothing and did not trust it.

Rudd sat on the wagon's rear lip with his hands clenched between his knees. His eyes kept returning to the smokehouse door the way a tongue returned to a sore tooth.

"He hasn't made a sound," Rudd whispered.

"Kellan?" Haines asked.

Rudd nodded.

Andrew watched the lane. A pair of townsmen passed once, carrying a coil of wire between them, and glanced at Andrew's wagon with the quick, wary look people gave to poverty and sickness. They did not slow. They did not ask questions. Their caution was practical, not kind.

"That's the point," Andrew said, mostly to himself.

Rudd heard him anyway. "The point of what, sir?"

Andrew did not answer at once. He could have said, The point is they leave us alone. But that was only the surface.

The deeper point was that they were rebuilding the old reflexes: step away from what might be contagious, accept a story that lets you keep your hands clean, trust a lock because it looks like responsibility.

Andrew looked at the smokehouse door, the iron bar seated in its brackets.

Locks cut both ways, Haines had said.

Andrew felt the wound under his bandage give a faint, anticipatory sting, as if the dark inside his life had leaned forward at the idea of being enclosed.

A lamp flared on Mrs. Harrow's porch. Another lit across the lane. One by one the houses decided to be visible, each small pool of light a stubborn announcement that night would not have everything.

Andrew told himself he should be grateful for that.

He was not.

When full dark settled, Rudd finally stood and approached the little fire they'd built in a shallow scrape beside the wagon. He fed it small sticks with the careful attention of a boy trying to earn a reason to be spared. The flame caught and rose. The light made the apple branches above them look like grasping hands.

Haines ate a heel of bread and a strip of pork without comment. He kept his back to the smokehouse, eyes on the lane and the gap between buildings where someone might appear.

Andrew took Whitcomb's ledger from the clerk's box and held it closed for a while, feeling its weight in his lap. He had written rules. He had written costs. He had written the shape of their day without writing its heart.

Now night had come, and with it the question he could not keep outrun by wheels: what did you do when you wanted help from something that did not answer?

Rudd stared into the fire until his lips moved soundlessly. Andrew watched him and realized the boy was praying.

Not loudly. Not theatrically. Just the small movement of a mouth making a request to the dark.

Andrew felt something tighten in his chest. It might have been pity. It might have been envy. He did not know which was worse.

Haines noticed too. He did not mock Rudd. He did not soften, either. He only said, quiet and flat, "Save your breath, boy."

Rudd's eyes flashed open. "Don't," he whispered. His voice shook, but it held a kind of stubbornness. "Don't take that too."

Haines's jaw worked. He looked away toward the lane as if prayer offended him less than hope did. "I ain't taking nothing," he muttered. "World already did."

Rudd swallowed, and his gaze slid toward Andrew as if expecting the lieutenant to decide what kind of camp this would be: one where faith was permitted, or one where it was treated like another dangerous noise.

Andrew did not give the boy permission. He did not deny him either. He only said, "Keep it quiet."

Rudd nodded, and his lips began moving again, slower now, as if he was afraid even God might draw attention if approached too directly.

Andrew looked down at his hands and saw faint ink stains along his fingers, half scrubbed, never fully gone. He thought of the chapel he'd entered months ago, the abandoned records, the relics that had felt heavy with promise. He had believed then that holiness was a kind of weapon if you held it correctly.

Now he knew better.

Holiness, like paper, worked only if the world agreed it did.

A soft knock sounded from the lane.

All three of them froze.

Haines's hand went to his knife. Rudd's mouth stopped moving as if someone had slapped him.

Andrew stood and stepped away from the firelight toward the sound. He kept his posture tired, irritated, as if being interrupted was only a nuisance.

Another knock. This one on the wagon's sideboard, polite and measured.

Andrew moved into the dim edge of the fire's reach and saw a man standing just beyond the firelight. He wore a black coat that had been mended at the elbows. His hat was in his hands. Behind him, the town was a low constellation of lamps.

"Evening," the man said.

Andrew did not answer the greeting with warmth. Warmth invited conversation. "Evening."

"I'm Reverend Baines," the man continued. His voice held the careful steadiness of someone used to being listened to, and used to being ignored. "Mrs. Harrow said you were passing through. Said you had illness with you."

Andrew felt Haines's attention sharpen behind him. Rudd's face went pale, and his eyes darted toward the smokehouse as if he expected the reverend to walk straight to it and lay a hand on the bar.

Andrew kept his voice flat. "We have sick."

The reverend nodded once, solemn. "I won't come close," he said quickly, as if reading the way Andrew's shoulders had tightened. "I won't ask to see anyone. But I thought…" He hesitated, and Andrew saw the man's courage flicker, not in the face of danger, but in the face of refusal. "I thought I might pray with you. For them. For safe travel."

Behind Andrew, Rudd made a small sound that was almost relief. A reverend meant rules. A reverend meant the old world hadn't entirely died.

Andrew's wound stung once, quick and clean, as if the offer of prayer had amused something listening.

Andrew stared at Reverend Baines and felt a bitter impulse rise: to say yes, to let the man pray, to borrow the shape of decency for a few minutes like a coat that still fit. He wanted to want it. He wanted it the way thirsty men wanted water even when they knew it was brackish.

But he could not unlearn what he had learned.

Prayer was a kind of door.

And Andrew had spent days learning how to keep doors shut.

"We don't need a minister," Andrew said.

The reverend's face tightened, but he did not retreat. "No," he agreed quietly. "Maybe you don't. But sometimes men don't ask for a minister because they think they don't deserve one."

Rudd's eyes flicked to Andrew, wide and pleading.

Haines stayed silent, but his contempt was visible in the angle of his jaw, not aimed at the reverend, but at the idea that words could fix what teeth had touched.

Andrew kept his voice controlled. "We're tired," he said. "We need sleep. That's all."

Reverend Baines nodded slowly. He did not look offended. He looked sad, and the sadness felt more dangerous than anger.

"All right," he said. "Then I'll pray on my own. For what it's worth."

Andrew wanted to ask him, worth what. Worth to whom. Worth against what.

Instead he only said, "Goodnight, Reverend."

The reverend stepped back, still holding his hat. “Goodnight,” he replied, and then, almost as an afterthought, “If you hear anything in the night, anything strange, you come to me or to the provost. People are… jumpy.”

Andrew nodded once, making his face blank.

Reverend Baines turned and walked away down the lane, his black coat moving between patches of lamplight like a shadow that still believed it had purpose.

Rudd exhaled shakily. “He wanted to help,” the boy whispered.

Andrew returned to the fire and sat down without looking at either of them. “He wanted to feel useful,” Andrew said.

Rudd’s eyes filled with frustrated tears. “Ain’t that the same thing sometimes?”

Andrew did not answer. He had no clean answer left.

For a while the three of them sat with the fire snapping softly and the town’s night noises drifting in: a door closing, a dog barking once, a brief burst of laughter that sounded forced and then stopped.

Rudd’s lips began to move again, but the prayer had changed. It wasn’t a child’s simple request now. It had the hurried, bargaining rhythm of a man trying to offer God a deal: I will be better if you will only keep the dark away.

Andrew listened and felt nothing answer.

Then, faintly, from somewhere deeper than the firelight, a thread of sound rose: singing.

A hymn, carried from the church or a parlor gathering, thin but steady. Voices joined and then separated again, imperfect and human. The melody floated above the lane like a fragile cloth held up to keep night from settling on the mind.

Rudd lifted his head, startled. For a moment his face softened. He whispered, "They're singing."

Haines muttered, "Let 'em."

Andrew stared into the flames and listened to the hymn until he recognized it. He could not have named when he'd last heard it. Before the war, perhaps. Before the cellar. Before the first chain bolts in stone.

The words, drifting on the air, were about shelter and deliverance.

Andrew felt his throat tighten. Not with faith. With a kind of grief that had nowhere to go.

Because shelter was exactly what he was building, and deliverance was exactly what he had stopped believing in.

His wound stung again, sharper this time, and the faint sweetness touched the air, subtle at first, like bruised fruit warmed by a palm.

Rudd's head snapped toward the wagon. His prayer stopped mid-word.

Haines rose slightly, tense. "No," he whispered, not to Andrew. To the dark itself. "Not here."

Andrew stood, his heart steady in a way that made him sick. He knew that steadiness. It was the steadiness of a man who had already decided what he would permit.

The hymn continued in the distance, unaware.

Andrew turned his head toward the smokehouse, toward the iron-barred door. He listened for Kellan. He heard only thin, uneven breathing through wood.

The sweetness deepened by a fraction, as if something nearby had smiled without showing teeth.

Andrew felt the shape of the night changing, not with a sudden attack, but with a slow settling into intention. A town full of lamps and hymns and fresh paint. A locked smokehouse behind apple trees. A weary lieutenant with ink-stained fingers and rules written down like scripture.

Unanswered prayers, Andrew thought, and the phrase did not feel like poetry. It felt like inventory.

Rudd whispered, voice breaking, "Sir… what do we do?"

Andrew looked down at the fire and then at the lane, as if the answer might be waiting in plain sight. He thought of Reverend Baines walking away to pray on his own. He imagined the man kneeling by his bed, asking God to watch over strangers with sickness.

Andrew almost laughed, and the almost was worse than laughter.

"We keep quiet," Andrew said.

Haines stared at him. "That's it?"

Andrew swallowed. His mouth tasted faintly sweet, and he hated his own body for reacting to it. "That's it," he repeated. "We keep quiet. We don't draw eyes. We don't make it a scene."

Rudd's tears finally fell, silent in the firelight. He scrubbed them away with the back of his hand as if ashamed of giving the night anything wet to drink.

The hymn in the distance reached its final line and faded.

The town's lamps burned steadily.

And somewhere close, something hungry and old adjusted itself to the new comfort Andrew had arranged: walls, locks, decent people singing about safety while the dark learned the layout.

Andrew reached for Whitcomb's ledger with hands that did not tremble and opened it to a blank line.

He stared at the empty space a long moment, listening to the quiet that had begun to feel occupied.

Then he wrote, small and neat, as if neatness could keep the night contained.

A reverend offered prayer. Declined.

And after a pause, he added another line beneath it, pressing hard enough that the pen scratched.

Hymn heard. No answer.

He closed the book and held it against his knee like a weight meant to keep him from floating away.

In the smokehouse, Kellan breathed on.

In the lane, the fire burned down.

And Andrew sat between the town's fragile light and the thickening sweetness of the dark, understanding with a calm dread that no one was coming to save them.

Not the reverend.

Not the provost.

Not God.

Only morning, when it arrived, would come for certain.

And even morning, Andrew had learned, did not banish what waited. It only made it easier to pretend it wasn't there.

Chapter 17

Resonance of Evil

Andrew kept the ledger closed after he wrote. The act of shutting it felt less like finishing a record and more like putting a lid on a pot that could boil over with one careless glance.

The fire gave up in slow stages. First the flame sank into itself, then the orange thinned to a faint red pulse, and finally even the coals looked like dull stones unless you leaned close enough to burn your face. Rudd slept only when exhaustion forced him, and even then his body jolted as if some part of him refused to surrender. Haines stayed upright, shifting his weight now and then, eyes on the lane and the darker shape of the smokehouse beyond the apple trees.

Andrew sat with his back to the wagon wheel and listened to the town's small nighttime sounds fade one by one. Doors closed. A voice carried and stopped. A dog barked once and then, as if corrected, went quiet. A nation practicing stillness again.

He did not hear Ambrose speak. He did not hear movement inside the smokehouse. But the faint sweetness remained in the air the way damp remained after rain. Not always strong enough to taste, never absent long enough to forget.

Just before dawn, the town gave a sound that made Haines stiffen: a single shout, far off, then the answering bark of another voice. Not a scream. Not panic. The ordinary, irritated sound of men discovering something they did not like and wanting someone else to come see it.

Haines looked at Andrew. "You hear that?"

Andrew nodded once. He did not rise. The worst mistakes were made by men who ran toward noise. He had learned that in battle and in cellars.

The light came slowly, thinning the shadows without fully banishing them. When the lane was gray enough to see faces, Mrs. Harrow's door opened and she stepped out with a pail in her hand. She paused on the porch, eyes scanning as if she could smell trouble the way she could smell smoke.

Rudd sat up, blinking. "Morning," he whispered, as if afraid to speak louder.

Haines said nothing. He only watched Mrs. Harrow.

She started down the steps, then stopped again and looked toward the road. More voices now, nearer, and a small cluster of townsmen moving quickly past the blacksmith toward the edge of the fields. A man in a blue coat, probably one of the provost's, walked with them, his posture impatient.

Mrs. Harrow's gaze flicked once to Andrew and his wagon. Not accusing. Measuring. Then she turned and followed the others at a distance, pail forgotten on the porch.

Rudd stood. "What happened?"

Andrew rose more slowly. His wound gave a small, clean sting, like a finger pressed lightly into his side. Not pain. Direction. Interest.

"Stay," Andrew told Rudd.

Rudd looked offended and frightened at once. "Sir, if something's wrong—"

"If something's wrong," Andrew said quietly, "it will still be wrong in ten minutes. You stay with the wagon."

Haines stepped up beside Andrew. "I'll go," Haines muttered.

Andrew shook his head. "No. You stay too. If someone comes nosing, I want two sets of eyes here."

Haines's jaw tightened, but he obeyed. Obedience had become the only structure left in him that wasn't anger.

Andrew walked toward the road with the posture of a tired man drawn by curiosity he did not want to admit. He kept his hands visible. He kept his pace unhurried. A man who moved too fast looked guilty, and guilt was a magnet for authority.

He followed the lane to where it opened into the main track that ran past the store and church. The town looked different in daylight. The whitewash on the church was too bright. The new wire on the rebuilt fences caught light and threw it back coldly. The provost building, with its crude sign, looked less like an office and more like a warning that someone still wanted to call themselves in charge.

The cluster of men had gathered near a small yard behind a house at the town's edge. A low shed, a trough, a patch of trampled earth where animals had been kept. Andrew saw the shape on the ground before he was close enough to understand it.

A hog lay on its side near the trough. Not butchered. Not torn. Its skin looked intact, save for a small, ugly wound beneath the jawline, dark as a puncture made by a tool. The ground under its head was wet, but not with the amount of blood an animal that size should have spilled. The wetness looked thin, like the last residue of something that had already been taken.

A man knelt beside it, fingers pressed to the puncture as if trying to decide whether he could explain it to himself. Another man stood with his hat in his hands, face pale with a kind of offended fear.

"That ain't a dog," someone said.

"Ain't a wolf neither," another answered.

The provost man cursed softly. He looked too young to hold authority comfortably, but he held it anyway, because someone had given him a pistol and a word to stand under. "It's probably some damned thief," he said, the way men named the easiest explanation first. "Somebody stuck it and bled it. For meat. For spite."

The kneeling man looked up, eyes tight. "Then where's the blood," he asked. "Where's the mess? You ever seen a hog slaughtered clean like that? It's like it just… emptied."

Andrew stayed at the edge of the gathering, letting other shoulders block him. He watched faces. Fear had its own rhythms. When people were afraid of raiders, they got angry. When they were afraid of hunger, they got desperate. This was different. This was the fear of something that did not fit the categories that made a town feel safe.

A woman stepped forward, apron over her dress, her mouth pinched hard as if holding back noise. “My hens too,” she said. “Two of them. Found them laid out like Sunday. No blood. Just stiff.”

The provost man looked around as if expecting a culprit to step forward and volunteer. “Any tracks?” he demanded.

A boy pointed at the mud near the trough. “There,” he said.

Men leaned in. The prints were shallow and half smeared by too many boots, but Andrew caught the detail that made his stomach go colder: the impression of a foot without a shoe. Bare. Long toes pressed into the mud as if the ground itself had been tasted. It could have been a child’s foot. It could have been a man who’d lost boots. It could have been a lie made by mud and imagination.

Andrew’s wound stung once, sharper, and the faint sweetness touched his throat like a memory of bruised fruit.

He did not have to ask what he already knew. The creature under his care could move unseen even when it was contained. Contained was a word people used to comfort themselves. Locks cut both ways. Walls were curtains. Ambrose had said it as instruction, and now the town offered proof.

The kneeling man stood, wiping his hands on his pants as if dirt could be scrubbed away by smearing it elsewhere. "It's the sickness," he said suddenly, voice rising. "Ain't you heard? Folks passing through with the flux, with fevers. Maybe it's in the animals."

The word sickness moved through the group like wind through dry grass. Men stepped back without thinking, hands rising as if the air itself might cling. Andrew felt their reflex, their desire for a story that required no monster, only bad luck and bad water.

The provost man seized it. "That's right," he said too quickly. "Could be disease. You," he pointed at the hog's owner, "you burn the carcass. Don't feed it to dogs. Don't touch it. You hear me?"

A few men nodded, relieved to be told what to do. Orders were comfort. Orders meant the world still had rails.

But the owner's face stayed tight. "Disease don't leave a hole like that," he said, and the stubborn honesty in his voice sounded like a sin.

Mrs. Harrow stood at the edge of the crowd now, her bonnet strings hanging loose, eyes fixed on the hog. When her gaze lifted, it found Andrew immediately, as if some part of her had been waiting to confirm a suspicion she did not want to admit. She looked at him and then, very deliberately, looked away again. Decency as refusal.

Andrew turned before anyone could decide to connect him to the convenient word sickness. He walked back toward the lane without hurrying, but the back of his neck felt exposed, as if the town's attention could become a hand.

As he passed the church, he heard voices inside. Not singing now. Talking. Low and tight. Men using God's house as a place to exchange rumor because rumor sounded cleaner when spoken under a steeple.

Two women stood outside the general store, speaking in quick bursts.

"Widow Lorne ain't opened her door," one said.

"She don't owe you—"

"No, listen. Her girl went by to bring bread. Knocked. No answer. Curtains drawn. She's always up early."

The other woman's mouth tightened. "Maybe she's taken ill."

"Maybe," the first said, and the word sounded like a prayer offered to an answer that would not come.

Andrew walked past them as if he hadn't heard, but his body heard anyway. The wound held its attentive ache, and under it something like satisfaction, faint and intimate.

Back at the wagon, Haines was standing with his arms crossed, eyes on the smokehouse. Rudd hovered near the canvas, hands clenched.

"What was it?" Rudd asked the moment Andrew came into view. "What happened?"

Andrew kept his voice low. "A hog. Found dead."

Rudd blinked. "Just a hog?"

Haines's gaze sharpened. "You don't look like it was just a hog."

Andrew didn't answer immediately. He looked down the lane. Mrs. Harrow's house stood quiet. The smokehouse door sat barred. A solid door. A lock that made townspeople feel safe.

He could almost hear Ambrose's calm amusement in the silence between sounds.

"There's talk," Andrew said finally, choosing each word as if placing boards over a hole, "of sickness in animals. And a widow missing from her morning."

Rudd's face went paler. "That's… that's him, ain't it."

Andrew's throat tightened. He could lie. He could reassure. He could offer Rudd the same disease story the provost man had grabbed with both hands. The impulse came, quick and practiced.

Instead he said the truth that mattered. "It's signs," Andrew replied. "That's all a town ever gets at first. Signs it explains until it can't."

Haines's voice came rough. "And what do we do?"

Andrew looked at the smokehouse door again, then at the town beyond, rebuilding its fences and offices like prayers nailed into wood. He thought of Reverend Baines offering words into the night and being turned away. He thought of Ambrose saying order was durable.

"We do what we've been doing," Andrew said, and hated himself for how natural it sounded. "We keep it ordinary. We keep it quiet."

Rudd's eyes filled, but he didn't cry this time. He only nodded, the way men nodded on battlefields when they understood the day's shape and knew they couldn't change it.

Andrew stepped closer to the smokehouse and rested his palm briefly against the rough boards, feeling the cold seep into his skin. A door that locked. A place meant for meat.

He felt the faint sweetness just on the other side of the wood, like breath through a crack. No voice, no movement, only presence.

Andrew withdrew his hand as if burned and walked back toward the wagon.

In the town behind him, men were already choosing their explanations. Disease. Thieves. Stray dogs. Anything that let them keep hammering posts into earth and calling it a future.

Andrew knew the pattern now. The first death was dismissed. The second would be argued over. By the third, someone would insist on prayer, on patrols, on searching every shed and cellar.

And when that searching began, Andrew realized with a cold, settling dread, the first place their eyes would come to was the locked smokehouse behind the apple trees, rented by a tired stranger who looked respectable enough to trust.

The wound at his side gave a small, clean sting, as if applauding the inevitability.

Andrew gathered the reins in his hands without moving the wagon yet. He watched the lane and listened to the town's morning sounds grow louder.

Somewhere, a hammer struck a nail.

Somewhere else, someone knocked on a widow's door and waited for an answer that did not come.

Andrew did not move the wagon immediately. The instinct to run was there, old and sharp as bayonet training, but running drew attention. It announced that there was something to chase.

He sat on the seat with the reins loose in his hands and watched the lane as if he were merely waiting for the day to decide what it wanted. Haines stood near the wheel, arms crossed, looking like a man guarding property that was not his. Rudd hovered in the strip of shadow between wagon and apple trees, eyes fixed on the smokehouse door as if staring could keep it shut.

From town came the restless sound of people choosing their panic carefully. Not screams. Not yet. Voices in clusters. Footsteps that kept changing direction. The provost man's barked orders carried once, then were swallowed by distance.

Andrew felt the wound at his side hold its attentive ache, the way it always did now when the world tilted toward consequence. Beneath that ache was something worse: familiarity. The shape of a town beginning to hunt, and the shape of himself already adjusting to it.

A man appeared at the top of the lane, walking quickly, hat in hand. He was broad-shouldered and red-faced, his shirt sleeves rolled, his boots still wet with trough mud. Mrs. Harrow followed him at a more measured pace, her mouth set as if she'd already decided what she would and would not admit.

The man stopped short of the wagon, as if the air around it might be foul.

"You," he said, pointing with his hat. "You the one hauling sickness?"

Andrew kept his posture tired. "Yes."

The man's eyes flicked toward the smokehouse. "That's your doing too?" he demanded, voice rising. "You bring plague into decent yards and then shut it up behind my cousin's apples like it's nothing?"

Mrs. Harrow snapped, "Eli Pruitt, lower your voice."

Eli Pruitt ignored her. "My hog's dead," he said, and his face worked with anger that had nowhere safe to land. "Found it this morning with a hole under its jaw like somebody put a nail through it. No blood. Like it was sucked dry. And now Widow Lorne ain't answered her door."

At the widow's name, Rudd flinched as if struck.

Andrew's mind measured the sentence the way it measured distances. My hog. Widow Lorne. The path people took from livestock to human was short when fear was hungry. And fear always needed a person to blame before it dared to name anything it couldn't.

"I'm sorry about your animal," Andrew said. He did not offer sympathy beyond that. Too much softness invited confession. "We didn't touch it."

"The provost says there's strangers bringing flux through," Pruitt pressed. "He says it could get into animals. That true?"

Andrew nodded once. "Animals get sick," he said. A true statement that did not answer the question asked.

Pruitt stepped half a pace closer, then hesitated, eyes narrowing at the bandage showing under Andrew's coat. "You got it too?" he demanded.

Andrew let the pause hang long enough to feel real. "I've had it," he said, and watched Pruitt's body recoil from the possibility. "That's why we keep away from folks."

Mrs. Harrow's gaze stayed on Andrew's face, steady, assessing. "You need to leave," she said quietly, not unkindly. Practical. "This town's already raw. They see what they want to see."

Haines made a low sound of agreement in his throat.

Andrew said, “We’ll go when the road’s clear.”

Pruitt’s anger searched for purchase again. “And the widow?” he asked, as if Andrew had been assigned responsibility simply by arriving. “You seen her? You been up that way?”

“No,” Andrew replied.

Pruitt looked past Andrew toward the smokehouse door again, and Andrew saw the moment suspicion fixed itself to a place. A locked building behind apple trees. A rented space. A stranger’s arrangement. A perfect object for a town’s fear.

“You got someone in there,” Pruitt said, voice tightening. “You keeping a man in there? That what you call convalescent?”

Andrew kept his face blank. “He can’t travel well. We keep him out of sight because people don’t want to see sick men.”

“That’s convenient,” Pruitt spat.

Mrs. Harrow held up a hand between them. “Enough. I saw them bring him in. He’s half dead with the runs, Eli. He ain’t walking out in the night draining hogs like a storybook devil.”

The word devil hung in the air. Pruitt's eyes flicked to Mrs. Harrow, then away, as if embarrassed by his own thought and angrier for the embarrassment.

Andrew felt the faintest sweetness brush the back of his throat, subtle as breath through a crack. A reminder that the thing people wanted to name in whispers did not care what they called it.

A second group came down the lane: the provost man and one of his companions, both moving with the irritated purpose of men forced to work too early. The provost's blue coat was unbuttoned, his belt hanging as it had yesterday, but his eyes were sharper now. He saw Andrew at once, then the wagon, then the smokehouse door.

"All right," the provost said, not greeting, only procedure. "Who are you?"

Andrew did not give his full name. He never did when the world began asking it loudly. "Mercer," he said. "Passing through. Hauling sick."

The provost's gaze dropped to the bandage. "I remember you," he said. "You came through town yesterday."

Andrew nodded once.

The provost jerked his chin toward the smokehouse. "You got them in there?"

"One man," Andrew replied. "He doesn't travel."

The provost looked at Mrs. Harrow. "You rent him that building?"

"I did," she said, chin lifted, defensive not of Andrew but of her right to set terms on her own property.

The provost's companion, a civilian with a pistol, muttered, "This is how it starts."

Andrew watched the provost's face harden with the satisfaction of finding something he could control. Towns were always like this. When fear rose, authority looked for a door to push on.

"We're checking outbuildings," the provost said. "Widow Lorne's missing. Livestock dead in odd ways. Folks are talking."

Andrew kept his voice even. "Talking doesn't solve anything."

The provost bristled at the implied criticism. "No, it don't," he snapped. "But searching does. Open it."

Rudd's breath hitched audibly.

Haines shifted his weight, and Andrew felt him readying for violence he didn't want but could not stop himself from preparing for. Old soldier reflexes. The body moving ahead of the mind.

Andrew held up a hand, not to stop the provost, but to slow him. "If you open it," Andrew said, "you'll have the whole town convinced the sickness is in your hands. You'll have men saying you brought it out of that building and spread it."

The provost hesitated. He did not look afraid of disease as a bodily reality so much as he looked afraid of losing the town's already thinning trust.

Pruitt seized the opening. "Then what, we just let him lock up plague behind apples?"

Andrew met the provost's eyes. "You want to keep order?" he asked quietly. "Then you keep people calm. You want calm, you don't make a spectacle of a sick man."

The provost's jaw tightened. He looked toward the smokehouse and then away again, as if the door itself offended him. "We could post a man here," he said. "Make sure nobody comes and goes."

Andrew felt the wound sting, quick and clean. Not warning. Interest, as if the idea of a posted guard was amusing.

"A posted man will get curious," Andrew said. "Curious men tell stories."

The provost stared at Andrew as if trying to decide whether he was clever or guilty. "You talk like you've done this before."

Andrew let a faint bitterness show, just enough to look human. "I wore a uniform," he said. "My job was keeping men from panicking."

Haines's eyes flicked to Andrew, sharp. He knew what the sentence omitted. Andrew's job now was keeping people from looking too closely.

The provost's companion spat into the mud. "We should run them out," he muttered. "Send them on."

Mrs. Harrow's voice snapped. "And if they go and the widow's still missing tomorrow, who you blame then? The next stranger that comes limping through?"

The provost rubbed his face with one hand, sudden fatigue showing through his posture. For all his authority, he was only a man in a town trying to pretend it had edges.

"All right," he said. "Mercer. You open that door enough for me to look. No going in. I want to see the condition of the man inside. And if I see anything that looks like you're keeping someone against their will, I'll have you in irons before noon."

Rudd's eyes went wide in silent horror.

Andrew's mind moved quickly, cataloging options that were all bad. If the provost saw

Kellan's emptiness up close, he would smell something wrong that no word like dysentery could cover. If he saw more than Kellan, if the air shifted with sweetness in a way that made the hairs on a human arm rise, the town's fear would become certainty.

And certainty would bring torches. Torches would bring crowds. Crowds would bring chaos that Ambrose would enjoy.

Andrew turned toward the smokehouse door. Each step felt like walking toward a mouth.

Haines moved closer, voice low. "Don't," he whispered, not a plea, a warning. "He sees inside, we're done."

Andrew did not answer. He could not tell Haines the truth, not fully. They had been done since the cellar. Since the first chain bolts. Since Andrew's wound learned to speak in stings.

Andrew slid his hand to the iron bar and stopped. He listened.

Through the wood he heard Kellan's thin breathing, the uneven rasp of a body still functioning. Under that he felt something else, not a sound but a presence, thick as folded cloth in the mind. The faint sweetness touched the air, then withdrew, like a tongue touching a tooth.

Andrew understood with sudden clarity that Ambrose was not surprised. This was not an accident spilling into daylight. This was a habit. A rhythm. A town rebuilding itself and a predator taking the first careful bites to test its new cover.

Old habits.

New victims.

Widow Lorne. The name returned to him like a hook.

He forced himself to move.

Andrew lifted the bar, slowly, and unlatched the door. The hinge complained as it opened, a sound like a throat clearing before speech. He pulled it just wide enough to reveal a slice of interior: dim boards, hanging hooks, straw in the corner where Kellan lay.

The provost stepped close, then stopped short of the threshold as if the air had a boundary. He leaned in, squinting.

Kellan's eyes were open. They always were. His face was pale, mouth slightly parted, the look of a man whose mind had been taken elsewhere and forgotten.

The provost's expression tightened. Disgust, fear, pity, all braided together. "Jesus," he muttered, and stepped back quickly. "How long he been like that?"

Andrew let his voice go flat with practiced medical fatigue. "Days," he said. "He can't hold food. He can't walk far without collapsing."

Pruitt peered over the provost's shoulder, saw Kellan's stillness, and recoiled as if the sight itself might infect him. "Shut it," he snapped. "Shut it now."

Mrs. Harrow's face had gone a shade paler, but she held her ground. Her eyes flicked over Kellan and then, just for a fraction, seemed to search the shadows behind him. Andrew saw it and felt cold respect. She did not know what she was sensing, but she sensed that the air inside that smokehouse was wrong.

Andrew closed the door and slid the iron bar back into place. The sound of it settling was heavier than before. Less like security. More like a seal.

The provost swallowed and wiped his hand on his coat as if he'd touched something unclean. "All right," he said, voice rough. "You keep him in there. You keep yourself out of town. If another animal turns up like that, if another person goes missing, I'll come back and I won't ask."

Andrew nodded once. "Understood."

The provost turned to go, already calling for his companion, already moving back toward problems he could name. Pruitt followed, still muttering about sickness and strangers. Mrs. Harrow lingered a moment longer.

She looked at Andrew, and in her eyes was the hard, practical fear of a woman who had survived by recognizing when a thing had no good answer.

"You leave today," she said quietly. It was not a demand. It was advice the way you told a man to step back from a rotten porch before it collapsed.

Andrew met her gaze. "Yes, ma'am."

Mrs. Harrow nodded once and walked away, shoulders stiff.

When the lane had cleared, Rudd let out a shaking breath. "They saw him," he whispered. "They saw Kellan."

Haines stared at the smokehouse door as if it might bulge outward. "And they didn't see what else was in there," he said.

Andrew's wound gave a faint sting, almost satisfied.

Andrew turned his face away so neither of them could read what moved behind his eyes. He tasted that faint sweetness again, subtle and calm, as if the world had merely completed a small, ordinary task.

The widow was still missing.

The town was still explaining.

And Ambrose, somewhere behind that barred door and those apple trees, had already begun living inside the new rules as if he had written them himself.

Andrew gathered the reins and stared down the road that led away from town, knowing with a slow, sinking certainty that leaving would not end what had started here.

It would only decide who the next victims were.

Andrew did not snap the reins at once.

He let the provost and Eli Pruitt and Mrs. Harrow's stiff-backed warning drift down the lane and away, and he sat with the leather loose in his hands like he was waiting for permission from the sky. The mules shifted in their traces, impatient to be moving. Rudd stood close to the wagon's rear corner, one hand gripping the sideboard as if the wood could steady him. Haines watched the road with a soldier's eyes, the kind that counted angles and exits even when there was no longer any army worth obeying.

Andrew tasted that faint sweetness again, not strong enough to make him gag, only persistent enough to remind him that the day belonged to something else now.

"Pack," Andrew said.

Rudd blinked. "Sir?"

"We leave," Andrew replied. He kept his voice flat, the way you spoke about weather. "Now. Before they come back with more men and less patience."

Haines nodded without argument and moved at once, tightening a strap, shifting a sack so the top layer still looked poor and carelessly piled. Rudd scrambled to gather the tin cup and the small bundle of oats. The whole time his gaze kept skittering toward the smokehouse door, as if the iron bar might lift itself.

Andrew stepped toward the smokehouse. He told himself he was checking the lock. He told himself he was listening for Kellan. Both things were true and neither was the reason his feet went there.

He stopped with his palm hovering near the rough boards and did not touch them. Touching felt like acknowledging ownership.

From inside came the thin, uneven sound of breathing. Human. Small. A man reduced to the bare proof of life.

Under that, Andrew felt something else, not a sound, not a movement, but the dense patience he'd come to recognize the way a man recognized a storm before he saw clouds. His wound answered with a quick sting, like a private signal.

Andrew turned away.

As he did, a voice called from up the lane. "Mr. Mercer."

Andrew froze for half a beat at the name. Too specific. Too clean. He turned slowly, face already arranged into weary irritation, and saw a man walking toward them with a leather satchel in his hand.

The man was in his forties, perhaps older, with a trimmed beard that suggested habit rather than vanity. His coat was brown and decent, patched at one elbow, and his hat was held low at his side the way a man held a tool he did not want to fumble. He had the careful eyes of someone who looked for signs before he asked for truths.

"I'm Dr. Finch," he said when he came close enough. He stopped a few paces short of the wagon, as if drawing an invisible line. "Town doctor. Provost told me you're hauling dysentery."

Andrew held still. "We are."

Dr. Finch's gaze flicked to Andrew's bandage. It lingered there with a physician's interest, not a friend's sympathy. "And you've had it," the doctor said.

Andrew kept his voice neutral. "I've had worse."

Haines shifted near the wheel, his posture tightening. Rudd moved closer to the wagon as if he could place his body between the doctor's eyes and the canvas.

Dr. Finch nodded once, as if he'd heard that sentence from too many soldiers. "I'm not here to pry," he said, and the word was chosen carefully, as if he knew it would matter. "I'm here because if flux is moving through the road traffic, I need to know what kind. And if your man in the smokehouse is in danger of dying, I'd rather he die with a name and a reason that won't set half the town to running."

Andrew stared at him. The doctor's mouth tightened when he said name and reason. Not morality. Not mercy. Administration.

"You want to see him," Andrew said.

Dr. Finch lifted one hand, palm out. "Not close," he said. "Not if he's as far gone as the provost claims. But I'd like to ask questions. How long. What he's passing. Whether there's blood. Whether he's fevered. It matters."

"It matters to who," Haines muttered, too low for politeness but loud enough to carry.

Dr. Finch looked at Haines without offense. "It matters to your host," he said, nodding toward Mrs. Harrow's house. "It matters to the mothers in town who will take one rumor and turn it into a week of sleeplessness. It matters to me because if there's a sickness, I can sometimes keep it from getting into the wells. Sometimes."

Andrew felt his wound sting, light and quick. The sweetness brushed his throat like a fingertip. He did not move.

Dr. Finch's eyes returned to Andrew's face. "You're leaving," the doctor said.

Andrew did not pretend surprise. "Yes."

The doctor nodded again. "That's wise," he said quietly. "People are frightened. They'll blame whoever is nearest. They always do."

Andrew watched the satchel in the doctor's hand and thought of holy relics in an abandoned chapel, of all the old tools men reached for when fear grew teeth. A doctor's satchel was another kind of relic now: proof that someone still believed in causes and cures.

"I'm not opening the smokehouse again," Andrew said.

Dr. Finch's gaze went past Andrew, to the apple trees and the squat shape of the building. "You barred a sick man in there," he said, and his voice held no judgment, only an assessment of the fact. "Is he yours?"

The question struck harder than it should have. Mine. As if people were property again, as if the war had not burned that word raw.

"No," Andrew said.

Dr. Finch studied him, then gave a slight, weary nod that suggested he'd heard enough to understand the shape without needing detail. "Then you're doing what you think keeps him alive," the doctor said. "Or keeps you safe. Either way, I won't ask to enter."

Rudd exhaled shakily.

Andrew kept his expression blank, but inside he felt the strange pull of the doctor's refusal. Not curiosity. Not insistence. Silence offered as a service.

"What do you want then," Andrew asked.

Dr. Finch reached into his satchel and drew out a small bottle wrapped in cloth. "Laudanum," he said. "A little. If he's in pain, it might quiet him. Quiet is valuable, as you've learned."

Andrew stared at the bottle. Quiet was valuable. The doctor said it the way a man said water was wet.

"How much," Andrew asked automatically.

Dr. Finch shook his head. "No charge," he said. "Consider it an investment. If your man screams, the town will come to look. If the town comes to look, I'll have more than dysentery to manage."

Haines's face hardened, but he said nothing.

Andrew took the bottle. The glass felt cold and too smooth. "You're careful with your words," Andrew said.

Dr. Finch's mouth tightened in something like a smile. "Words are most of my work," he replied. "And paperwork."

The mention of paperwork landed like a weight.

Andrew saw it then: the doctor wasn't merely offering medicine. He was offering a kind of quiet arrangement, the same kind Ambrose had described by the creek. Doctors sign. Clerks sign. Ministers sign. The doctor's silence was part of the town's curtain.

As if hearing his own thought, Andrew felt the faint sweetness rise and settle again. Not strong. Patient. Pleased.

Dr. Finch looked toward the road, as if checking whether anyone was watching him stand this close to strangers. "There's another matter," he said, lowering his voice.

Andrew said nothing. He waited.

"The widow," Dr. Finch continued. "Widow Lorne. They've forced her door. She isn't there."

Rudd went rigid. "She's gone," he whispered, voice breaking.

Dr. Finch's gaze flicked toward Rudd and softened by a fraction. "No blood," he said. "No signs of struggle, they claim. Just… absence. Her girl's shawl left on a chair. Bread on the table. The kind of scene that makes men want to invent a reason."

Andrew's wound stung again, sharper. Interest. A predator's satisfaction in a clean removal.

"And you'll give them a reason," Andrew said. He did not mean it as a question.

Dr. Finch held his gaze. For a moment his physician's composure cracked, not into fear, but into fatigue that went down to the bone. "I will try to keep them from forming a mob," he said. "If that's what you mean."

"That isn't what I mean," Andrew replied.

Dr. Finch's eyes narrowed slightly. "Then what."

Andrew chose his words carefully. "If she turns up," he said, "and she's… harmed. You'll write something down that makes sense to them."

Dr. Finch did not answer at once. He looked past Andrew at the road again, at the rebuilt fences, the town trying to be legible. When he spoke, his voice was low and even.

"I will write what keeps panic from spreading," he said.

The sentence was a confession and a defense all at once.

Andrew watched him and saw a man already practicing the role Ambrose preferred: a respectable hand, steady ink, an explanation that let neighbors sleep. Not because the doctor loved evil. Because he feared chaos. Because chaos destroyed the fragile structures that let a town feed itself. Because people begged for lies when the truth would require action.

Rudd whispered, "That ain't right."

Dr. Finch heard him. He looked at the boy, and his expression held something like sorrow. "No," he said. "It isn't. But I've watched men die of fever while their families tore the house apart looking for witches. I've watched a whole street decide one woman was cursed and burn her out to feel clean again. Panic doesn't heal anyone. It only chooses a sacrifice."

Haines's voice came out rough. "So you'll sacrifice truth."

Dr. Finch met Haines's gaze without flinching. "Truth," he said quietly, "doesn't always arrive with proof. Sometimes it arrives as a shape you feel in your gut, and if you speak it without proof you become the monster in the story. I will not become the monster today."

Andrew felt the words settle in him with a cold recognition. That was exactly how the curtain held: men refusing to become the monster, even when the monster was already in the room.

"You should leave," Dr. Finch said to Andrew, the practical tone returning like a coat buttoned up. "Go north or east or wherever your road leads. Don't stop here again."

Andrew nodded. He kept his face still. "Thank you for the medicine," he said.

Dr. Finch hesitated, then added, almost reluctantly, "If your man dies in that smokehouse, don't bury him in our ground. Take him with you."

Andrew's wound gave a small sting, almost amused, as if the creature listening found the doctor's request quaint.

Andrew did not promise. Promises were roots.

Dr. Finch stepped back, hat still in his hand. "Good day," he said, and turned away before anyone could see him lingering.

As the doctor walked up the lane, Andrew watched the straightness of his back. A man carrying medicine and silence in the same satchel.

Rudd whispered, "He knows something's wrong."

"He knows enough," Andrew replied.

Haines stared after the doctor. "He'll cover it," he said, voice flat. "Whatever happens, he'll cover it with ink."

Andrew gathered the reins, the laudanum bottle tucked into his pocket like a small, poisonous kindness. He looked once at the smokehouse door, barred and ordinary in the morning light. He imagined Widow Lorne's kitchen with the bread left on the table. He imagined the doctor's pen moving over paper, shaping absence into a story that would let the town keep building fences.

Andrew clicked his tongue, and the mules leaned forward. The wagon began to roll.

Behind them, the town would keep searching for the widow in all the wrong places, and Dr. Finch would keep his voice calm and his hands clean. He would do it for order. He would do it to prevent mobs. He would do it because in a rebuilding country, silence was often mistaken for stability.

Andrew felt the faint sweetness linger at the edge of his breath as they passed the apple trees and the smokehouse slipped behind them.

Civilization is a curtain, Ambrose had said.

Andrew understood now that the curtain did not hang itself.

It was held up by men like Dr. Finch, who could look at a wound that made no sense and decide, for the sake of keeping the town from burning itself down, to give it a name that lied.

And Andrew, driving the wagon away with steady hands, knew with a slow, sinking certainty that if the widow's body was found, the doctor's silence would not be the end of the story.

It would be the beginning of how the town learned to live with it.

Chapter 18

Epilogue – A New Orchard

Andrew kept his journals where other men kept their guns.

Not on a shelf where dust could settle into the grooves of the spine and announce neglect. Not in a drawer where a curious hand might rummage. Not in the house at all, when he could avoid it. Paper was too honest in the wrong light.

He stored them in the cellar.

The cellar had once been a root place, a square of earth beneath a respectable building where potatoes could be kept cool and apples could be kept from rotting too quickly. Now it was something else: a controlled dark, a domesticated pit. A place that could be explained by any man with a hammer and a wife to impress, and understood by Andrew as the only kind of architecture that lasted.

Outside, the town was rebuilding itself into habits. Five years of new fences and repaired storefronts had taught people how to look forward without daring to look down. There were children who had no memory of marching columns. There were men who spoke of the war as if it had happened to somebody else, somewhere else, and ended neatly on paper.

Andrew lived among them with a name that belonged here.

Mercer was not a common name in the town, but it was not uncommon either. It fit in ledgers. It fit on receipts. It fit on the small brass plate by his door that read S. MERCER, CLERK AND ACCOUNTS, a phrase vague enough to be harmless. He did work, too, the kind that let him be seen during daylight: tallying shipments, writing invoices, translating a man's confusion into a number a creditor could accept. He had ink stains on his fingers often enough that no one questioned them.

The wound at his side had stopped throbbing years ago. It did not ache the way it had in Virginia. It had become a quiet instrument that tightened when the air turned wrong and loosened when the world turned cooperative. It could sting at the scent of fear. It could warm at the proximity of fresh grief. It did not hurt him so much as keep him tuned.

Tonight, after the last customer had left and the street had gone quiet, Andrew locked his front door and took the lamp down the narrow stairs into the cellar. The lamp's light was small and yellow and deliberate, like a lie you carried in your hand.

At the bottom, he paused and listened.

He heard the house above him settle with its ordinary noises. Boards contracting. The faint tick of cooling metal. In the distance, a wagon wheel rolled over planks laid down to keep mud from swallowing commerce. Somewhere a dog barked and then, after a brief hush, barked again. The town proving it was still awake.

In the cellar, the air held that faint sweetness, never quite strong enough to offend a guest, always strong enough to remind Andrew that the darkness here was occupied.

He set the lamp on the small table he kept near the wall. Its circle of light did not reach the far corners. It never did. He had learned not to push light too far into places it did not belong. People who did that lost their appetite for denial, and denial, Andrew understood now, was a kind of mortar.

He took the newest journal from the wooden box, the one lined with oilcloth to keep damp out. His handwriting had changed over the years. It was still neat, still disciplined, but the edges of the letters had softened. The hand of a man who no longer wrote battlefield reports, who no longer expected another man to read his words aloud to an officer with a clean shirt.

He opened to the last page.

The entry from two nights ago stared back at him in calm ink.

May 1870. Widow Harland. Milk cow found down by the creek. Puncture under jaw. No blood. Town says wolves.

He had written the next line smaller, as if shrinking it would shrink its meaning.

Doctor Wilkes signed the cause as "infection."

Andrew had paused after that line, pen hovering, and added what felt like an indulgence.

Doctor Wilkes did not look at me when he spoke.

He read it again now, not because it was new, but because repetition made the brain accept what it could not change.

He turned the page and found the clean paper beneath. Blank lines waiting like rows in a graveyard. He set the tip of his pen to it and wrote the date.

May 14.

Then he stopped and listened again, because sometimes the cellar was quiet enough that he could pretend he was alone, and sometimes it made that pretending costly.

The sweetness deepened slightly, as if the air had been stirred by a slow breath.

Andrew's wound tightened, a small internal tug, not painful, not sharp. Expectant.

"Not yet," Andrew said, and hated himself for speaking into the dark the way one spoke to a man resting in the next room.

The response was not words. Ambrose did not waste words when he did not need to. But the shadows at the far edge of the lamp's circle seemed to thicken, to fold. The sensation was faint, but Andrew had spent too long learning to interpret faint things.

He dipped the pen again and forced his hand back to the page.

A child taken from the path near the mill, he wrote, then stopped.

He did not want to put the sentence down. Once ink held it, the town became a little less salvageable in his mind. If it remained unrecorded, he could still pretend it might be reversed.

But it had already happened. Reversal was a childish hope. Even Rudd, if he had lived, would have understood that by now.

Andrew wrote it anyway.

A child taken from the path near the mill. Name: Josie Lark. Age: seven. Mother says she turned to pick flowers. No scream. No tracks except bare print near creek stones. Provost says "drifter." Offers reward.

He paused at provost and felt something cold settle in him. Provost. The word had followed him north like a stain. New coats, new badges, the same need to assign order to fear.

The same need to find a human culprit.

He added another line.

I gave the provost a description. Tall man. Ragged coat. Smell of whiskey. Told him I saw him on the road two days ago. He believed me quickly.

The pen pressed hard at quickly, tearing the paper slightly. Andrew forced his grip to loosen. Anger did not help. Anger was only noise.

He leaned back and stared at the lamp flame until his eyes watered. The flame bent and straightened with a tiny internal wind.

"You didn't have to take the child," Andrew said quietly, not pleading, not accusing. Stating the fact like an account that did not balance.

A sound came from the dark. Not a laugh, not a sigh. Something softer. A small shift, as if cloth had been adjusted.

When Ambrose finally spoke, the voice seemed to come from just beyond the lamp's reach. Polished. Calm. Almost courteous, as if he had been waiting for Andrew to finish his writing before answering the question.

"I did not have to," Ambrose said. "But you are mistaken if you think necessity is the only law."

Andrew swallowed. The taste of sweetness touched the back of his tongue. He had not eaten since morning, but the sensation was not hunger. It was contamination, intimate and unavoidable.

"She was small," Andrew said. "She was not—"

"Convenient?" Ambrose's voice held mild amusement, like a man correcting a clerk's arithmetic. "You have grown sentimental about the shape of my appetite."

Andrew tightened his jaw. "I have grown careful," he replied.

A pause, and then Ambrose spoke again, and the words landed with the same calm certainty they always did, the certainty that came from never having to bargain for breath.

“Care is your religion,” Ambrose said. “It is why you still write.”

Andrew stared down at the journal. The ink glistened wetly on the last line. His hand was steady. That steadiness was no longer a victory. It was simply a fact.

He thought of Virginia, of the estate that burned and did not burn enough, of the smokehouse behind apple trees, of Dr. Finch’s satchel and his practiced silence. He thought of Elias, somewhere in the country, perhaps living, perhaps not, but certainly older, and certainly still carrying the knowledge like a stone. Andrew had not heard his brother’s name spoken in years.

The ribbon Elias had given him was still in Andrew’s possession. It was folded in the small tin box he kept with the journals, as if cloth could be archived like guilt. He did not take it out. He did not need to touch it to feel it press against his memory.

“I write so I remember,” Andrew said, and the sentence sounded too close to prayer.

Ambrose did not answer that immediately. When he did, his voice was nearer, the shadows at the edge of light seeming to take on a finer shape, a suggestion of a man sitting comfortably where no man should.

"You write," Ambrose said, "because some part of you still believes in a judge."

Andrew felt the wound at his side give a small, sharp sting. Not pain. Mockery.

"There is no judge," Andrew said, and he did not know whether he meant God, the government, history, or the part of himself that still tried to speak.

Ambrose's voice softened by a fraction. "And yet," he murmured, "you keep minutes."

Andrew lowered his gaze to the journal again. He turned back a few pages, to entries that had nothing to do with blood.

April 3. Church roof repaired. Hymn on Sunday carried through the street. I did not go in.

April 9. Doctor Wilkes complains about the smell in the creek bottom. Says dead animals foul the water. He will write letters.

April 12. Mrs. Lark brought eggs as payment for accounts service. Said she is grateful someone can still make numbers behave.

Beneath those, in smaller ink, as if confessing to the paper rather than the world:

They think I am decent.

Andrew's throat tightened. He shut the journal slowly, as if closing it could close the night that sat inside it.

The lamp flame trembled once. The sweetness deepened. In the far corner, where the light could not reach, the dark seemed to shift with the subtlety of a man standing up from a chair.

Andrew did not turn. He had learned that turning too quickly made the body betray itself. The body wanted to flinch. He would not give it that satisfaction.

"What now?" Andrew asked.

Ambrose answered as if the question was only about schedule.

"Now," Ambrose said, "you will go above and wash your hands. You will sleep for a few hours. In the morning you will speak to the provost again. You will suggest the drifter has gone east. You will tell them to search the river road, not the mill path."

Andrew's fingers tightened on the journal's cover. "And the mother?" he asked, because he could not help it. "What do I tell her?"

A pause. Then, smoothly: "Tell her what men always tell mothers when they cannot return what was taken," Ambrose said. "Tell her to keep faith."

Andrew felt something in him go very still, a hardening that did not feel like strength. It felt like the last stage of rot, when wood became light enough to snap.

He stood, journal in hand, and placed it back in the box. He closed the lid and latched it. The sound was small but decisive.

He lifted the lamp. Its light shook on the cellar walls, making the shadows dance in ways that looked briefly alive.

As he turned toward the stairs, Ambrose spoke one last time, and the voice was so close it could have been breath against Andrew's ear, though there was no warmth, only that faint sweetness that carried the memory of old fruit and old cellars.

"You were right once," Ambrose murmured. "War did not kill you."

Andrew paused on the first step and did not look back.

Above him, the house waited with its ordinary furniture and its ordinary dust. Above him, the town waited with its fences and its hymns and its signatures on paper. Above him, morning would arrive and everyone would pretend, with disciplined hunger, that the world could still be made decent if they chose the right culprit.

Andrew held the lamp steady and climbed.

In the dark behind him, the cellar settled into comfortable quiet, as if satisfied to know its journals were kept, its keeper trained, its new orchard already taking root in a country that had learned, again, to look away.

Andrew washed his hands at the kitchen pump until the water ran cold enough to sting.

The ritual had become precise over the years: lift the handle, feel the iron shift, watch the first cloudy spurt clear into something that looked clean. Scrub the ink from beneath his nails. Scrub the cellar's faint sweetness from his skin, though it never fully left. Dry with a cloth that had once belonged to a house he did not own and now could not imagine leaving.

He did not eat. He did not trust his mouth with anything that required savoring.

Upstairs, the house was still. The street beyond the curtained windows offered only the distant hush of wheels and the occasional call of a man starting his day. Normal sounds, meant to be comforting. Andrew listened to them the way a man listened to the creak of ice, measuring where the surface would hold.

He sat at his small desk and opened the account book he used for daylight work. Lists of names. Amounts. Deliveries. Honest numbers that gave him a place in town. He stared at the columns and saw, behind them, other columns that existed only in his journals: puncture under jaw, no blood, missing woman, missing child, doctor signed infection.

Ambrose's instructions ran through his mind with the calm inevitability of a timetable. Wash. Sleep. Speak to the provost. Suggest east. Not the mill path.

Andrew did not like how little of it involved Ambrose doing anything visible. That was the change that had taken years to understand. At first Ambrose had been a presence you could imagine stopping if you could only find the right trap, the right sunlit hour, the right consecrated ground. Now Ambrose moved through a town the way rot moved through wood: quietly, patiently, using the structure itself as cover.

He lay down for a few hours, but sleep did not take him. It only pressed on him, heavy and unhelpful, like a hand held over his face. His mind kept returning to the same image: a child bending to pick flowers, and the moment the world decided not to notice her vanishing because noticing would require an explanation too large for a day.

When he rose again the light had shifted. Midmorning. The time when men decided what kind of day it would be. He put on his coat, checked the brass plate by his door as he always did, the little lie that declared him to be only a clerk, and stepped into the street.

People were already talking.

They did not talk loudly. Loud talk demanded an answer. They talked in controlled tones, in doorways and beside wagons, in the pauses between transactions. Fear did not stop commerce. It adjusted it.

A woman with flour on her hands stood outside the baker's, her face drawn tight. A boy carried a bucket and looked over his shoulder too often. Two men argued softly near the feed store about whether it was wolves or drifters or something worse, and neither man said the word they both wanted to avoid.

Andrew walked as if he belonged, because he did. That was the foulest part. He had earned belonging the way he earned everything now: by being useful, by keeping his voice calm, by providing answers that kept the town from tearing itself open.

At the end of the street the provost's office squatted in its familiar ugliness. The sign had been repainted since Dr. Finch's day, but it was the same word nailed into wood. Someone still wanted the comfort of a badge and a ledger.

Inside, the air smelled of sweat, tobacco, and paper. The provost on duty was not the same man from years earlier. That one had either moved on, died, or been replaced by the slow turning of bureaucracy. This provost was older, his hair thinning, his hands stained with ink as if he wanted the town to believe he was a man of rules rather than a man forced to improvise.

He looked up as Andrew entered.

"Mercer," he said, and it was not a greeting. It was recognition of a tool.

Andrew nodded once. "Provost."

The man's eyes were tired. "If you're here about the reward, there isn't one for clerks."

"I'm here about the search," Andrew replied.

The provost leaned back in his chair, the wood complaining. "Search," he echoed, as if the word tasted bitter. "You got something to say, say it."

Andrew chose his tone carefully. Concerned. Practical. Ordinary. "They're looking in the wrong direction," he said.

The provost's eyes narrowed. "And you know that how?"

Andrew let a small pause hang, just long enough to suggest reluctance. Reluctance read as honesty to men who didn't know any better. "I do accounts," Andrew said. "I hear who owes who. I hear who's passing through. There's been talk of a man on the east road. Not from here. Big fellow. Rough."

The provost's mouth tightened. He wanted it. Andrew could see the hunger for a shape he could chase.

"What kind of talk," the provost demanded.

"Drinking," Andrew said, and watched the provost's eyes settle on the word like a hand finding a weapon. "Stealing small. Nothing that got written down yet because folks don't like paperwork unless it saves them."

The provost made a sound through his nose. "Don't preach to me about paperwork."

Andrew kept his face blank. "I'm not. I'm telling you where the town's eyes are already turning."

The provost stared at him a moment longer, weighing whether this was help or manipulation. Andrew had learned long ago that most authority did not recognize manipulation unless it came with flattery. He offered neither.

Finally the provost reached for a pen. “Name,” he said.

Andrew gave a name that belonged to nobody, a plain string of syllables that fit the region and would snag on no known family. He watched the provost write it down. Watched the ink become official.

The provost shoved the paper aside and leaned forward. His voice dropped. “They say there’s no tracks. No sign she fought. No sign of a man. Just gone.” He stared hard at Andrew. “What do you think happened?”

Andrew felt the wound at his side tighten faintly, a subtle internal tug that warned him to keep the curtain heavy.

“I think people vanish easier than we like to admit,” Andrew said. “Roads are full of holes. Woods are full of places a voice doesn’t carry.”

The provost’s jaw worked. He did not like the uncertainty. Uncertainty made his job impossible. “And the creek?” he asked. “Them cows. Them hogs. That puncture.”

Andrew let his shoulders lift in a small, helpless shrug. “I’m a clerk,” he said. “I’ve seen men do strange things for meat. I’ve seen sickness do stranger things.”

The provost stared a moment longer, then looked away first. "All right," he muttered. "I'll send men east. Keep folks from wandering. Keep the mothers from flooding my doorway with crying."

Andrew nodded. "That's wise."

As he turned to go, the provost said, "Mercer."

Andrew stopped.

The provost's voice was rougher now. "You ever get tired," he asked, "of being calm?"

The question hit Andrew harder than it should have. Not because it was insightful, but because it was close to something he could not afford to touch.

"Yes," Andrew said simply.

He left the office and stepped back into the street. The air outside smelled of horse, bread, and early spring damp. He walked toward the mill path without going down it, circling instead toward the creek road where he knew people gathered when they had nothing else to do but stare at water and try to see their fear reflected in it.

He found Mrs. Lark near the edge of a small crowd.

She stood with her shawl pulled tight over her shoulders though the day was not cold enough to require it. Her face looked older than the year, as if time had chosen her as a place to show its cruelty. Women around her murmured and touched her arm. Men stood nearby and did not touch anything, as if grief was a contagion.

Andrew stayed at the edge and watched. He did not approach at once. Approaching would make him a participant. Participation created obligations he did not want and could not keep.

Mrs. Lark turned suddenly, as if sensing eyes. She saw Andrew and stepped toward him with startling directness.

"You do accounts," she said. Her voice shook, but it held. "You write things down."

Andrew nodded once. "Yes."

Her eyes were red-rimmed, but dry. "Write this," she said. "Write that she didn't run. Write that she didn't wander off. Josie was afraid of the creek. She never went near it alone."

Andrew felt his mouth go dry. The urge to reassure rose in him, automatic and useless. He pushed it down.

"I believe you," Andrew said quietly.

Mrs. Lark's face tightened as if she hated belief. "Belief don't bring her back," she whispered.

"No," Andrew admitted.

Her gaze searched his face. For a moment Andrew thought she might see something in him that she could not name, the way Mrs. Harrow had once looked through smokehouse shadows. But Mrs. Lark's pain was too sharp to leave room for intuition. She only saw a man who wrote, and she needed writing to make her daughter's disappearance real enough that it could not be smoothed away.

"They say drifters," she said, bitterness creeping in. "They say wolves. They say anything that makes it simple. Tell me you'll write her name so she don't become just a story people trade for a week."

Andrew thought of his journal in the cellar. The neat lines. The list of names and ages. The way he kept minutes like a man who still believed in a judge.

"I'll write her name," he said.

Mrs. Lark's mouth trembled. "And if they find her," she whispered, and her voice broke on the sentence, "if they find what's left, don't let them say she deserved it. Don't let them say she wandered. Don't let them say it was God's will."

Andrew felt the wound at his side give a small, sharp sting, like a private laugh shared between him and the dark.

He held Mrs. Lark's gaze. "They'll say what they need to say to keep living," he replied, and the honesty in it felt like a cruelty. He tried to soften it. "But I'll write what you told me."

Mrs. Lark nodded once, as if accepting the only mercy on offer.

Andrew stepped back into the crowd's edge and let other bodies fill the space between them. As he did, he felt it: the faint sweetness in the air, not from blossoms or fruit, but from something older. Something that did not belong in daylight and yet moved through it as if daylight had finally learned to stop objecting.

He turned his head slightly.

A man stood across the road near the shade of a budding tree, his posture relaxed, his hands loosely clasped behind his back as if waiting for a late appointment. His clothes were not fine, but they were arranged with an elegance that made their plainness look intentional. A dark coat. Clean collar. Hair neatly kept. A face pale enough to look unwell to the casual eye and composed enough to make unwellness seem like refinement.

No one stared at him. A few glances slid over him and away again, the way eyes slid off men who looked like they belonged to paperwork and parlors, not to violence.

Ambrose met Andrew's gaze without any effort at secrecy.

He did not smile. He did not need to. The calm in his face was worse than a grin. It was the expression of a thing no longer required to hide in wagons or cellars unless it chose to. A thing that had learned the rhythms of the town and now stood among them as an option, a respectable shadow.

Andrew felt his heart slow rather than race. His body had learned the wrong lessons. Fear had become less useful than obedience.

Ambrose inclined his head slightly, a gesture so polite it could have been exchanged between two men passing on a street.

Then he looked past Andrew to Mrs. Lark, to the cluster of women holding grief like a bucket that kept spilling, to the men who wanted a culprit they could hunt.

Ambrose's gaze moved with mild interest, like a man assessing a market.

Andrew understood, with a sinking clarity, what ascendance looked like for a creature like this. Not a throne. Not worship. A town that kept working. A doctor who signed what kept panic contained. A provost who wrote down a name and called it progress. Mothers told to keep faith. Men sent east to chase a drifter that did not exist.

Ambrose turned slightly and began walking down the street, unhurried, neither skulking nor bold. A man among men. A shadow that did not need darkness to persist.

Andrew watched him go, the sweetness lingering in his breath, and felt the old wound tighten in a way that was not pain but alignment, as if his own body recognized that the creature's place in the world had shifted upward, becoming less dependent on hiding and more dependent on being accepted.

The crowd behind Andrew murmured about search parties and river roads. Someone said they'd heard of a big man seen east. Someone else repeated the name Andrew had given the provost as if it had always been known.

Truth, Andrew thought, was not only what happened. It was what a town agreed to write down.

He turned and walked back toward his house, already feeling the pull toward the cellar, toward the journals, toward the place where he could admit in ink what he could not admit aloud.

Behind him, Ambrose continued down the street with the ease of a man who had finally found a country that would rebuild itself around him. Not because it loved him.

Because it was tired.

Because it wanted fences and hymns and signatures more than it wanted to look too closely at what fed beneath them.

Andrew reached his front door and paused with his hand on the knob. He looked once more toward the street, toward the ordinary daylight where Ambrose had just walked unchallenged.

Then he went inside and closed the door, shutting out the voices and the spring air and the grief.

The click of the latch sounded small.

But it sounded, to Andrew, like a vow being kept.

The house settled around Andrew as soon as he shut out the street. The latch's small click did not quiet the town, not really, but it cut the sound into something muffled, distant enough to pretend it belonged to someone else's life.

He stood with his back to the door for a moment longer than was necessary, hand still on the knob. The air inside smelled of lye soap and old wood and the faintest ghost of lamp smoke. Ordinary scents. Domestic. The kind that made a man think of supper, of worn chair legs, of a coat hung in the same place each evening.

They were the smells of a curtain.

Andrew removed his hat and set it on the hook by the door. His hands hesitated over his coat buttons. In the street he had worn his calm like armor; in here he did not know what he wore. He unbuttoned anyway, slowly, as if a sudden motion might draw attention from the spaces that did not need light to see him.

On the small table in the hall sat an unopened letter he had meant to answer yesterday, a note about flour deliveries and credit terms. There were men who still believed the world could be corrected by ink and arithmetic. Andrew had once been one of them, or had pretended he could become one.

He did not touch the letter.

He crossed the kitchen and paused at the pump as if the sight of it could return him to the ritual that made him feel, for a few minutes, less contaminated. He lifted the handle once, then let it drop without pulling water. The metal's hollow clank sounded too loud in the quiet. He did not want the sound to travel downward. He did not want to announce himself to the dark like a servant stamping his feet before entering a parlor.

He took the lamp from its bracket and lit it with a practiced motion. The flame caught, small and steady, and the glass chimney warmed. He watched the glow for a beat, trying to decide whether it comforted him or disgusted him. Light was honest only when men were willing to look at what it showed. Otherwise it was merely another tool for pretending.

He carried the lamp to the cellar door and stopped there with his fingers on the latch.

Above him, the house was quiet. Beyond the walls, the town would be thick with quiet talk, with mothers speaking through their teeth, with men making plans for search parties that would travel in the direction he had given them. The provost would already be writing down the name of a drifter that did not exist. Dr. Wilkes would already be preparing his face, his voice, his clean, useful explanations.

And Ambrose had walked in daylight, unhurried, as if the street belonged to him.

Andrew opened the cellar door.

Cool air breathed up at him. Not merely the cool of earth, but the cool of a place where time collected. The sweetness was there too, faint but immediate, as if it had been waiting just on the other side of the wood.

He descended the steps carefully, lamp held low. The stairs creaked in their familiar places. He had learned the noises of his own house the way a soldier learned a rifle's parts: what could be trusted, what would misfire, what would betray you by being louder than it had any right to be.

At the bottom, the cellar spread out in a rough square. The lamp's circle did not reach the corners, and he did not try to force it. He set the lamp on the small table where he kept his journals and stood still, listening.

He heard the house above him settle. He heard, faintly, a wagon's wheels over distant planks in the street. He heard nothing in the cellar itself but his own breath.

That was never the whole truth.

Andrew opened the wooden box and took out the newest journal. The oilcloth lining whispered against paper. He sat in the chair and turned to the last page as if he might find a different story written there, one that did not include a child's name.

May 14 stared up at him.

The ink he had written last night was dry now, set into the page like a verdict. Josie Lark. Age: seven. No scream. Bare print near creek stones. Provost offers reward.

He read it once, then again, and the act of reading felt like punishment. Not because it changed anything, but because it made him admit that he had become the kind of man who catalogued a mother's grief and then used it, later, to steer search parties away from where grief had become evidence.

He dipped the pen and added a line, forcing his hand steady.

Spoke to provost. Sent men east. Crowd at creek. Mother asked me to write her name.

He paused, pen hovering, and listened again. The cellar did not answer with sound, but the sweetness deepened by a fraction, the way a room's air changed when another person stepped closer.

Andrew did not look up. He did not want to see a shape at the edge of the lamp's reach. Seeing made it too much like a conversation between equals, and nothing in his life was equal anymore.

"I wrote it," Andrew said quietly, because the words demanded an outlet. "Her name. Like she asked."

The darkness seemed to fold slightly, a soft change in density. Then Ambrose's voice came, calm and composed, as if he had been present the whole time and merely waited for silence to become an invitation.

"You have always been meticulous," Ambrose said. "It is one of your few virtues."

Andrew's fingers tightened around the pen until his knuckles ached. "Virtue," he echoed, and the word tasted wrong.

A pause, and the faintest sound that might have been amusement if amusement could be bloodless. "Not virtue in the way your reverends mean it," Ambrose replied. "Virtue as in function. You do what must be done, and you do it neatly."

Andrew forced himself to breathe evenly. He thought of the creek road, of the crowd's murmur, of how quickly his invented name had become a rumor that men repeated with relief. He thought of Mrs. Lark's dry eyes and her voice cracking on a sentence she could not finish.

"There were other ways," Andrew said, and he did not know what he meant by it. Other ways to feed. Other ways to survive. Other ways to be a man in a town without becoming part of the curtain that hid a predator.

Ambrose's reply was patient. "There are always other ways," he said. "That is the lie you tell yourself to feel choice. Choice is a luxury. You have not had luxury since Virginia."

The word Virginia pulled at Andrew's memory like a hook. Rain-choked night. A locked cellar door. Boot tracks ending at wood and iron. Broken chains bolted into stone. A rumor that became his life.

He looked down at his bandaged side through the layers of cloth, as if he might still find the wound there in its original shape. It was only skin now. Scar tissue. An instrument. It tightened faintly, responding to Ambrose's nearness with a familiar, intimate signal.

"You walked in daylight," Andrew said, and his voice was flatter than he intended. He had meant accusation. It came out like a report.

"Yes," Ambrose replied simply. "Because your town has become ready."

Andrew's mouth went dry. "Ready for what."

"Ready to believe the right things," Ambrose said. "Ready to insist upon causes that can be written down. Ready to chase men on roads instead of looking into their own cellars."

Andrew's gaze flicked toward the journal box. Toward the ribbon tin nestled inside it, folded cloth pressed into a hard square of remembered shame. He did not open it. He did not touch it. He only felt, as he always did, the ghost of Elias's voice: a funeral between the living.

"And Dr. Wilkes," Andrew said. "He'll sign whatever they need."

Ambrose's tone did not change. "He will sign what keeps him employed," he said. "He will sign what keeps mothers from becoming mobs. He will sign what makes the town feel clean."

Andrew's pen scratched lightly across paper without ink, the motion unconscious, a twitch of habit. "You're making me part of it," he said.

"You made yourself part of it," Ambrose corrected, gently enough to be cruel. "You believed you could contain me by arranging me. You believed locks and schedules and papers could become a cage."

Andrew swallowed. "They were supposed to."

The darkness thickened a little more, as if leaning in. The sweetness was clearer now, bruised fruit and old cellar air, refinement applied to rot until it became almost tolerable.

"Nothing is a cage," Ambrose said, "if the world agrees not to look inside."

Andrew stared at the lamp flame until his eyes stung. He thought of fences hammered into wet ground. Of provost signs nailed to old boards. Of hymns sung like cloth held up against night. Of how easily a town accepted sickness as explanation because sickness required no enemy you could shoot.

He set the pen down and closed the journal with care, as if respect for the object might substitute for respect for what it contained.

“What do you want now,” Andrew asked.

Ambrose’s answer came at once, like a man reciting a plan he had already written.

“You will go above,” he said. “You will eat enough to keep your face from hollowing. You will speak to Mrs. Lark again if she seeks you and you will tell her what she needs to hear in order to live through the next day without setting fire to the town. You will continue to steer them away from the mill path.”

Andrew’s throat tightened. “And if they find her.”

A pause, small and deliberate.

“If they find what remains,” Ambrose said, “the doctor will name it. The provost will file it. The minister will pray it. And you will write it. That is how your country heals. By turning wounds into stories it can survive.”

Andrew felt something inside him go cold and still. He wanted to argue. He wanted to spit the words back, to insist there should be a difference between survival and complicity. But he had lived too long in the narrow space between those words to pretend they did not overlap.

He stood slowly, lifting the lamp. The light shook slightly against the cellar walls, and the shadows moved in response, but he did not turn his head toward the corners. He had learned, over years, not to demand shapes from darkness when darkness was content to remain only presence.

He took a step toward the stairs.

"Andrew," Ambrose said.

Andrew stopped with one foot on the first step, the lamp's heat warm on his knuckles.

"Yes," he answered, and hated himself for how instinctive the obedience was.

Ambrose's voice softened, intimate, almost courteous, as if offering a benediction.

"You will not be forgiven," Ambrose said. "But you will be useful. Do not confuse those."

Andrew's fingers tightened around the lamp handle until metal bit skin. He thought of forgiveness as something men begged for when they still believed in a judge. He thought of usefulness as something he had once despised in officers who cared more for outcomes than for lives.

He climbed the stairs without answering.

At the top, he paused and looked out into his kitchen. The daylight that filtered through the curtained window was ordinary, pale, full of dust motes. The table held its simple scratches. The pump waited. The unopened letter sat where it had before, patient as paperwork always was.

Andrew turned back and pulled the cellar door shut.

The wood met frame with a dull, final sound. The latch slid into place with a click so small it could have been mistaken for nothing at all.

He kept his hand on it for a moment, feeling the vibration settle out of the boards, as if the house itself was accepting the new arrangement again: light above, dark below, and a man in between who knew exactly what was kept under his feet.

Then Andrew released the knob and walked toward the window to watch the street without being seen, already arranging his face into calm.

Outside, the town would keep searching east. Men would keep repeating a false name with grateful certainty. Mothers would keep their children closer and call it vigilance. Dr. Wilkes would prepare his pen.

And down below, in the controlled dark, the sweetness would linger, patient and at home.

Andrew stood in the kitchen, listening to the faintest hum of the world trying to behave, and understood with quiet clarity that the door he had just closed was not only a barrier.

It was a promise being kept.

www.ingramcontent.com/pod-product-compliance
Lightning Source LLC
La Vergne TN
LVHW050908080826
845145LV00001B/14